# DEBT OF AGES

# STEVE WHITE

BAEN

DEBT OF AGES

A Baen Books Original

Baen Publishing Enterprises
P.O. Box 1403
Riverdale, NY 10471

ISBN: 0-671-87689-9

Cover art by Stephen Hickman

First printing, October 1995

Distributed by Simon & Schuster
1230 Avenue of the Americas
New York, NY 10020

Printed in the United States of America

To Sandy, as always.

❧❧

To David Weber, for suggestions too
numerous to mention.

❧❧

And to Geoffrey Ashe. If you love a
story enough, you don't care if it's
true; but finding out that it was true
all along is one of the little bonuses
that make life so much better than
merely "fair."

# PROLOGUE — 491 A.D.[2]

The Restorer was dying.

*I knew him for the Restorer at the moment I first met him,* thought Sidonius Apollinaris, known to the world these past eight years as His Holiness Gaius II, keeper of the keys of Saint Peter.

Behind him stood most of the Consistory, filling the incense-heavy air with that sense of numb disbelief with which the entire Sacred Palace, the entire City of Constantine around it, and the whole of Rome's reunified and expanded empire beyond that awaited the passing of him who had brought it all back from the edge of the abyss. But Sidonius was aware of none of the overdressed dignitaries with whom he shared the Imperial bedchamber. He stood over the bed and looked down into his old friend's face, worn down by war, the cares of empire and sixty-four winters, as well as by the sickness that was killing him.

The dark eyes fluttered open, glittering with recognition as much as with fever. "Sidonius," he said in a dry whisper to which he still managed to give a kind of firmness.

"Yes, Augustus, I am here."

The shockingly aged face formed the famous grin whose boyishness had never seemed incongruous and still didn't.

"There you go again, Sidonius! I never persuaded you to stop addressing me as 'Riothamus' even though I kept telling you we Britons only used the title on formal occasions. And after that it's always been 'Augustus'! Will you let me go to my grave still refusing to call me by my name, at least in private?"

All at once, Sidonius was no longer in the ornate room that the doctors insisted on keeping so stifling. He was on a beach at the mouth of the Loire twenty-two years before, standing in the chill salt wind with the men—all dead now, besides him—who had awaited the arrival of the High King of the Britons whose army was the Western Empire's last hope against the Visigoths.

*I can still see the afternoon sun blazing forth through the first break in that day's overcast as he stepped from the boat, silhouetting him against the divine fire. But that fire burned even more strongly within him, burned with a force that could snatch back that which had been consigned to the irrecoverable past and defy the Fates themselves* (as always, Sidonius automatically chided himself for his lifelong weakness for pagan mythology). Yes, he had known that the British ruler with whom he had corresponded was destined to restore the Empire. He had known it with a simple, absolute certainty that, he guiltily acknowledged, not even the Church's doctrines could inspire in him.

That moment had remained with Sidonius through all the tumultuous, unbelievable years that had followed. His certainty had faltered that very winter when he had learned of the treason of the Praetorian Prefect of Gaul, whom he had once called friend. (What had his name been? Oh, yes: Arvandus.) But the Restorer's destiny was not to be deflected by betrayal, and the matter had been forgotten in the jubilation following the great victory at Bourges. That victory had banished the terrifying Visigothic threat to the realm of old nightmares from which one had awakened. And then had come a potentially disastrous digression, with rebellion calling the High King back to Britain. But he had returned to the continent somehow strengthened by his campaigning in the island's wild western hills. After that, events had moved with the seeming inevitability of a river's journey to the sea.

The Restorer had never ceased to insist that he had not sought even the Emperorship of the West, much less of a reunited Roman Empire. Sidonius was inclined to believe him. Looking back, it was hard to see how he could have avoided any one of the steps he had taken, or how each of those steps could have failed to lead to the step that had followed. After his ally the Western Emperor Anthemius had been murdered, Odoacer—who had succeeded Ricimer as Master of Soldiers at Rome—had moved against him. With no alternative save extinction, the Restorer had advanced into Italy, where on the victorious field of Pavia his British and Gallic and Frankish troops had proclaimed him Augustus of the West. That had been in 474, the year the Eastern Emperor Leo had died; his successor Zeno had never acknowledged that he had a legitimate fellow in the West, and after six years of uneasy coexistence had come the inevitable clash. Thinking back, Sidonius wondered how he could ever have doubted its outcome. *Me and most of the world,* he reflected, which always made him feel a little better. But if his confidence had wavered, his loyalty never had. And when old Pope Simplicius had died in 483, the ruler of the miraculously reunified Empire had let it be known that in his opinion the churchmen and citizenry of Rome could make no better choice for their new bishop than his old friend and supporter, that noted prelate and man of letters Bishop Sidonius of Clermont. For some odd reason they had agreed.

No, he could never forget those years. Nothing could dim their luster in his memory—not even the uncomprehending hurt and disappointment he had felt all too often during the years that had followed. And he heard himself form the same words he had spoken on that windy beach twenty-two years before, when it had all begun. "Very well . . . Artorius."

The Restorer smiled again. "Better! There may be hope for you yet, Sidonius!" Then he raised a hand from the bed and grasped the papal forearm with surprising strength. When he spoke, the whisper was fainter than before, but not with the faintness of failing strength. No, it was deliberate—these words were for the two of them alone.

"Sidonius, you will see me again."

"Why, of course, Augustus." Sidonius reverted to formality in his puzzlement. "There can be no doubt of it. We will see each other again, before the throne of God, when—"

"No!" The grip tightened on his arm, and the whisper took on a compelling urgency. "I don't mean that. I mean in this life! I'm telling you this because I want you to be prepared, and not doubt your sanity nor fear for your soul. You must dismiss all thoughts of the black arts, and accept what your eyes and ears and mind and heart tell you. . . ."

The whisper faded to nothing and the grip went slack, for the effort had been too much. Damasius the Syrian stepped forward and examined his imperial patient with that look of sharp concentration which all physicians cultivated, a mask behind which yawned bottomless ignorance.

"He must rest now, Your Holiness. I fear he has exhausted himself."

Sidonius nodded and stepped back from the bedside. *Whatever was he talking about?* he wondered. *Nothing, probably. His mind is going, and he can no longer command it to reason. Not even the force of will which hauled back the outgoing tide of history can hinder death in its work of dissolution.*

"Remember," he told the physician, "I am to be notified when the end is at hand." Then he turned from the bed and looked around the room, so very Greek in its massive, mosaic-encrusted somberness. Equally Greek were most of the men and eunuchs in the room, the high officials of state and church. Then he saw a new face, and he froze.

It seemed amazing that Acacius could have entered the room silently, moving under the weighty vestments of the Patriarch of Constantinople. Even more amazing was his audacity in being here at all, knowing that the Pope of Rome, his bitterest enemy, was bound to be present. *Well*, Sidonius thought, his habitual good nature reasserting itself, *perhaps he feels sincere affection for this dying man. He certainly has every reason to. And I will* not *create a scene here!*

He nodded stiffly to the Patriarch, who acknowledged with what he had to admit was probably superior grace. Then he turned and left the room, moving with that natural stateliness that people assured him he had acquired by virtue of the weight he had put on in recent decades. *I hope that's true*, he thought as he made his way along corridors and past the occasional statue-like figures of white-uniformed Scholarian Guards. *It would be good to have some recompense in exchange for wind and vigor! But I mustn't complain. At fifty-nine I should be thanking God that I'm still alive, not whining to Him about the loss of youth.*

He reached the top of the marble stairs that led down from the imperial apartments to the first floor. Here he paused, and gazed out the wide windows that gave light to the landing. They gave little light now, for it was approaching twilight. Sidonius looked out at the terraced gardens that sloped down to the Sea of Marmara, where lights were winking to life on passing ships. He liked this view, for the palace itself and the adjacent hippodrome blocked from sight the teeming hive that was Constantinople.

*At one time I dared hope that he'd move the principal Imperial residence back to Rome, where it was in the great days before the world began to go wrong, when the first Augustus ruled as* Princeps *among his fellow citizens, not as an Asiatic god-emperor inhabiting a world of ceremony and splendor far above his subjects' cringing heads. But Rome was always hopeless as a location for the Imperial capital, from the military standpoint. The logistics were all wrong. And, of course, most of our wealth and people—and our most dangerous enemies—are in the East. All of this was as true for Artorius as it had been for Constantine. As in everything else, he made the only possible choice.*

*Later, though . . .*

At first Artorius had been a breath of fresh air in this place. But then the wind had settled, and everything had been as before: the eunuchs, and the ceremonies and hierarchies they had devised and eternally elaborated (*A substitute for what they've lost?* Sidonius wondered); and the clerks and notaries who did the everyday business of the state with an inefficiency they defended with a stubbornness fit to shame the Saxons, for any change could only be to their disadvantage. *There's no way the empire can function without them,* Sidonius reflected bleakly. *No one else knows how to play the games they themselves have invented for the purpose of making themselves indispensable.*

He sighed and shook his head. He shouldn't complain about the way the restored empire was governed. *It's like my advancing age,* he reminded himself. *Consider the alternative!* No, the decisions that had wedged him and his old friend apart over the last few years had concerned not the things of Man but those of God. . . .

"Sidonius! Your Holiness, I meant to say!"

Sidonius turned and smiled at the man bounding up the staircase. The clouds lifted from his mind for the moment. It was impossible to stay depressed around Ecdicius.

"Noblissimus," he greeted, using the proper form of address for the heir to the Empire.

"Well, now that we've got all *that* out of the way—greetings!" Ecdicius reached the landing, not even breathing hard after an ascent that would have reduced Sidonius to a state of gasping exhaustion, and clasped forearms with his brother-in-law. Ecdicius flashed the smile that transfigured his engagingly ugly face, and Sidonius reflected as always on how much he was like his adoptive father the Augustus.

Ecdicius had not yet reached adolescence when the twenty-year-old Sidonius, scion of another of the aristocratic Gallo-Roman families of their set, had come to seek the hand of his older sister Papianilla. Sidonius still thought of him as the wiry, restlessly energetic boy for whom the villa in the Auvergne had seemed too confining. *God, what a brat he was,* he recalled, in the wake of every man who ever courted a girl with a younger brother. But that boy had survived the whirlwind of events that had soon followed—his father Avitus' brief reign as Augustus of the West and subsequent murder, and the "Marcelliana" conspiracy in which Sidonius had almost been implicated. And later, in his mid-twenties but already grown into the kind of man that other men instinctively follow, he had raised a private cavalry unit that had distinguished itself at the Battle of Bourges. He had subsequently become one of Artorius' leading cavalry officers, with a reputation for taking hair-raising risks and emerging alive through sheer dash. When the childless Restorer had found it politic to adopt an heir, he hadn't found the choice a difficult one.

"I got back as quickly as I could," Ecdicius said, sobering. "I wouldn't have left for the Danube a fortnight ago, except that he seemed to be getting better and insisted that I not let it disrupt my schedule. Of course, when I heard he had taken a turn for the worse . . ." He indicated his dusty, travel-worn clothes. "How is he?" Without waiting for an answer, he abruptly started in the direction of the imperial apartments. Sidonius placed a restraining hand on his arm.

"Sleeping now. You can't get in to see him, so you may as well change and rest." Ecdicius nodded, but continued to move, pacing as though to vent his excess vitality.

Sidonius couldn't swear that he had *ever* seen Ecdicius hold still, and it was no different now that he was in his late forties.

"Come with me to the Daphne Palace," Sidonius continued, gesturing at the garden vista outside the window and to the right, toward the residence that had been placed at the disposal of the Pope and his entourage. "We can dine . . . and we need to talk. Acacius has been hovering like a circling vulture. I fear that he and his supporters are planning some move after Artorius is . . ." He let the sentence die.

Ecdicius' face grew stormcloud-dark, and he unconsciously gripped the hilt of the cavalry *spatha* that never left his side. "I can't imagine what he thinks he'll be able to pull off, after I assume the purple. Maybe he hopes to take advantage of a confused transition."

"Well, then, we must assure that the transition is a smooth one," Sidonius declared as the two of them descended the stairs. There was still just enough light to see by, and the spring night was warm. So they didn't wait to summon lantern bearers but proceeded toward the Daphne unescorted, through gardens that the dusk transformed into a realm of pagan enchantment and mystery, its deepening shadows inhabited by nameless dangers. . . .

*Ridiculous!* Sidonius chided himself. *What danger can there be in the grounds of the Sacred Palace?* But for once he felt no inclination to ask Ecdicius to slow his pace in deference to the papal dignity and years.

Ecdicius seemed oblivious to the *frisson* Sidonius felt, for he alternated between brooding and talking. "What can Acacius and his lot possibly hope for?" he wondered aloud. "Maybe they think they can persuade me to inaugurate my reign by calling a new Council, where they can do even more harm than was done at the last one. . . ." He cut himself off. "I know, Sidonius. I shouldn't speak ill of him, at this of all times. But we wouldn't be worrying now if he hadn't made that snake Patriarch of Constantinople

again! And some of his other appointments . . . !"
Bewilderment entered Ecdicius' voice. "Why, Sidonius?
What's happened to him over the last few years?"

"Well," Sidonius spoke in the conciliatory tones of
lifelong habit, "we can hardly blame him for the Council
of Chalcedon. It was in 451, when he wasn't even High
King of the Britons yet. That was where the great mistake
was made, declaring the See of Constantinople equal to
that of Rome, even though our Lord expressly delivered
the keys of the Kingdom into the hands of Peter. . . ."
Exertion overcame indignation, and he had to pause for
a gasping breath as he tried to talk and keep up with
Ecdidius at the same time. "Well, at least they did one
thing right at Chalcedon by rejecting the Monophysite
heresy. But later it came back to haunt the East."

"Yes . . . with Acacius carrying its standard! I tell you,
Sidonius, I can't understand it! That devil-begotten
'Declaration of Union' Acacius drew up in 482 was one
of the reasons for Artorius' final break with Zeno, Acacius'
patron. After he'd won, Artorius tore it up and deposed
Acacius as Patriarch. So why, just four years later, did he
restore the goat-bugger to the Patriarchate?"

Sidonius frowned. A prelate of Holy Church—even
Acacius!—was entitled to a certain respect. He was framing
a stern admonition when the four darkly cloaked figures
stepped from the bushes ahead of them and deployed across
the pathway.

Ecdicius wordlessly motioned Sidonius back and laid
his hand on the hilt of his *spatha*. He cast a glance backward
and Sidonius, following it, saw that three more strangers
had blocked the path behind them.

One of the quartet to their front stepped forward and
spoke in cultivated Latin. "Noblissimus, a plot against you,
and against the sacred person of the Augustus, has been
uncovered. I must ask that you accompany us to a place
of safety."

" 'Uncovered' by whom?" Ecdicius inquired as he

unobtrusively twirled his cloak around his left forearm. He did not draw his weapon—none of the strangers had—but he stood in a fighting stance that was as relaxed-seeming as his voice, and measured distances with his eyes. "Who are you, and who sent you?"

"That is immaterial, Noblissimus. For the safety of the Empire and Holy Church I'm afraid I must insist that you cooperate." He gestured to his followers, and swords appeared with a scrape of metal.

Sheer, flabbergasted outrage brought Sidonius out of shock. He stepped forward to stand beside Ecdicius. "How dare you?" he thundered—or intended to thunder, but it came out closer to a gasp. "As you hope for salvation, I command you to let us pass!"

They evidently recognized him. Blades wavered, and one of the men turned to the leader and muttered something. Sidonius couldn't understand it, but he recognized the bastard Greek of Constantinople's slums. The leader snarled back in a Greek that was educated enough for Sidonius to follow. "You cowardly dung-eaters! Take both of them!"

Ecdicius exploded into action, shoving Sidonius back into the bushes with one hand as he drew his *spatha* with the other. He was of only average size, but his body had lost little of its whipcord toughness to middle age. Positioning himself to shield Sidonius, he held the three-and-a-half-foot cavalry sword at the ready as the six bravos closed in with their shorter weapons. Two of them moved to flank him while two others leapt in.

Ecdicius' response was too quick for Sidonius to follow, as he suspected it would have been even in bright daylight. Almost simultaneously with a quick clang of blades, one bravo was on the ground gurgling his life out through a slashed throat and Ecdicius was grappling with another who had gotten in under his long sword. With a vicious move, he dislocated the bravo's shoulder and sent him staggering sideways into his companion who was moving in from the right. That was all the time it took the bravo from the left to grab him from behind, as the remaining two moved in.

Sidonius had never encountered physical violence in his entire adult life, and it was as though he moved through a world of unreality with the rock he couldn't remember picking up. He brought it down on the head of the bravo holding Ecdicius. At the same time, the latter kicked out with both feet, sending the two new arrivals staggering backwards, then fell in a heap with the unconscious man who had grasped him. He rolled free in time to grab Sidonius, who was staring openmouthed at the blood-smeared rock he still held, and haul him back against a thick shrub, then turn to face their attackers once more.

Things began to register on Sidonius. Ecdicius still had his *spatha*. Three bravos were out of action, but the other three had picked themselves up. Now, in company with their employer—who was holding his sword as though he knew how to use it—they were closing in warily. They'd make no more mistakes. And—final detail—Ecdicius was bleeding from a superficial but doubtless painful wound in his left side.

Sidonius managed to form words. "Guards ho!" he croaked. "To me!"

"Save your breath, Sidonius," Ecdicius said quietly. "They must have made certain no one would be in earshot. Otherwise somebody would have heard this fight."

The leader of their assailants gave an unpleasant smile that provided confirmation. His face still wore the smile as he started forward . . . but then went blank as he crumpled, without fuss, to the ground.

Sidonius became aware of a strange buzzing sound, not really like the swarming of bees. He wondered what it could be, with a small part of his reeling mind, as he watched the three bravos collapse.

He and Ecdicius looked at each other.

Two men stepped from the shadows.

Sidonius and Ecdicius started, and the latter raised his

*spatha* again. The new arrivals halted, and the shorter of them—they were both big men—spoke in the Latin of the army with an accent not unlike that of the Augustus.

"Relax, Noblissimus! We're here to save you." He indicated the motionless forms of their erstwhile attackers. "Sorry we didn't arrive sooner—although you weren't doing so badly yourself! And you, Your Holiness—you're pretty handy with that thing. Have you considered you may be in the wrong line of work?"

Sidonius dropped the rock like a red-hot cinder and tried to draw a cloak of dignity around his brutalized sense of reality. "Who are you, my son? Step closer so I may see you."

The pair did so. They wore nondescript civilian garb. Oddly enough, for men supposedly embarked on a rescue, they were unarmed. Instead, each held a short metal rod of no apparent function—and yet, in an undefinable way, they carried the useless-seeming objects like weapons.

The man who had spoken was very dark considering the British origin his accent suggested, but his features and his blue eyes were not inconsistent with it. The other, aside from his robust size, could have passed unnoticed in the streets of Constantinople. Sidonius spared him barely a glance. He could only stare at the Briton—for such he seemed to be—and try to decide where he had seen him before, where he had heard that voice. For he was morally certain that he had met the man.

Ecdicius spoke without preamble. "How did you do that to them . . . with those?" he indicated the little metal rods. Sidonius felt his eyebrows rise; what could make Ecdicius think the strangers had incapacitated the would-be kidnappers with *those* things? It was manifestly impossible. And yet . . . what else *could* they have done it with? And Ecdicius and the Briton were gazing intently at each other, with a look that went beyond mutual respect, though that was very much present.

"Noblissimus," the other stranger spoke, "I know you

have many questions, but we haven't time to answer them. This city isn't safe for you—nor for you, Holy Father. Your only hope of safety is to follow us down to the Boucoleon Harbor." He gestured toward the darkling waters of the Sea of Marmara, barely visible through the trees. "We have a ship ready to take you to Italy."

"Italy?" Ecdicius blurted. "I can't just run away from Constantinople in the night like some footpad! The Augustus needs me. And Faustina, and—"

"Noblissimus," the big stranger cut in, "the Augustus is going to be beyond your help, or anyone's, very soon. And your wife and children are already on our ship."

"And," the Briton added, "you can accomplish nothing by staying here. Ah . . . here comes someone you know, Holiness. I think he may be able to persuade you."

A man emerged from the darkness. He was middle-aged, very tall, with features and coloring that must draw glances in even so cosmopolitan a place as Constantinople. . . .

"Tertullian," Sidonius breathed.

Ecdicius shot him a glance. "You know this man, Sidonius?"

Sidonius nodded. He heard his voice answer for him. "He was my secretary, long ago, before the Battle of Bourges. He was never heard of after the battle. We all assumed he had been killed."

"Well, Your Holiness, as you can see I'm very much alive. I regret that I had to leave your employ so abruptly. But there's no time for apologies now. This man—" he indicated the Briton "—is absolutely correct. The Noblissimus Ecdicius will not be allowed to live to assume the purple. You must both take refuge in the West, where support for his claim—and for the true Catholic faith—is concentrated."

Sidonius barely heard the last two sentences, for recognition had smote him again. "You!" He stared at the Briton. "I remember you now. You're that mercenary Tertullian hired as a bodyguard while he was travelling with Artorius. What was your name . . . ?"

"Bedwyr, Your Holiness. And my comrade here is Andronicus. And now can we *please* go?" His eyes met Ecdicius' again, and he raised, ever so slightly, the metallic rod he held.

For a heartbeat their eyes locked. Then Ecdicius' face broke into the familiar devil-may-care grin. "Lead on, then! I never was much good with my books—isn't that so, Sidonius?—but I like to think I can tell a good man when I see one."

"But Ecdicius," Sidonius stammered, feeling the solidly built structure of his life begin to pitch and heave like the deck of the ship these impossible people were leading them toward. "We can't . . . How do we know . . . ?"

"Ah, come on, Sidonius!" Ecdicius slapped the pontifical shoulder. "Is life really worth so much worrying?" And he was off behind the strangers, again the wiry, restless boy in the Arvernian villa.

Afterwards Sidonius could never remember much of the scramble through the darkened gardens, illuminated by the lighthouse to their right, down to the Boucoleon Harbor with its semicircular artificial mole. How these people had gotten access to the private imperial harbor was the least of the impossibilities that swirled through his mind. But underneath it all there seemed to lurk something very prosaic and obvious, something he should have noticed. Even as he stumbled over tree roots and half-slid down the final slope to the quay, he couldn't stop worrying about it.

Then they were approaching a ship, and Ecdicius was rushing ahead to embrace his wife and children, and Tertullian was conferring with a strongly built man on the quayside . . . and it finally came to Sidonius. Tertullian didn't look a day older than he had when Sidonius had last seen him. Bedwyr was somewhat older-looking, but not as much so as he should have been after twenty-two years. He stepped forward to ask Tertullian about it.

Then the strongly built man turned to face him, and the question fled his mind, along with everything else.

Tertullian must have seen his expression. "Ah . . . Your Holiness, I'm afraid I haven't been entirely candid with you."

Sidonius didn't hear him. He grew aware that he was on his knees, making the sign of the cross with frantic repetition—and, with his other hand, older signs such as the peasants of the Auvergne still made when no priest was looking. "*In nomine Patris,*" he began.

Strong hands grasped his arms and raised him up. "Don't be afraid, Sidonius." Yes, it was the same deep baritone.

"But . . . but . . . but *Augustus?!*"

As always, the boyish smile looked somehow right on that face—the face of a man in his early forties, the same face that the thirty-seven-year-old Sidonius had seen by the mouth of the Loire.

"Sidonius, you never change! If we're going to be fugitives together, I think you can address me by my *name!*"

# CHAPTER ONE

The battlecruiser had come out of continuous-displacement drive in the cold dark domain of the outer system. But now its sunward hyperbolic orbit had carried it into the regions where liquid water could, under certain circumstances, exist. Rear Admiral Robert Sarnac, Pan-Human League Space Fleet (Survey Branch), standing under the curving armorplast transparency that was a prerogative of his rank, was bathed in the light of the sun Loriima that flooded his quarters.

To an observer, he might have seemed to be talking very clearly and distinctly to himself. In fact, he was dictating a report for Fleet Ops. The computer wasn't really sentient, of course—that still lay in the realm of science fiction, where Sarnac privately hoped it would remain. But it was programmed with his personality and handled most of his routine business on its own, conversing with people mostly too young to care about their inability to tell whether they were talking to him or to his silicon-based familiar. It could be trusted to edit reports like this one, bleeping out all facetiousness, sarcasm and other assorted wise-ass-isms that he himself wouldn't have allowed onto the final hardcopy. He sometimes wished it wouldn't.

". . . And so," he concluded, "as per orders, I proceeded

with all possible speed to Starholm where I picked up my augmented staff. There, I learned that it has been confirmed that the hostile forces encountered in the Torlaerann Chain beyond Loriima are, indeed, of Korvaash race. I thereupon continued to Loriima, where, pursuant to orders, I have contacted Battle Group Thirty-Seven and assumed command, effective this date, Terran Standard 24 June, 2275." The computer would, of course, insert the Raehaniv half of the paired standard dating. "Upon arrival at Loriima III, I will receive a full report of the Battle Group's status, including progress made in repairing the recent battle damage. My first-sense impression is that the initial reports of the extent of that damage were not exaggerated.

"I therefore urgently request that the reinforcements I have been promised be dispatched as expeditiously as possible, since any delay in mounting a counterattack will only allow the Korvaasha to consolidate their position in—"

The door chimed for admittance. "Cease recording," Sarnac ordered—regretfully, for he hated to break such an uncharacteristic flow of pompous formality. *The computer must be proud of me*, he thought. *I haven't given it anything to clean up. Or maybe it thinks I'm up to something.* "Enter," he added. The door slid open, revealing his chief of staff.

Senior Captain Rimaeriy zho'Dornaeriel looked as Raehaniv as her name: tall, slender, sharp-featured, with skin of a coppery shade not quite like that of any of Earth's ethnic types. Her features were a caricature of those which, in Tiraena, were smoothed and muted by an infusion of Terran blood. It was a thought Sarnac couldn't let himself dwell on, for it reminded him of how long it had been since he had seen Tiraena. Too long. *And now we've got another goddamned war.*

"Well, Rimaeriy," he greeted her, "is everything set for our arrival? And don't tell me about any last-minute hitches—I don't need it!"

"Not to worry, sir," was what Sarnac heard inside his skull, overriding Rimaeriy's liquid Raehaniv. The ubiquitous implanted translators had swept away language barriers and allowed the wartime alliance between the two branches of humanity to ripen into the League.

"Our people have been in contact with what's left of the Battle Group Thirty-Seven staff," Rimaeriy continued, "and it looks like we'll be able to put together a combined staff without hurting too many feelings—the seniorities of the people involved worked out right. And we haven't gotten any trouble after the initial raised eyebrows over a Survey officer assuming command."

"Come on, Rimaeriy! It was more than 'raised eyebrows,' and I know damned well what these Line types really call 'Survey officers'! But they couldn't argue with the general order amalgamating Survey and Line and everything else for the duration and making seniority apply across the board regardless of branch."

"No, sir, they couldn't. And . . ." She hesitated. "They naturally stopped grumbling when they heard who the Survey admiral was."

Sarnac grimaced. He and Rimaeriy had been together too long for any possibility of brown-nosing, and they both knew it. The chief of staff was just stating facts. But he'd never overcome an inability to wear special status well. Maybe it was a matter of national character, for he was a child, however irreverent, of one of the North American successor-states, and the traditions of aggressive egalitarianism and "aw-shucks" self-deprecation had never quite died. Still, he reflected, fifteen years should have been time enough to adjust to it. He'd had to live with it since the day he and Tiraena had arrived in a stunned Solar System with the news that the beleaguered Solar Union had allies among the stars—human allies who had no business being there, including descendants of the Russian-American Mars Project people whose disappearance had mystified Terran humanity for two centuries. It had been the beginning of the end for the late unlamented Realm of Tarzhgul, and he had seen Fleet action in the final campaigns of the war—experience which should stand him in good stead now.

But, as always, notoriety had been a decidedly mixed blessing for a junior officer. There had been times when he had come close to quitting the service. The lure of new frontiers had kept him in, just as it had kept Tiraena in the affiliated civilian agencies, specializing in alien contact as she had done before they—and, through them, their peoples—had met. It was what she was doing right now, on the far side of the League from the Torlaerann Chain.

"And," Rimaeriy went on, sensing the Admiral's discomfort and changing the subject, "the fact that we've got an ops officer who's Line should make them feel better."

Sarnac nodded. Captain Draco had joined the staff at Starholm, and the death in action of Battle Group Thirty-Seven's operations officer had left a vacancy he would fill in the combined staff. Sarnac didn't know him, but on the basis of his service record he'd been glad to get him. An altogether impressive man . . . and one whom Sarnac couldn't stop thinking he had met somewhere, long ago and far away. For the sight of him had aroused unwelcome, tantalizing echoes of the dreams. *They've been getting worse lately. Why?*

"All right, Rimaeriy," he said, dragging his mind back to the here-and-now. "Let me finish this report for Fleet Ops. Then I'll want to go over the new staff postings with you."

A couple of Terran weeks passed, and the combined staff was, if not quite a band of brothers (and sisters), at least a smoothly functioning unit. Rimaeriy had worked wonders, Sarnac thought as he entered the briefing room—Rimaeriy, and Captain Draco.

He studied the officers who rose to their feet in the afternoon Loriima-light that streamed through the tall windows. The majority were Raehaniv-looking. However integrated the League's military had become, units still tended to retain their original ethnic character. Battle Group Thirty-Seven, based here at an old Raehaniv colony, had always been a predominantly Raehaniv outfit. Of course, a certain number of them showed the blood of those Terran exiles for whose descendants fighting for Raehan had become a tradition. . . . Sarnac sternly dismissed the image of Tiraena.

In an instant's flash of clarity, he wondered at the way these humans, originating on two planets a light-millennium apart, could function so matter-of-factly in the face of the inexplicable. But that was the point, of course: the existence of *homo sapiens sapiens* on two different planets *was* inexplicable, and the peoples of the League couldn't let themselves dwell on the mind-numbing impossibility of it. They could only agree that the human species—and certain others—had evolved on Earth and somehow appeared on Raehan thirty thousand years ago, apparently through the agency of a palpably impossible prehistoric human starfaring culture, and let it go at that, assuring each other that future discoveries would undoubtedly clear up all the mystery. Only thus could they concentrate on immediate practicalities.

*Like the fact that we've just turned up another Korvaash successor-state,* Sarnac thought. *Yeah, the other end of creation is probably the best place for Tiraena to be right now, just like school on Earth is the best place for Claude and Liranni.*

Two centuries earlier the Korvaash empire, the Unity, had sprawled over an unknowable expanse of this spiral arm, and had extended one tentacle to crush the life out of Raehan. Varien hle'Morna, the eccentric genius who had invented the continuous-displacement drive that allowed interstellar travel without recourse to fixed displacement points, had taken his discovery to Earth and offered it as payment for help for his world. In one of history's little ironies, he had arrived to find a world turning its back on space as it sought a return to a totalitarian womb. But the exiled American and Russian terraformers had taken up his offer, departing with him and destroying all evidence of their origin so as to place their homeworld beyond Korvaash reprisal in the event of failure.

Against all odds, they had succeeded in lopping off the Korvaash tentacle that had clutched Raehan. And then had come one of the recurring realignments of the galaxy's displacement structure. It had put an end to the Unity, but it left the Terran exiles in the same state of ignorance as to Earth's location that they had intended for the Korvaasha.

So matters had stood until fifteen years ago, when Earth's recovered humanity, fighting for its life against one of the surviving fragments of the Korvaash Unity, had encountered their cousins of Raehan. This time the reunion of the two humanities was to be permanent, because Lieutenant Robert Sarnac and Tiraena zho'Daeriel DiFalco had evaded Korvaash pursuit to reach Earth.

As Sarnac looked his staff over, they studied him in turn through the lens of that story. They saw a man of barely average Terran height—his female Raehaniv chief of staff overtopped him by an inch—with dark complexion and strikingly contrasting light blue eyes. By grace of the Raehaniv biotechnology now available throughout the League, his curly hair was as black as ever at forty-three, and thicker than it had been fifteen years before. Middle-aged solidity had not yet overlaid a kind of athletic rakishness.

"As you were, people," he said briskly. "After all the shared VR hookups, I thought it was time we had an in-the-flesh meeting of the entire staff. Unfortunately, Commander Tarluin can't be present." A freakish shipyard accident had put the intelligence officer into the regen tank for at least another week. "But his boss will give us the update. Captain Draco, you have the floor."

"Thank you, sir." Captain Geoffrey Draco, though dark

of hair and eyes, didn't have the kind of Latin look his surname suggested. But names were only coincidentally related to origins in the ethnic bouillabaisse that was present-day Earth. He looked European, and you couldn't narrow it down much more than that. He wasn't tall, but he was very strongly built. He was about Sarnac's age; his record said he was ex-enlisted, which explained why he was still just a captain despite his obviously exceptional abilities. It also explained why Sarnac had never met him during the war against the Realm of Tarzhgul—they had been serving at different levels.

In fact, nobody in the staff had ever met him . . .

"Everybody knows the general background," he said, derailing Sarnac's train of thought. He used a pocket remote unit and a holo of the Torlaerann Chain appeared between the table and the ceiling. "When a survey squadron probing along the Chain failed to report, heavy elements of Battle Group Thirty-Seven investigated. Fortunately, some of them got back, with a small hostile craft they'd tractored. No prisoners to interrogate, of course—they had automatic suicide implants. But enough was left to identify them as Korvaasha. Commander Tarluin and his people have had a chance to analyze the tapes of the battle. At a minimum, they're more advanced than the Realm of Tarzhgul was. For one thing, they've got deflector technology."

"Hm . . . inventive Korvaasha," Sarnac mused. "Not too good."

"No, sir. But not entirely unanticipated. When the shifting of the displacement network left the various pieces of the old Unity on their own, most of them simply died. They'd been locked into a rigid totalitarian structure so long that they couldn't function in the absence of higher authority. The ones who survived were the ones who, for whatever reasons, *could* adapt. The dangerous ones. There must be a lot of variation among the surviving Korvaash cultures in the galaxy by now." A bleak smile. "Maybe there are even some we can get along with. But not these, it seems."

"Hardly," Sarnac agreed. The deflectors worried him. The device was an application of gravitics, fending off incoming objects with a force proportional to their own kinetic energy. Varien hle'Morna had gotten the idea from relics of the prehistoric spacefaring culture that was one facet of the enigma of Raehaniv origins. That the Korvaasha—whose lack of inventiveness relative to humans was widely thought to be not merely a cultural trait but a racial one—had apparently come up with it on their own was disturbing.

"Could they have the continuous-displacement drive?" Rimaeriy asked.

"Unknown. The fact that it came before deflectors in *our* history is immaterial; our development was shaped by a quirky genius working with archaeological hints. But even if they do have it, it's of limited use to them in the current tactical situation, because they have no knowledge of where we come from in realspace."

Heads nodded around the table. Exploration was something that the League did with great caution. Survey ships carried no astronomical data that were not rigged for instant cybernetic lobotomy in the event of probable capture.

"We, on the other hand, know exactly where they are," Draco continued. One of the holographic star-symbols flashed obligingly. "And we *do* have the continuous-displacement drive. This sets them up for the classical trap used in the liberation of Raehan by Eric and Aelanni DiFalco."

*Tiraena's great-grandparents*, Sarnac thought. Aloud: "Yes—come at the defenders of a displacement point from a direction where you've got no business being, and *then* come through the displacement point like you're supposed to. One problem, Captain: we're talking a displacement connection that bypasses a realspace distance of over three hundred light-years. Any units we send there via continuous-displacement drive are going to have to be units built for speed and endurance and little else."

"Yes, sir," Draco acknowledged unflinchingly. "Also, there's the possibility of an additional problem: if they *do* have continuous-displacement drive, the maneuver won't come as a surprise to them. Even if they've never used it themselves, the theoretical possibility should be apparent to them, and we have to assume that they'll have taken precautions against it.

"But," he continued after letting the silence stretch just long enough, "we've developed an operational plan that takes both of these considerations into account and, I believe, offers a very high probability of success. I invite your attention to the folders in front of you, marked 'Most Secret.' "

He continued, holding everyone's attention. Sarnac found himself admiring not just the plan itself—without question a brilliant piece of work—but also the dynamism of Draco's presentation. No doubt about it, he was a man who had that indefinable thing called "charisma" coming out his ears.

And he was also a man Sarnac had known before. He was surer of that than ever. But every time a gesture or a mannerism awakened the insubstantial wisp of familiarity, it flitted elusively away like the tatters of an old dream.

But the dream didn't lie comfortably in the past—it was new and it came to renew itself more and more.

*Blossoms swirling in the wind of our passage as we rode through the spring under a cloudless sky when the world was young . . .*

*Armies grinding together in a roar of pain and terror and blood . . .*

*The circle of faces wavering ghostlike in the flickering campfire . . .*

*The still lake . . . the sword tumbling end over end through the air, flashing in the westering sun, dazzling my eyes so that I nearly miss the ripples spreading from*

*where it had struck the water—where surely it must have
struck the water . . .*

Sarnac's head jerked upward from his desk, spinning
with the disorientation of sudden awakening. For an instant
his skin prickled as he looked beyond the pool of light
from the desk lamp into the shadows. Then he shook his
head in annoyance as the familiarity of the office registered.
Served him right, working late and falling asleep at his
desk!

He shook his head again, to clear away the last cobwebs
of sleep. What was he going to do? He couldn't fight a
war distracted by insomnia! He knew he'd been resisting
sleep lately, since the recurring dreams had ceased to be
the once-in-a-while thing they had been over the years.
But eventually his body's need caught up with him—like
just now. And the dreams would come again, leaving him
with an aching need to find a missing part of himself.

*What's the matter with me? In the Middle Ages they
would have said I was being tormented by demons. In
the twentieth and twenty-first centuries they would have
said the same thing, only phrased in terms of their
established religion of psychoanalysis. Either way, I could
have gone to the local priesthood and gotten sprinkled
with holy water or psychobabble. Nowadays, we've finally
admitted that we really don't know diddly about what
goes on underneath the surface of the human mind—which
is wise but not too awfully helpful.* Tiraena had always
been a willing listener but an uncomprehending one, for
she had never had such dreams herself. It was something
she couldn't really share with him, and that inability had
come more and more between them. *And, at any rate,
she's not here now.*

He straightened. He certainly wasn't going to get any
more work done tonight. He needed to get back to his
quarters; maybe, having gotten in its licks already, the
dream would leave him alone for the rest of the night.
He stood up.

It was then that he saw the figure in the open door, silhouetted against the light from the outer office.

"What the . . . who are you?" he demanded. There shouldn't be anyone else in this office, they'd all gone home earlier.

Instead of answering, the figure stepped forward into the private office, entering the circle of light from the desk lamp. He was a nondescript middle-aged man in nondescript civilian clothes, medium-tall and ethnically unidentifiable—he might have had some Raehaniv blood, but Sarnac couldn't be certain. What *was* certain was that he had no business being here. *I'm gonna have a few words for Security*, Sarnac vowed to himself . . . but then the thought died as he realized he was feeling the same thing he always felt in Captain Draco's presence: a tantalizing certainty that he had seen the face before, in the country of his dreams.

The man smiled gently. "Good evening, Admiral Sarnac. I apologize for approaching you in this manner. But you're an important man, and it was the only way I could catch you alone."

"If you're a reporter, this is *not* the way to get an exclusive interview," Sarnac snapped. "And you never answered me. Who are you? And how did you get in here?" He made the unobtrusive jaw movement that activated his implant communicator, and was about to subvocalize a call to Security when the stranger replied.

"To answer your questions in order, Admiral, I am not a journalist; and my name is Tylar."

"Just . . . Tylar?"

"Actually, my full name is rather long. But 'Tylar' is quite sufficient."

"I'm relieved." It didn't come out as sarcastic as Sarnac had intended, and he missed the fact that Tylar had omitted to answer his final question. For the sense of recognition was back, this time with the force of certainty.

"May I sit down, Admiral? I'm afraid I'm not as young as I once was." Evidently taking assent for granted, Tylar lowered himself into a chair. Feeling slightly foolish, Sarnac followed suit. As he did so, he subvocalized a code which would bring a Security team. There was no acknowledgment. He frowned with a puzzled annoyance which Tylar's gentle smile did nothing to ameliorate. Could the man read his mind?

He forced patience on himself. "All right, Tylar. Tell me what you're doing here."

"I'm here in connection with a matter of mutual interest, Admiral: the dreams that have been troubling you."

There was a long moment of absolute silence. "What are you talking about?" Sarnac finally managed.

"Come, now. We both know. And we also know that you need help. I'm here to offer it."

"Why should you want to?"

"A matter of ethics, Admiral. I'm fulfilling a moral obligation. You see, I'm responsible for the fact that you're having the dreams." Tylar raised a forestalling hand as Sarnac's mouth started to open. "Let me hasten to add that this result was entirely unintended on my part. The fault lies with an inherently fallible process—to wit, selective memory erasure. I'm afraid yours simply didn't take very well. This became clear upon your return to the Solar System fifteen years ago, when you rendezvoused with the battlecruiser *Excalibur*."

Sarnac was in the process of signalling Security to send medical personnel as well—for Tylar clearly was raving mad in a calm, professorial sort of way—and wondering why he was still getting no acknowledgment, when the stranger's last sentence brought him up short. It had been years since he'd thought of that rendezvous, at the conclusion of his uneventful voyage from Sirius. But now the memories came flooding back, bearing with them the certain knowledge that there was a connection with the dreams.

It had been customary in those days to decorate the wardrooms of Sword-class battlecruisers with murals illustrating the legends of the blades after which the ships were named. *Excalibur's* wardroom had been adorned with a painting of Sir Bedivere throwing his dying king's magical sword into the water, to be caught by the Lady of the Lake. He had no clear recollection of what the sight of that mural on the comm pickup had awakened in him. All he could remember was regaining consciousness in Tiraena's arms and being asked what he had meant about the artist not having gotten things right, and about the sun having blinded him. . . .

*. . . The flash of reflected sunlight, strangely dazzling considering that the blade had been encrusted with dried mud and gore . . .* He shook himself free of the maddening half-memories. Tylar was smiling his irritatingly gentle smile.

"Yes, I see that you remember. It was just one of those things. No one could have foreseen that out of the entire Solar Union fleet you'd be met by that particular battlecruiser! I suspect it was that instant of recollection that prevented the unavoidable mnemonic residue from dissipating over time as it usually does, crowded out by the press of day-to-day sensory impressions—"

"Wait a minute, Tylar! Talk sense!"

"Believe me, Admiral, everything will become clear after it has been adequately explained . . . for which purpose, I must ask you to accompany me."

"What? Look, Tylar, I admit you've displayed knowledge that requires me to take you seriously. But I can't just go off with you to God knows where! In case you hadn't noticed, we've got a war on here—and I, God help me, am the on-scene commander! I don't know if a sense of duty has any place in your value system, but—"

"Be assured, Admiral, that the twin concepts of 'honor' and 'duty' are basic to my culture—as they must be to any culture which lasts long enough to contribute to that ongoing accumulation of worthwhile ideas that certain immature societies try so gropingly to conceptualize with the notion of 'progress.' " The voice had ceased to have anything of the absent-minded professor about it. Indeed, it was as the voice of many trumpets. But then the moment was past, as was Sarnac's memory of it, and there was only Tylar, sitting across the desk and looking faintly embarrassed.

"But, my dear fellow," he said diffidently, "you need have no worries concerning your discharge of your duties. When our business is concluded, I will return you to this place and time . . . whatever time this is." He glanced at an ordinary-seeming timepiece. "Loriima III's 28.6 hour rotation period is frightfully confusing, don't you agree?"

Sarnac blinked. All right, that settled it: Tylar was mad as a hatter. But then the stranger rose and reached into a pocket. Sarnac stiffened . . . but the device Tylar produced was clearly not a weapon. He placed it on the floor. Sarnac waited for him to do or say something. But all that happened was that a doorway-sized rectangle, outlined in glowing insubstantial bars of refracted light, formed with its lower left-hand corner resting on Tylar's device. Sarnac blinked repeatedly, for through that outline he saw not the room beyond but . . . what?

"Shall we go, Admiral?" Tylar asked pleasantly, and stepped through the immaterial portal. Then he turned and beckoned. "Here lie your dreams."

As though in a dream, Sarnac followed him.

# CHAPTER TWO

They had passed through two more of the portals before Sarnac called a halt. One had led into a corridor in what Sarnac was somehow sure was a space vessel—although there were no sensations that he could have pointed to in support of his conviction—and the second had given entry through what had been a solid bulkhead into . . . this place.

"Wait! Wait, Tylar!" He stood stock-still in the gentle breeze under the blue vault of sky, looking around at the intricately landscaped grounds of what seemed to be a villa whose gracefulness transcended all canons of architectural form and, indeed, somehow incorporated them. He tried to speak again, but no words would come—how does one frame questions about the patently impossible? He could only drink in the heart-stopping loveliness of it.

There was an indefinable oddness about every perspective, and an even more indefinable sense that there were things here he was not seeing, not because they were invisible but because they were incomprehensible—his brain simply edited them out, refusing to process the input of his eyes. But none of this detracted from the almost unendurable perfection of the scene.

Tylar turned around and faced him. "Yes, I know this is all a bit much, Admiral. For now, suffice it to say that we are in an artificially generated pocket universe . . . and that you have been here before."

The odd thing was, Sarnac never for an instant doubted him. For this was one of the impossible settings he glimpsed in his dreams as if by flashes of lightning. But he could accept no more. He closed his eyes, shutting out the vista of achingly unattainable beauty, and forced himself to speak.

"Tylar, before I go another step you've *got* to tell me more. I want to know who you are and where you're from and what you once did to me."

Tylar regarded him for a couple of heartbeats, then spoke briskly. "If you think about it, I'm sure you'll conclude that the question of my origin can have only one possible answer, however fantastic that answer may seem in light of your civilization's understanding of reality. I am from your future—your quite remote future. As for what I did to you, I took you and your Tiraena into the timestream that my people have learned to navigate, after rescuing you from your Korvaash captors near the end of your voyage from Sirius to Sol fifteen years ago—"

Sarnac came out of his paralysis with a jolt. "*What?* Tylar, what the hell are you talking about? We left the Korvaasha eating our dust at Sirius! *Nothing* happened on our trip from there to Sol; it was almost anticlimactic."

"Yes," Tylar nodded. "So you remember. It was at the instant before the Korvaasha overhauled you in the outliers of the Solar System that we cut off your memories. The battlecruiser you thought you had eluded had in fact followed you from Sirius using a captured Raehaniv continuous-displacement drive. It was commanded by a Korvaash officer with whom you had previously crossed swords, on Danu."

A chill struck into Sarnac. "The Interrogator!"

"Yes, I believe that was what he called himself. At any rate, we maneuvered a temportal, as we call it, into the path of the Korvaash ship, thus transposing them—and you—seventeen centuries into the past. You see, we had need of you in the fifth century of the Christian Era, for reasons I later explained to you. Afterwards, we regrettably had to delete your memories of everything except your humdrum voyage from Sirius. We then returned you to your own time, on course for Sol. After which you, to use a traditional and deservedly popular phrase, lived happily ever after . . . except for the recurring dreams that resulted from a faulty job of memory erasure."

For a long moment, the silence stretched to the snapping point. Then Sarnac spoke in a voice choked with rising fury.

"So you used me and Tiraena for God-knows-what purposes of your own, and then stole our memories! Why, you cynical, dishonest, manipulative old bastard!"

"Actually, I'm not all that old—at least not on the standards of my own society. And it would be more accurate to say I *borrowed* your memories." His sheepish look would have been funny on anyone else under any other circumstances. "You see, while your minds still held those memories I took the liberty of recording them. It wasn't exactly 'by the book,' as I believe you'd put it, but it seemed a shame to let them simply vanish into oblivion."

"So on top of everything else you're a mental voyeur!"

"My dear fellow, I should think you'd be grateful to me." Tylar sounded deeply hurt. "If I hadn't artificially preserved your memories, it wouldn't be possible to restore them to you, as I now propose to do."

"What? You can do that? You can, uh, 'play back' recorded memories into the brain?"

"Yes . . . with some difficulty, and some initial disorientation for the individual involved. You'll still have your memories of the years since then, of course; so you'll remember fifteen years of *not* remembering the events you'll now remember! I'm told it can be quite disconcerting at first. Knowing this, are you willing to undergo it? I'll not compel you."

Another interval of strained silence passed. Then Sarnac

grinned crookedly. "Yeah . . . you know damned well you don't *have* to compel me, don't you? There's no way I could possibly turn back now."

"Well then," Tylar beamed, "shall we?" He gestured toward a foot path, and they proceeded toward the villa.

*The brutally massive Korvaash ship looming impossibly astern, laden with its cargo of nightmare . . .*

*The torus of reality-distortion they flashed through, and the impossible little ship that overtook them at a substantial fraction of lightspeed and then stopped dead and tractored the great hulking Korvaash battlecruiser . . .*

*Tylar being his inimitable self . . . "We were so concerned, after this dreadful mix-up . . . Dear me! This is going to be even more difficult to explain than I thought . . . It occurs to me that if you prefer to make some use of your time in this era, you could perhaps assist us in our research . . ."*

*The three of them, moving dreamlike through the nearly forgotten Gallic campaign of the British High King Riothamus: Tylar as Tertullian, secretary to tinsel-age litterateur Sidonius Apollinaris; Tiraena as Lucasta, a lady-in-waiting to Riothamus' consort; and Sarnac as the British soldier of fortune Bedwyr, bodyguard to Tertullian and later confidant of sorts to Riothamus . . .*

*His dawning realization of just who Riothamus really was . . .*

*The Battle of Bourg-de-Déols, where Riothamus fell victim to treachery . . .*

*The mountain lake and the thrown sword that had flashed in the westering sun so many times in his dreams . . . and after he had thrown it, his words to his friend Kai, welling up from he knew not where: "His name will live longer than you can possibly imagine . . . in a way, he can never die . . ."*

*Tylar's final explanation of what they had been put through, and of his own people's policing of the past to assure that history followed the course that had eventuated in their own existence—including their planting of the ancestral humans on Raehan, where history said they had to be present in defiance of all evolutionary logic . . .*

*"Tylar . . . aren't you going to change history by returning us to our own time. I mean, when we get back there knowing what we now know, knowing all you've just told us . . ." "Ah, but do you?"*

*And the sinking into unconsciousness, as Tylar looked on with unmistakeable sadness . . .*

"How are we feeling today?"

"What's this 'we' stuff?" Sarnac growled as Tylar entered his quarters. He wasn't about to give over being mad at the time traveller, but he couldn't complain about the accommodations.

He was sitting in a kind of solarium, suffused with simulated sunlight from the holoprojection that was the "sky" of this few-kilometers-wide pocket universe. It was midmorning of the local twenty-four-hour day—Sarnac wondered if that was for his benefit—and he was digesting both his breakfast and his new knowledge.

Tylar crossed the inner living room and joined him in the solarium, obviously in no hurry. Sarnac allowed himself only a moment's glare before giving in and answering the time traveller's question.

"Pretty good. You didn't exaggerate about the 'initial disorientation,' that's for sure. Besides the problems you mentioned, there's the freshness of these fifteen-year-old memories—I can remember it all more clearly than I can the births of my children, or things that happened just last year!"

"But you're over the sensation by now, I trust?"

"Yeah, I've gotten things more or less sorted out." He gave the time traveller a hard, level look. "And I've been doing some thinking."

"Oh?" Tylar seated himself across the low table from

Sarnac, as though settling in for a discussion he had known was coming.

"I've been thinking," Sarnac repeated, "about the reason you wiped our memories: we couldn't be allowed back into our own historical period with knowledge like the origin of Raehaniv humanity that our era isn't supposed to have. And yet you *had* to let us return, because your history said we had gotten through to Sol. I suppose that's why I'm not exactly slobbering with gratitude for your having saved us from the Korvaasha. You had your own reasons; in fact, you needed us as much as we needed you."

Tylar spread his hands. "What can I say? You're correct, of course—as far as you go. But I hope you can also remember that my motivations regarding you and Tiraena were, at bottom, benign."

"Oh, yes, I can accept that. And I think I've more or less gotten over being pissed at you. But that's not the point now." He leaned forward intently. "The point is that the same reasons for not letting anybody with the knowledge you've just given back to me run around loose in the twenty-third century still apply with equal force. So *why* have you given me back the memories? And please don't tell me it's out of an altruistic desire to relieve me from my nagging dreams!"

"Ah." Tylar settled back in his chair, steepling his fingers in a gesture Sarnac now remembered. "Well, I'm afraid I haven't been entirely candid with you. . . ."

Sarnac lowered his head into his hands with a low moan and spoke without looking up. "Tylar, one of the things I remember is that every time you say that I end up taking a barge pole up the ass!"

"Oh, nothing as alarming as all that, my dear fellow! It's just that you needed to have the memories restored in order to fulfill a certain obligation."

"Obligation?"

"Yes. An ethical obligation—an extremely important one. I should add that it's primarily mine. But it is in some small part yours as well. And it is my intention to give you the opportunity to set matters aright—to pay a debt that you otherwise wouldn't even have realized you owed."

*He actually looks proud of himself,* Sarnac thought in a haze of unreality, *as though he's doing me some tremendous favor.* "Uh, Tylar, maybe you'd better explain things one at a time . . . starting with just what the hell you're talking about."

"Of course. In fact, I'm waiting for someone who will help me with the explanation. . . . Ah, here he is now."

"May I come in, Admiral?" a familiar deep, resonant baritone spoke from the entrance.

Sarnac sprang out of his chair and whirled to face the figure in Fleet uniform. "Captain Draco! What are you doing here . . . ?" His voice jolted to a halt and he grasped his chair for support as belated recognition crashed into him.

*How could I have not made the connection with "Captain Geoffrey Draco" as soon as Tylar poured the memories back into my skull? Well, he does look different without a beard. And I'm still integrating all these suddenly reacquired memories with my subsequent life. . . .*

Even as the strangely calm thoughts were making their unhurried way through the storm center of his brain, his throat struggled to form words. "But . . . but . . . but you *died!*" he finally got out.

"Ah, but you know what people say about me! You should; it's largely because of you that they say it!"

Tylar cleared his throat. "I suppose I should have given you some warning, Robert. You see, we evacuated him and took care of his wounds. I'd intended to mention it to you and Tiraena, but . . ."

"But it somehow slipped your mind. Right." Sarnac gave the time traveller a quick, poisonous look and then addressed his operations officer. " 'Draco.' Of course. Cute. But where did the 'Geoffrey' come from?"

"Oh, that. Well, it's my way of paying tribute to Geoffrey

of Monmouth. His account of my life was highly fictionalized, but I rather like it."

"You would! You always had a vain streak, as I recall. Not that I would have said so out loud, back then. I wasn't exactly on your social level."

"No, you weren't," Draco acknowledged affably. "But now we're both officers and gentlemen of the Pan-Human League." The voice held not a hint of irony. "In fact, you outrank me! I'll have to wait for you to invite me in."

"Huh? Oh, yeah. Sure." Sarnac gestured expansively at the table and chairs. "Come on in! *Mi casa es su casa*, and all that! Make yourself at home. . . ." He realized he was babbling, but he thought he was doing about as well as could be expected under the circumstances.

After all, he told himself, it's not every day you invite King Arthur into your quarters.

"So those three ladies who came to take you to the convent in the town were Tylar's people?" Sarnac fortified himself with another sip of the wine Tylar had earned his relieved gratitude by supplying. He was remembering with special vividness the Britons' retreat into the Burgundian lands with their mortally wounded High King, ending outside a town perched on a crag at the eastern end of a valley . . . the town called Avallon.

"Precisely," said Draco—or was it Artorius? (Arthur? Somehow, no.) "You were gone at the time."

"Yeah, tossing your pig-sticker into that lake. By the way, what should I be calling you?"

"Oh, make it 'Artorius'; it *is* my birth name, after all. Anything but that honorific 'Riothamus,' which I never much liked." He took a sip of wine. "And I've been wanting to thank you for that business with the sword. As you gathered at the time, it meant a lot to me. I was intermittently delirious by then, and my mind kept returning to the old Sarmatian hero-tales I'd grown up on."

"Tales that I implanted into the Western tradition,

dressed in Celtic clothes—as *you* intended all along," Sarnac added with a sideways glare that didn't put a dent in Tylar's visible self-satisfaction.

"Yes," the time traveller nodded. "It was necessary. And the whole episode worked out very well indeed, from the standpoint of establishing the mythic elements of the story. It was a nice touch, if I do say so myself, to simulate those three ladies who've kept turning up in myth—finding Christ's tomb empty, for example—ever since the Bronze Age."

Sarnac, a lapsed Catholic, wasn't offended. "Only, they didn't really take King Arthur off to Avalon, however you spell it. They took him through your portals to a sickbay where his wounds were a snap to fix. As much as I hate to admit it, that was pretty decent of you."

"True," Tylar allowed. "But I can't claim it was pure, disinterested altruism. The fact is, Artorius was simply too valuable to be allowed to die. I really *am* a historical researcher, you know—among other things. And in the course of our time in Gaul in 469 and 470 I came to the conclusion that he was an even more remarkable individual than we had previously thought."

"Yeah, I remember you mentioning something about it, at the Battle of Angers," Sarnac said. Artorius, he noted, was handling all this very well. But then, it was hard to imagine him not doing so. *Never mind the Romans and their Sarmatian cavalry auxiliaries crowding the Celts in his family tree*, he thought, as he often had in the fifth century. *This guy wrote the book on the charm of the western isles.*

"So," Tylar continued, "after restoring him to physical health, we gave him an up-to-date education and employed him as a field agent. You see, our experience with you and Tiraena had convinced us of the usefulness of operatives from prim—ah, from backgrounds more typical of most of human history than our own. We expected Artorius to display tremendous aptitude for the work. I might add that he's more than fulfilled those expectations. Indeed, he's made himself indispensable to me in the years that have followed—more subjective years, by the way, than the fifteen that have passed for you."

Sarnac nodded. He was still readjusting to the consequences of time travel. And he noted that Artorius seemed no older than he remembered. *Well, with the kind of medical science Tylar's people must have . . . and of course anybody looks younger clean-shaven than with a beard. . . .*

"It must have been a hell of an adjustment for you," he suggested to the former High King of the Britons.

"It was all of that," Artorius agreed with the emphatic nod that Sarnac recalled. The shadow of a wind-blown cloud seemed to cross the strongly marked features. "At first it was like a continuation of the delirium. Afterwards . . . I can't tell you what it was like, because I can't clearly remember myself. It would have been worse, I think, if I'd been taken directly into *your* world. There would have been just enough that was, if not familiar, at least comprehensible, to make the rest seem *wrong*. And the wrongness might have driven me mad. But in *his* world, where *everything* is beyond dreams, I could just . . . let go, and accept things as I found them."

"Yes," Tylar nodded. "*You* could. Not everyone would have been so resilient. In this, too, you lived up to our expectations. I for one wasn't surprised in the least at your subsequent success in the field."

"Well," Artorius said easily, "I've tried to do well by you, for I owe you a debt. Not just for saving my life, but for giving me a new one, one which is . . ." For the first time since Sarnac had known him—in any century—he was at a loss for words. "The things I've seen," he finally half-whispered.

"I can certainly vouch for how good you are," Sarnac said. "Your performance as my ops officer . . . well!" He paused for a moment while they all partook of the wine.

"Satisfy my curiosity about something. When did you tumble to me?"

Artorius raised one dark brow. "Tumble . . . ?"

"Maybe you don't remember it clearly, but at the end you told me you knew I wasn't just a simple merc. How long had you known? And what gave me away?"

For a moment their eyes held each other, and Sarnac remembered those same eyes staring out of a blood-stained face while the dying High King whispered, *"Bedwyr, I know you're not what you claim to be, though I know not what you really are—nor do I wish to know, for I believe that knowledge lies beyond the proper ken of mortals."*

"There had been a lot of little things," Artorius finally answered. "But what finally convinced me was the exchange we had just before the army set out from Bourges. It was obvious that you knew more than you were telling. You wanted to persuade me not to advance into Berry without waiting for reinforcements from Soissons, but you couldn't say so openly. It kept nagging at me. And, of course, when your unspoken prophecy came true . . ." He let his voice trail off with a shrug.

Sarnac remembered very well that spring morning in Bourges, looking up into the face of the man he must watch be destroyed as history required. The forbidden hint had been out of his mouth before he could shut it.

"Artorius," he asked softly, "have you ever wished, in the years since then, that you could just say to hell with history and go back to that morning and act on my not-quite-advice? Wait inside the walls of Bourges for the Romans and Franks, then go out and kick the Visigoths' butts . . ."

"No!" The vehemence rocked Sarnac physically back in his chair, and he saw in that face what many others had seen above a shield-rim across a battlefield, though far fewer had lived to remember seeing it. And then Artorius' smile was like the sun breaking through thunderclouds.

"Sorry, old man, but you're talking about things that mustn't even be spoken of. Besides, I've learned a lot about history since then, and I know what a calamity it would have been if I had succeeded."

"Yes," Sarnac nodded. "Tylar explained it to me and Tiraena. In defeat you bequeathed the emerging Western culture a legend that helped give it shape. If you had won . . ."

"It wasn't comfortable knowledge, I can tell you! But Tylar helped me to become reconciled to it, to realize that all I had done hadn't been in vain or worse." Artorius smiled again. "I understand you tried to do the same for Kai. Good old Kai! That's something else I meant to thank you for."

"Well," Sarnac said uncomfortably, "he was a friend. It was the least I could do. I imagine I broke some rules," he added with a glance at Tylar, "but it didn't matter. I doubt if he understood a word I was saying."

"That's usually the way it is," Tylar acknowledged. "He took the parts he *did* grasp back to Britain with him, and they entered into the legend as was intended. That, too, is usually the way it is. However, I'm glad you've raised the point, because it's closely related to the reason I've brought you here again and restored your memories."

"Oh, yeah; I'd almost forgotten, in all this . . ." Sarnac waved vaguely in Artorius' direction. "So tell me about this 'obligation' or 'debt' of mine."

"Well, it's rather complicated . . ."

"Things generally are, with you," Sarnac interjected drily.

". . . so let me begin at the beginning. You recall my little lecture to you and Tiraena on my people's experiences with time travel and the various theories we'd developed and then discarded concerning the nature of reality and the potential effect of time travellers upon it?" Sarnac nodded, and Tylar resumed, clearly uncomfortable. "Well, it turns out that our most recent theory still needs some fine-tuning."

❖        ❖        ❖

An awkward moment passed as Sarnac waited for an explanation of that statement, so fraught with disturbing implications. When none was forthcoming, he broke the silence. "You mean that time travellers can't affect history at certain critical times after all? But Tylar, that would invalidate the whole rationale for your people's policing of the past. . . ."

"Oh, no," the time traveller cut in emphatically, seeming to look around for something to mop his brow with as he waved away Sarnac's near-obscene suggestion. "Absolutely not! That's not what I mean. *That* aspect of the theory is still good. As I explained to you and Tiraena, throughout most of history reality possesses a very strong 'fabric,' impervious to being 'torn' even by seemingly brutal applications of force." He shifted into discursive mode. "Remember I mentioned that we have research tools beyond your understanding, whereby we can extrapolate the outcomes of theoretical interventions in history? Well, we used these methods to plot out one of the favorite daydreams of early time-travel theorists: going back and killing Adolf Hitler in his cradle. You'd be surprised how little would have changed. The Germans of the post-World War I era would have found somebody else like him. Likewise, doing the same to the infant Christopher Columbus would accomplish little except to satisfy certain American Indian revanchists. The European discovery of America around that time was inevitable. Oh, some unimportant things would have been different; the Spanish language might have become less widespread, Portuguese and Dutch perhaps more so. But the Native American societies were doomed."

"At the same time," Sarnac said, in an effort to get Tylar back on track, "you told us that at certain points history has a weak, frayed 'fabric' that can be torn with minimum effort. You indicated that Artorius' Gallic campaign that we were mixed up in was one of those points in history."

"Indeed it was. History was at a turning point, and its

momentum could have been deflected by the lightest touch and sent careening off onto a whole new course."

"But it *wasn't*," Sarnac stated. "Your policing operation was a complete success, wasn't it? You told us as much. So what's the big deal?"

"Well, it seems that some areas of 'weak fabric' in the historical tapestry are even weaker than others, and that your conversation with Artorius in Bourges represented a moment of extraordinary—perhaps unique—weakness. Our theorists don't understand why—there's *so* much we don't understand!—but evidently reality can only tolerate that degree of instability for the briefest instant; it only lasted a few seconds after you spoke to Artorius, while he wavered. But for that moment in time, the future teetered on a knife-edge!"

"Scary," Sarnac admitted. "But, again, so what? The moment passed, Artorius decided as history said he did, and that was that. 'God's in his heaven, all's right with the world.'"

"Well . . . yes and no. You see, the discovery of that area of unprecedentedly weak 'fabric' led us to the realization that our theories held the flaw to which I alluded earlier." He seemed to gather himself. "Remember my mentioning that 'branches of time' are fantasy, and that any given act can have but one outcome?"

"Yeah. Too bad; no 'parallel universes' with 'alternate histories.' I've always been a science-fiction fan—the classic stuff from the twentieth century—and they used to dream up some . . ." His voice came to a horrified halt. "Wait a minute, Tylar! Are you about to tell me that . . ."

"Oh, the theory is still good—under almost all circumstances. But it turns out that truly extreme weakness in the 'fabric' of reality does, after all, allow the same event to have multiple outcomes, all of equal mathematical validity. We'd never had occasion to become aware of this fact because we'd never encountered such conditions before. That moment with you and Artorius in Bourges may have been unique. I devoutly hope so." This time Tylar did mop his brow, using his sleeve.

"So you're saying," Sarnac continued faintly, "that there's an alternate reality in which Artorius decided, at that moment, not to deploy his forces into Berry? And that . . . ?"

"Yes." Tylar nodded. "And the resulting changes in history were at least as momentous as I had speculated."

"But," Sarnac continued, head spinning, "in that case there must be alternate versions of me and Tiraena! Or were, in the fifth century of this alternate universe, with God knows what happening to them!"

"By no means. The two of you, and I, ceased to exist in the alternate universe at the instant it branched off from our own. For in *that* universe, my people can never come into existence; the history that culminates in us is stillborn. Hence, there are no Raehaniv; we weren't there, thirty thousand years before your time, to plant their ancestors on Raehan."

"I imagine," Artorius put in, "the alternate Artorius wondered what had become of you."

Sarnac's head was starting to ache. "But, Tylar, how can you be sure of all this? How can you know about this alternate universe?"

"Because," Tylar answered gravely, "we've received a visitor from it. Or we *will*, that is, in the twenty-ninth century. He will come from the twenty-ninth century of his universe seeking help—for, to repeat, my fears concerning the consequences of a victory by our friend here turn out to have erred on the conservative side."

"Seeking help? You mean . . . ?" Sarnac didn't finish the question because he didn't really want to hear the answer. Tylar supplied it anyway.

"Yes. The Korvaasha. Remember, in the alternate universe there are no Raehaniv. Hence no Varien hle'Morna—and no technologically advanced civilization on twenty-first century Earth for him to have found even if he *had* existed."

Sarnac's head felt as though someone was driving a railroad spike upward between his left eyeball and the frontal bone. "Tylar, I think I can see where this is heading. You're going to say that *I'm* responsible for the existence of this alternate reality because I shot off my mouth to Artorius . . ."

"Not altogether. Not even primarily. As I admitted earlier, the principal fault is mine. If not for me, you wouldn't have been there in the fifth century at all. Nevertheless, to a certain extent you share my responsibility. Therefore," he continued, the inexplicable look of self-satisfaction back at full force, "instead of simply proceeding on my own— with Artorius' help, of course—to set things right, I came to this era first, to make you aware of your debt and enable you to pay it."

Sarnac wasn't even fully aware of his headache as he groped for a handhold on reality. "Uh, Tylar, let me make sure I'm clear on the situation. Our own history, in our own universe, came out okay, right?"

"Oh, certainly! As I explained . . ."

"Then," Sarnac pressed on, "whatever has happened, or is happening, or will happen in this alternate universe isn't *real* from our standpoint, is it? So, why should you or I feel this moral obligation? I mean, so what?"

The time traveller spoke in the puzzled tones of a man encountering unexpected difficulties in explaining the obvious. "You don't seem to understand, my dear fellow. In the context of its own metrical frame, the alternate universe is as 'real'—however one chooses to define the term—as our own. The historical development it has followed is an . . . abomination. A *wrongness*. The ethical responsibility borne by those who—however unwittingly— called it into being is, of course, intuitively clear to anyone of moral sensibility, regardless of cultural background." Artorius gave Sarnac a covert wink of commiseration. "So surely," Tylar continued, "you can see . . . can't you?" He seemed to deflate. "Well, perhaps it isn't as self-evident as I supposed. But surely you can at least see that the people of the alternate universe are as human as you or I, as capable of feeling pain. Surely you can grasp the reality of their tragedy. If nothing else, the one who has visited us should make their common humanity obvious."

"Oh, yeah," Sarnac temporized. "This visitor you mentioned. How can it be possible for him to be in our reality?"

"Why don't we let him explain that?" Tylar beamed.

"Huh? You mean he's here now?"

"Quite. I thought a little preparation would be in order before letting you meet him, so I asked him to wait." He drained his wineglass and rose to his feet. "Shall we go?"

# CHAPTER THREE

Andreas Ducas was thirtyish, olive-complexioned, regular-featured, solidly built, clad in a utilitarian one-piece garment on loan from Tylar. As he rose to greet them in the lakeside pavilion, Sarnac couldn't avoid the irrational feeling that someone from the future of an alternate timeline ought to have something just a little bit out of the ordinary in his appearance. But Andreas didn't.

Nor was there anything remarkable about the fact that he had been born on Alpha Centauri A III. "We've known for some time that there was a planet with water and free oxygen at Alpha Centauri," Sarnac explained to him after the introductions were complete. "But since there's no displacement point there . . . uh, are you familiar with displacement points?"

Andreas nodded—up and down for affirmation, Sarnac noted with relief; he'd once tried to communicate with a Bulgarian. "Yes, Tylar has explained the concept to me." He spoke in the fifth-century military Latin that was the only language they had in common. He had acquired it courtesy of the same kind of implant which had, fifteen years before, conferred it on Sarnac. Tylar had decided against cluttering his mind with unnecessary languages like

49

Standard International English. "It accounted for what happened almost three centuries before my time. But continue, Admiral Sarnac."

" 'Robert,' please. Well, until fifteen years ago that was the only means of interstellar travel available to us. Then we acquired the continuous-displacement drive from the Raehaniv . . . uh . . ."

"Yes," Andreas smiled encouragingly. "Tylar explained about them too. And about the drive."

"Then you know it freed us from dependence on displacement points. There's now a thriving infant colony on your planet . . . or what is, or will be, your planet in your reality." Sarnac's head was starting to throb again.

"Yes," Tylar put in. "It will be quite an important place by the twenty-ninth century. We'll have a kind of listening post in the outer system, and it will . . ." He stopped and shook his head in annoyance. "Latin is even more impossible for discussions of time travel than Standard International English, you know—the same lack of several requisite tenses, including 'subjective-past,' which is what I should be using now. I'll have to use past tense. Better still, I'll let you use it, Andreas. Why don't you explain matters to Robert, starting with an overview of your history?"

"I'll try, but as you know I'm no historian." Andreas frowned with concentration as he organized his thoughts. "Tylar has described your history to me, so I know that by the twenty-first century *your* Earth was engaged in interplanetary exploration. We were only up to steam pumps and black powder firearms at that time—sixteen centuries after the Restorer."

"The Restorer?" Sarnac glanced at Artorius, who gave a rueful nod. "So, Tylar, you were right after all. . . ."

"Yes. Instead of messy but technologically fruitful political disunity, Europe got a reunited and expanded Roman Empire which imposed a kind of . . . Byzantine Mandarinism is as good a term as any. It was as deadly to innovation as the restored Chinese Empire in the same era of both timelines. The result was as Andreas has described. Naturally, none of this affected the Korvaash Unity in any way—except that there were no Raehaniv for it to encounter, and no Raehaniv navigational data for it to capture. So its expansion in Earth's direction was somewhat slower in the years before the great realignment of the displacement network. Pardon me, Andreas—do continue."

"Of course we knew nothing of these events beyond the solar system. But in the subsequent five centuries, we mastered the scientific method and began to forge ahead technologically." His voice held a kind of forlorn, defensive pride. Sarnac belatedly understood that he was looking at a man who had been cast, all alone, among strangers whose kindliness only underlined the fact that they wielded powers beyond the dreams of gods. "By the twenty-sixth century," he continued, "we were ready to launch our first interstellar expedition, toward Alpha Centauri."

Tylar's face took on the abstracted expression that, Sarnac had come to realize, meant he was in whatever unimaginable linkage he maintained with his sentient machines. The image of a space vessel appeared in midair above the table around which they sat, although there was no apparent holo projection equipment nor any place for it to be concealed. Sarnac couldn't worry about that as he stared in fascination. It was like what Jules Verne might have visualized had the notion of an STL interstellar ship ever occurred to him.

Tylar seemed to read his thoughts. "Yes. The technology of the alternate Earth developed in ways that were idiosyncratic to say the least, from your standpoint or mine. Those divergences make a fascinating story in themselves."

"It looks big," was all Sarnac could say, even though he had no familiar objects to give a sense of scale.

"Indeed," Tylar affirmed. "It had to be, for it was what those science fiction writers of whom you're so fond called a 'generation ship.' It required a century to reach Alpha Centauri, and one of the things of which its builders were

ignorant was cryogenic suspension. Given those builders'
capabilities, it was really a technological *tour de force*,
and like all such was incredibly expensive. I gather it was
at least in part a symbol, carrying with it the prestige of
the Empire—which included the Americas and large parts
of Africa and Russia as well as all of Europe and the Near
East, and was locked in rivalry with its Chinese counterpart."

"Sort of like the mid-twentieth-century space programs,"
Sarnac opined.

"It was expensive," Andreas acknowledged. "But it turned
out to be a better investment than its builders imagined,
for it put a small portion of the human race out of reach
of what happened twenty-five years into its voyage. That
was when the Korvaash ships inexplicably appeared in
the outer Solar System and descended on Earth."

"The Realm of Tarzhgul?" Sarnac made it as much a
statement as a question.

Tylar nodded. "Remember, the displacement network
is the same in both universes. And the Realm arose in the
same manner after the disruption of that network put an
end to the Unity."

"Yeah," Sarnac grinned crookedly. "Founded by a
Korvaash dissident who thought the Unity's problem was
that it was being run by a bunch of bleeding-heart liberals.
After the displacement points went blooey and his planet
found itself cut off from its higher-ups, he and his disciples
were in a position to step into the power vacuum. They
may have heard, in our universe, the news that something
funny was going on at Raehan; but that had nothing
important to do with their takeover. It would have happened
anyway."

"Precisely," Tylar affirmed. "Later, with no Solar Union
to oppose them, the Korvaasha of the Realm expanded
slowly along the displacement chains, taking until the
twenty-sixth century to reach an Earth that could not hope
to resist them."

"The generation ship's occupants could only listen in

horror to the broadcasts from Sol," Andreas resumed. "They continued on their predetermined course to Alpha Centauri, constantly expecting the Korvaasha to pursue them using whatever mysterious space drive had brought them to Sol. After all, the Korvaasha must have learned about the expedition after occupying Earth, where it was common knowledge. But even after the ship arrived at Alpha Centauri seventy-five years later, nothing happened."

"Naturally," Tylar interjected. "As in our universe, Alpha Centauri has no displacement points in the current epoch. Clearly, the alternate Realm of Tarzhgul had not discovered the continuous-displacement drive in the twenty-sixth century, and still has not in the twenty-ninth.

"But," he continued somberly, "that is no guarantee for the future. The continuous-displacement drive is merely an application of the same gravitic technology that allows displacement-point transit. No matter how uninventive the Korvaasha of Tarzhgul are, they'll stumble onto it eventually. And they'll remember the hitherto-inaccessible human colony at Alpha Centauri."

"Even if they never discover it," Artorius interjected, "don't forget the *other* Korvaash successor-state that's come to light in Robert's era. It must also exist in the alternate universe. And *those* Korvaasha are more inventive than they're supposed to be! I may as well tell you, Robert, that they don't have the drive in your time. But with no Pan-Human League to run up against, they're bound to discover it eventually. For all we know, they've already discovered it by Andreas' lifetime and are gradually expanding toward an inevitable meeting with the Realm of Tarzhgul. Whether that meeting results in amalgamation or war makes no difference to Andreas' people. They're living on borrowed time."

Andreas' face gleamed with a sheen of sweat in the simulated sunlight and he licked his lips before continuing. "We didn't know any of this, of course. But for the entire two centuries since the landfall on Chiron—that's what we call the third planet of Alpha Centauri A—our lives have been built around preparation for the eventual arrival of the Korvaasha. Among other things, we've tried to develop a means of faster-than-light travel. But we've never discovered the secret of artificial gravity; that's one of the many ways in which our courses of development have differed since your timeline branched off." He looked around at the other three as though challenging anyone to take exception to that particular phraseology, but no one did. "Our efforts were aimed at translating a ship into a parallel space in which the speed of light was higher, or ignorable altogether."

"Oho!" Sarnac smiled. "The old 'hyperspace' idea. It was a favorite with Terran science-fiction writers before the discovery of displacement points."

"The Chironites were wrong about faster-than-light travel," Tylar said. "But in pursuing their erroneous theory they blundered onto something concerning which not even my people have ever had an inkling: the ability to access an alternate reality. Tell him what happened, Andreas."

"Theory predicted that our experimental drive would not work deep in a gravity well, so the experiments were carried on in the outer reaches of the Alpha Centauri system. At last a robot probe was launched—with apparent success, for it vanished and later reappeared on schedule at the same location. But its recorded data showed that it had emerged in exactly the same spot in the outer Alpha Centauri system! But not the *same* Alpha Centauri system, for all the regular communications channels were dead. Instead, there was an enormous volume of incomprehensible broadcasts from Chiron."

*Lirauva*, Sarnac mentally corrected him. *That's what we call Alpha Centauri A III, because Varien hle'Morna's daughter Aelanni named it that when she used it as her base for studying twenty-first-century Earth, back in the days when Alpha Centauri had a displacement point.*

*Nowadays, being a nice place and just a short continuous-displacement hop from Sol, it's a rapidly growing colony. What will it be like in the twenty-ninth century?*

"At first we thought we had inadvertently discovered time travel," Andreas was saying. "But the probe's photographic record showed absolutely no difference in the relative positions of the stars. Only one conclusion was possible: our probe had travelled not up or down the timestream but *across* to the same point of a different timestream."

"A conclusion that showed great intellectual courage and flexibility," Tylar approved.

"I suppose becoming hidebound is one of the many luxuries we've never been able to afford. At any rate, the video broadcasts the probe had picked up showed that the inhabitants of Chiron—the *other* Chiron—were human. Their language was indecipherable, although one of our more eccentric philologists claimed to discern, in part of the vocabulary, a remote kinship with the languages spoken by the barbarians of northwest Europe before their final incorporation into the Empire. Of more immediate concern was the fact that they possessed technology beyond our utmost horizons. We resolved to contact them and seek their help against the Korvaasha, perhaps enlisting their aid in liberating Earth.

"The energy cost of the transtemporal breakthrough is enormous, and the generating machinery is almost prohibitively massive relative to the payload. It was out of the question to send more than one emissary, especially given the tonnage of life-support equipment he'd need for the voyage insystem to Chiron . . . or whatever you call it. The competition for that posting was fierce, despite the danger; we had no way of knowing for certain that a living organism could survive the transposition. Senior government officials were generally too old or otherwise disqualified. So they turned to those of us who had been in training for the projected faster-than-light interstellar expeditions. In the end, I was selected for good physical and mental health, lack of ties to my own world—I have no living relatives—and broad-based scientific knowledge. *Not* for historical expertise, as Tylar can attest!

"As it turned out, I successfully made the transit and emerged into your reality. Then, just after I had set a course for Chiron, I was met by a ship which made even the technology of the alternate Chiron seem primitive."

"You," Sarnac stated flatly to Tylar.

"Yes. The emergence of the unmanned probe had set up a kind of dimensional fluctuation which our listening post could not fail to detect. The energy flux was quite unprecedented; we had no idea what was happening. So I was sent for. We were fully prepared for Andreas' appearance. We couldn't allow him to contact the twenty-ninth-century inhabitants of Lirauva, of course; our own history said nothing about any such contact. It was clearly a case where intervention was required to keep history on its proper course—the course that eventuates in *us*. So we picked him up."

"I can imagine that scene," Sarnac remarked. He really could. (*"Oh I'm so sorry about this dreadful mixup, my dear fellow. . . ."*)

"It soon became clear what had happened," Tylar continued, oblivious, "as incredible as it all seemed. The next step, of course, was to determine the exact point at which the two histories had diverged. Andreas, as he has admitted, is no historian. But he has an educated man's familiarity with the salient events and personalities. He knew that in the late fifth century the Roman Empire was being reunified. And he knew who had done it."

"Yes," Andreas said. "The man who bestrides the ages. When I met *him* . . ." He gazed across the table at Artorius. "Of course, I know that he isn't really Artorius Augustus the Restorer, that in your history he died—or was supposed to have died—at the same time he was winning the Battle of Bourges in mine. But still . . . do you know I was born in a city on Chiron called 'Artoriopolis'?" Artorius gave a gesture that was all offhand graciousness, while Sarnac tried to imagine meeting a George Washington who had been hanged by Lord North and lived on in legend.

"Given this information," Tylar resumed, "I accessed Robert's recorded memories of that period. It wasn't hard to pinpoint that brief conversation."

"Wait a minute, Tylar," Sarnac protested. "Are you really *sure* that for just those few moments the future was teetering on such a knife-edge, as you said earlier, that a few words from me could have tipped the balance?"

"Yes," Tylar stated shortly. "Those moments may have been unique in all the timestream. I devoutly hope so. But at any rate, the inarguable fact is that an alternate timeline *was* created, by application of precisely the right stimulus at precisely the right instant. Our subsequent researches leave no room for doubt on the matter."

After a few heartbeats, Sarnac decided it was incumbent on him to break the silence. "So, Tylar, what do you propose to do? Take me back to that same place and time and make sure that I keep my big mouth shut?"

"Oh, no. I'm afraid it doesn't work that way. We've had a chance to investigate these matters in some depth, and while there's much we don't understand, one thing is clear: once an alternate timeline branches off, it can't be unmade."

Sarnac felt that sensation of groping for an understanding of the basic fundamentals that was all too familiar when dealing with Tylar. "Uh, I don't quite get it. If what happened can't be undone, then what's the use of all this?"

"Andreas' timeline can't be obliterated, true. But it can be *altered* under the right circumstances, just as ours can. It's precisely what my people and I are constantly on guard against, in our own reality. Well, in the alternate reality I'll have to bring about that which I've dedicated my life to preventing, and change history so as to assure that by the twenty-sixth century the alternate Earth is prepared to defend itself against the Korvaasha. I fear I'll be hard put to manage with equanimity such a . . . reversal of orientation."

"So you're saying we should enter the alternate reality and go back to a point in time just after the branching-off, and talk the alternate Artorius into changing his mind? Well, it shouldn't be too hard." He turned to Artorius. "The decision you made was entirely reasonable, given the information available to you at the time."

"So I've frequently assured myself," the former High King said drily.

"Ah, I'm afraid it's not quite that simple." Tylar sounded apologetic. "You see, after the crucial turning point the 'fabric' of the alternate reality becomes *very* strong for some time, as one decision leads with inexorable logic to the next. We've investigated the matter thoroughly, and the next area of 'weak fabric' when history can be changed occurs twenty-one years later, in the alternate year 491 A.D."

"*What?* But that's a lot of time, Tylar—time enough for a lot of water to have flowed over the dam. Won't the changes that lead to Andreas' world have accumulated a lot of, uh, momentum by then?"

"Indubitably. There will be certain difficulties, and I anticipate an extended stay in the alternate universe to assure ourselves that matters are proceeding as planned. But," he added brightly, "anything worth doing is worth doing properly, as someone once said."

"Your mother," Sarnac supplied. *If you had one*, he didn't add.

"Ahem! Well, to business! You'll need to be supplied, via implant, with updated knowledge that Artorius and Andreas already possess. Then these data will have to be supplemented with a conventional briefing concerning the precise state of affairs at the moment when we'll—"

"Tylar." Sarnac's tone achieved the not-inconsiderable feat of stopping the time traveller in his verbal tracks. "Look, I think I understand all this, at least on a superficial level.

And I'm not blind to the ethical implications—I'm willing to admit a degree of responsibility. But like all adult human beings, I have to balance my responsibilities. And, as you know, I'm in command of a naval force that is shortly going into battle against some very dangerous enemies of the human race—*our* human race." His glance at Andreas was rueful but not apologetic. "That has to be my first priority."

"But, my dear fellow, there's no conflict! As I explained, after your obligations are fulfilled I'll return you to your office at the precise time we left it."

"Yeah, if I'm still alive! You've implied that changing the alternate history is going to involve a lot of difficulty and danger as well as an 'extended stay,' and I know from experience how rough that era can be." He took a deep breath. "Look, I'm not afraid of personal risk—not as an individual. But my life isn't strictly my own to risk. I'm not even talking about the fact that I've got a wife and children; I'm talking about—"

". . . the just cause which is entrusted to you to defend," Tylar finished for him. It sounded like a quotation, but Sarnac couldn't quite place it. "Yes, I can respect that. But I cannot let it weigh in the balance against the fate of an entire reality—a reality in which the human race is doomed to be slaves and meat-animals for all that remains of its existence. You are, at this point in time, the guardian of an ephemeral polity called the Pan-Human League. *I* am the guardian of universal reality!"

Memories of which he had been robbed not once but twice came back to Sarnac, for once before, in this very place, Tylar's eyes and voice had seemed to fill this artificial continuum of his own creation. And now, once again, the eyes and the voice were all that was or could be, and he was in free fall through a bottomless cosmos of the incomprehensible. . . .

But then there was something else. There was a face in which the blood of Earth and Raehan blended into a harmony of coppery skin and dark-red hair and features which held all that that was worthwhile in Sarnac's personal universe. And all at once he knew where he was and who he was.

"Tylar." He heard his own voice as though from a great distance. "Tylar!" he shouted—or at least the rasping in his throat told him he was shouting. Abruptly, all was as before in the elegant lakeside pavilion. Artorius and Andreas looked on in silence, and Tylar smiled slightly.

"You've grown up," the time traveller observed. Then he leaned back, head tilted to one side, as though inviting Sarnac to speak.

Sarnac forced steadiness on himself. "Tylar, I know there's no point in trying to refuse you. So I'll go along—on one condition. Tiraena comes too."

Tylar's eyebrows lifted. "But that's really not necessary. She bears no part of the responsibility; she was in Britain at the time when . . ."

"Yes, I know. But that's not the point. The half-memories you left in my subconscious but not in hers have been like a . . . a fault line between us. I don't want to take the chance of that happening again. And besides, Tylar—you *owe* her! I won't *let* you give me back my memories of what we went through together without giving them back to her as well, even if it's only for a little while for both of us." He took a deep breath and plunged ahead. "You may be able to compel my cooperation—but you can't compel my *willing* cooperation! The only way you're going to get that is by going along with me on this!"

There was a moment's silence, while Andreas looked lost and Artorius' face wore an expression that Sarnac had never thought to see there. Tylar finally spoke in a conversational tone. "How can you be sure she'll *want* to go along on this expedition?"

"I can't. But it has to be her choice. You have to give her memories back to her and then let her decide. So help me, that's the only way you're going to get my wholehearted participation."

There was another pause. When Tylar spoke, it was at least half to himself, and with seeming irrelevance. "My work requires me to violate my own ethics far too much as it is, you know. In your case, I think I've already violated them quite enough." He seemed to reach an inner decision. "I believe what you request can be arranged."

# CHAPTER FOUR

The grav raft swept in out of the red sunset, knifing through the mists under the ghostly outline of the giant close moon that hung where it always hung over this planet whose rotation it had long ago halted.

Tiraena zho'Daeriel DiFalco-Sarnac watched the Survey base come into view as the raft slid silently over the flatlands. It lay near the estuary of Naeruil II's greatest river, surrounded by native dwellings that had sprung up around it. The Naeruilhiv were at least the equal of their human discoverers in their appetite for novelty, and had little attachment to a particular place to deter them from moving close to where that appetite might best be satisfied. Maybe their disinclination to stay in one place long enough to form elaborately stratified societies had contributed to keeping them in the Bronze Age despite their high intelligence—it seemed to get higher every time the neural-scanner technicians recalibrated their equipment.

Of course, it wasn't easy to measure the intelligence of a race that consisted of two symbiotic species, so that each "individual" was, in fact, a duality. By the same token, it gave them a natural gift for communication. . . .

"Cleared for landing," the pilot broke into her thoughts. She nodded absently and the native settlements (Camps?

Something else?) vanished behind structures that seemed to rise up as they settled like a falling feather onto the landing stage.

"Very smooth, Nicky," she approved. Nicole Hunyadi grinned in response.

"Hard to go wrong with these new models," the pilot admitted, slapping the console affectionately. "My dad—he used to pilot the old Solar Union drop shuttles during the war—keeps telling me that my generation's got it soft."

"Well, you do," Tiraena stated firmly. Hunyadi's grin was unabated in its infectiousness, and it duly infected Tiraena. She found it easy to share the pilot's irreverence, having grown up with the kind of refined grav repulsion to which the peoples of the former Solar Union were still adjusting.

*Still,* she thought, *have a little respect! I'm more than old enough to be your mother.* But, she assured herself as she swung herself out of the raft under Naeruil II's 1.18 G pull, she didn't feel it, nor look it. She had, from birth, had access to the best bioscience Raehaniv money could buy, and at fifty-four Terran years her hair was as darkly auburn and her body as lithe as ever. Though chronologically older than Bob, she was almost certain to outlive him. It was a dilemma that linked her with her great-grandmother Aelanni zho'Morma, and they had both made the same decision.

She swung her satchel over her shoulder, waved goodbye to Nicky, and started toward the headquarters building with the cautious stride that was her natural gait's compromise with the local gravity. The sun seemed almost as stationary as the moon—this planet's sidereal day was longer than four of Earth's—but it *was* setting, and there was some relief from the heat that had, over the last few watches, made Tiraena thankful for her utility suit's ability to "breathe." Soon would come the long night when it would get as close to cold as Naeruil II ever got. The enormous moon kept this hemisphere's night from being very dark, but still it was good to get as much done as possible in daylight. *Which*, she told her conscience, *is a perfectly valid reason for me to go out and pitch in with the field work, rather than spend my whole time back here doing my administrative chores like a good little station director. Plenty of time during the night to catch up on all that* rhylieu *shit.*

Rationalization completed, she grinned to herself as she checked in at her office and proceeded on to her quarters, thinking back over all the wonders she had seen in the hinterlands. The universe was full of planets with the right conditions for life, but most had not yet existed long enough to bring it forth. Earth's Sol and Raehan's Tareil were exceptionally old members of that exclusive club of F, G, and K type main-sequence stars which could sire living worlds. Prebiotic planets were everywhere, readily terraformable but as yet barren. And of the life-bearing worlds, most held only primitive marine microorganisms that made scummy the seas that lapped their landmasses of naked sand and rock. A planet with a mature, highly developed and richly diversified biosphere was a rare and precious thing. And rarest and most precious of all were the worlds which had brought forth sentience—like this one. *Every one of the sentient races we've found has been a new adventure—a new perspective on reality. Every one of them has been unique, showing us one more road that leads beyond what we had thought were the boundaries of the possible.*

*And then,* came a thought like a blighting chill, *there were the Korvaasha—the living confirmation of Goethe* (she had learned of him during the last fifteen years) *for they showed that sentience can enable its possessor to become beastlier than any beast.*

The thought led her consciousness back to Bob, where she had resolved not to let it wander. The details hadn't made their way across the Pan-Human League yet—messages were limited to the speed at which the combination of displacement points and continuous-displacement drive would allow a ship to carry them; humanity left instantaneous communications behind when it emerged onto the interstellar stage. But it was clear enough that the mysterious menace that had emerged from the unexplored spaces beyond Loriima was yet another surviving fragment of the old Korvaash Unity. (*How many more?* some inner self that had never left girlhood behind asked God.) And Bob was now on the far side of the League organizing humankind's resistance. . . .

She shook her head, for she knew the futility of wishing to be with him at this moment. They had learned to live with the long separations their careers mandated, and the realities of space travel had made humanity relearn the patience of the Age of Sail. *And it wouldn't really matter if it weren't for the sense of something unresolved, of feelings he has that are always hidden from me, a part of him in which I can't share. If it weren't for that I could face the possibility of never seeing him again without this gnawing feeling of incompletion.* Her thoughts remained far away as she entered her small suite of rooms and dropped her satchel on the bed.

"Hello, Tiraena."

She whirled around at the impossible voice, her sense of reality reeling. *"Bob?!"* She knew it came out as a ridiculous squeak, but she could no more worry about that than she could doubt that it was really him—she had known him too long for the idea of an imposter to even enter her consciousness. Then she was in his arms and for an instant no mysteries or impossibilities existed . . . or, at least, mattered. But only for an instant. She disengaged and held him at arm's length so she could look at him. It was only then that she noticed the other man, also in Fleet uniform.

"Ah, Tiraena, this is my operations officer, Captain Geoffrey Draco."

"Charmed," she said mechanically. "Bob, what are you doing here? How did you get here?" The figures for the voyage from Loriima ran through her head, and she didn't even have to activate her implanted calculator to see that he *couldn't* be here.

"Tiraena," he said with apparent evasiveness, "you don't know Captain Draco, do you?"

She looked at the ops officer closely for the first time. "No. Should I?"

"We've only met once, Ms. DiFalco-Sarnac. And I wasn't at my best at the time—in fact, I was only semi-conscious. You see, I was dying. Prior to that you may have gotten a bad impression of me, since you knew my wife, from whom I was estranged." ·

"Well, there're always two sides to these things," Tiraena said with ritual politeness. "And I'm glad you got to the regen tank in time." She turned back to Sarnac. "Bob, you didn't answer me. What's this all about? How could you have gotten here from Loriima? And why didn't anyone tell me you were here? And how did you even get into this suite . . . ?"

"Tiraena," Sarnac stemmed the flood of questions, "you remember the recurring dreams I've had—the ones that didn't really seem like dreams at all, but rather like incomplete memories?"

She blinked twice. "Of course. In fact, I was only just thinking of it. I know they've been getting worse."

"Well, they *were* fragments of memory, Tiraena. Memories that were taken from me. Memories of incredible experiences we went through fifteen years ago. You see, the memories were taken from both of us by someone you don't remember named Tylar." A crooked smile. "It's just that in your case he did it right. So there's been more to our lives together than we knew—more than you *still* know. But I've had the memories restored, so I know that part of our lives together has been missing, without us even knowing it was missing. Only, I think we *did* know it was missing, on some level beyond even Tylar's understanding. That's why there's always been—let's be honest—a kind of incompleteness about our life together, something we both knew was absent."

Tiraena started to speak, but then her mind flew back over the last fifteen years—the heady days after their arrival at Sol, the end of the war, the children, everything—and her mouth closed again and she nodded slowly.

"Now," Sarnac continued, "you can also regain those memories. It won't be easy, I can tell you. But it's very important to me that you do it. I don't want it to come between us again, this . . . this *lack* that we can't even put a name to. Especially since I've got to do something for Tylar now, and I need very badly for you to be a part of it. For that, you're going to need your memories back."

For a time they looked levelly into each other's eyes— they were almost exactly the same height. When Tiraena finally spoke, her words awoke in Sarnac the joyful realization that he *did* know her after all, for they held neither fear nor confusion nor doubt.

"Who's this 'Tylar'?" was all she said.

"Let's go meet him," Sarnac replied with a smile.

She smiled back. "Well, as long as we don't have to go too far—I have a ton of work waiting for me, you know. I can't exactly go to Loriima with you!"

"Oh, no, we're not going to Loriima. Just to Sol."

Her smile vanished, for he had spoken deadpan. "You're serious, aren't you? Bob, didn't you hear me? I've got work to do here. . . ."

"And I've got a war to fight," he cut in. "Tiraena, you're just going to have to take my word that this isn't going to interfere with our duties. Don't ask me to explain—you'll understand when you have your memories again."

She visibly kept a thousand questions penned within her, only releasing one. "Well, how are we going to get there? You never did explain how you got *here*, you know!"

"There's a ship waiting for us, outside this base." Sarnac gestured to the mysterious Captain Draco, who placed a device unfamiliar to Tiraena on the floor. What followed didn't register at first, for the luminously bordered hole in the universe was too far beyond what was right and ordinary and proper. But then Sarnac had stepped through it, then turned and beckoned. Without stopping to consult reason, she followed. There was a slight resistance as she entered what lay beyond—it was the inside of an artificial construct, but there was nothing to identify it to her mind as a spacecraft. Equally unfamiliar was the late-middle-aged man who stepped forward to greet her.

"Tiraena, my name is Tylar. . . ."

Sarnac was the first through the door and at her bedside when she had awakened and was able to receive visitors.

"Tiraena, darling, it's me. Are you all right?" He desperately wished for something besides banality. But, contrary to the opinion of innumerable generations of playwrights, intense and genuine emotion poses for most people an impassable barrier to style.

Her eyelids fluttered open and she gave a drowsy smile. "Yes, I'm fine," she assured him. "The disorientation was bad at first, but I've had time to integrate it all. And you were right—there *has* been something missing all these years, and I could never even identify a gap, much less know what belonged there. And," she continued, reaching out a hand and grasping his with all the strength she could manage, "you're the only thing these new-old memories have in common with the ones I've had all along. That's why I know they're genuine."

Sarnac felt himself nodding as he returned the pressure of her hand. "Yes. Naturally it occurred to me to wonder if the memories were fake—but I never seriously considered it for a minute. You see, I already knew exactly what it felt like to fall in love with you—I'd done it in the life I already remembered. And now I know I've done it twice, never knowing the second time that it *was* the second time. And you know what? It felt exactly the same both times. Not even Tylar could fake that."

As though illustrating the old adage about speaking of the Devil, Tylar's voice came from near the door. "Yes, I'm sure she'll recover faster than you did. In her case the process was not complicated by residual scraps of memory to which extraneous recollection had accreted from the dreams in which they had been incorporated for years. So you see, my dear, it was simplicity itself by comparison."

Tiraena looked up at him. "Hello, Tylar. Yes, you and your people obviously did a superlative job. And," she continued, still smiling sweetly, "the first time you tell us you haven't been entirely candid with us, I'm going to personally wring your scrawny neck, you lying old *grolofu*!"

"Yup," Sarnac drawled, with a wicked grin at the time traveller. "No question about it. She remembers *everything*!"

"I can already see one problem."

The four men at the table turned toward Tiraena, their heads moving against the backdrop of star-blazing blackness. Three walls of the meeting room in Tylar's villa had vanished to show the view outside the ship that was bearing them toward Sol at a speed that gave the closer stars a visible relative motion.

Tylar had explained that the ship generated around itself a bubble of accelerated time, within which a modest velocity became incredible multiples of $c$ relative to the outside universe. Sarnac could believe it, having once utilized the effect on an individual scale, and his intellect was able to assure the rest of him that God hadn't really rescinded general relativity and the Doppler phenomena.

Still, his skin prickled as he watched what looked to be a type A giant give new meaning to the term "shooting star," hurtling impossibly past and dwindling astern.

"What problem is that, my dear?" Tylar asked.

"Well," Tiraena said, "as I understand it, you intend to go back to the late fifth century A.D. of the alternate timeline and change things so that its future will turn out differently. I can provisionally accept the possibility of doing that.

But if we succeed, then what happens to Andreas?" She gave the young transtemporal voyager a smile that Sarnac sternly reminded himself was maternal. "I mean, if we wipe out his history . . ."

"I assure you that the philosophical problems have been taken into consideration. In particular, the fact that Andreas himself will be one of the people doing it makes the situation reminiscent of the 'grandfather paradox' that time-travel theorists were raising centuries before your time. Nevertheless, it is our considered opinion that his existence will be placed in no danger."

"But Tylar," Sarnac protested, "didn't you tell me that you and I and Tiraena ceased to exist in the alternate history the instant it branched off, because its future couldn't have produced us?"

"The present situation is entirely different. We're not going to be creating yet a third timeline, which would hardly fulfill our ethical obligation to Andreas' people and which, as I've pointed out, is almost never possible. Instead, we're going to be changing the future course of an existing one, which we believe *is* possible at certain times in history. And we believe that the 'grandfather paradox' is chimerical, that one who travels back along his own timestream as Andreas will be doing possesses a personal existence rooted in a reality which cannot be affected by any history-altering actions he takes. The future in which Andreas was born came 'before'—in some absolute sense—the 'new' future in which he will never be born."

Through his developing headache, Sarnac heard Tiraena speak challengingly. "But you can't really be sure, can you? Andreas, has he made all this clear to you?"

The emissary of a desperate reality looked at her gravely. "He has explained it, Tiraena. I don't pretend to understand the theory, but the possible consequences are clear enough. I'm willing to take the risk." He gave one of his infrequent smiles. "It's no more of a risk than I took when I ventured into your reality!"

"But," Tiraena persisted, "even if Tylar's right about your personal existence, we'll be wiping out your world. It has to be your decision."

Andreas seemed to gather himself. "As I've told Robert, I have few close ties with my world. It's one of the reasons I volunteered for the mission. And . . . my world isn't worth having close ties with." He kept pushing the words out, despite what each of them obviously cost him. "We've lived our lives knowing what's been happening on Earth for almost three centuries—the last furtive broadcasts after the Korvaasha landed made it clear enough—and knowing that sooner or later it will happen to us or our descendants. Do you have any idea what that does to a society? You hardly ever hear even children laugh on Chiron—it affects them early. Not that there are as many children as there used to be! There is a growing movement among us, men who emulate certain ancient orders of fanatical monks and—" he looked at Tiraena and blushed "—render themselves incapable of siring children. They claim it is a sin to bring new lives into a universe where Satan obviously reigns triumphant. It's hard to argue with them. We constantly wonder what the human race has become on Earth, if they're still human at all in any but the biological sense. But we also have to wonder how much worse they can be than ourselves."

For a moment he could not continue, and no one else broke the silence. Sarnac stole a glance at Tiraena, whose Raehaniv ancestors had endured a mere few years of Korvaash rule, and saw her jaw muscles clench.

Finally, Andreas recovered his usual self-possession and spoke in an unwavering voice. "My world is a world without hope, without joy, and without a future for humanity save as a species of livestock that won't even be allowed the mercy of extinction. There are only a few people in it who I care about, but I know they would all join with me in saying to you: 'Erase it, if there's any chance at all of replacing it with something better!' "

There was another silence as the simulated stars streamed by. Then Sarnac drawled, "Well, what about it, Tylar? How exactly do we go about the erasing? Since you're not worried about preserving history, and in fact setting out to change it, I suppose we can just go in and use all the high-tech goodies we want."

"By no means! Any blatant display of magical-seeming technology would blight and distort the alternate Earth's subsequent development, giving rise to unforeseeable social pathologies. An open announcement of our presence, implying the existence of alternate realities and time travel, would be even worse. No, we must be at least as subtle and inconspicuous as we were before."

"Uh-*huh!*" Sarnac nodded fatalistically. "I don't suppose this has anything to do with those little 'difficulties' you mentioned to me before, Tylar?"

"Ah, well, I'm afraid I haven't . . ." Tylar saw Tiraena's expression and caught himself just in time. "As you pointed out, my dear fellow, twenty-two years of the alternate timeline will have passed by the time change becomes feasible. History will have diverged too much for us to have any hope of forcing it onto the exact road ours travelled. Instead, we must set in motion events that result, not in Western history as it transpired in our timeline, but in a similar state of political pluralism that is equally conducive to uncontrolled technological innovation. The ultimate aim, of course, is an advanced civilization capable of standing alone against the Korvaasha in a universe without the Raehaniv. Hopefully, Terran humanity will have built an interstellar empire of its own which will crush the Realm of Tarzhgul long before the latter reaches Earth in the twenty-sixth century." He smiled, and a K type orange dwarf star that must have been *very* close to their course to be visible at all whizzed mischievously past his head. "I daresay the alternate world's future historians will devise theories of 'historical inevitability' to account for what we will have done! If they do, then we will have succeeded, for the

course their history has taken will seem entirely natural—
the 'only possible' one."

"Okay, so how do we accomplish this subtle nudging?
How can you be clear on the details of Andreas' history,
about which he doesn't claim to be an expert?"

"He's not—but we were able to access his memories,
including all the history he was ever taught, whether or
not he consciously retained it. Most of it was valueless,
as is generally true of the history that filters down to
educational bureaucrats for dissemination in required
courses. But one fact stood out: when the Restorer died in
491, his adopted successor was assassinated. I'll let Artorius
trace the steps our research has taken from there."

"You'll be pleased to know, Robert," Artorius smiled,
"that our inquiries led us to the alternate version of an old
acquaintance of yours: Sidonius Apollinaris."

"Oh, yeah, Sidonius! He seemed much too nice a guy
for the lousy fate Tylar told me was in store for him."

"Well, his fate was a happier one in the alternate reality—
up to a point. In 483 he was elected Pope."

"Pope! Uh, did that mean as much then as . . . ?"

"Perhaps not officially; the Bishop of Rome was elected
locally like any other bishop of the period. Until the early
fourth century, he was known as just that: Bishop of Rome.
But then, in the bishopric of Silvester, the pontifical title
was added as a recognition of the primacy he had always
been accorded as successor of Saint Peter. So the election
was a matter of wide importance, and Artorius . . ." Artorius
trailed to a rueful halt. "Let's call him 'the Restorer' to
avoid confusion. The Restorer took steps to assure the
election of his loyal supporter, Bishop Sidonius of Clermont.
Then, in 491—"

"Wait a minute!" Sarnac sifted through his new-old
memories. "Tylar, didn't you tell me that Sidonius died at
age forty-eight? Wouldn't that come to 480 or so?"

"Ah, but that was in *our* reality, in which he endured
appalling hardships withstanding several Visigothic sieges

of Clermont, only to be sold out by the Western Empire for which he had held the Auvergne—one of that empire's final sellouts before its richly merited demise. And afterwards he was imprisoned for years by the Visigoths. It's scarcely surprising that he lost his will to live. In the alternate timeline there were no sieges, no imprisonment, and no heartbreak at witnessing the death of the empire in which he'd believed."

"I'm glad *somebody* had a better life in my history," Andreas said bitterly. Then he remembered himself and gave the former High King an apprehensive look. But Artorius took it with his usual affability.

"Actually, quite a lot of people did. My counterpart forestalled the Dark Ages, which was certainly a good thing in the short run. Of course, after witnessing enough history one grows skeptical of good things in the short run."

"Didn't somebody once say, 'In the long run, we're all dead'?" Sarnac couldn't resist putting in.

"John Maynard Keynes," Artorius replied unhesitatingly. "Author of an economic theory which infallibly bankrupted any nation that embraced it and led directly to the fall of the West little more than a century after his time. You'll forgive me if I view his aphorisms with a degree of irreverence. But, to continue, the alternate Sidonius was only better off until 491, when he was killed by an aristocratic clique with its own ideas about who should succeed to the purple. Killing the Pope hadn't been part of their plans; he just happened to be in the wrong place at the wrong time, with his brother-in-law the heir."

"Brother-in-law?"

"Yes. You'll recall that I was childless," Artorius continued evenly. "So to secure the succession, the Restorer revived the custom of the Antonine emperors and adopted an heir. He chose Ecdicius, one of his top cavalry generals."

"Anybody I know?" Sarnac asked, reviewing his memories.

"No. I never met him, myself, although I knew of him

as the brother of Sidonius' wife Papianilla. They were the children of Avitus, who had been Augustus of the West from 455 to 457. After my . . . departure, he formed a small private unit of cavalry, financed by the income of his own estates, to resist the Visigoths. His aggressive, hit-and-run operations were the reason it took King Euric five years to conquer the Auvergne. On one occasion, he lifted one of the sieges of Clermont with only eighteen men!"

"Sounds like quite a guy," Sarnac remarked, summoning up from his own land's history the image of Nathan Bedford Forrest.

"Indeed," Tylar nodded. "He was a swashbuckler born long before his time—a proto-Musketeer. By sheer gallantry, he held back the night for a little while. But he could not halt it. In the end, he escaped into the land of the Burgundians and entered their service. His struggle had been hopeless from the first."

"I like him more and more," Sarnac said. "Blame it on my background. Where I come from, we've always been suckers for lost causes."

"Yes, his was a lost cause—in *our* reality. In the alternate timeline . . . well, imagine what the man who fought the Visigoths to a standstill for five years with no resources except his own private ones could have accomplished on the *winning* side, with the full support of a triumphantly resurgent empire!"

Sarnac thought about it. Tylar observed his expression and nodded. "The alternate Ecdicius led his band of cavalry to join the alternate Artorius in time to help smash the Visigoths before the walls of Bourges."

"All *right!*" Sarnac exclaimed, carried away. Tiraena rolled her eyes heavenward.

"In the subsequent campaigns he became the Restorer's right-hand man," Tylar continued. "His military prestige plus his connections—son of an Augustus and brother-in-law of the Pope—made him the logical choice as the adopted heir. The fact that he wasn't a Briton also helped; the Restorer needed to broaden his base of support. And then in 491, with the Restorer on his deathbed, Ecdicius was assassinated."

Sarnac's face fell. Tylar continued relentlessly. "This is the point at which it is possible, using minimal overt force, to effect a change in the alternate history's course. We will save Ecdicius and Sidonius from death."

"Wait a minute, Tylar," Sarnac said hesitantly. "Don't get me wrong; from everything you've told me about Ecdicius, I'd like nothing better than to save his life. But how is this going to fundamentally change the course of the alternate history? I mean, if Ecdicius survives he'll just succeed to the throne of the reunified Roman Empire you want to torpedo!"

"Oh, my! I see I haven't made matters altogether clear." Tylar seemed to gather his forces. "You see, my dear fellow, we're going to have to lay a bit of groundwork first, to assure that Ecdicius, after having been saved, will be more than willing to act as our instrument to set in motion the changes we want."

"Just what changes *do* we want?" Tiraena wanted to know.

"Consider: in our reality, the Roman Empire split into Eastern and Western halves, and subsequently the Western part devolved further into the competing nation-states in which the scientific and industrial revolutions could occur. In the alternate history, the Restorer aborted this process by reuniting East and West. Well, we're going to make sure the process resumes. Ecdicius is going to lead the West into secession!"

# CHAPTER FIVE

The transtemporal vehicle traced its cold, dark orbit through regions where Sol was just another zero-magnitude star. Its remoteness, as much as the stealth technology of Tylar's people, had concealed it from the sensors that kept watch on the borderlands of one of the Pan-Human League's two capital systems.

They gazed at it in silence, standing on the immaterial force-field floor of what Sarnac had decided to think of as the observation deck of Tylar's ship. The spherical chamber had, at the touch of the time traveller's thoughts, seemed to vanish. Their eyes told them that they stood, impossibly, in empty space, silhouetted against the star-fields. But from some unidentifiable source came enough light to see each other and the mammoth construct they were approaching.

"We decided it would be most straightforward to equip it with a time-distortion drive—not a very efficient one, but it only had to travel from Alpha Centauri to Sol," Tylar explained. "Then we brought it back from the twenty-ninth century to the twenty-third when we came to fetch you."

"Gee," Sarnac attempted lightness. "A temporal just for little old me!"

"Scarcely," Tylar said deflatingly. "We already had one

at Sol at this particular time—a rather crucial time, given the discovery of a second Korvaash successor-state, though not to be compared with fifteen years ago. So we decided to use it. Can't just go anywhen, you know!"

"So that's why you picked me up fifteen of my years later, and not right after our last acquaintance when I was still young and full of beans. I'd wondered about that."

"Also," Tiraena spoke up from the semidarkness, "it explains why you moved this monstrosity to Sol instead of just leaving it at Alpha Centauri, which in our time is just a newly established colony that doubtless doesn't rate a temporal."

"Precisely," Tylar affirmed. "Temportals are quite expensive—even for us. Having to emplace one in 485 A.D. expressly for this operation was bad enough."

"485 A.D. . . . ?" Sarnac began on an interrogatory note. But Tylar hurried on in his patented question-deflecting way.

"We then equipped this vehicle with our power sources so it can operate with a lower probability of failure— Andreas was very lucky to survive the transition to our reality! Fortunately, we didn't have to rebuild it to carry a larger payload, since this ship is actually smaller than the one-man craft that was to have carried Andreas to the inner system of Alpha Centauri A. Still, it's been through a few changes.

"I can tell." Sarnac couldn't take his eyes off the huge artifact toward which they seemed to be magically gliding through open space. The original structure was like a colossal junk-sculpture representing pathologically overcomplex technology. But the Baroque massiveness was here and there overlaid by the jarringly contrasting additions of Tylar's people, which like all their machines didn't look like machines, having been grown in nanotechnological embryos. As Sarnac watched, one of them reconfigured, its unfamiliar metal writhing as it shape-shifted to perform the next stage of the preparations for departure.

"I hardly recognize it." Andreas sounded lost.

Then they seemed to swoop around it and begin their approach, entering a kind of open latticework funnel that reminded Sarnac of the front end of a twentieth-century artist's conception of a Bussard ramscoop—one of the many concepts that unanticipated discoveries had left behind in realms of the hypothetical and the irrelevant. The massiveness of that delicate-seeming framework became apparent as they settled into its enclosure, which easily held the ship that, despite the evidence of their eyes, surrounded them.

"And now," Tylar said briskly, "we can proceed to the temporal."

There was no sensation of motion. But the stars precessed around them, and ahead Sarnac could see that which he had uncomprehendingly glimpsed fifteen years earlier: a torus of space-distorting force, visible only by the wavering and twinkling of the stars beyond it. It began to grow as the transtemporal vehicle that held their ship in this clenched magnetohydrodynamic hand accelerated toward it under the reactionless drive he kept meaning to ask Tylar to explain.

"Must be a tight fit," he remarked, gesturing aft at the stupendous mass of the construct that bore them.

"Not really," Tylar assured him. "You'd be surprised at the temporal's diameter."

In fact, the barely perceptible circle was enclosing more and more of the sky as they neared it. They were moving slowly compared to the Korvaash battlecrusier aboard which Sarnac had previously made such an approach, and he had time to brace himself for what he knew was coming.

It was as bad as he remembered—like the disorientation that accompanied a displacement transition, only worse. The sensation of wrongness was somehow only heightened by the fact that the sky was still the familiar one of Sol, not the new one that greeted one who emerged from a displacement point into a different stellar system.

But not quite the same sky. A before-and-after photographic comparison would have shown the slight changes wrought by eighteen centuries of random stellar motion. And as he regained his mental equilibrium his eyes swung toward Canis Major. Yes, its brightest star was even brighter than it was supposed to be . . . and it was red, not blue-white. What Sarnac's epoch knew as Sirius B had not yet collapsed into the white dwarf stage, bequeathing some of its mass to its companion. Far outshining the future Sirius A, it was still the red giant that the ancient astronomers had observed. And he knew that at this moment, far sunward, lay an Earth whose people still believed the sun and planets and stars revolved around it. An Earth where the Western Roman Empire had met its overdue end nine years earlier and Europe was a swirling barbaric chaos within which the future gestated—at least in this, his own familiar reality.

As though reading his thoughts, Tylar harrumphed. "The next step is the transition to the point in the alternate timeline congruent to this one. Robert and Tiraena, I should warn you to expect the same phenomena we just experienced, only in intensified form."

"Oh, shit!" Sarnac breathed.

"You have almost a minute to prepare yourselves," the time traveller assured them. "It takes that long for our power sources to charge the capacitors that make up most of this vehicle's mass, making possible the truly titanic power surge required."

"It took us days," came Andreas' faint voice. No one else commented. The silence stretched. Sarnac's left hand felt the pressure of Tiraena's grip. He returned it.

"It is time," Tylar stated. And within Sarnac's head, Creation went mad.

When he could think again, he found himself crouched on the immaterial floor, staring at the stars light-years beneath him. They were unchanged. And Sirius was still as ruddy as when he had last glanced at it. But there was no room for doubt that *something* had happened.

" 'Intensified form' my left one," he muttered as he got to his feet, noting with sour satisfaction that Tylar was recovering his composure with as much difficulty as the rest of them—except Andreas, who was seemingly unaffected.

"Andreas, didn't you *feel* that?"

"Oh, I know what you just experienced. It affected me when I entered your reality. But no, this time there was nothing."

"You see," Tylar explained, back in form, "Andreas is returning to the place in which he *belongs*. The psychic sensation of outraged reality only seems to affect someone making a transition to a timeline other than his own."

"So we won't feel it on our return?" Tiraena asked.

"No, you won't. By the same token, you'll find that a transposition via temportal back to your own twenty-third century—which you've never done in a state of consciousness—will be less unpleasant than one to an era foreign to you. And no, we don't understand the 'why' of it."

"To hell with the 'why' of it," Sarnac grunted, "as long as we've got some light at the end of the tunnel." He turned to Tiraena. "What did you feel?"

"It's hard to describe." She shook her head slowly. "Sometimes, at the moment you wake up from a deep sleep it's as though you're looking at yourself from the outside. You remember your name, and the face in the mirror, but for the barest instant you wonder: 'Who *is* this person?' Well, this was like that . . . but for the *universe*."

The last aftershocks ceased reverberating around Sarnac's skull, and he noted that they were no longer surrounded by the vast metal basket. Instead, the Brobdingnagian mass of hybrid technology that had brought them to this reality was falling away astern. The starry firmament seemed to rotate around them as their ship realigned itself. Then the bright yellow-white star that was the alternate Sol lay dead ahead.

"Now," Tylar announced briskly, "we can proceed to Earth."

There was, as always, no sense of motion. But the transtemporal vehicle seemed to recede from them with impossible rapidity, vanishing from sight before Sarnac could even try to calculate their velocity. The tiny flame of Sol began to grow perceptibly brighter.

"We should be entering Earth orbit in a few hours," Tylar explained. "We may as well stop wasting time by talking of the 'alternate Earth' and the alternate this and the alternate that. As for the alternate Artorius, I suggest we adopt Artorius' suggestion and refer to him as 'the Restorer.' At any rate, we have time for—"

"For listening to you answer a few questions," Sarnac cut in. "For openers, why have we come to the year 485 A.D.? You've been saying all along that 491 is the first year when the course of this timeline's history can be changed."

"Ah, but we want it to *stay* changed. And for that, it will be necessary for us to lay a bit of groundwork, as I mentioned before."

"Groundwork?" Tiraena queried suspiciously. "Yes, I remember you saying something about assuring that this Ecdicius would be inclined to do what you want him to do. . . ."

"Yes: break up the Empire by setting up a separate Western Empire. But there must be more behind the breakup than one man's understandable annoyance at being almost assassinated. Ecdicius will merely provide the leadership for a movement with a genuine East-West incompatibility behind it."

"What 'incompatibility' is that?"

"In our own history, what sundered the two halves of the Empire irrevocably was the schism between their two forms of Christianity. This suggests our obvious avenue of approach."

"Uh, hold on, Tylar," Sarnac said hesitantly. "I'm no history buff, but I do know that the religious wars in European history were pretty damned nasty. Is that what we're going to be starting here?"

"Oh, we won't be starting it, my dear fellow. It started before the timelines branched off, at the moment the Empire took the road of intolerantly exclusive monotheism. Andreas' history doesn't include the Thirty Years' War, but you can be sure that it holds comparable horrors."

"He's right," the young transtemporal explorer admitted. "Instead of wars between sovereign nations espousing different religions—Tylar told me about those—we've had repeated, bloody suppressions of embryonic heresies. Whole ethnic groups were exterminated because they had been 'infected with error.' Doctrinal unity has always been seen as a pillar of Imperial unity, and no challenge to it has ever been tolerated."

Tiraena shook her head. "I still have trouble imagining this kind of thing, in either version. I never heard much about it as a child—I suppose it was something my Terran ancestors weren't proud of in their heritage. And while the history of Raehan has its share of stupidities and brutalities, the Raehaniv have never been inclined to slaughter each other over their various religions."

"The religious atmosphere on Raehan has always been more like that of eastern Asia," Tylar explained. "It was once said that a Chinese gentleman was a Confucian in public and a Taoist in private. But after he died, he expected to enter a Buddhist afterlife. And he was always careful to sacrifice to Animist deities. All, be it noted, with complete sincerity. This seems odd to a Westerner—but no odder than formulations like 'Thou shalt have no other gods before Me' or 'There is no god but Allah' seem to a Chinese . . . or a Raehaniv."

"My background is Western," Sarnac said defensively,

"and I'm not intolerant of anybody's religion, or lack of it."

"Of course not. You're a modern, secularized Westerner, a product of the scientific and industrial revolutions and their resultant social disintegration, otherwise known as 'freedom.' We're going to make that possible here. But it will take more preliminary work than I may have indicated. And now—" he indicated Sol, grown to the proportions of a sun "—we have much to do and little time, so you must forego further explanations until after we land."

Sarnac had approached the night side of fifth-century Earth once before, and no longer felt a bottom-dropping-out-of-the-stomach sensation at the nighttime blackness of an Earth innocent of electric lighting.

The ship dropped down and settled like a feather. It was stealthed against all sensors, including the Mark One Eyeball and Mark One Eardrum that were the only sensors currently available to humans. But Tylar made sure there was no one present to see the hatchway open before he let them step through and emerge into the moonlit spring night beside the old Roman road.

As soon as the hatchway closed behind them, Tylar took out a small device and regarded it silently for a moment. Then they felt a breeze of displaced air as the invisible ship soared silently upward into the low orbit where it would patiently await recall. Then they looked around at each other.

They were all in the same kind of nondescript contemporary clothing, including Tiraena. Tylar had decided that for the moment it would be simplest for her to masquerade as a young man—a simple matter for her in this ill-nourished milieu. She was of average height for a twenty-third-century Raehaniv woman, which made her tall on the standards of her Terran female contemporaries and taller than the average man of the fifth century. She had acquiesced with no good grace. Sarnac, for his part, was looking forward to the newly remembered sensation of being a big guy—it was restful, somehow.

He activated his light-gathering contact lenses, and the moonlit scene became as clear as though seen by daylight. The road ran northeast toward Constantinople, their destination. Off to one side was what had been a roadside shrine to Hermes, long since desecrated by the Christians and its idol removed. The moonlight had invested the crumbling little structure with a flesh-prickling aura of romantic, mysterious antiquity. In the pitiless clarity of the optics, it was merely dilapidated. To the other side, a low cliff overlooked the Sea of Marmara.

The device in Tylar's hands shape-shifted, stretching out to form a staff such as a middle-aged man might use when journeying on foot. A quick calculation told Sarnac that its total volume had increased significantly; it was probably less dense than the wood it now appeared to be.

"Where are we?" Tiraena wanted to know. "I thought we were going to Constantinople."

"As I intimated, we've been researching this era—the temporal we used has been in place for over a year. This is as close to Constantinople as I thought it prudent to land, so I had the portal device left here. We've also infiltrated an agent into the city, with whom I've already been in contact." He didn't say how.

"An agent?" Andreas looked puzzled. "I thought we were going to be on our own."

"In operational terms, we are. Quite simply, I can't risk involving any of my own people except Artorius, whose background is unique. I'm not at all certain of their ability to function effectively in a mission which flies in the face of all their training and conditioning. Imagine a dedicated veteran museum custodian who was suddenly ordered to start smashing the exhibits! But for reasons which will become apparent, we need a contact. So I'm using one of my best men in a supporting capacity. We're to meet him this morning. We'll have a bit of a walk, but we should reach the city just after dawn."

Tiraena ran a hand through her hair, cut even shorter than its norm. "Tylar, should we be travelling in the dark like this? Aren't you worried about, uh, highwaymen, or dacoits, or whatever they're called in this part of Earth?"

"No, I expect no such trouble this close to the capital of an empire as vigorous and effective as this one has become. And if we do encounter any unpleasantness, our ability to see in the dark plus these——" he took from the pouch at his side a slim metallic tube such as they all carried "——should give us whatever advantage we need." He set out along the road, and the other four followed, moving slowly along the coastline of what would one day be called Turkish Thrace in *their* reality. What it would be called in this reality—and, indeed, everything else about the future of this reality—was about to become unpredictable.

They first glimpsed Constantinople silhouetted against the dawn. By the time they reached the Golden Gate, the city had awoken to roaring life.

They passed through a polyglot throng as they crossed over the sixty-foot-wide moat—dry now, as was normal— and through the outermost of the three-mile-long triple walls Theodosius II had built early in this century to protect a city that had long since outgrown Constantine's original wall. They continued on up a ramp through the twenty-seven-foot second wall, and before them stood the *real* wall of Constantinople, with its massive seventy-foot towers, thick and solid enough to withstand the discharge of the torsion-powered missile-throwers atop them.

Sarnac's experience of the fifth century was limited to the provinces of western Europe, whose rusticity was seldom varied by even so much as a town. Perhaps that was why he—child of a civilization which tamed the energies that powered the suns and the gravity that shaped space—found himself impressed by these walls, remains of which could still be seen in his timeline. In *that* history, nothing had overcome them for a thousand years . . . and even then it had taken the gunpowder artillery of which Theodosius II had never dreamed. He tried to imagine what the construction of these walls had meant to a society on this technological level, but soon gave up.

"Artorius," he asked the former High King, who was wearing a hood lest anyone should notice that his profile was the one on all the coins, "how did your counterpart ever take this place?"

"He didn't. He defeated Zeno in the field. Afterwards, Zeno died during the retreat, and the Sacred Consistory—that's sort of the Emperor's cabinet—unanimously concluded that the Augustus of the West was his late enemy's undoubted heir apparent. The Senate ratified the decision, which is its only remaining function, and the Restorer made a triumphal entry through this very gate."

Sarnac shook his head. "So it was as though the civil war had never happened. This must be a pettifogging lawyer's paradise—as bad as twentieth-century North America!"

"Oh, I don't know if I'd go *that* far. But it's true that the Roman Empire, from its inception, had no clear-cut law of succession. The 'Tetrarchy' scheme that Diocletian set up in the third century only muddied the waters. So it's always been necessary to come up with rationalizations for the current power grab—especially since the Empire became Christian. It's believed that the emperor holds office by virtue of God's will . . . and who's to say how He'll express His will? Nowhere is it written that He has to act through heredity! So whoever currently occupies the throne, however he got there, is by definition the rightful emperor." He paused. "The Restorer is trying to solve this problem by returning to the system of adoptive heirs that worked for a little while in Rome's great days. In Andreas' history, he succeeds."

They continued on, wending their way through

obviously new construction to the Old Golden Gate in what was left of the Wall of Constantine, largely cannibalized for its stones. Then they proceeded along Middle Street, the greatest of the thoroughfares that crisscrossed the dense mass of narrow, crooked streets—urban footpaths, really—that made up most of Constantinople. The teeming warrens were visible beyond the porticoes that lined Middle Street. Sarnac's implanted knowledge included a map showing only the main routes; he wondered if one even existed which showed every detail of what might jokingly be called a street plan—it would have looked like a plate of spaghetti.

The deeper they penetrated into the city the harder they had to push through a colorfully dressed crowd which was as diverse socially as racially. Glancing to left and right, Sarnac saw that the dwellings of rich and poor interpenetrated as thoroughly as did their occupants. That was something else he "remembered": Constantinople, unique among big cities (including those of his own twenty-third century) had no fashionable residential districts. Of course, the rich didn't have to huddle together to find privacy from the rabble—the architecture of their homes, organized around a central court and presenting a blank stone face to the tenements around them, saw to that. But Sarnac wondered if there might be something more to it, in this empire which recognized only the god-emperor and his subjects, of whom the richest was as much a slave as the poorest.

As they walked on through the urban throng, the only certain indication that they were getting anywhere was the series of squares onto which Middle Street unexpectedly opened—the Forum of Arcadius, the Forum Bovi, the Amastrianum, the Forum of Theodosius, and finally the oval Forum of Constantine, with its red porphyry column topped by a colossal statue of the city's founder.

"Constantine was in pretty good shape," Tiraena observed, eyeing the statue's classically perfect body.

"Actually," Artorius explained, "It's a statue of the god Apollo, with the head knocked off and replaced by Constantine's—badly, as you can see. He was vain as the devil. I imagine nobody ever dared to tell him that the locals call the statue 'old dirty neck.'"

Tiraena sputtered with laughter, which Sarnac was glad to see. It was the first sign that she was thawing where Artorius was concerned. She'd never been precisely hostile toward the former High King since regaining her memories . . . just cool and distant. Artorius might not even have noticed—he'd certainly given no indication of noticing—but Sarnac knew how utterly unlike her it was. He wondered what her problem was, but there had never been just the right opportunity to ask her—and there still wasn't. Instead, he addressed Artorius.

"What did the Christians have to say about this statue? I mean, isn't it sort of, uh, blasphemous?"

"Where their imperial patron was concerned," Artorius deadpanned, "the Christians were prone to uncharacteristic tolerance."

Then they were out of the forum, and soon the massive bulk of the Hippodrome loomed up ahead and to their right. Beyond it, Sarnac knew, the Sacred Palace sprawled in all its labyrinthine profusion of buildings, courtyards and gardens down to the Sea of Marmara. A little further and they emerged into the Augustaeum, the colonnaded public square bounded on the southwest by the main entrance to the Sacred Palace, over which floated the sleeve-like blood-red dragon standard that Artorius the Restorer had brought from Britain. At right angles to the palace, and appropriately dwarfed by it, was the Senate house. To the northeast was the church of Saint Sophia—impressive enough, but nothing like the transcendent edifice Justinian would raise in its place in the other reality.

Already, under the porticoes and around the central statue of Constantine's mother Helena, the Augustaeum was filling with lawyers, officials, and everyone who wanted to meet someone. A figure detached itself from the crowd and started toward them.

"Koreel!" Tiraena exclaimed, at the sight of the familiar face.

"Ventidius," Tylar corrected. "Remember, cover names! He's still using the same one he did when he was your fiance. It's safe enough, as he's quite a distance from Britain and unlikely to meet anyone who'll want an explanation of the alternate Ventidius' abrupt disappearance twenty-two years ago."

"You haven't changed," Sarnac told Koreel after the greetings were completed. "Of course, I only met you once."

"Yes, I remember: the night Tiraena and I departed for Britain." He had arranged for her a position in the household of Artorius' consort, where he himself was established as a merchant and distant cousin of Tylar/Tertullian. "But now," he said to Tylar, "we'd better get to my house. You'll want to eat and rest, and later we can discuss plans for getting you into the Sacred Palace."

They left the Augustaeum and moved northward through a maze of narrow streets toward the Phosphorion Harbor on the Golden Horn. Sarnac quickened his pace and got alongside Tylar. "Get us into the palace?" he queried. "What are you and Koreel up to, Tylar? Is this the 'groundwork' you've been so mysterious about?"

"Precisely! We're going to meet none other than the Restorer himself. You see, we need to secure his cooperation."

"You're going to ask for his cooperation in undoing his own life's work? That ought to go over like a turd in a punchbowl, Tylar."

"Granted, I wouldn't expect him to listen to me. But we have one with us who may very well be able to persuade him."

Sarnac stole a backward glance. Within his hood, Artorius' face was unreadable.

# CHAPTER SIX

The house of Koreel/Ventidius was typical of the dwellings of the moderately well-off: a wooden two-storied structure with balconies like the one Sarnac now stood on in the late afternoon. The house blocked his view of the sunset, but he could see to the east, where the hill that had been the acropolis of the old Greek city-state of Byzantion rose above the maze of roofs. By leaning over the railing, he could glimpse the hills beyond Pera to the north, on the other side of the Golden Horn. Directly below him was one of the narrow alleys that he couldn't bring himself to call streets, thronged with people as usual.

Sarnac had confidently expected some vague similarities of overall outline to his world's Istanbul that would confer a comforting familiarity on this city. His expectations had been dashed—if anything, his disorientation was worse than it would have been if he had never had them. He should have approached fifth-century Constantinople as he would have approached contemporary Ctesiphon or Ch'ang-an, which it might as well have been for all he recognized of it.

He heard a rustle behind him. "Hi, Philogius," he greeted with a smile. Tiraena snorted at the name Tylar had decreed for the tall teenaged boy that was her current cover identity—a nephew of "Ventidius" and distant cousin of "Tertullian." All were members of the rather mysterious merchant family of remote Indian origin that was the time travellers' device for explaining their ethnically unidentifiable looks. It was more than sufficient in the hayseed West, and should work even in this cosmopolitan city. Artorius was a business associate from Gaul, and Sarnac and Andreas were bodyguards.

"At least *I'm* not semi-barbarian hired muscle, Bedwyr," she gibed as she settled in beside him on the balcony and looked around. "Taking in the view?"

"Yeah. I was just thinking how little good my knowledge of this city in our time is doing me. You've never been here, of course. I was, in the dim mists of my youth." (Another more-or-less ladylike snort.) "It'll be called Istanbul then."

"Somebody conquers it?"

"Yes—in our reality. But there's a lot of diverging history between *that* city and this one. I've got a list of questions I want to ask Artorius. You know, if he lived in our time and didn't go into politics or the Fleet, he'd be a natural as a tour guide!"

Her face instantly lost some of its mobility. "Yes. Artorius." There was a couple of heartbeats' worth of silence. Then she turned. "The sun's setting. We'd better get inside."

"Hold on a minute. We need to talk about this. You never knew Artorius before—never even *met* him, just saw him once. And he couldn't have done anything to piss you off then, he was too busy dying. But it's pretty obvious you've got a problem where he's concerned."

"I've never . . ." She stopped abruptly and her mouth snapped shut, cutting off any pointless denials. After a moment's stiffness in which she seemed to collect her thoughts, she relaxed and even gave a crooked smile. "The truth is, I find myself liking him more than I expected to."

"Huh?" Sarnac shook his head. "How could anybody *not* like him?"

"You've got a different perspective. You and he were comrades-in-arms of a sort. And I don't think you can separate him in your mind from the legendary figure he became in our timeline. The culture you grew up in made that figure its personification of nobility and greatness and human aspiration. To meet the living original of that figure and find he's as affable as *this* character . . . Well, I can see how it must be an irresistible combination."

"It's not just that," Sarnac insisted. "Even in his own time, when he was just another warlord and didn't carry any mythic clout, people could feel his personal magnetism. It was so strong that it left a permanent imprint on legend."

"Yes . . . with a little unwitting help from you and a lot of very witting help from Tylar. But, yes, I know what you mean. And what he—in his alternate version—has done in this timeline speaks for itself about his abilities."

"So," Sarnac asked, perplexed to the point of exasperation, "what's the problem?"

"You were never in Britain," she answered obliquely. "You never met Gwenhwyvaer."

"Uh," he began cautiously, "whatever you may have heard from her, you've got to discount it for bitterness."

"Oh, no! She wasn't bitter about him. In fact, she was still very much in love with him. Yes, she had other men, in the lonely years after he drifted away from her. And that fixed *her* role in legend, with the help of Ambrosius Aurelianus, who was a prick on wheels." Her years on Earth had done wonders for her vocabulary, Sarnac thought, not for the first time.

"No," she continued, "the problem wasn't hers. It was mine." She gazed moodily out over the darkening city, and Sarnac didn't interrupt her thoughts. "Sexual equality has been taken for granted on Raehan for a lot longer than it has on Earth. Or it *will*! Or . . . something." Her smile was like the sun through a rift in clouds. "Give me a good, swift kick the first time you hear Tylar-like noises about tenses! But you know what I mean. And . . ."

Abruptly, the clouds were back. "I don't think you ever fully understood what a shock fifth-century Earth was for me. If, like you, I'd at least had a clear idea that things had once been that way, I might have been able to use the dry historical facts as emotional antibodies. But the whole thing hit me without warning. And Gwenhwyvaer focused it for me. So I suppose this faceless figure of Artorius, who'd apparently lost interest in her when she failed to produce an heir for him—naturally it was the woman's 'failure'—became, for me, the symbol of everything I didn't like about this milieu."

"He didn't invent the culture he was born into," Sarnac pointed out. "And, for what it's worth, I think you're talking about a problem that would have existed in any era. Artorius can charm the 'gators out of a swamp, but he's a political animal to the core. Given an objective, he has a kind of focus that excludes a lot of really deep human attachments. People like this—I won't say *men* like this, although most of them for most of history *have* been men, if only for reasons of opportunity—don't tend to have very secure personal relationships, whatever kind of society they live in. So I hope you can accept it as simply being the way he is, and not resent him as a symbol of this age, which would make working with him pretty difficult."

"Oh, I think I can work with him. I just can't stop thinking about Gwenhwyvaer. I wish you could have met her, Bob! What makes their story such a damned shame is that they were really so well-matched. She was a remarkable woman. . . ."

"Actually," came the diffident voice from within the curtained entrance, "you shouldn't speak of her in the past tense. She's very much alive this very evening. Not as young as she once was, of course . . . but who among us is?"

"How long have you been eavesdropping, Tylar?" Tiraena inquired with a glare.

"Oh, not long at all. I'd just come to collect the two of

you for a final briefing. We'll be entering the Sacred Palace tonight."

"I need to be certain," Tylar addressed the group, "that everyone remembers the implanted data concerning this timeline's recent history, especially the circumstances surrounding the Restorer's final break with the Eastern Emperor Zeno."

It was a reasonable question. The synthetic memories were like things actually experienced . . . but that wasn't necessarily the same thing as *remembering* them, unless one was blessed (cursed?) with total recall. Sarnac frowned with concentration.

"Well, there had been a lot of accumulating friction. But wasn't the final straw something to do with a religious dispute . . . the, uh, Declaration of Union?"

"Precisely. In the year 482 of both realities, Zeno promulgated the *Henotikon*, which was really the work of Acacius, Patriarch of Constantinople. And in both realities it caused a religious crisis by compromising with the Monophysite heresy which dominated Zeno's Eastern provinces but which the Council of Chalcedon had anathematized in 451."

"The Mono . . . uh . . . ?"

"Essentially, the Monophysite position is that Christ had only one nature, the divine, after His incarnation. In our reality, Pope Felix III, who took office the following year, excommunicated Acacius for deviating from the doctrine of Christ's dual nature, in which the divine and human components are separate but commingled; and Acacius then excommunicated the Pope. In *this* reality, the Restorer took up the cudgels of orthodoxy and, after becoming sole Augustus later the same year, deposed Acacius as Patriarch."

Tiraena shook her head. "I simply can't believe that anyone would go to war over such insane metaphysical hairsplitting!"

"Oh, you'd be surprised," Artorius said, almost too softly to be heard.

"It *is* hairsplitting," Tylar acknowledged. "But in this era, cultural or ethnic conflicts generally come disguised as abstruse theological disputes. Monophysitism seems to be an early expression of a Near Eastern tendency toward a kind of austere monotheism foreign to the West. In our reality, this impulse will find its ultimate expression in Islam, and Monophysite Christianity will die of terminal irrelevance while the Eastern and Western churches move toward their final break in the eighth-century Iconoclastic controversy—another reflection of the same basic East-West dichotomy."

"In my history," Andreas spoke up, "the Restorer's prestige plus his close relationship with Pope Gaius II— your old friend Sidonius Apollinaris—were sufficient to impose universal orthodoxy, with the Church as an arm of the Empire. The Popes were so delighted at not having to share ecclesiastical primacy with the Patriarchs of Constantinople that they scarcely noticed their total subordination to the Emperors." He smiled disarmingly at the others around the table. "No, I didn't really remember all that until Tylar's people retrieved it from my unconscious."

"Tonight," Tylar said, "all that is going to start to change."

"Right," Sarnac said decisively. "So let's get down to the practicalities of how we're going to change it. I gather we have to get the Restorer alone. That's surely going to take some doing in itself."

"Quite. The Augustus follows a rigidly prescribed daily round of ritual and ceremony designed to emphasize his remoteness from ordinary mortals and surround him with a semi-divine aura that, hopefully, discourages would-be assassins and usurpers. And he's *never* alone . . . except when he sleeps. That's why we're going in at night."

"Which leads to the question of how we're going to get into the Sacred Palace. I mean, that place must be guarded like you wouldn't believe. And you've made it clear that we can't simply use your technology to reduce any local opposition to a grease spot."

"Ventidius," Tylar yielded the floor to Koreel.

"Through my business contacts, I managed to get myself admitted to one of the Restorer's semi-public audiences. Once inside the palace, I proceeded inward toward the imperial apartments."

"Just like that?" Sarnac didn't even try to keep incredulity out of his voice.

"You'd be surprised how easy it is to infiltrate a place if you don't need to be concerned with getting out afterwards," Koreel smiled. "Admittedly, it also helped that I was wearing a field-generator that bends incoming light one hundred and eighty degrees around itself, thus conferring invisibility. I got as close to the imperial apartments as possible, emplaced the portal device I was carrying, and used it to return to this house. The guards were left very puzzled, of course, and security was tightened up. But it all died down after a while."

"So," Tiraena said, "you simply left this device in the palace? I can't believe no one's found it."

"This is a rather special device. After I departed, it activated an invisibility field of its own. The only way anyone in the palace would find it would be by stubbing a toe on it. And it can avoid that—it has a limited self-motive capability, and it's sentient. You will be wearing similar invisibility devices tonight."

"And," Sarnac drawled, "hopefully we're also sentient."

Unseen in an alcove in a deserted corridor, the immaterial doorway opened and two segments of reality came into dimensional congruency. Sarnac emerged, stepping from Koreel's house into the heart of the Sacred Palace. He looked around, trying to see as much as possible of the fabled magnificence of which the pillaging Crusaders and Turks of his history would leave not a trace.

But he could only see it in blurry shades of gray—his magic cloak of invisibility had a little drawback Tylar had neglected to mention until the last minute. (The time traveller had blandly expressed surprise at his lack of gratitude for the compensating effect that enabled him to see at all from within the field.) And, of course, he couldn't see other wearers of the field-generators at all.

All of which meant that they were going to have to do without the gizmo as much as possible.

The portal vanished, and Tylar winked into existence beside him. "Well, we're evidently alone in this corridor, so we can deactivate our stealth fields." Sarnac did so— his, like Tiraena's and Andreas', was manually operated— and all five of them stood revealed. The corridor was dark, but the light-gathering optics enabled them to see it in all its ornateness, stretching endlessly off to both sides. Sarnac called up his implanted infobase, and a floor plan seemed to float before his eyes. A cluster of five red dots showed their location.

"This way," Tylar commanded. They set out toward the right, keeping close to the wall, and the red dots began to move.

They hadn't gone far before Tylar motioned them to a halt. The time traveller then sidled forward to a corner and reactivated his stealth field. Sarnac heard the disturbed-beehive sound of a stunner. Then Tylar reappeared and motioned them forward. Rounding the corner, Sarnac saw two Scholarian Guards lying motionless before elaborately carved double doors.

"This is the entrance to the imperial apartments. They're not as heavily guarded as you might think, as it's normally impossible to get this far without passing through many outer layers of security." He brought a small instrument to bear on the lock, and soon the doors swung ponderously open.

"This is too easy," Tiraena whispered as they passed through spacious outer chambers. "I mean, in a society where an assassin is the legitimate successor as long as he can prove it's 'God's will' by making it stick . . ."

"I know what you mean," Sarnac whispered in reply. "But we've got to assume Tylar knows what he's doing."

"You've *got* to be kidding!" she muttered.

Then they were at a second door. "The imperial bedchamber," Tylar announced. He brought the little instrument to bear. "This should only take a moment."

They waited—with no good grace, at least in Sarnac's case. Tiraena's words had awakened worries he hadn't let himself contemplate. He hadn't had a migraine for years—his era's medicine was up to dealing with them—but he wondered if one might be coming on, for the pseudo-light of the optics was starting to hurt his eyes, as though with an intensifying glare. . . .

The glare became blinding at the same instant as the shouts rang out, and the guards were on them.

Sarnac frantically deactivated his optics at the same time he fumbled to get out his stunner. *Yeah*, some detached part of him took a split second to think, *that's the trouble with light-gathering technology. When it's got a lot of light to gather—like that lantern this patrol is carrying—they can blind you. These guys must have just found the unconscious guards outside the outer door and followed us in here.*

Then there was no time to do anything but react. He stopped trying to tug the stunner out and brought up his left arm to catch the downward-chopping sword. The impact jarred through his shoulder, but the material of his sleeve stiffened into a hardness exceeding that of steel at the touch of the sword-edge. His right arm brought a fist up into the stunned guard's gut. *Good thing the Scholarians don't wear body armor with their palace-service whites*, he thought within his inner storm center. But then a second guard was on top of him from behind. As he struggled in the man's grip, he caught a glimpse of the total scene. Tiraena and Andreas had managed to bring their stunners to bear and were scything down their assailants—Tiraena got the lantern-bearer, and managed to catch the thing as it fell from his limp hand. She almost stumbled over the man Sarnac had punched, and put an end to his gasping with her stunner. Artorius was on the floor, throttling the guard he was atop. Tylar was standing strangely aloof from it all . . . but his expression told Sarnac he was up to something. But then he could spare no thought for anything except fumbling with his stunner and jamming it up against the disconcertingly strong guard whose arm was around his neck.

He had just managed it and felt the weight on his back go limp, and simultaneously saw Andreas' last attacker fall stunned, when the bedchamber doors crashed open.

"What's this?" roared the man who stood there, clad in a nightgown but with a very businesslike sword in his hand. He took in the scene in a glance, then drew a breath. "Guards! To me!" he thundered. He might be old for this era—fifty-eight, Sarnac automatically calculated—but there was nothing wrong with his lungs.

Tylar faced him equably. "No one can hear you, Augustus. I have . . . well, suffice it to say that no sound can escape these chambers."

The dark eyes narrowed. "Witchcraft? Ha! Save it to frighten children, assassin! In the meantime, come and get me!" He raised his sword and fell into what Sarnac remembered as correct fighting stance.

"We mean you no harm, Augustus." The words came from across the room in the same baritone. Artorius stood up from the unconscious guard and faced the Emperor of Rome.

For a time that lasted so long that Sarnac began to suspect Tylar of using some sort of temporal-distortion trick, the tableau held. Then the Restorer's sword lowered inch by inch until the point scraped the floor. Then his features firmed and the sword came up again.

"So, you plan to substitute an imposter for me, do you?

Well, as plotters go you're a poor breed! You might have gotten a man old enough, and not clean-shaven!" Then his face took on a thoughtful look and he addressed Artorius. "Ah! I see. You're to pose as a long-lost son of mine, a by-blow of my youth, after I'm dead. Well, I'm not dead yet, mountebank! Come for me, or are you as gutless as you are faithless?"

Artorius stepped closer, heedless of the sword, until their faces were only a few feet apart, like mirror images save for the emperor's beard, wrinkles and uniformly gray hair. "You don't really think that, Augustus," he said softly. "You know—oh, yes, you know!"

Again, time seemed to freeze as the two identical profiles faced each other and no one else dared break the silence that had congealed around them.

"No," the emperor finally whispered. "It can't be possible."

Artorius sighed. "What shall I tell you of, Augustus? Of the little mole on the inside of Gwenhwyvaer's left thigh? Or of your fourteenth summer, when you went riding with the men into the hills southwest of Ribchester to buy horses from the Ordovices, and at night while your father was dickering with the chieftain a roan-haired girl whose name you never learned led you off beyond the campfires and . . ."

"Stop," the Restorer croaked.

"Or shall I go further back and tell you of your childhood friend Perdius, who you later watched bleed his life out through the gash of a Saxon throwing-axe? Of the time you and Perdius . . ." Artorius stopped and swallowed hard. When he resumed, his words were like soldiers advancing to face whetted steel, first hesitantly, then in a rush. "Of the time you and Perdius—no longer really children, though you didn't understand that just yet—were wrestling, and all at once your eyes met his, and you knew he was feeling the same strange, frightening things you were, and without a word you both . . ."

"As God is my witness, that was the only time in my

entire life . . . !" The Restorer's voice shuddered to a halt. For a long moment his eyes stared wildly into Artorius'. Then he smashed a fist against the door-frame. "No dream," he muttered to himself. "Am I mad, then. Or dead and in a hell of madness? Or . . . ?" He faced Artorius with a strange calm. "Can a man see his own ghost while yet living? Is that what you are—the spirit of my own younger self?"

"No, Augustus. I'm older than I look. I am not truly yourself, although . . ." He hesitated, as though realizing the inadequacy of all their planning for this moment. "I am the same man as you, but in a world which is a . . . a different thought in the mind of God."

The Restorer shook his head slowly, looking every day of his age and more. "You talk of things I can't understand, spirit. This is madness indeed, for if you speak truly then the world itself is mad and no man can say for certain that he himself is sane." He shook his head again. "I believe I'll continue to think of you as a spirit, for I own that I lack the courage to face the alternative!"

"Very well, Augustus. You may even be right; perhaps I *am* a spirit of the air to you, as you are to me. Some would explain it otherwise and speak of *quantum mechanics* and *superposition of functions*, but it's all one. For now, let it suffice that my world, and my life in it, ran the same course as yours until your forty-third year, when you waited with your army in Bourges until Syagrius of Soissons arrived with his forces and those of his Frankish allies, and together you smashed King Euric's Visigoths."

"Ah, yes!" The Restorer's eyes gleamed with memory. "Syagrius! He was a faithful ally! His death before Bourges almost made the victory too costly."

*Even though with his dying breath he made you his heir to the Kingdom of Soissons, and your power base was secure,* Sarnac thought with his implanted knowledge. *Now, now, let's not be cynical. Maybe he really was sorry to see Syagrius go. Who am I to say otherwise?* But then Artorius was speaking again.

"Know, Augustus, that in my reality I advanced from Bourges and placed my own army in a forward position in Berry, not knowing that our plans had been betrayed to Euric by Arvandus, former Prefect of Gaul. At a place called Bourg-de-Déols the Visigoths came against us in overwhelming force. We gave better than we got in the course of a long afternoon's slaughter, but in the end the army of Britain was routed and I was mortally wounded. Six years later, that Odoacer who you defeated in your world deposed the last Western emperor, and Europe descended into chaos."

The Restorer's eyes grew round. "Again, spirit, you speak madness! If you were mortally wounded fifteen years ago in this spirit-world of yours, how come you to stand here now looking, I'll swear, no older than I did then?"

"I was saved from death, and later from the ravages of time, through the mercy of God." (Sarnac searched Tylar's face in vain for any trace of embarrassment.) "But I was . . . called away from the affairs of my world after that. There are others here who can attest to what happened in those days in my past." He motioned Tylar and Sarnac forward. The Restorer's eyes widened still further.

"Tertullian! I remember you—Sidonius' secretary. And Bedwyr! of course I remember you. You saved my life in a Saxon ambush just before the Battle of Angers, where you did good service." He looked bewildered. "Tertullian, you look the same as you did then, like . . ." He waved vaguely in Artorius' direction. Then he smiled at Sarnac. "At least you, Bedwyr, look somewhat older now, as is proper!" *You could have gone all night without saying that, Your Imperial Majesty,* Sarnac thought sourly.

"Augustus," Tylar interjected, "do you recall what made you decide to stay in Bourges, that spring of 470, and wait for the reinforcements from Soissons?"

The Restorer looked blank for a heartbeat, then blinked. "Of course! I hadn't thought of it in years, but seeing Bedwyr reminded me. Yes, a few words I had with him as we were preparing to advance into Berry. He didn't really tell me anything I didn't already know—his words just crystallized certain doubts I had had all along." Suddenly, his eyes widened and he rounded on Artorius. "Are you telling me, spirit, that those few words made the difference between the real world and this nightmare spirit world of yours? That the merest instant of wavering on my part separated the empire from oblivion . . . ?" He came abruptly to a halt, silenced by what he had seen on Artorius' face. For he, and he alone, knew with a knowledge beyond the need for thought what the expressions of that face meant.

"Augustus," Artorius said slowly, "I've asked you to accept much this night. Now I must ask you to believe one more thing that defies belief. Since my . . . departure from the world, I have been vouchsafed a vision of the future—the future of my world and also of yours." The Restorer crossed himself, while Artorius gathered himself to say that which he knew he himself would once have found unacceptable. "You have achieved all that I once dreamed of—no, more than I ever dared dream of. I swear that my ambitions stopped with making the British High Kingship secure . . ."

"Yes, I swear," whispered the Restorer.

". . . but I can't deny that in my private moments, in my thoughts that I never shared with Gwenhwyvaer or anyone, I saw myself as the world-restorer that all my teachers had held up as the ideal. Well, you *are* that ideal. And now I know that what you have done—what I *would* have done but for one blunder—will blight the future beyond redemption, dooming it to . . ."

"No!" The Restorer drew back, and his sword came up again. "Now I know you for what you are, spirit: a demon, sent to sow the seeds of doubt! But you confound yourself out of your own lying mouth, for you admit that what I've done saved the empire . . ."

"Yes," Artorius said flatly. "You saved it, as I would have

in your place. And now you've seen it at its core. Are you certain that it really ought to be saved?"

"More madness," the Restorer said, but unsteadily, not with a roar of full-blooded outrage. "Oh, aye, I've seen the corruption, and the waste, and the way the emperor has been made into a gilded idol served by a fat-gutted priesthood of officials and eunuchs . . . I've seen it all, and tried to change it, only to find that it's like the scaffolding that can't be changed without bringing the whole house crashing down." His voice took on something like a beseeching note. "And it *must* stand! If what you say is true, you saw everything I saw up to the Battle of Bourges. You saw what the barbarians leave of a town they sack. You saw . . ."

"Augustus, I of all people know what you were trying to accomplish. I—you—grew to manhood knowing only empire or chaos. But since my life sundered from yours I've learned that there are other ways. I've also learned a very wise saying: 'Be careful what you wish for—you may get it.'" Artorius drew a deep breath. "In my world, the fall of the empire was so complete that men lost sight of the truth of my life. But that only let them read whatever meaning into my story they wanted or needed. And because I had failed, they didn't have to face the reality of what my victory would have meant . . . what yours *will* mean, as you've come to suspect in the innermost secret places of your heart. Instead, they made me the embodiment of all their aspirations for the unattainable. So I lived on in memory, not as I really was but as men needed to believe I had been. God knows I was unworthy of what my name came to mean . . . but I like to think the legend they made of me helped light their way through the dark years after Rome's fall."

A long time passed before the Restorer spoke. "So, spirit, we both live on—I in history, for I gave Rome back to the world, and you as a fable in a world that will have to do without Rome . . ."

"Aye, *Pan-Tarkan*," Artorius cut in, shifting to the British tongue and to the title of the hereditary commander of that originally Sarmatian cavalry unit which now included the Britons on whose tongues it sounded something like *Pendragon*. "And my empire of woodsmoke and fairylight, unlike yours of stone and laws, will let that world grow into something Rome could never have allowed."

"Aye, it's in my heart that you've the right of it," the Restorer said in the same tongue, barely above a whisper. "But what was I to do? What *am* I to do? For whatever the future may hold, there are many this night who are sleeping under their whole roofs in the knowledge that they can reap a whole harvest tomorrow. What of them?"

"Leave them in the peace you've given them, *Pan-Tarkan*. Let them raise their children behind your shield. But for the sake of those children, and their children for more generations than you can know, I ask you to do one thing. In the name of all that we share—a sharing beyond ordinary ken—I ask this of you." He made a smooth transition back to Latin. "Reinstate Acacius as Patriarch of Constantinople."

"What?! But it was only three years ago that I sent him packing! I'd never hear the end of it from Sidonius, from all my Western supporters . . ."

"That's precisely the point, Augustus," Tylar cut in. "The West must go its own way. This will make it *want* to do so. And Ecdicius will lead it."

"Ecdicius!" The Restorer's eyes shone. "I have no son, but he makes me feel . . ." He stopped. "But you say he's to lead the West into rebellion?"

"He won't see it that way, Augustus. He'll be barred from succeeding you by conspirators. He'll simply be doing the only possible thing—as you did for all those years following the Battle of Bourges."

"Yes." The Restorer nodded slowly. "Yes. Well, spirit," he addressed Artorius with the famous grin, "if I can't trust *you*, who can I trust? But it can't be at once. What about the current Patriarch, who I appointed to replace him?"

"The world knows that the old man was just a transitional appointment, Augustus. He'll not live to see another summer. Wait until he's gone and then call Acacius back."

"Well, I suppose I can come up with some kind of reasonable pretext to do it. And I suppose you'll want me to give him the same kind of support I would a Patriarch of my own choice?"

"Just so, Augustus." Artorius' grin was like a mirror of the other's. "It shouldn't be too hard. We both know how much you *really* care about doctrinal disputes!" He gestured at the unconscious Scholarians. "When we leave, summon more guards and tell them that your cry for help frightened off the intruders who fought these. I fear the palace will be turned upside down for a few days' searching."

"Very well." The Restorer looked at him long and hard, one more time, and then said, simply, "Farewell." Then he turned to Tylar and Sarnac. "Tertullian and Bedwyr! I never knew what became of you two. No one could find you at the time of the Battle of Bourges. But yes, Bedwyr, I do remember talking to you shortly before that . . ." He seemed about to say more, but Tylar forestalled him.

"Don't brood overmuch about what has passed before this night, Augustus. Just remember that your place in history, and in the hearts of the people for whom you won a time of peace, is secure. And now we must go. In fact, we must leave Constantinople. But our companion Andronicus will remain in the city." He indicated Andreas, who had been gaping. "He will be in contact with you from time to time over the next few years—after which we may well see you again."

"Will you be going far?" the Restorer asked. "I can give you a pass to use the imperial post."

"It is better if we travel in our own way, Augustus, though we must indeed journey far. All the way to Britain, in fact."

"Britain!" The imperial face wore a look as far-off as that misty island. "It's been so many years . . . Will you, perhaps, see the Regent?"

"It is entirely possible that we will see the lady Gwenhwyvaer, Augustus," Tylar said smoothly. "Is there any message you would like us to convey?"

"Tell her . . ." The glow went out of the Restorer's eyes, and he gave Artorius an odd look. "Tell her only that . . . I wish it had been better with us."

Artorius returned the look gravely. Tiraena regarded them both with an expression Sarnac could not read.

# CHAPTER SEVEN

"Are you sure Andreas will be all right?"

"Oh, quite." Tylar responded to Sarnac's anxious question in an abstracted manner, standing in the field beside the old Roman road beside the derelict shrine of Hermes and guiding his ship in by mental command. "He'll stay at Koreel's house and get regular reports on developments over the next six years. It won't be a tedious wait for him; Koreel has a stasis chamber which will allow him to skip the intervening periods. By the time we see him again, in 491, only a month or so of subjective time will have passed for him—and, hopefully, even less for us. Ah!"

"Hopefully?" Tiraena's worried query was cut short by the breeze from the descending spacecraft. Dawn was breaking over the Sea of Marmara, and even without their light-gathering optics they could see the grass being pressed flat over a wide expanse of meadow.

"Well," Tylar remarked offhandedly, "one can never be absolutely sure about these things, however carefully one tries to plan them." A portal appeared, with the ship's interior visible beyond it. They hurried aboard. The portal vanished, a sudden breeze caused the grasses to sway, and the abandoned shrine of Hermes was left to its decay.

❖   ❖   ❖

They proceeded at moderate altitude and leisurely velocity—no need to spread rumors of Judgement Day with a sonic boom—on a west-northwest heading, keeping pace with the dawn. The land unfurled beneath them, growing more and more corrugated as they passed over the Balkan Mountains and what would, for a little while in their reality, be called Yugoslavia. Then they were over the titanic masses of the Dinaric Alps. On they went, over mightier and mightier snow-capped ranges that held nary a ski chalet, until somewhere below were the headwaters of the Rhine. Then they were over the middle reaches of that river on both of whose banks Rome's writ now ran, for the Restorer had incorporated the Franks and fulfilled the dream of the first Augustus by advancing the imperial frontier to the Elbe.

Sarnac knew better than to look for engineering works visible from this altitude. There was an occasional glimpse of a line too straight to be anything but a Roman road, but there was nothing like the artificial environment that clothed his Earth. For all he could see, this might as well have been the year 485 A.D. of his own history, with West Rome nine years fallen. But he fancied that he could sense something of the quickening imperial life in the regions below him, over which dawn continuously broke as they flew west.

"How did he do it?" he asked Tylar. "Oh sure, he put down the barbarians. But that wasn't what was fundamentally wrong with the empire."

"Don't underestimate the importance of stopping the constant depredations," the time traveller told him. "But you're right; what's really been causing civilization in the West to collapse into feudalism is a tax system that shortsightedly treated the Western cities as revenue sources, killing a fragile yearling by trying to use it as a beast of burden. Under such circumstances, the cities died and their inhabitants attached themselves to some powerful landlord or other, who could protect them from the state's taxgatherers. In our reality, the process continued, with the Roman landowning class being replaced by a Teutonic one. The Restorer's fiscal reforms have been far more important than the battles the chroniclers will record."

Tylar gazed at the sunrise for a moment and then continued. "Also, there's the matter of timing. The Huns have withdrawn to the steppes, where their clans bicker over the sorry remnants of Attila's empire. And the Avars won't arrive in Europe for another generation or two. So Europe is getting a respite from central Asian invaders while the imperial structure is still just barely salvageable. That's why this period is so uniquely crucial—why the fabric of reality is so very weak."

They swept on over the Flemish lowlands and out over the channel. The sun had caught up with them, and far below gleamed the white cliffs of Dover.


"Silence! In the name of God and of the Augustus, I will have order here!"

The shouting and fist-brandishing halted, and in the sudden silence the two groups of men on opposite sides of the long table turned to the woman at its head. She had risen from her high seat to shout them down, and now she stood glaring at them, silently defying anyone to disobey her. None did.

Gwenhwyvaer, wife (albeit long-separated) of Artorius Augustus and his regent here in Britain, was still magnificent in her fiftieth year. She still stood regally erect to the full stature that had, in her youth, reminded old men of her great-grandfather Magnus Maximus. The red-gold blaze of her hair had been damped down by the invasion of gray. But her eyes were still the same vivid blue which now flashed dangerously at the Britons to her right and the Saxons to her left. Seeing her, these men saw the visible presence of the empire.

*The visible presence of the empire! What a colossal irony! Ambrosius, I hope you're watching now from*

*whatever corner of Hell is reserved for censorious prigs—
you, who always saw me as a separatist enemy of the
Rome you worshipped, and hated me for it.* Gwenhwyvaer's
features stiffened as usual at the thought of the general
who had been Artorius' regent until his death; but then
they relaxed just a bit, and a slight smile crept out. *And
yet, you old bastard, the greatest irony of all is that now
that I sit in this seat I almost wish I had you back. Not
quite . . . but almost.*

She shook her head to clear it of old memories.
Ambrosius' victories over the rebelling Saxon *foederatii*
had laid the groundwork for Artorius to restore the High
Kingship that Ambrosius himself had refused to accept.
But marrying a descendant of Maximus had given the young
High King legitimacy, in this land with its matrilinear
traditions that the Romans called "Celtic" but which dated
back to forgotten peoples before the coming of the Celts.
So, to the Britons at least, she represented not just the
Augustus of Rome but the High King as well. As for the
Saxons . . . well, they had only recently settled into the
role of imperial subjects, and the British High Kingship
meant nothing to them. But the name of Artorius did. And
they knew her for an ally.

*More irony,* she thought. *By trying to smooth the Saxons'
assimilation into Britain, I've alienated my own natural
supporters, the British diehards.* She turned to those
diehards' leader.

"Cador, I see that I was wise to order all weapons turned
over to my guards at the start of these conferences. I know
it's folly to expect young hotheads to hold their tempers—
but you? At your age?"

"Forgive me, Lady," Cador of the Dumnonii mumbled.
"But I'm not too old to stand up for what we fought for
under Ambrosius and your husband the High King . . . er,
the Augustus. Nor will I be, as long as I'm above the
ground!"

"Nor are some of us too young!" Cador's son Constantine

was a younger replica of his father in his dark fieriness. "We've heard from our sires and grandsires the tale of how the Saxons broke their faith and ravaged this land for years. And now that Artorius stands triumphant, first here in Britain and then in the Empire beyond . . ." All at once his hurt showed and he seemed as young as he was. "Is this what we Britons fought and bled for? Bad enough that these pigs continue to wallow in the eastern lands that they'd already seized. Are we now to let more of them in?"

"And give them lands all too close to Dumnonia?" his father put in, glaring across the table at the two relatively new arrivals who led the Saxon delegation.

"Pigs, is it?" Aelle of the South Saxons spoke in Latin even more heavily accented than usual, and his lined face grew florid behind its luxuriant growth of gray-blond mustache. "Our folk had held those eastern lands, as loyal allies of Rome, for generations. Why do you think the old Romans named that land the 'Saxon Shore'? But then your own High King Vortigern brought in the Jutish freebooter Hengist and his cutthroats! If you knew anything about our lands beyond the North and Narrow Seas, you'd know that a younger son of a *jarl* who wants to go raiding can always gather a crew of men outside any family—the kind of scum who can be found in any nation!"

"All Saxons are scum!" Cador leaned forward, gesturing his son back. "And if they held the Saxon Shore for generations, it was only to breed mongrels with our women!" He glared directly at the young man beside Aelle—very young to be an *ealdorman* among the Saxons, but more and more prominent in their councils since his arrival in Britain the previous year.

Cerdic of the West Saxons smiled at him easily, then responded in fluent British. "Well, now, I'm thinking that in my case at least you've the wrong shore for mongrel-breeding, Cador of the Dumnonii. And the wrong men doing it! My mother was of those Saxons who've settled along the lower Loire, in Gaul. She always told me my father was a Briton, which was why she'd given me a name of his people. That was after Artorius had broken her people—and yet she and hers were among those families which, through his intervention, weren't moved off their land afterwards to serve Childeric the pig-king of the Franks! Ah, Lady," he addressed Gwenhwyvaer, "I could find it in me to pray to your cross-god if he'd grant me the boon of having known that man before he moved on to Romaburg, far beyond the ken of the likes of me . . . and of you also, Cador, so you needn't be so high and mighty! And," he added with a flash in his eyes that was pure Celtic, "if it's Saxons stealing your women that worries you, you might well ask yourself why they're *willing* to be stolen!"

"You damned pagan half-breed!" Cador yelled, groping instinctively at his side for the weapon that wasn't there.

"Enough!" Gwenhwyvaer's voice cut across the rising hubbub like a sword-slash. "Cerdic, your mouth will talk you into trouble yet. And you, Cador—and all your house!— whether you wish it or not, the Saxons are here to stay, however or whenever they first came. Whatever future Britain is to have, they will be a part of it. All those of their race who now live in this island are citizens or allies of Rome; to strike at them is to strike at Rome—and at Artorius who *is* Rome! Will you defy *him*, Cador?" The western chieftain dropped his eyes. After almost a decade and a half, the memory of how Artorius had dealt with the rebellious Silures was still fresh. *Yes, irony piled upon irony! Ambrosius, are you listening to me invoke the iron fist of Rome? Is that your ghost I can almost see, looking too stunned to haunt? Or could it be the ghost of my own younger self?*

All at once exasperation overtook her. "We will meet again tomorrow and see if you fools can attend to the business at hand. And know this: I will have an end to this endless paying of blood-debts, before there's no blood left to be paid! In the meantime, remember my ban on all quarreling within these walls and for five miles around! This conference is adjourned." They all rose to their feet as she swept out, followed by her guards.

"I need to breathe air that isn't thick with stale old hates," she declared. "I'm going riding."

"I'll summon an escort, Lady," the guard captain said.

"The Devil take escorts! I need a time by myself."

"But, Lady, alone . . . ?"

"Sweet Jesu! Will no one obey me this day?" The captain inclined his head. He belonged to the Artoriani, the elite heavy cavalry Artorius had commanded by right of birth before he had become High King, much less Augustus. A small detachment of them remained stationed here, a reminder that he had not forgotten the island of his birth.

A few minutes later, she was cantering away from the stables, her full ankle-length skirt hitched up so that she could use the stirrups that Artorius' Sarmatian ancestors had brought from the steppes long ago. He had taught her how when they'd been young, in the years that seemed a solid blaze of happiness in her memory against which all the hurtful wrongnesses since were silhouetted like dead trees against the sunset. *I wonder how much longer I'll be able to do this,* she thought. *I'm not getting any younger. But compared to most women my age . . . ! Of course, they're mostly worn out from childbearing. . . .* Automatically, from long practice, she thrust the thought back down into the cavern where it dwelled.

She rode through the southwest gate, under the tower Ambrosius had designed to resemble a work of Rome, and down the hillslope past the four rings of earthworks that attested to this place's past as a Celtic hill-fort. Today, she had to thread her way among encampments—the chieftains had brought far too many retainers for Ambrosius' walls to hold. Ahead, the River Cam snaked among the scattered stands of trees, ablaze with the reflected afternoon sun. She wanted none of the old Roman road to the north of the hill, where travellers would distract her with their salutes. No, she would seek the old trail alongside the Cam, where she might find solitude—and remembrance.

But the day's cares would not leave her. *Yes, Artorius, you were right. The things that drove the Saxons to this island—too many mouths to feed from too poor a land— didn't stop driving them when you conquered that land. So where they once came as raiders, you let them come as immigrants to join their kindred already here—most recently Cerdic and his fellows from the Loire. Yes, it has been as you commanded. But not even you can command old blood-feuds to quietly die. Not from your golden City of Constantine, far away beyond the sunrise.*

She tried to imagine what the City must be like—she'd heard descriptions, but discounted them as typical travellers' exaggerations—as she rode slowly along the trail, dappled with late-afternoon sun that slanted through the trees. Then, up ahead she saw a group approaching on foot. She urged her horse forward to see them more clearly, and they halted. The leader—a tall middle-aged man whose exotic appearance reminded her of someone, she knew not who— motioned his three companions to a halt with his walking staff. One of them was a tall lad, also foreign-looking, who Gwenhwyvaer felt she ought to know. Another was a big, dark, rakishly good-looking man in the prime of life, evidently a bodyguard but seeming in an indefinable way to be something more than your typical hiresword. And finally there was a powerfully built man whose face was obscured within a hood.

All in all a decidedly odd group of wayfarers, Gwenhwyvaer decided. And something about the hooded man—was it a movement he had made, or the way he held himself?—caused her to feel, just below the level of thought, a shuddering fear that was absurd in the absence of any threatening or hostile move from these men. Indeed, the leader bowed with every evidence of respect and addressed her in cultured Latin.

"Greetings, Lady. I am Tertullian, cousin to Ventidius, known to you of old."

Ventidius! Of course this man had looked familiar. "Yes, I remember now, although it was . . . what? Fifteen years ago? He was a merchant, close to my household. In fact . . . yes, his fiancee was briefly one of my ladies-in-waiting. But then they both disappeared abruptly. It was quite a mystery. What ever became of them?"

"Alas, Lady, they were never seen again. They must have fallen afoul of brigands. It was a terrible blow to our family. But I've come trying to rebuild our British business. That's why I've brought my young kinsman Philogius—time he was learning something of the world." The maddeningly familiar-looking boy bowed. "And this," Tertullian continued, indicating the hooded man, "is Gerontius, a business associate who met us after our arrival from Constantinople."

Gwenhwyvaer's eyes widened. "Constantinople? You've come all the way from the City? What news of . . . of the Augustus?"

"The divine Augustus was, God be praised, very well at the time of our departure. In fact, I was privileged beyond measure to be presented to the Sacred Presence. He commanded me to convey his greetings to you, and to deliver certain messages."

"Well, then, you must stay with us this night! We'll talk on the morrow."

"You are too kind, Lady. But surely there's no room for us. We've heard since our arrival that you are hosting a great gathering. . . ."

"Yes, to discuss border adjustments to accommodate the latest Saxon arrivals." Her expression momentarily darkened. "But no matter. We'll find room for someone who brings word from the Augustus! Your bodyguard can be lodged with my personal troops."

She turned her horse around, leading them back toward the hill at a slow walk. Tertullian walked beside her, answering her avid questions. If she had torn her attention from him and looked back, she might have seen the bodyguard—who Tertullian naturally hadn't introduced—move up alongside the youth Philogius and mutter in an unfamiliar tongue.

"This is something I've been meaning to take up with Tylar," Sarnac groused. "Why is it that you always end up hobnobbing with the social elite while I'm billeted with the grunts?"

"Seems reasonable to me," Tiraena replied judiciously.

They proceeded up the hill of Cadbury, passing through the concentric rings of earthworks and the camps; they got stared at by what Sarnac thought were some very tough-looking hombres. Then they were at the summit with its twenty-foot-thick rampart of stone-faced earth topped with a timber palisade.

"This gate-tower is a damned clever design," said Sarnac, who fancied himself an authority on low-tech military engineering since his last sojourn in this century, as they entered the fortress.

"Yes," Tiraena nodded. "But from the standpoint of Ambrosius Aurelianus, who designed it, it was even more important that it reflect Roman patterns, and even incorporate some recycled Roman structural elements. He was a fanatic, you see—a brilliant fanatic, but a fanatic."

They entered the enclosure. "I guess this all looks familiar to you," Sarnac remarked.

"Mostly," Tiraena acknowledged. "But I was here fifteen years ago, before the timelines branched off. There have been a few changes. That proto-Byzantine cruciform church, for instance. I remember it as little more than a foundation. It never got finished in our timeline, or so I gather from the implanted historical data I've now gotten back."

They approached the timbered hall that had been the primary headquarters for Artorius as High King of the Britons and for his viceroys—first Ambrosius and now

Gwenhwyvaer. It was the nucleus of this stronghold at the summit of Cadbury, already known by the name which, a millennium later in their timeline, the Tudor antiquary John Leland would hear from the local people and make famous: Camalat.

"So you were at the Battle of Angers?" The youngster in the red-and-white uniform of the Artoriani gawked at Sarnac. "Did you know my father Caradoc?"

"I did indeed," Sarnac said truthfully. "Does he still live?"

"No," the young *cataphract* replied with the fatalism of an era when death usually came early. "Disease took him during the campaign against Odoacer in Italy. I can barely remember him, for I had not long been weaned when he departed for Gaul with the *Pan-Tarkan*." This reality's Artorius might be Emperor of Rome, but these men would always call him by the title that they alone were privileged to use.

A somewhat older man looked at Sarnac narrowly. "You hardly seem old enough to have fought at Angers, Bedwyr."

In point of coincidental fact, Sarnac had spent just about the same amount of subjective time since his participation in that battle as had elapsed in this timeline. But a decade and a half meant far less to one with access to twenty-third century bioscience than it did to these men. "Well, I was little more than a stripling then. My parents, settlers in Armorica, had been killed by the Saxons. I had some training in arms, and a mercenary who knew my family took me on. He'd just been hired as a bodyguard by the Bishop of Clermont's secretary, who was travelling with the High King. It got confusing—his name was Bedwyr too." To his relief, no one reacted. He'd been counting on this era's mortality rate to assure that none of the men he'd served alongside—or, rather, their counterparts—would still be on active service. And nobody had, it seemed, heard of him. *There'll be no Sir Bedivere in this world's legends. Bummer.*

"But what about the later campaigns?" the young man persisted. "I've heard that at Bourges . . ."

"Sorry," Sarnac shook his head. Now came the tricky part. "Just before the Battle of Bourges, our employer was called back to Clermont by the Bishop—now His Holiness Pope Gaius, you know—and we had to go with him. After that there was plenty of employment for us in the south of Gaul as the old Visigothic kingdom broke up and bands of their survivors were everywhere. But now," he said firmly, "I've got to take a trip outside." The facilities were holes in the ground. He didn't really feel a need to use them, but his head needed a respite from the hot, smoky interior. This common room was used for sleeping and all other purposes, including cooking at the fire that was kept smoldering under a hole in the roof through which the smoke would rise when the wind was right. Tonight it wasn't.

He stepped out into a night which, like the day that had just ended, was unusually clear for this land; he could actually see some of the stars to which he had voyaged. On impulse, he ascended the rampart and leaned on the timber palisade, looking out over the darkened landscape. Yes, there were more stars visible up here above the scattering of torches that gave some illumination to the enclosure.

He heard a rustle from below and looked down. A cloaked man, his head not far below the level of Sarnac's feet, had emerged from the shadows and was proceeding toward the gate tower from the direction of the great hall. Then three other figures stepped unsteadily from the shadows and crossed his path. One of then staggered into a collision with the cloaked figure—Sarnac couldn't tell whether or not it was intentional—then sprang back, glowering. "Who do you think you're running down, dog?" he said in alcohol-slurred British.

"Your pardon," came the reply in the same language. "The night is dark." The cloaked man made to go around, but the trio moved to block his path.

"Oho! The Saxon pig can grunt in a human tongue," another of them said in the careful way of a drunk who is trying to convey a particular tone—in this case, sarcasm.

"He still needs to be taught manners," said a bystander who, like the drunks, belonged to the visiting tribal contingents and not to the Regent's guards.

The Saxon, as he evidently was despite his facility with the British language, spoke calmly. "I'll remind you that the Lady Gwenhwyvaer has forbidden all fights within these walls." The bystanders were gathering, in a way that bore an odd resemblance to an attempt to surround him.

"Aye," one of them said. "So it's too bad you started one by attacking Brychan here." The man who'd collided with the Saxon nodded with drunken profundity, endeavoring to look very much the injured party.

The Saxon looked around. "You may be too drunk to fear the Regent, but my men—who, fortunately for you brave lads, are camped outside the walls—will come looking for you. On that you have the word of Cerdic of the West Saxons."

It was evidently the wrong thing to say, because an ugly rumbling arose in which Sarnac could pick out the phrase "half-breed." Suddenly, the Briton who'd been doing the talking lunged for Cerdic. The latter's sturdily shod left foot shot out and caught him below the belt. Then the Saxon twisted around and fed another attacker a knuckle sandwich before disappearing under a knot of kicking, punching men.

Sarnac reminded himself that he had only one purpose in being here, and that any actions that might jeopardize the mission were to be avoided at all costs. He reminded himself that the rights and wrongs of the local residents' disputes could not be his concern. He even reminded himself that he didn't have all that much use for Saxons.

He was still telling himself all these things as he leaped off the parapet and landed feet-first on the back of one of Cerdic's attackers.

He scrambled to his feet and waded in, pulling two men

off Cerdic and bringing their heads together with an authoritative clunk. It gave the Saxon the break he needed to get free of the tangle, and he began laying about with swings that were as powerful as they were unscientific. Nobody here knew the deadly hybrid form of unarmed combat that the PHL military taught its people, and Sarnac had enough presence of mind to avoid using it.

All at once, Sarnac felt a brain-rattling jolt against his jaw and the world turned to spinning galaxies of stars. He managed to get his right arm up in time to block a second powerful but clumsy blow, and his head cleared enough to recognize his opponent as Brychan. With all the force he could muster, he drove his left fist into the boozy Briton's gut. Brychan doubled over and proceeded to rid himself of his battered stomach's contents. At the same time, Sarnac took a blow from behind to the kidneys. Scarcely noticing the pain, he thrust backward with his right elbow, connecting with something, then spun around and squared off with his new foe, wishing he was wearing the impact armor on which the fellow would have broken his knuckles. *I'm getting too old for this shit*, he thought. *Why didn't I think to remind myself of that?*

"Halt! Enough, I say!"

As though by magic, the clarion-like voice transformed the scene into a still life. Everyone still conscious—except Brychan, who continued retching—turned slowly toward the approaching group of torch-carrying guards and the tall woman who strode forward at their head.

"By all the demons of hell! Did I, speaking with the voice of Artorius Augustus, not prohibit all brawling?" Gwenhwyvaer was in a splendid fury, and as her blazing blue eyes swept the scene, nobody met them. Instead, these hulking warriors studied the ground, looking exactly like boys who'd been caught playing with their pee-pees.

"Er, it's *his* fault, Lady," somebody finally managed, pointing at Cerdic. "The Saxon. He attacked Brychan, over there."

"Bullshit!" Sarnac remembered to say it in British. "Brychan and two others, all drunk out of their minds, decided to pick on Cerdic. The rest joined the fun." Brychan had reached the dry-heaves stage and was in no condition to give evidence.

Gwenhwyvaer stepped closer and recognized the young Saxon through the battering he'd taken. "Cerdic! What in God's name have you done now?"

Cerdic gave a grin which obviously cost him some pain. "It's as this man says, Lady. By the way, friend, what's your name?"

"Bedwyr," Sarnac muttered, hoping Gwenhwyvaer wouldn't make any connections.

"Well, Bedwyr, if you ever need a favor, remember that Cerdic of the West Saxons owes you a rather large one. You did me quite a good turn, even though your name couldn't be more British. But, then, neither could mine. . . ."

"Shut up, Cerdic!" Gwenhwyvaer muttered through clenched teeth. Then she stepped closer to Sarnac. "Haven't I seen you before? Aren't you . . . ?"

"My bodyguard, Lady," Tylar finished for her. He hurried forward into the torchlight, followed by Tiraena in full "Philogius" kit. Following behind came the hooded figure of "Gerontius."

"Well, Tertullian," Gwenhwyvaer said imperiously, "he knew the ban on fighting. He must be turned over to the guard captain for judgment."

"I beg you to be merciful, Lady. I've known this man for some time, and I'm certain he would not have disobeyed your commands had it not been in defense of himself or others."

"He claims he was defending the *ealdorman* Cerdic of the West Saxons here against an unprovoked attack. These others say it was Cerdic who did the attacking."

"Well, Lady, I appeal to your common sense. How likely is it that the *ealdorman* would, in the teeth of your prohibition, single-handedly begin a fight in the stronghold of his people's blood-enemies? He would have had to be either mad or a fool, and I have yet to hear that he is either."

Gwenhwyvaer said nothing and neither did anyone else. Again her eyes swept the group, and again none met them. For once, Cerdic left well enough alone.

Tiraena stepped forward. She was wearing a broad-brimmed hat which helped her carry off the "Philogius" role. "I, too, beg you to show Bedwyr mercy, Lady. He's a rough, common fellow, but he means well." (*You'll pay*, Sarnac thought darkly.) "And I ask it as a favor, for you've known me before."

"When have I ever known you, lad?" Gwenhwyvaer asked, puzzled.

Instead of answering, Tiraena took off the hat and relaxed from simulating the body-language of an adolescent male. For a long moment, the two women stared at each other in the firelight and the silence.

"Lucasta," Gwenhwyvaer finally whispered. "But you're . . ."

"Lady," Tylar broke in quietly but firmly, "we need to speak to you in private. There is more at stake here than you perhaps realize."

At first it seemed that Gwenhwyvaer hadn't heard. Then she nodded. "Yes. . . . There are many questions that must be answered. Come with me to the hall." She turned to the puzzled onlookers. "The rest of you, disperse. Guards, see to it."

"Ah, perhaps I'd best be getting back to my men's camp, Lady." Cerdic began to sidle off.

"Ha! So the sight of your face can stir them to anger? No, you'll come to the hall as well, you can sleep there. We'll send a messenger to let them know you're spending the night." Without even waiting for an acknowledgment, she swept off. The four time travellers followed.

By the time they'd entered her private chambers and she'd shooed out a gaggle of ladies-in-waiting,

Gwenhwyvaer's self-possession had returned. She turned to face them unflinchingly. "I know not what's afoot here, but you *cannot* be Lucasta, however loudly my mind shouts that you are, for you look no more that a few years older than you . . . than *she* did fifteen summers ago. I'll know the truth! And you, Gerontius or whatever your name is: remove that hood!"

"Is that my lady's command?" came the deep baritone.

For a time beyond time, there was absolute stillness as terror and denial and emotions less easily defined struggled back and forth across the battlefield of Gwenhwyvaer's face. Then she amazed all of them by speaking firmly. "Remove it."

The hood fell from Artorius' face. Sarnac managed to catch Gwenhwyvaer as she fainted.

# CHAPTER EIGHT

She didn't entirely lose consciousness, at least not for more than a moment. Artorius was instantly at her side, and he and Sarnac got her to a chair. She blinked only a few times before her eyes steadied and her face lost its disorientation. Sarnac wondered at her lack of hysterics. *Well, Tiraena said she's a remarkable woman. And maybe this era's people find all this easier to take than those of my time would. After all, they don't think they understand the universe. For them, the world is full of unexplained mysteries, so what's one more?*

Finally, Gwenhwyvaer extended a hand—not altogether steady, Sarnac was oddly relieved to note—and touched Artorius' cheek where the nascent facial hair had reached the bristly stage. "I'd almost forgotten what you look like without a beard," she whispered as though thinking out loud. "It's been so long . . . we were young then. . . ." She shook her head again and her voice firmed. "But otherwise you look much the way you did the last time I saw you, on your return to put down the western rebels after the Battle of Bourges. Not long after I last saw you, Lucasta." A smile flickered to tremulous life. "Does the journey from Constantinople restore one's youth, then? Perhaps I should try it."

"Gwen," Artorius began, "you must believe me, even though what I speak sounds like madness. On this night, Artorius Augustus lies abed in his palace in Constantinople."

"You . . . an imposter? No! I know you, Artorius—I think I knew you when I first saw you cloaked and hooded on the trail by the Cam where we once . . . No! Unless I am mad indeed, it is you."

"Yes, I am Artorius—but I last saw you before leaving for Gaul in 469."

"Madness," Gwenhwyvaer began. But Artorius pressed on, overriding her attempts to speak.

"I have, indeed, come from Constantinople—where I spoke to Artorius the Restorer. I tell you now what I told him: that I'm the same man as he, but in a world in which God ordered events differently. In my world, I was delivered by treason into the hands of the Visigoths. And a few years later, Rome-in-the-West ceased to be. Men believed I'd died. Then they made a legend that I was not dead but merely waiting until I was needed again; and they were right, but not in the way they thought. For, though I was grievously wounded, a most unlikely manifestation of God's mercy had spared me and also preserved my appearance as it was then."

"But," Gwenhyvaer finally got in, "you say that *you* met *me* just before leaving on your expedition against the Saxons and Visigoths in Gaul in 469 . . ."

"Yes. For you see, Gwen, this world and the world I've been speaking of weren't sundered from one another until the spring of 470, shortly before the Battle of Bourges in this one. Until then, I was in truth the man you knew, and you were the woman I knew. But at that moment, my life and memories parted from those of him who this world knows as Artorius Augustus, the Restorer."

Gwenhwyvaer's eyes grew haunted. "If what you say is true—and I believe it must be, for no one could invent a tale so strange—then there must be another of *me* as well, living in this shadow-world you speak of, who heard of your death even as I was celebrating your triumph at Bourges! What of *her*? Does she still live?"

"I know not, Gwen. It may be so. In my world, Britain took a while to go down into the dark, and she may well have lived on. But I can't say for certain."

She stood up, eyes aflame. "*What*? Do you mean to say that you escaped death, unknown to all, and left me . . . her to continue to believe herself a widow? That you never even took the trouble to learn if she was dead, or living in degradation? By God, I swear you'd show more interest in a favorite horse!" As though with the breaking of a petcock, decades of bottled-up hurt began to gush out. "I know your love died years ago, as well I should, having watched it die while trying in vain to give you the heir who might have kept it alive—"

"No, Gwen, no," Artorius whispered.

"—but I'd have thought that the very *memory* of love would have made you go to Britain, or send someone, to learn how it went with her who you once called—" She remembered the others in the room and cut herself off before resuming. "The loss of love I'd long come to accept. But hatred and contempt? Dear God, Artorius, what have you even been *doing* for these fifteen years in your world?"

*And that,* Sarnac thought, *is going to be a tough one to answer in terms she can understand and accept, especially considering that it's been a hell of a lot more than fifteen subjective years for him. She's taken all this amazingly well so far—but time travel . . . ?* He watched as the man who looked to be in his early forties raised his head and locked eyes with the woman of fifty who had been born eight years later than he.

"You've the right of it, Gwen; I could have found out how it fared with my Gwenhwyvaer. Tertullian here could have found out for me. And I never let him." She took a sharply indrawn breath. He hurried on. "You ask why? It wasn't because my love for you had died. Indeed, I don't think it ever truly died."

"Don't lie to me, Artorius," she said in a voice almost too small to be heard. "Not that."

"It's no lie, Gwen. I sometimes wish I had lost my love, or never had it at all. Either would have been more merciful than feeling it but never being able to give it as much of myself as it deserved and needed."

"What do you mean?"

"In Constantinople I told the Emperor of Rome, who is my own self, that he gave Rome back to the world while I gave a legend to a world that had to do without Rome. But in both worlds, my life has been what posterity required it to be, not what I might have wished."

"I married a man, not a Purpose!"

"Did you, now?" Artorius' eyes hardened. "Don't *you* lie to *me* Gwen, nor to yourself! You fell in love with what you saw in me. And you knew—or should have known—that the man you saw could never be purely yours. Be honest: could you have loved a man who would have been satisfied with a life which held you and naught else?"

"I was just a girl!" she stormed. "I understood nothing of such things."

"Oh, I think you did . . . and do. For we're alike in this, Gwen. Remember what I just said, about the legend people in my own world will make of me, when they think I'm gone? Well, you're in it too. You reign forever in men's minds as Guinevere, queen of a wondrous city called Camelot where, for just a little while, men attained the unattainable." His gaze gentled. "So we're both caught in the same doom, Gwen my love. We were put in this world to fill not our own needs but those of unborn generations."

She slumped into the chair again and ran a hand through hair that had once been the color of flame. "I understand none of this," she muttered. "I'm old and tired and lonely, and anyone who believes I reigned over some ideal kingdom conjured up by bards from hot air and heather beer will be an even greater fool than I am for continuing to love you all these years! All I understand is that you never sent this Tertullian to inquire after me in a world where I might have been dead, or some barbarian's slave. . . ."

"Don't you see? That's the very reason I couldn't ask how you fared! If I'd learned my Gwen was in peril or in want I'd not have been able to do otherwise than come to her aid—which wouldn't have been possible. You asked what I've been doing in my world in the years since I . . . departed from men's knowledge. Well, all I can tell you is that I've been in a kind of indenture, working off the debt I owe for my rescue from death. And I won't pretend that I haven't enjoyed the work, for I've seen things that make all the legends of magic and wizardry seem insipid. But it carries a curse: I can't take any action that would change the appointed course of my world's future. If I'd learned that Gwen must die, I'd have had to stand by and let it happen."

She crossed herself. "This has a pagan ring to it, Artorius—like the Fates of Roman myth and the tapestry they weave, or the Norns the Saxons tell of. I like it not."

"No more do I, Gwen, for I've always held that men make their own destiny. But now I've learned that things aren't always so simple. I've accepted that . . . but I couldn't face the possibility of having to let you die. For it *would* have been you, Gwen, in whatever world."

"Ah, Artorius!" Again she reached out and touched his cheek. "Is that truly the reason?"

"Truly, Gwen. The bards will lie about your having been queen of an enchanted many-towered city, but they'll speak the truth about one thing: you were always queen of my soul."

She smiled, allowing them all an instant's glimpse of what the young Artorius had once seen. "You always did have the power to move me with words, you scoundrel! Like the time . . . But no, I'll not let myself recall that which lies beyond the veil of years. For it's all done with now, isn't it? Oh, Artorius, what a waste! All those years of living, as you say, the lives the future required . . ."

"Gwen," Artorius cut in gently, "I've come to you this night to tell you that we're not through doing it." She stiffened. "I must ask you to believe what I asked Artorius the Restorer to believe: that I've been vouchsafed a vision of the future, and—"

She rose abruptly. "You ask too much of me . . . at least without further explanation in private, without these others. Come." She led the way toward her inner chamber. He followed.

Left to their own devices in the antechamber, Sarnac, Tylar and Tiraena sat down on whatever was available. Sarnac squirmed uncomfortably on a stool obviously intended for a lady-in-waiting, his bruised kidneys protesting. After a time he spoke.

"Well, er, Tylar, I suppose they're, uh . . ."

"I'm sure they're discussing the possible geopolitical options," Tylar stated blandly.

"No doubt! All in pursuit of whatever your objective is here in Britain—about which you've never been 'entirely candid,' as usual!"

"It's straightforward enough. We need to make Gwenhwyvaer aware that The Restorer has only a few years left to live, and that when he dies a usurping tyranny will seize power at Constantinople. The time will then be ripe for her to make her bid for British independence."

"Huh! But why? I thought you were betting on Ecdicius to set up a separate Western empire. Won't a British rebellion just be an extra headache for him?"

"All will become clear in good time," Tylar intoned. Sarnac was about to wax sarcastic, but Tiraena spoke up.

"Tylar, does he mean it? Or is he just bullshitting her?"

"Oh, he means it. I've heard him on the subject often enough over the years. And I've come to know him very well. He's quite capable of 'bullshitting,' as you so elegantly put it. But I can tell when he's not."

"Then he never really stopped loving her." Tiraena shook

her head slowly. "I suppose I should be glad that we gave this night to her, but I can't help thinking about the *other* Gwenhwyvaer, who may still be alive. . . ."

"She's not." Tylar's flat declarative took them both by surprise. "In point of fact, she died two years ago in our reality, and now lies buried on Glastonbury Tor, in a tomb beside which the abbey will one day stand. And Artorius lies beside her."

The last sentence didn't even register at first. When it did, Sarnac spoke cautiously. "Uh, Tylar, I think I must have misunderstood you . . ."

"Artorius will live quite a long time on your standards," Tylar said obliquely. "But not very long on mine. He was introduced to civilized medical care only after having spent his first forty-two years among . . . this." Tylar's gesture encompassed fifth-century Earth. "Eventually, he'll grow old. And when he does, I'll take him back to the early 480s of our timeline, while he and Gwenhwyvaer still have life in them. The monks of Glastonbury will lay them to rest together. Their tomb will be rediscovered in the twelfth century. Later it will be generally written off as a hoax, despite certain annoying facts that will stubbornly defy explanation." He blinked. "Dear me, I must be growing garrulous with age! I must, of course, insist that you not mention any of this to . . ." He gestured at the door through which Artorius had passed.

Tiraena spoke while Sarnac was trying to find his tongue. "Tylar, how can you know you'll do this?"

"Oh, my! The problem of tenses again! You see, in terms of my own subjective consciousness I've *already* done it. Just another bit of historical policing, you know; history required that those bones be found in the abbey graveyard at Glastonbury. But there's no regulation that prohibits me from sometimes enjoying my work—or from doing a good turn for a valued associate." He settled back with a faint smile and composed himself to wait, politely ignoring the other two's expressions.

Presently, the door opened. Artorius and Gwenhwyvaer emerged in mid-sentence. ". . . but it still can't work," she was saying. "It comes to grief on the same hard reality that defeated Carausius two centuries ago."

*My God,* Sarnac thought, *they really* did *find time to talk politics!*

"You mean the inability of Britain to survive a serious attempt at reconquest?" Artorius said—Artorius whose corpse lay beside his Gwen's on a hill twelve miles northwest of here this very night in his native reality. It was, Sarnac thought, like looking at a ghost.

"Yes. Any usurper who arises in Britain must either conquer the Western Empire or be conquered by it. Maximus tried and failed. Constantine the Great succeeded. But Britain can't remain aloof in a state of . . . of . . ."

" 'Splendid isolation'?" Tylar offered with a smile. "The situation will be different this time, Lady."

"In what respect?" Gwenhwyvaer asked, gazing at him narrowly. "I don't know who you are, Tertullian, but there's clearly more to you than I can see, or understand. Speak!"

"Artorius has already told you that after the Restorer dies his designated heir Ecdicius will be prevented by usurpers from coming into his inheritance and will lead the West into separation. In exchange for your recognition of his legitimacy as Augustus of the West, he will acknowledge Britain's independence."

*Mighty free with Ecdicius' commitments, aren't we Tylar?* thought Sarnac. Gwenhwyvaer looked thoughtful. "Ecdicius," she said with a slight frown.

"You can rely on him, Lady. And without his guarantee, your dreams of an independent Britain are only dreams." Tylar looked Gwenhwyvaer unflinchingly in the eyes. "Don't hold it against him that he's the Restorer's heir in place of the son you never had."

The Regent's eyes flashed blue fire, but Tylar's continued to hold them. The flames subsided, and she said only "How can you know this?"

"As to that, Lady, I can only ask you to trust me. As you yourself have admitted, there are mysteries here that are beyond ordinary understanding. But . . . he will vouch for me." Artorius nodded. "And this much is no mystery: the Restorer cannot live forever. Even if I'm wrong about the nature of the storms that will follow his passing, you'll want to prepare against some such storms. During the next few years, Lucasta will visit you from time to time with counsel concerning those preparations."

Sarnac started, for he hadn't been told about this part of the plan. But Tiraena evidently had, for she showed no surprise. She and Gwenhwyvaer regarded each other levelly.

"So you are in truth Lucasta. Indeed, there is a mystery here that I cannot fathom." Gwenhwyvaer spoke with the fatalism of all the ages before humankind had begun to *expect* to be able to fathom mysteries.

Abruptly, the outer door swung open. "Oh, am I interrupting? Your pardon, Lady, but I was anxious to know if the messenger had assured my men that I'm all right within these walls. My son Cynric is out there, and he's only seen eight winters . . ."

"They have been informed, *ealdorman*," Tylar said smoothly while everyone else wondered how to handle the new arrival. "By the way, I am Tertullian, employer of Bedwyr, who I believe is already known to you."

"He is indeed!" Cerdic stepped all the way into the room, walking a little stiffly and beginning to show a spectacular mouse under one eye but managing a certain raffishness. "And this gentleman?" He indicated Artorius.

"My associate Gerontius." Tylar spoke quickly and firmly, forestalling everyone else. "And now, *ealdorman*, I suggest you close the door, for we are discussing matters which are not for every ear. I believe, however, that they are for yours."

Cerdic gave Gwenhwyvaer an uncertain look. "Lady . . . ?"

"Do it, Cerdic," she sighed. "I don't know how Tertullian finds things out, but since he knows so much else he probably knows how deeply you are in my counsels regarding the future of Britain."

Sarnac took his first close look at Cerdic of the West Saxons. He was in his mid-twenties, dressed in a version of his people's standard tunic-and-trousers garb that was less drab than most. He was darker than most Saxons—Sarnac recalled hearing that he was half-British—but had the sturdy build and sweeping mustaches that typified them. And his quietly thoughtful expression would have surprised most of those who knew him.

"Well, Tertullian," he finally said, "however you may have learned it, it's true. The Regent has tried to smooth my people's path in this island, so that we may perhaps—" he seemed amused at the thought "—become a new sort of Britons ourselves. And I'm with her." He grinned in his usual public way. "If all my thoughts were widely aired, I know not whether my own people or the Britons would bellow the loudest. At least it would give them something to agree on!"

"No," said Gwenhwyvaer. "It would just give them one more thing to fight over: the right to hang you! And it would probably serve you right. But I have no heir, and the Britain that is to be will need leaders. Sooner or later you're going to have to become a Christian, of course—and spare me that pained look! Quite a lot of your people have been receiving baptism. It has to come, you know. We need all the sources of unity we can get. All the more so given Tertullian's news. I'll call for some wine, then you can hear it yourself."

The wine level was a good deal lower by the time Tylar finished his account of what was to be, carefully hedged about with "in all probability" and "I have reason to believe." Cerdic silently sipped his wine. ("Don't tell my men I've turned traitor to ale!" he'd joked.) Then he cocked one eyebrow at Gwenhwyvaer.

"I don't suppose I need to ask what *your* course will be, do I?"

"The question is," she retorted, "what will *yours* be?"

Instead of answering, he turned to Tylar. "What if the East reconquers the West and then turns on us?"

"That could be," Tylar admitted. "And even if Ecdicius wins in the end, you may well suffer an invasion in the course of the war that's bound to come. I can't promise you that these things won't happen. But I *can* promise you this: you'll never see a more auspicious moment to make your bid for British independence. Such an opportunity will not come again."

"Well," Cerdic said after a moment's silence, "a little invasion might do wonders for unity in this island. And my people have known Rome for too short a while to have developed much attachment. But," he turned to Gwenhwyvaer, "what of the Britons?"

"Remember, we were independent of Rome for a pair of generations, after Honorius graciously permitted us to arm ourselves against the invaders Rome was no longer able to keep from our shores. For the last few years, we've convinced ourselves that *Rome* rejoined *us* since it was our High King who restored the empire." She shook her head in rueful acknowledgment of the Celtic genius for self-deception. "As long as he lives, you'll not find a more loyal set of imperial subjects. But after he dies" —an involuntary side-glance at Artorius— "and especially if Tertullian is right and his heir is denied the purple by a usurper . . . yes. If I know men like Cador and his son, they'll be ripe for rebellion."

"Well, is there no end to this night's surprises?" Cerdic grinned through his mustache. "I've found something in common with Constantine ap Cador! For I, too, have no stomach for rebellion against an empire that still has Artorius the Restorer on its throne."

"And why would that be?" asked "Gerontius," speaking for the first time. "Did he not smash your people by the banks of the Loire?"

"So he did. But that was war. Oh, yes, I hated him then—

I was only a lad of eleven, and his name was used to frighten us children. Actually, I hated Britons in general, for I'd learned early enough that my mother had been used by one of them—you can be sure the other boys let me know from whence I'd come! When my mother and I were forced to leave our home, I could have killed him. But later I learned that we'd been moved to keep us out of the clutches of the Franks. Still later, he allowed our people to emigrate to join our kin in Britain. And as I grew to manhood I followed the tale of his rise to empire. It was like a hero-saga that was really happening! I suppose that was why I felt more and more drawn to him, and wished with all my heart that I could meet him." He shook his head. "I know that can never be. And I know that after he's gone the Empire of Rome will have no hold on my loyalty. Yes, Lady I'm with you." He reached for the amphora and refilled his winecup. "Shall we drink to a war that will see Briton and Saxon on the same side?"

As they drank, Sarnac sought to read Artorius' expression. But there was none to be read.

"So Tylar's set up a temporal stasis device for you?" Sarnac kept his voice down even though he and Tiraena were probably out of earshot of the others. Tylar and Artorius talked with Gwenhwyvaer and Cerdic where the latter two sat their horses a good distance ahead on this little-used stretch of road.

"You'd better believe it. There's no way I would have spent six subjective years here! My 'periodic visits' will be between spells in stasis. At that, I'll be aging several months more than you will, since you won't emerge from stasis until 491."

"Seems only reasonable to me," he quoted. She dug him in the ribs.

Tylar had spoken the truth (*Always a first time for everything*, Sarnac thought) about the limitations of his people's time travel technology. Their temporal vehicles, used for emplacing temportals, incorporated a hideously expensive, highly specialized capability which Tylar's ship did not possess. But the temporal stasis field was, in effect, a kind of passive, strictly one-way time travel into the future. While the field was activated, no time passed within it (well, maybe a second for every billion years of the larger universe) and its contents were invisible and impalpable from the outside—in effect, it dug a hole in the space-time continuum and pulled the dirt in over it.

"Where is this gizmo?" he asked.

"A very convenient spot: a cave near the base of Cadbury, not far from the River Cam." Tiraena smiled. "Artorius mentioned that in our reality there'll be a local legend that that cave is where King Arthur is sleeping, waiting until Britain needs him."

"Could Tylar's little activities possibly have anything to do with getting that story started?" Sarnac wondered out loud.

"He also mentioned," she continued, "that the Cam is the root of the name Camlann, the place where, in the 530s of our reality, the last of the Artoriani will effectively wipe themselves out in internecine fighting. By then they'll just be a well-armed band of freelance brigands. The High Kingship will have ended with him." She sighed. "This landscape holds a lot of sadness for him, knowing what he knows now."

"I gather you've resolved your feelings about him by now."

"Oh, yes. If Gwenhwyvaer can do it, I can do it!" She smiled wanly. They fell silent, both thinking of that dim battle beside the Cam, the last battle of those *cataphractarii* who, as King Arthur's knights, would ride their richly caparisoned steeds into legend. Somebody named Medraut would incite them to slaughter each other over God knew what quarrel—some tribal feud, someone's wronged sister— within sight of Glastonbury Tor, where they would never dream that Artorius lay with his lady.

Up ahead, Tylar motioned them forward. "I fear we must part company here," he told Gwenhwyvaer. "We have business which requires us to return to Constantinople." Which, Sarnac reflected, was true as far as it went, as Tylar's statements so often were.

"I still can't believe you wouldn't let us give you some horses," Cerdic remarked. "Will you be returning to Britain?"

"I think not. But remember, I'll be sending messages to you through Lucasta, whom you'll be seeing from time to time. I have means of getting information to her." *Do you ever!* Sarnac thought.

"Then this is farewell, Tertullian," Gwenhwyvaer said. "And . . . and you, too, Gerontius." She and Artorius held each others' eyes for a length of time that Cerdic couldn't have missed, although he gave no sign. Sarnac wondered what he made of it, in his ignorance of who "Gerontius" was. *Tylar could have invented the term "need to know,"* he thought. *Come to think of it, I wonder if he did?*

"Farewell, Lady. And . . ." Tylar hesitated. "As we've all acknowledged, Britain may not be allowed to go its own way in peace. You can depend on Ecdicius' guarantee for the Western Empire, but he may not be able to shield you from the East. So the peoples of this island may need inspiring to arise in the common defense. I've taken the liberty of loosely translating certain possible sources of rhetorical inspiration for you, including a speech given by a queen who found herself in a position not unlike yours." He reached into a pouch and withdrew two scrolls of the Egyptian papyrus which, along with parchment and vellum, served this world in place of the paper that had not yet made its way west from China. He handed one of them to Gwenhwyvaer. "It helped to unite her people. And, *ealdorman*," he added, handing Cerdic the other scroll, "I thought you might find this useful. It was used to inspire an army to fight and win against seemingly impossible odds."

"Thank you," Gwenhwyvaer said, putting her scroll away. Cerdic examined his with frank curiosity—having become one of the few Saxons to have mastered the written word, he couldn't get enough of it. "When you get to Constantinople," she continued, taking out a scroll of her own from her saddlebag and proffering it not to Tylar but to Artorius, "give this to Artorius." For an interval whose silence no one felt inclined to break, two pairs of eyes once again held each other, blind to all else. The byplay, including her use of the name rather than the honorific "Augustus," was lost on Cerdic, who had become absorbed in his scroll.

With a final gaze, Gwenhwyvaer straightened in her saddle and turned her horse around. "Come, Cerdic."

Cerdic came up for air from the scroll and made to follow her. Then he halted his horse and turned to Tylar, holding up the papyrus. "You know, Tertullian, this isn't bad. 'We few, we happy few, we band of brothers.' Yes, I like that! Of course, it *can* be improved. I'll work on it." He nudged his horse forward, and he and Gwenhwyvaer vanished around a turn in the road.

Sarnac stared at Tylar. "What did you give *her*?"

"Oh, this and that. And now . . ." His walking staff shape-shifted into the recall device. Presently there came the faint breeze which was the only announcement the ship gave of its arrival.

"This device," Tylar told Tiraena after the portal that would allow them ingress into the ship had formed, "will reconfigure into a staff after we've passed through. Take it to the cave and leave it with the stasis generator. And now we must be going."

Sarnac and Tiraena clasped hands. "Hey," she said, "it'll only be a few subjective months—even fewer for you. We've been apart that long lots of times."

"Yeah, I know. But the fact that it's really going to be six years as far as the rest of the universe is concerned makes it different, somehow." He sought for something brilliant to say, but only managed: "Take care of yourself."

"Come, come," Tylar fidgeted. "Someone might happen along this road." He and Artorius stepped through the portal into the ship. Sarnac followed.

Once aboard, Artorius excused himself and went off—to read Gwenhwyvaer's scroll, Sarnac suspected. He himself followed Tylar to the "observation deck," where they seemed to be standing in mid-air a few yards above the ground. Tiraena was still beside the road, holding the nondescript walking staff and gazing toward the ship she could not see. Then she gave the self-conscious wave of one who can't be sure if the gesture is being seen, and turned to go. Feeling foolish, Sarnac waved back.

"Well," Tylar said conversationally, "the ship's stasis field should finish building any time . . ."

In less than an eyeblink, Tiraena's retreating figure vanished from the panoramic outside view, the leaves disappeared from the trees, and the ground acquired a covering of snow.

". . . now." His sentence finished, Tylar looked concernedly at Sarnac's face. "Oh, dear! I should have warned you of what to expect."

Sarnac shook his head, mental equilibrium reasserting itself. "No . . . it's all right. I had no reason to expect anything else, I suppose—I've been told often enough that no time passes inside a stasis field." He took a deep breath. "So it's now . . . ?"

"February of 491," Tylar confirmed. "We haven't been able to pinpoint the exact date of Ecdicius' assassination. But various facts allow us to infer that it's no earlier in the year than March, and probably later. So . . ." In response to his silent command, the ship rose in the air and swung around into an eastward course. Looking aft, Sarnac glimpsed Cadbury before it receded into the distance.

"Tylar, do you think they'll pull it off?"

"Oh, yes. Gwenhwyvaer is, as you'll have gathered,

formidable. And she's been wise to groom Cerdic for leadership of the future ethnically mixed Britain."

"Yeah, Cerdic's a character. Uh, I suppose that, like everybody else, he also existed in our reality."

"Indeed! He's *the* Cerdic. Cerdic of Wessex." Tylar looked at Sarnac expectantly but saw only blankness. "Hmm. I keep forgetting that your knowledge of history isn't all it might be. Well, in our timeline Cerdic didn't arrive in Britain until 495. Aided by his son Cynric—an adult by that time—he carved out the kingdom of Wessex which would later unify England. All subsequent English royalty have claimed descent from him."

"Huh? You mean James III . . . ?"

"Oh, yes, that's right; they *had* restored the Stuarts by your lifetime, hadn't they? But yes, he's a descendant—although the connection will be extremely tenuous by then."

"Well, well!" Sarnac shook his head. "All from an illegitimate son fathered on a Saxon girl by some Briton. . . ."

"Yes. It was in the course of his first Saxon-fighting expedition to Armorica."

"Uh, what do you mean, Tylar?" Sarnac couldn't make any connection between the bland statement and what they were talking about.

"Artorius," Tylar said patiently. "It was in 457, three years after he became High King."

For a second or two, Sarnac still didn't get it. Then little things he should have noticed before—a certain way of cocking the head, a peculiar outward flare to the eyebrows, the body build—began to come to him. "Wait a minute, Tylar! Are you telling me . . . ?"

"It's not uncommon in this era," Tylar said pedantically, "for victorious troops to share out the women of the vanquished after a battle. An old Roman custom, in fact, which includes the proviso that the commander gets a share. Artorius didn't take advantage of it very often—usually he'd pick some child and set her free. But he's only human, after all, and he was in the process of adjusting to the fact that Gwenhwyvaer couldn't bear him children. And I have reason to think the Saxon woman in question was exceptionally beautiful."

*I wonder,* was all Sarnac could think. *Did she tell her son stories about Artorius the ogre who ate naughty Saxon children with horseradish? Did she even know who the father had been?*

"Tylar," he finally asked, "does Artorius know?"

"No, and I'll be obliged if you don't tell him. It might prejudice his judgment at some crucial time."

"But . . ." Sarnac glanced aft, where the British landscape had yielded to the gray winter sea. "Does *she* know?"

"Gwenhwyvaer? She hasn't been told, if that's what you mean. But . . . oh, yes, I think she knows."

# CHAPTER NINE

The merchant Ventidius had servants because it would have seemed odd for him not to have them. They cleared away the remains of a meal that bore little resemblance to Sarnac's recollections of Greek cuisine (except perhaps for the prevalence of olive oil) and withdrew, leaving their kindly but mysterious master alone with his guests.

Koreel activated the device that would safeguard them against eavesdropping. Then he settled back with a sigh and poured more wine all around—*not* retsina, to Sarnac's relief.

"So," Tylar asked Andreas, "his health seems to be getting steadily worse since he restored Acacius to the Patriarchate? I fear the Western clergy will see that as divine justice!"

"Well," the young transtemporal voyager replied, "the deterioration hasn't really been steady. But the trend is downhill. Nevertheless, nobody thinks his life is in any immediate danger, and there's been no talk of recalling Ecdicius from the Danube."

"Given what passes for medical science here, that's not too reassuring," Sarnac said dourly. "A turn for the worse could kill him in no time."

"That's true," Andreas acknowledged. "I don't think I'll ever get used to watching what these people endure under

147

the name of medical care." But his tone was that of a man admitting a flaw in a milieu to which he seemed to have taken like a duck to water. He'd changed dramatically in the time since they'd been apart—cheerier and generally more alive. Of course, Sarnac reminded himself, it had been a considerably longer subjective time for Andreas than for the rest of them. But he wondered what had happened during that time to banish the moody, withdrawn Andreas he remembered.

"Nevertheless," Tylar put in, "we can't be taken by surprise even if that should happen. We don't know many of the details, but we do know that the Restorer doesn't die until after Ecdicius returns to Constantinople and is assassinated. Speaking of Ecdicius, I trust you've gained the confidence of his family as we'd planned."

"Oh, yes," Andreas nodded. "The Restorer introduced me to them as a nobleman from Bithynia, in Asia Minor. I could get away with it because Ecdicius' wife Faustina is also from Gaul and this is the furthest east she's ever been. In the years since then, I've gotten to know them well on my various 'visits to Constantinople' between spells in stasis. I don't mind telling you it's bothered me, deceiving them. Faustina's a true lady. And Julia—that's the oldest child, eighteen now—is so charming that . . . ! Well, you've met her, haven't you, Koreel? You know the way she . . ."

*Aha!* thought Sarnac.

Tylar dragged Andreas back to earth. "Now, now! Remember, all the dissembling is in a good cause."

"Of course! We can't leave them behind in Constantinople when we get Ecdicius out!"

"Indeed not," Tylar affirmed. "If captured, they could be used as hostages, giving the usurpers potentially disastrous leverage with Ecdicius." Andreas blinked; he clearly hadn't been thinking of that aspect of things. "Which leads to my next question: how are the preparations for our flight progressing?"

"On schedule," Koreel said. "The Restorer has let us

use the Boucoleon Harbor, adjacent to the Sacred Palace. I've bought a ship, allegedly for my 'trading fleet,' and quietly moored it there. The Restorer secretly supplied a crew; they're all Britons, old salts from the Saxon Shore Fleet but with a lot of experience in these waters. Just as importantly, they're personally loyal to him. All they know is that they're to perform a mission of vital importance to him, and that's enough for them. They'll keep their mouths shut and ask no questions. We're holding them on standby; money's no object, of course."

"It seems you've both done well," Tylar approved. "And now comes the most difficult part for all of us: waiting for Ecdicius to return to Constantinople. As soon as he does, we must activate the plan and get him out at once, for we've no idea how long he's in the city before the assassins strike. So some of us at least must be active and on watch at all times. We can use stasis to alleviate the tedium, but only in shifts."

For a moment they all sipped their wine in silence. Then Artorius finished his, set the cup down with a click and excused himself. If Andreas had become more animated, the former High King had become less so. Sarnac wondered if it was related to reawakened feelings where Gwenhwyvaer was concerned and a too-brief reunion. But his moroseness didn't seem precisely of that sort. Then understanding came, and Sarnac bit his tongue at the thought of his earlier "sudden death" remark as he belatedly recalled *whose* death was under discussion.

Presently Koreel and Andreas also said their goodnights. Sarnac, who didn't feel sleepy and got the impression that Tylar didn't either, poured another round of wine for the two of them. The time traveller inclined his head in grave thanks and they regarded each other in the wretched light of the room's oil lamps. *People must wear their eyes out young, trying to read in what this era uses for artificial light,* Sarnac thought. *And spectacles won't be invented for another eight hundred years in my timeline, God knows when in this one. Well, it's not a problem for the majority, I suppose; they're illiterate.*

"Well," he broke the silence after a moment, "we've settled one question." Tylar raised an interrogatory eyebrow. "Andreas," Sarnac amplified. "He's still with us. He didn't vanish with a pop or anything like that the instant we first changed this timeline. And we *have* changed it, you know."

"Our program of directing this history's flow into a desired channel is very far from completed," Tylar cautioned. "Indeed, it's barely commenced."

"Yeah, I know. If we dropped dead tonight, the divergences from recorded history as Andreas knows it would be unpredictable. But there would *be* divergences! Acacius' restoration to the Patriarchy in 486 and the Restorer's subsequent pro-Monophysite moves didn't happen according to Andreas' history books. And we've planted the notion of separation in Gwenhwyvaer and Cerdic."

"There's no way to know whether those changes are sufficient to preclude Andreas' existence, on the assumption that it *can* be precluded. But I'm quibbling. In general terms, you're right. This history has, to some extent at least, been irrevocably changed. It is now up to us to direct the change."

"Tylar," Sarnac said after a pause, "you mentioned earlier that most of your people wouldn't be able to handle this mission, which flies in the face of their whole history-preserving orientation. How are *you* handling it?"

"Better than I expected," the time traveller answered briskly, "considering that my life has, as you say, been devoted to preserving the past. We were firmly convinced that alternate realities were impossible—and I continue to believe that this is the only one in existence. But it *does* exist, and in it the rationale for my life's work doesn't obtain. I can . . . it's almost . . . well, I hardly know how to describe it. There's something deliciously wicked about it."

"Hey," Sarnac said, alarmed, "this isn't going to become habit-forming, is it?"

"Oh, no." Beneath Tylar's reassuring tones, Sarnac detected a faint sigh. "I'm doing this to fulfill an ethical obligation, as you know. But I can't claim I'm sorry to have come." He gave Sarnac a look whose sharpness was visible in the room's dimness. "And what about you, Robert? Are you glad you came?"

The quietly spoken question was so unlike Tylar that it took Sarnac aback. He hadn't often had conversations like this with the time traveller, for his awareness of the gulf between them was a barrier to intimacy. *My supply of conversation openers has always been kind of limited. "What's your world like, Tylar?" doesn't quite make it. Could I go back fifty thousand years, sit down at a campfire and tell the Cro-Magnons about the twenty-third century?* But now Tylar had, uncharacteristically, come forward with a question about his own thoughts and feelings.

"Yes," he finally said. "I think I am. And I'll tell you why. You once said that your people always had to suppress any impulse to take sides, regardless of what they witnessed in history. You explained that this wasn't just because history as recorded was sacrosanct, but also because your projections of probable outcomes suggested that things generally seemed to work out for the best in the long run. So intervening on the side of the good guys was as likely as not to have catastrophic long-term consequences."

"Yes, I recall commenting on the irony involved. Of course," Tylar continued, settling back into his accustomed pedantic mode, "you must bear in mind that it's difficult to generalize on the subject. Historically, the 'good guys' have won so seldom that the total of such instances doesn't make for a very meaningful statistical universe."

"Yeah, so I'd gathered. Well, I accepted what you said. But I didn't have to like it! Now, this time . . ." He leaned forward, and the disconcertingly light-blue eyes in his dark face held Tylar—and all at once the time traveller understood why the human race had endured long enough to give birth to his own people.

"This time," Sarnac repeated, "the good guys are going to win! They're going to win, and there's going to be no ambiguity about the consequences of their victory. We're going to make history do something right, for a change— and we're going to make history *like* it! I personally guarantee it, Tylar!" The cold flame that shone through his eyes died down and he spoke more softly. "Yeah, I'm glad I came."

Winter gave way to spring and the Restorer's health continued to fail. Pope Gaius came to Constantinople to be present at the end—Sarnac glimpsed his arrival from among the street crowd and observed that Sidonius Apollinaris had put on weight. And the death watch, as he thought of it, went on.

*At least the weather's better for it now*, he thought as he swung over the gunwale of their ship and gazed around at the Boucoleon Harbor and the imperial gardens that rose in terraces above it to the Sacred Palace's eastern front. He'd had the good fortune to spend most of March in stasis. Now, the arrival of the Pope—who they knew had been around for the assassination—had set off warning bells, and Tylar had decreed that only one of them could be in stasis at any given time. At the moment the carefully hidden device held Artorius.

He considered the ship with the eye of one who'd done some sailing in his youth. She was a hundred-footer, whose twenty-five-foot beam gave her the stubby lines typical of Roman merchantmen. Many such ships were over twice as large in both dimensions, but *Nereid's Wake* was large enough for their needs, and would attract less attention at what was basically a yacht harbor than would one of the massive grain ships. She lacked the mizzenmast possessed by some larger ships, having only a mainmast with a large square sail and two little triangular topsails, and a rakishly forward-slanted *artemon* foremast that was more for steering than anything else. Despite her tubby dimensions, *Nereid's Wake* had a certain grace of line, with her sternpost rising in a smooth curve to a carved swan-head.

"Quite a beauty, isn't she?" he remarked to Andreas as the latter climbed up from below decks. "In spite of . . ." His gesture took in a paint job and assorted decorations that were, from his standpoint, typical of the place and time: garish and overdone.

"No doubt," Andreas replied in carefully neutral tones. The colonists of Chiron had had neither time nor wealth to spend on recreational revivals of obsolete technology, and he'd never set foot on a sailing vessel in his life. At least, Sarnac thought, he'd never experienced seasickness and was therefore blissfully ignorant of what he was in for.

Tylar had explained why they had to use this kind of transportation. Meeting the younger image of Artorius was the sort of marvel Ecdicius and Sidonius could be made to accept; but as for stepping through a glowing door from Constantinople into Italy . . . no. The miracles to which they would be exposed must be held to a minimum, to avoid contamination of this world's intellectual development. The scientific mind-set is born of the dawning realization that the universe is orderly and predictable, subject to laws which can be understood; it might well be aborted if these people had their noses rubbed in things too far beyond their horizons (*Or mine*, Sarnac thought ruefully) to be fitted into a rational world-picture. The last thing Tylar wanted was to revive the notion that the world is a terrifying chaos of incomprehensible forces wielded by capricious deities.

Still, Andreas looked as though he had some vague idea of how little he was going to like this voyage.

"Aw, come on!" Sarnac jollied him, leaning against the gunwale and grasping a shroud just above the deadeyes— a Roman invention, he recalled Tylar saying. "It's a beautiful afternoon, everything's in readiness, and we can relax for a while."

Naturally, it was at that moment that the emergency chime of his implant communicator tolled inside his skull.

He and Andreas exchanged a sharp look—the other had clearly been signalled also—and he glanced around the deck. The only crew member aboard was old Corineus, the skipper. He wasn't paying any particular attention, so he must not have noticed their startlement. But there was, Sarnac decided, no need to arouse the Briton's curiosity by appearing to talk to himself. He activated the communicator and subvocalized.

"What is it, Tylar?"

"It's happened." The time traveler's voice held an uncharacteristic repressed excitement. "Ecdicius has arrived in the city. He should be arriving at the sacred palace shortly."

*So all the pieces are in place,* Sarnac thought. *Let the games begin.*

"We have no idea how much or how little time we have before the assassins make their move," Tylar went on. "So we'd best set the plan in motion at once. I'll deactivate the stasis field. Are any of the crewmen immediately available?"

"Yeah. Corineus is aboard."

"Excellent. Send him to gather the rest of the crew. Artorius and I will be aboard shortly."

"Right." Sarnac broke the connection and spoke aloud in British. "Corineus, Tertullian sent me to tell you that we'll be departing sooner than we expected. Go ashore and round up the rest of the lads."

"Aye, Bedwyr." Like most contemporary people over thirty or so, Corineus looked older than he was. He also looked tough as well-aged oak, and the Mediterranean sun had burned his skin a like color. Given the right clothes and the right language, he would have fit in aboard a pirate ship of the seventeenth-century Spanish Main like part of the rigging. "Will we be departing this night? If so, I'll have to find some rowers to warp us out of this harbor."

"I can't say for certain, but probably so. Ask Tertullian. He should be here by the time you get back, and Gerontius." They had used Artorius' cover name with the crew, adding the detail that he was a relative of the Restorer. The imperial face was too well known for them not to notice a close family resemblance. But these weren't exactly men who moved in the Emperor's social circles; they wouldn't realize that it was *too* close.

"Aye," Corineus repeated, and clambered over the gunwale onto the pier. As soon as he was gone, Sarnac and Andreas went below decks to the cabin that the crew had been told, in no uncertain terms, was off-limits. They had barely entered when the portal glowed into existence. Tylar and Artorius emerged.

"That's cutting it pretty close," Sarnac observed. "Corineus only just left."

"No doubt." Tylar didn't sound too concerned. "But we have no time to lose. I want you and Andreas to proceed to the heir's apartments and bring his family back to this ship. Artorius and I will enter the palace and make contact with Ecdicius when the time seems ripe."

"Faustina and the children may not be willing to come with me," Andreas protested, "if I just show up unannounced and—"

"You must persuade them!" Tylar's voice was charged with urgency. "We have no time to lose. And when the conspirators move against Ecdicius, you can be sure they'll attend to his children as well. As I've already explained, we can't let them become hostages for Ecdicius' good behavior."

*Of course*, Sarnac did not say, *if they were dead rather than captured they wouldn't provide the usurpers with any leverage. In fact, their deaths would just get Ecdicius seriously mad—which might well be to our advantage. I'm proud of you, Tylar, for not mentioning that. I'd be even prouder if I thought it had never crossed your mind.*

*I think there was a time when it wouldn't have crossed mine.* He was still thinking about it as they made their way through the gardens and entered the palace complex. "Andronicus" was evidently known to the few people they encountered, and no one questioned their presence. Twilight was gathering when they reached the courtyard-surrounding outbuilding that housed the heir's family.

An elderly male servant opened the door. Andreas cut off his greeting. "I must speak to your mistress, Chares. It's urgent."

"But, but," the old fellow sputtered, "the Lady Faustina is awaiting the return of the Noblissimus Ecdicius. We've received word that he has already entered the city . . ."

"What is it, Chares?" The voice was followed by Faustina herself, coming around a corner into the entrance hall followed by her three children. Andreas pushed past the outraged Chares with Sarnac in his wake. "Why, Andronicus! We didn't know you were in Constantinople! And this other gentleman . . . ?"

Faustina was younger than her husband—not uncommon, when a woman's life expectancy was considerably less than a man's provided that the latter avoided violent death. But she was in her late thirties, and had begun to put on weight as the women of this place and time tended to after a decade or two of repeated childbearing. Faustina had had another three children and buried them in early infancy, as was normal—so normal that for most of history people hadn't dared to let themselves become too attached to children. *Tylar once mentioned that in the late twentieth century, when it was first becoming possible to live like a human being, intellectuals used to bleat about the "dehumanizing" effect of advanced technology,* Sarnac recalled. *God, what silly jerk-offs they were in those days!*

Still, Faustina remained a handsome woman, reflected in the slender eighteen-year-old replica who peeked over her shoulder and smiled at Andreas. The latter surprised Sarnac by not becoming tongue-tied.

"Lady Faustina, this is Bedwyr, a cavalry officer of your husband's staff." *Gee, not a hired bodyguard for once,* Sarnac thought. *Can it be that I'm picking up a little class?* "He's not in uniform because the Noblissimus Ecdicius and his escort have had to enter the city unnoticed," Andreas improvised freely. "We have reason to believe his life is in danger, now that the Divine Augustus is—I must speak bluntly—dying. The vultures are gathering, as must be expected. You know what this city is like."

"Oh, yes—*how* I know!" sighed the woman from the provinces.

"Is . . . is father all right?" Julia asked in a trembling voice. Eight-year-old Helena began to whimper, and ten-year-old Avitus strove to look like the man of the house.

"He is," Andreas assured them. "But he's sent Bedwyr to take all of you to a ship in the harbor, where he'll be meeting you soon. It's necessary for all of you to return to Italy."

"Leave Constantinople? With the Augustus on his deathbed?" Faustina shook her head in confusion. "Andronicus, what's your part in all this? I never knew you'd even *met* Ecdicius!"

Andreas was opening his mouth, and Sarnac was wondering what would come out of it, when a choked scream brought all their heads around to stare at old Chares, still standing in the doorway. He toppled forward, a dagger-hilt protruding from between his shoulder blades. The first of the bravos followed him through the door.

Sarnac and Andreas fumbled for their stunners, but the attackers swamped them. Andreas was clouted on the head and fell to his hands and knees. Sarnac managed to get the harmless-looking little rod out, only to have it knocked from his hand and sent spinning across the floor by a bravo who shoved him against a wall and levelled a short sword at his midriff. He forced calmness on himself and looked around the entrance hall, crowded with intruders. One stood over the slowly recovering Andreas, idly swinging a cudgel. Three others had Faustina and her children backed into a corner. One of this group seemed to be the leader.

"What do we do with these two?" the man pointing the sword at Sarnac asked. The common Greek was one of the languages "Bedwyr" had picked up a smattering of in his mercenary days in the East.

"They may be wanted for questioning or something," the leader replied. "We'd better take them along with these." He indicated the three children and the woman trying to shield them.

"Nobody said anything about any big hurry to bring them back, did they?" another bravo asked with a leer in the direction of Helena. The child stood sucking her fingers in numb shock, as unable as her mother and siblings to understand a word of the gutter argot.

"Ah, you rotten bastard," the leader joshed indulgently. "Your crazy yen for young stuff has always gotten you in trouble! Now *there's* what a *real* man wants!" He swept the shrieking Faustina aside with one arm and lunged at Julia. "Come here, bitch!"

Julia screamed and twisted away from the groping hand. Avitus flung himself at the bravo, who smashed him aside with a backhand slap to the laughs and cheers of his comrades. Then he advanced, grinning, toward Julia, whose back was to a wall. Suddenly the girl's groping hand closed over a vase on a side-table. With a convulsive motion, she flung it at her tormentor's head. It missed him, but hit the man guarding Sarnac.

As the momentarily stunned bravo staggered, Sarnac kicked out at the short sword, sending it flying. Then he flung himself sideways and rolled along the floor toward his stun rod. He had just enough time after grabbing it to thrust it practically into the face of his nearest pursuer. Then he swept its beam across two others. As they collapsed in a heap, he had a split second to see that Andreas had revived and was grappling with the cudgel-wielding bravo, before the one remaining opponent got in under his stunner.

Sarnac let trained reflexes think for him. He dropped the useless stunner, blocked a blow with his left forearm and formed his right hand into a blade which he thrust into the man's solar plexus. As the bravo collapsed with a thin, whistling shriek, Sarnac clasped his hands behind his head and forced it down while bringing a knee up, hard. It was the man who'd indicated an interest in Helena. Sarnac brought his knee up twice more for good measure, feeling facial bones splinter. As he let the body fall to the floor, he saw Andreas release his grip from his motionless opponent's throat and stand up.

Helena's eyes were marbled with shock—hysteria might come later, but Sarnac was quite prepared to use the stunner. Julia stood against the wall, heaving as she sought to bring her breathing under control. Andreas ran to her, and in his arms she gave way to gasping sobs. Faustina looked up from Avitus, who was regaining consciousness, and gave Sarnac a calmer look than he would have believed possible.

"What *is* that?" she asked steadily, pointing at the stun rod.

"That's unimportant, Lady. At least, you don't need to know it just now. What you *do* need to do at once is get yourself and your children to our ship. Surely you can see now that there's no time to waste."

"Yes," she said matter-of-factly. "Come, children." She gathered them up and herded them out the door, shushing complaints of favorite toys left behind. Before the two of them left, Sarnac noted that Andreas gave each merely unconscious bravo a hard kick to the temple. He felt not even an abstract objection, though he would have rather left them to face their employers' displeasure at their failure. *Don't tell Andreas he's done them a favor,* he cautioned himself. *Why ruin his day?*

As they proceeded through the darkling palace grounds,

Sarnac reported to Tylar via implant communicator. "Oh, dear!" the time traveller exclaimed. "Was it *really* necessary to use the stunners? I fear that will take some explaining!"

"Tylar!" Sarnac saw Faustina's quizzical look and realized he'd spoken aloud. "We weren't exactly in a position to worry about 'intellectual contamination,' you know," he subvocalized. "It might have helped if you'd monitored us with your life-form sensor and let us know that those thugs were approaching!"

"Quite right, my dear fellow. I am in the process of remedying that omission even now." Sarnac could visualize the process, although he didn't pretend to understand it. The device Tylar was readying displayed on a small screen the returns generated as a byproduct by neural activity above a certain level. And it could tag the returns of individuals for whom it had a genetic scan—a simple, non-invasive matter for the time traveller's technology.

"Ah," came Tylar's voice after a moment. "Yes, I can identify you and Andreas, and the four with you. And . . . wait a moment." There was silence inside Sarnac's skull, then the voice resumed, this time in tones of repressed alarm. "I've also picked up the returns of Ecdicius and Sidonius, walking toward the Daphne Palace—they must have set out practically the instant Ecdicius arrived." Sarnac wondered how Tylar had obtained the genetic readings of heir and Pope, but he knew he'd get only evasion if he asked. "And seven unidentified individuals taking up positions alongside the pathway they're using! Robert, this is terrible—we weren't expecting matters to reach a crisis so quickly!"

*Jesus Christ, what else can go wrong?* Sarnac chopped the thought off and subvocalized hurriedly. "Tylar, get a grip on yourself! Are we in a position to get to them before they reach the assassins, from where we are now?"

"No," Tylar replied. "But if you hurry you should be able to reach the location of the ambush shortly after they do."

"Give me the bearing."

"I'll do better. Turn about seventy degrees south of your present route." Sarnac stopped and did so, ignoring his companions' stares. A red dot seemed to appear in mid-air in front of his eyes. "I'm downloading data to your contact-lens display," Tylar explained. "As long as you're proceeding in the right direction, you'll see the dot. Send Ecdicius' family on ahead. I'll come as quickly as possible—I may be able to persuade Sidonius of the need for immediate flight."

"Faustina," Sarnac said aloud, "can you make it the rest of the way to the harbor?" He pointed ahead. The woman lacked his light-gathering contact lenses, but she could see the harbor lights through the trees. She nodded. "Good. Get the children down there—someone will meet you on the dock." He hoped they'd be too disoriented to recognize Artorius—this was *not* the time for lengthy explanations! "Andronicus and I have business, but we'll be along soon."

Faustina nodded again and shepherded the children along after a last eye-contact between Julia and Andreas. Sarnac slapped the latter on the shoulder, none too gently. "Come on! I'll explain as we go."

They ran through the gloom of the gardens, well-illuminated for them, and the ghostly dot seemed to constantly recede before Sarnac's eyes. Presently they heard shouts and clashing steel, and soon they saw Ecdicius hauling Sidonius away from the bravo he'd sapped with a rock and backing the two of them up against a tall thick hedge. Three bravos were on the ground, but four others closed in on the pair, clearly unconcerned by Sidonius' call for help.

Sarnac pulled out his stun rod. "Well, shall we?" Andreas nodded and they stepped forward.

# CHAPTER TEN

Homer had sung of the "wine-dark sea," and Sarnac could see exactly what he'd meant as he looked into the swirling, foaming Aegean depths far below.

He stood on the footropes that the ever-practical Romans had first strung behind yards, and wrapped one arm around the swaying mast. The mainsail was taken up as per Corineus' orders and he could take a moment to gaze around from his high vantage, shielding his eyes from the Mediterranean sun with his free hand and letting the warm wind blow through his hair. The brilliance and clarity of the day, and the blueness of the sky, were just short of hurtful. Off the starboard bow he could glimpse Cape Sounion, its cliff topped by the white temple that was now in the first stages of the decay that would eventually leave only a few stark columns, lovingly preserved in his day because the worship of beauty had outlived that of Poseidon.

"Can we get down now?" Andreas pleaded. He stood on the other side of the mast, grasping the yard for dear life and resolutely not looking down at the ship—and the world—that seemed to swing back and forth like a pendulum. They had departed Constantinople in haste minus a couple of crew members, and when Sarnac had volunteered to help take up the slack the younger man had

163

swallowed hard and stepped forward beside him. By now
he'd learned enough to be useful, and his experience with
other forms of motion sickness had helped ease him past
his initial *mal de mer*. But he'd never like it.

"Sure," Sarnac said reluctantly, grasping a shroud and
sliding down to the deck. Andreas followed more slowly,
just as a wave buffeted the ship. He succeeded in hanging
on; the fact that Julia was watching from below might have
had something to do with it.

Sarnac surveyed the deck, looking aft where the steersmen
stood in the projections at the quarters. They had already
made the course change needed to round Cape Sounion
in response to Corineus' commands; now they kept the
handles of their rudders steady (not even the Chinese had
the stern-post rudder yet) while the skipper held Avitus
and Helena spellbound with imaginative lies about his
youthful sea-fights with Saxons, Frisians and the occasional
monster. *Yup*, Sarnac thought, *all he needs is a parrot and
a wooden leg*. Between the steering stations was the long
deckhouse that held most of the living quarters. Sarnac
entered it and descended the ladder to the sanctum.

Tylar, Artorius, Ecdicius and Sidonius sat around the
little table in the lamplight. Ecdicius fidgeted in the cramped
space. On learning of the attack on his family he'd been
all for going back ashore and spilling blood in large
quantities, even before his own wound was tended to. But
Faustina had been able to calm him down, and their
departure hadn't been too delayed. Afterwards, when
Artorius had given him and Sidonius the same story they'd
used on the Restorer, he had accepted it more readily than
Sarnac had dared hope. Clearly, Ecdicius was one of those
fortunate souls with the ability to file apparent miracles
away under the heading "Inexplicable—not to be worried
about" and get on with practicalities.

Sidonius, though, was still deeply troubled.

"But is it not heresy?" he was asking as Sarnac entered
and closed the hatch. "Surely there can be no warrant in

the scriptures for supposing *two* Saviors! So is one of these worlds of which you speak not irrevocably damned?"

"No, Sidonius," Artorius spoke patiently. He'd grown up in this century, and knew the depths of what Sidonius was undergoing while Sarnac could only glimpse the surface. "Remember, the forking of the roads I've spoken of happened twenty-one years ago—four hundred and seventy years *after* the birth of our Savior, and almost four hundred and forty after His resurrection. So all men, whichever history they are playing out, are redeemed."

Sidonius wrung his hands in anguish. "But now, after these 'roads' of which you speak have indeed parted, are there two trinities? How could the divine essence be so subdivided?" Sarnac tried to imagine what a nightmare this must be for Sidonius, in an age when so much ink and blood had been spilled over the precise nature of *one* trinity. He himself couldn't feel these concerns, but he knew distress of soul when he saw it.

"Not at all, Sidonius," Artorius assured him. "The Father, being infinite, is well able to comprehend two—or, for that matter, infinitely numerous—realities." The former High King had had to become something of an amateur theologian to deal with this problem, which they'd known was coming. Luckily, doctrine had never been Sidonius' strong point. He'd started his ecclesiastical career at age thirty-eight as a political bishop. A trained theologian would have been a lot harder to deal with.

Ecdicius squirmed. "This is all very well, but the question now is what we are to *do*! You say these damned conspirators were part of a Monophysite plot?"

"Well, Noblissimus," said Tylar, "it stands to reason, doesn't it? In view of your well-known fidelity to the true Catholic faith, the Monophysites could hardly have welcomed the prospect of your accession, could they?" Sarnac shot the time traveller a sharp glance, but Tylar continued without a break. "Their obvious objective would be to bestow the purple on an openly Monophysite emperor, one who would call a new Council which would undo Chalcedon and make the Monophysite position canonical, anathematizing all others. One might also suppose that they would wish to elevate the Patriarchy of Constantinople to supreme primacy, reducing Rome to the kind of subordinate position now occupied by Antioch and Alexandria."

Ecdicius and Sidonius had been showing signs of gradually rising blood pressure throughout, but the last sentence brought the latter surging to his feet, doctrinal concerns forgotten. "*What!* But everyone knows that our Lord explicitly gave into the hands of Saint Peter . . ."

Ecdicius wasn't far behind him. He stood up with a roar, trying to draw his *spatha* and banging his funny bone against a bulkhead of the little cabin, which did his mood no good at all. "By the mercy of Christ, when I return to Constantinople to claim my inheritance my horse will walk fetlock-deep in the blood of these damned traitors and heretics!"

"Noblissimus," Tylar smiled, "are you absolutely certain you *want* to return to Constantinople?"

"What are you saying, Tertullian? I'm the rightful heir to Artorius the Restorer!"

"And," Sidonius added, "he is our only hope for crushing this foul conspiracy and the Monophysites behind it! Otherwise, the usurpers will impose their devil-begotten heresy on the West, and we will all face damnation."

"Yes! When I'm back in Constantinople with the support of the West, like . . ."

"Like the Restorer was." Tylar's quiet interjection stopped Ecdicius short, and he and Sidonius were suddenly quiet. Tylar smiled. "Noblissimus, I don't question the legal rightfulness of your claim to the purple. But we must consider reality. And reality is that the East, with its multitudes and its wealth, will always dominate a unified empire. This is so even if the Augustus comes from the West and bases his power on Western arms."

"My people," Sarnac put in, "have a saying about the tail wagging the dog."

" 'The tail wagging the . . .' Ha! Good one, Bedwyr! I'll have to remember that!" Ecdicius' mercurial mood-changes no longer caught Sarnac flat-footed. "All right, Tertullian, what are you advising me to do?"

"If the West is to stand as the stronghold of the true faith, Noblissimus, it must stand alone. Once in Italy, declare the resumption of Constantine's division of the empire. Your troops will eagerly proclaim you Augustus of the West, for yourself as well as for the love they bear the Restorer, whose choice of a successor is well known to them. And you, Your Holiness, can lend your support by anathematizing the Eastern Church and excommunicating anyone who adheres to the *Henotikon*."

"Yes," Sidonious nodded. "And specifically excommunicating the Patriarch Acacius and whoever the conspirators set up as Augustus." He turned to his brother-in-law. "Ecdicius, I believe Tertullian is right. We can't save the East from error, but we can . . ." He sought for a word, but of course his world held no such concept as *quarantine*. "I've watched what the East has done to my old friend. The reunified empire of which he—all of us—dreamed can never be anything more than a Greater Eastern Empire, with the West as a set of provinces. I see that clearly now. I think I've seen it for years. But no old fool ever wants to admit that his youthful ideals have been discredited, or were mistaken in the first place, for that admission is the final relinquishment of youth." He sighed deeply, in a silence which no one cared to break, then gathered himself and actually smiled. "Ecdicius, I'm still enough of an old fool to believe that we can preserve what is of value in Rome's heritage. But we can only do it in a separate Western Empire." He smiled again, with infinite sadness. "I hope Virgil will understand," he whispered.

After a space, Ecdicius cleared his throat. "All well and good, but there's one practical point we have to dispose of first." He looked Artorius unflinchingly in the eye. "The Restorer adopted me as his heir in the belief that he had no heir of his body, indeed no close blood-relatives who might be able to set up rival claims. Now, as I understand it, you and he are closer in blood relation than any men have ever dreamed of being." Sarnac thought he could see a sheen of sweat in the lamplight, of a kind that had nothing to do with the cabin's stuffiness. But Ecdicius pressed on, as fearless in the face of the unknowable as he had ever been in battle. "Indeed, unless I misunderstand, you *are* . . ."

Artorius raised his hand. "Set your mind at rest, Ecdicius. It's true that for my first forty-two years I was one and the same as he who adopted you as his heir. But now I belong to another world—or, perhaps, another story of the same world—and as soon as may be I mean to return to it. I have no intention of seeking to rule this one. I could give you a written statement of support for your claim to the Principate of the West if you like, but it would be a meaningless formality. Let me instead tell you this: I know of what you've done, and what he who you became in my world has done in that world." Ecdicius crossed himself, in a way that Sarnac recognized as something more than mere conventional piety, for which Ecdicius had never been particularly noted anyway. "And I tell you now that had my life followed the same course as that of the Artorius you know, I'd have chosen the same heir he did."

Tylar let the two men regard each other for a moment before filling the silence. "So, Noblissimus, you see that there will be no difficulties in this regard. Furthermore, you will have an ally: Gwenhwyvaer, wife of Artorius the Restorer and his regent in Britain. I'm empowered to tell you that she will support your claim—on one condition."

"Condition . . . ?"

"Only one. You must agree to accept Britain's independence from the Western Empire." Sarnac gave Tylar another sharp glance, but held his tongue. "In exchange, she will recognize you as legitimate Augustus of the West."

Ecdicius frowned. "Independence? Tertullian, I can't set a precedent like that! Britain has been a Roman province since the time of Claudius . . ."

"Once again, Noblissimus, let us leave the legalisms to the lawyers." Ecdicius' eyes flashed dangerously, but Tylar hurried on. "Practically speaking, Britain has been independent since 410, when the Emperor Honorius gave permission for the provincials there to see to their own defense. Everyone recognized that as a *de facto* abandonment of the island, for an armed Britain would inevitably be a self-ruling Britain. And remember how the Restorer came to Gaul in 469 as High King of the Britons, ally of the Western Emperor Anthemius, who dealt with him as the separate sovereign he was. So you can acknowledge this accomplished fact with no loss of dignity."

"But, Tertullian, the precedent! What if other provinces start getting ideas?"

"Given the uniqueness of Britain's history over the last eighty years," Tylar said smoothly, "no valid precedent will be created. So the matter need not concern you, Noblissimus; rather, you should concern yourself with the implications of having a hostile Britain to your west at the same time you're facing an attempt at reconquest from the east."

"Hmmm. . . ." Ecdicius stroked his not-inconsiderable nose thoughtfully. He didn't look happy, but he gave a slow nod. "Very well—so be it. I'll pay Gwenhwyvaer's price." He stood up and stretched, catlike. "Plenty of time to work out the details later. I need a turn on deck." He paused at the hatch and looked back at Sarnac. "The tail wagging the dog!" He shook his head and chuckled as he left the stifling cabin, followed by the others. But Sarnac touched Tylar's sleeve, and the two of them remained.

"I seem to recall you saying," Sarnac began without preamble, "that the plotters who tried to assassinate Ecdicius were an aristocratic clique motivated solely by power politics. You never mentioned anything about them being a bunch of Monophysite fanatics."

"Quite." Tylar pursed his lips. "Strictly speaking, I never actually told Ecdicius that the assassins were Monophysite conspirators, did I? I merely pointed out that their course of action would be a logical one for Monophysite conspirators to take. If he chose to jump to conclusions . . ."

"Also," Sarnac interrupted, "I remember you telling Gwenhwyvaer that Ecdicius would accept British independence on condition of her recognizing him as Augustus of the West—which is exactly the reverse of what you just told him."

"Ah, well, I'm afraid you have me there. But look at it this way, my dear fellow: each of them will get what he or she wants from the other. And these, um, *hypothetical* conditions will cancel each other out, as it were. So in the end . . ."

"In short," Sarnac cut in again, "you've been lying your ass off, as usual!"

"It could be argued that I haven't been entirely candid with them. But it's all for the best, you know. In fact, it's necessary if all we've done isn't to go for nought. Ecdicius must be provoked into a separation from the East, not into an attempt to assert his right to the throne of a unified empire which he'd probably succeed in keeping unified, as the usurpers did in Andreas' history. And Britain's independence must be assured."

"You've never explained that. Why is an independent Britain so crucial to your plans?"

"Isn't it obvious? Our whole object here is to bring about the kind of political pluralism that arose in our world and prevented any one entrenched power structure from stifling scientific innovation to preserve the status quo. The division of the Roman Empire into East and West is a start—but it isn't enough; the two empires might reach some kind of *rapprochement* in the coming centuries. In our history, Europe was carved into nation-states by the invading barbarian tribes. Our friend the Restorer put a stop to that here. So the same result must be obtained through provincial separatism. With the example of an independent Britain . . ."

"But you just told Ecdicius that Britain is a special case and won't constitute a precedent!"

"That's quite true—in the legal sense." (Sarnac snorted.) "But in men's minds, the empire will have irrevocably given up its claim to universality. Britain will stand as irrefutable proof that political existence apart from Rome is possible, that chaos is not the only alternative to imperial centralization."

"I still think it's a rotten trick to play on Ecdicius."

"Oh, the long-term effects won't manifest themselves in his lifetime. Probably not even in his son's. But his more remote successors will, I think, be living in interesting times, to quote the old Chinese curse."

"I suppose," Sarnac said slowly, "that bringing 'interesting times' to this world is what we're here for."

"Well put. And now we need to confront another problem: Artorius' emotional state."

"Oh, yeah. I could tell he's been down in the dumps because his counterpart is dying."

"Is dead," Tylar corrected bluntly. "Koreel informed me last night. We can't let Ecdicius and Sidonius know, of course. But Artorius knows."

They had passed between the Peloponnese and Crete and set a westward course into the Ionian Sea when Sarnac found Artorius standing alone in the bows, one arm draped around the *artemon* mast, staring fixedly ahead into the setting sun.

He'd been present when Tylar had tried to help the erstwhile High King past the news from Constantinople. But this was the first time he'd found himself alone with the man who, alone of all the human race in all the ages, knew the feelings he now felt. *Well*, Sarnac reflected, *he always had something unique about him.*

He searched desperately for something brilliant to say, but Artorius came to his rescue by noticing him and smiling. "Ah, Bedwyr," came the musical British, "it's a rare fine sunset, is it not?"

"It's all of that," Sarnac replied in the same tongue. For a while he gazed at the sun toward which *Nereid's Wake* seemed to be steering. When its lower edge touched the watery horizon, he gathered himself. "Look, Artorius, I realize I can't possibly know what you're experiencing . . ."

"No, you can't." Artorius gave his head a shake of self-reproach. "Sorry, old man. I know how that must have sounded. And I can't claim I didn't have time to prepare myself; I've known from the first that this was going to happen while we were here. But . . ." He shook his head again. "I've lost friends in plenty, and relatives, and parents. We never used to let ourselves be bothered too much by death; it came so easily, and so early for most people. A human life can only hold so much tragedy. Besides, we believed the dead were only passing on to a better world. We really did believe it, you know. Even *I* believed it, and I was never especially devout. Since then, of course . . . the things I've seen, the things I've learned . . ." His voice trailed off, then firmed up again. "And besides, another person, however well-loved, is still someone *different*. He doesn't remember what my mother's loom looked like when the afternoon sunlight came through the window, aswarm with dust-motes, as I played at her feet. He doesn't know how a remark someone made when I was twelve felt. He doesn't know the innermost thoughts and feeling that can never be shared with anyone, for they define the true self that none of us ever really reveals. Well, that man—" he gestured vaguely toward the northeast, toward Constantinople where Artorius the Restorer lay in state "—held all of that in his head. And when he died, it all *vanished*." He smiled wryly. "Or whatever it does. I don't know, anymore. Not even Tylar's people know."

"That universe of memory he held within him hasn't really been snuffed out," Sarnac said cautiously. "Not as long as *you* hold it. And he wasn't really you—not anymore. He had a different destiny. In our world, you passed into legend. In this one, he'll be locked into mere history, like an insect in amber."

The sun had sunk into the Ionian Sea, and Artorius' expression was hard to read. "Yes; very astute of me to fail before emerging from obscurity, leaving posterity to fill the vacuum with fables I wouldn't have dared invent myself! I constantly amaze myself with my own cleverness!" Sarnac started to say something reassuring, but thought better of it. He'd never seen Artorius in this mood. Then he was relieved to see a smile flash in the light of the ship's lanterns. "Ah, well, you've the right of it: the poor sod that I became in this world *is* stranded in documented history, of all the dreary things! So the least we can do is make that history *better!*" Artorius stood up straight and clapped Sarnac on the shoulder. "Instead of mourning my own death, I should be seeing to my future reputation!"

They entered the Tiber and landed at Ostia, the seaport of Rome, amid dumbfounded jubilation.

The news of the Restorer's death had reached Italy overland, along with rumors of the death of the Pope and the Heir. A pall of depression had hung over this land and radiated outward through the Western provinces at the speed of couriers' horses. When they established their identity, it was like a summer thunderstorm over Ostia that dissipated a stifling, stagnant closeness.

"You say there's a new emperor in Constantinople?" Sidonius had to shout at his secretary Gelasius to make himself heard over the ecstatic roar of the crowd that hemmed them in, straining for a glimpse, as they left the harbor.

"Yes, as we only just learned," Gelasius shouted back. He was a native of North Africa, dark to the point of duskiness, with tightly curled iron-gray hair. It was sheer good fortune that he was in Ostia on business, though the local clergy could have provided positive identification of Sidonius. "Since the Augustus died, the conspirators who tried to murder you have seized the initiative and now dominate the Sacred Consistory. At first they squabbled among themselves, trying to agree on a successor. But now they've agreed to bestow the purple on Wilhelmus, governor of Illyricum."

"Wilhelmus!" Ecdicius exploded. "But he's a *joke*! A nobody! The army will never accept him—everyone knows he's a coward who used influence to avoid military service in his youth."

"And," Sidonius put in, "everyone also knows that his word means nothing—even if anyone could divine what his word *is*, under all the qualifiers that obscure everything he says!"

"Perhaps," Tylar put in diffidently, "that's precisely why the conspirators settled on him as a compromise choice. Since no one is ever quite clear as to what he's saying, everyone distrusts him equally. And, being weak, he should be controllable."

"Maybe that's what they think," Ecdicius replied. "But they're wrong if they think *they* can control him. They'll find they've just turned the empire over to his rabid bitch of a wife!"

Koreel had notified Tylar two nights before that the power struggle in Constantinople was over. But of course they couldn't reveal that knowledge. Instead, Sarnac subvocalized to Tylar via implant communicator. "Gelasius seems pretty well informed, given the comm technology—or lack of it—he has available."

"Quite. A most impressive man. It's easy to see why he became Pope in our history."

"He *what?!*"

"Oh, yes. He was secretary to Felix III, who was Pope from 483 to 492, and was elected to the pontificate after Felix died. In this world, he serves the same secretarial function for Sidonius, and it's entirely possible that he may become Pope when Sidonius is gone. I certainly wouldn't disapprove. He's death on heretics—he originally fled from Africa to escape the rule of the Arian Vandals, you see. And he's an intellectual champion of papal supremacy within the church, including the Eastern church. In short, he's precisely the sort of man we want in the position in the immediate future."

They and the prudently hooded Artorius stayed in the background as they made their way through the cheering crowd, with the local troops—whose commander had recognized Ecdicius—running interference. Ahead of them, Gelasius talked animatedly. "No one in Rome knew what to do when the demand for homage to Wilhelmus arrived. Everyone thought you were dead, though there was no proof. But now that you've been returned to us through God's mercy, the armies of Italy will rise as one man and acclaim the Restorer's adopted heir as Augustus. Especially when they hear what a viper's nest of Monophysite heretics were behind the attempt on his life—and that of the Holy Father! You must proceed to Rome without delay."

"Yes," Ecdicius nodded. "And we must send word to Gaul."

"Of course, Noblissimus . . . er, *Augustus*," Gelasius agreed. From some men it would have been blatant brown-nosing, but from Gelasius it wasn't. "Being your native land, Gaul will be the center of your support."

"And we have to get it consolidated as quickly as possible. It's only a matter of time before it has to face the Army of Germania."

Sarnac knew what he meant. The newly organized province of Germania, between the Rhine and the Elbe, was now Rome's first line of defense against Europe's unconquered barbarians, and accordingly it held an army that was in a different class from the garrison troops of Gaul and the other Western provinces. He quickened his step and touched Ecdicius' arm.

"Any chance of getting the support of that army's commander?"

"I wish to God there were. He's a good man, and a friend." Ecdicius shook his head regretfully. "But those snakes in Constantinople know how crucial he is, and I'm sure they've already sent word to him. We can't possibly get to him first. And they'll play on his loyalty to the Restorer. They'll lie and say they're carrying on the work of the man he worshipped. Yes, that will be the way to win Kai over . . ."

He talked on, but Sarnac heard nothing more. Nor did he see the thronged streets of Ostia, for he was suddenly beside a forest lake in the Burgundian uplands watching the sword he'd thrown flash in the afternoon sun as it tumbled end over end through the air into legend. And beside him was bluff, honest, decent Kai, who'd subsequently carried the tale home to Britain.

After a while he became aware of Artorius' grave regard. "I don't suppose you knew, did you? I never thought to mention it. But I remember that he was your friend."

Sarnac nodded mutely. *Well, what did you expect?* he asked himself. *What made you think he didn't exist in this world as well, like everybody else?* He shook free of the thought. "So he's made general here?"

"Indeed," Tylar affirmed. "He's become an important man in this timeline. And I fear you and he are going to find yourselves on opposite sides of the war that's coming."

The chamberlain Nicoles entered the imperial dressing-room, bowing profoundly as was proper when entering the Sacred Presence. Wilhelmus Augustus acknowledged him absently, most of his attention on the shapely servant-girl who was bringing more of the regalia that would be draped over the somewhat overweight imperial form. The pudgy face formed the vacant smile that seemed to ooze insincerity like a kind of pus.

"Ah, Nicoles. What do you think of the adjustments they've made to the coronation regalia for me? It's very important that everything be just so, don't you agree? Especially in light of . . ." He gestured vaguely, leaving the circumstances of his accession unstated.

Wilhelmus' ancestors had been among those Teutonic soldiers who had come to dominate the empire late in the last century—the Romanized German name was typical of his family. A classic case, the chamberlain decided, of passage from barbarism to decadence with no intervening phase of civilization. Aloud, Nicoles spoke in the voice that had been carefully trained to be pleasing. "Rest assured, Lord" —Wilhelmus preferred this form of address to "Augustus"— "that your coronation will be . . ." Nicoles hesitated, then reminded himself that no flattery was too blatant for this creature. "Your coronation will be Rome's next moment of greatness."

Wilhelmus considered this and nodded. "Yes, I rather like that. Although, of course, I would not in any way denigrate my illustrious predecessor. But on the other hand . . ."

*Good God, he even does it in private! It must be sheer habit by now*, Nicoles thought, and composed himself to listen until the Lord of the World had finished qualifying all trace of meaning out of what he'd said. He was saved by the arrival of the empire's ruler.

"Augusta," he murmured, bowing particularly low.

Hilaria acknowledged with a nod as she swept into the room, and Nicoles raised his head. She wore her usual fixed smile. Most people never saw her closely enough to be startled by the way that expression extended no higher than the mouth. Nicoles, who was taken aback by very little, was still stunned by the distilled bitterness in those eyes.

"Ah, my dear," Wilhelmus said, hastily waving the

servant girl away. "I'd sent for the chamberlain to receive his report concerning the courier who's just returned from General . . . ah, General . . ."

"Kai, Lord," Nicoles prompted. "A difficult name to remember, of course. He's a Briton, an old follower of the late emperor Artorius—and, like him, descended in part from Sarmatian cavalry auxiliaries, which is the origin of the name."

"Yes, yes," Hilaria cut in, forestalling her husband. "But what was his response to our message?"

"Favorable on the whole, Augusta." Nicoles decided to dispense with the middleman and address her directly. "His personal loyalty to Artorius extended to his adopted heir, so he had searching questions concerning Ecdicius' fate. But the courier reports that he's provisionally accepted our story, and is prepared to give his allegiance to y . . . to the Augustus."

"Excellent," Wilhelmus spoke up, reentering the conversation. "The Western provinces are still wavering, and it may well become imperative for the Army of Germania to intervene in Gaul and Britain to . . . assure an orderly transition. Naturally, we hope that none of our subjects will be harmed any more than necessary. In fact—" he paused momentarily and sought for just the right phrase "—I feel their pain. Nevertheless, any disturbances that might arise would probably work even greater harm, so it is our Christian duty to maintain order in this difficult period. But at the same time . . ."

Hilaria's schooled smile had begun to resemble a rictus. "Run along, Wilhelmus," she got out through gritted teeth. The Lord of the World complied with visible relief, exiting by the same door the servant girl had used. Hilaria's eyes followed him with an expression that was no more venomous than usual. *She doesn't hate him, except to the extent that she hates everyone,* Nicoles reflected. Indeed, in many ways it was a marriage made in heaven. She, so eaten away by the lust for power that nothing else was left inside her, had always egged him on to rise higher and higher up the ladder of office; which suited him well enough, if only for the access to women that came with exalted status.

"Now, Nicoles," she said briskly, "given our inability to locate Ecdicius and his family since those stupid thugs failed to kill them, and the persistent rumors that he is in Italy or en route there, it is necessary that we move without delay to stamp out any possible spark of rebellion in the West. The armies of the East will be concentrated at Sirmium and then move to secure Italy. In the meantime, I want you to go to Germania and meet with Kai personally."

"Germania, Augusta?" Nicoles squeaked in horror.

"Germania," she repeated with a malice that was as habitual as her husband's compulsive equivocation. "You must impress upon him the importance of acting with total ruthlessness in pacifying the West. We are confident that, with your well-known powers of eloquence and persuasiveness, you will be able to make these matters clear to him—in spite of . . ." She let the sentence fall off into a well of innuendo.

*In spite of being a eunuch,* Nicoles thought behind the seamless mask of his face. *Why don't you come out and say it, you demented bitch?* "But Augusta," he said aloud, "surely the word of a fellow military man would carry more weight with the general!"

"Unfortunately, we cannot be certain of the . . . enthusiasm of most professional officers for the Augustus. Many of them are still troubled by his youthful military record. On the other hand, your absolute commitment to us is unquestionable." She left the reason unsaid: having been deeply involved in the plot, he now lived or died on Wilhelmus' sufferance—meaning Hilaria's.

"Afterwards," she resumed, "you will accompany Kai and make sure he remembers that his duty to the Augustus supersedes any loyalty he may feel toward his old comrades-in-arms in the Western provinces. Naturally,

Kai himself—along with the Britons under his command—should attend to Gaul and leave Britain to a subordinate." Nicoles nodded; this was standard imperial practice. "Also, I understand that you and the Master of the Offices have been making arrangements to employ barbarian auxiliaries."

"Yes, Augusta." Nicoles, knowing the matter was closed, had resigned himself to the hardships of the Germanian forests. "Our agents have been active among the savages of Hibernia. It should be possible to arrange an invasion of Britain from that direction to coincide with our own landing there. You may rest assured that that island, and Gaul, will be devastated beyond any hope of mounting a successful defiance of your Lord's divinely appointed authority. And any other potential rebels should be deterred by the slaughter there."

For once, Hilaria's smile was one of unaffected happiness. There was, Nicoles thought, something oddly pure about it.

# CHAPTER ELEVEN

They rode north along the Via Ostiensis past the Basilica of Saint Paul-without-the-Walls toward Rome, and the word of their coming sped ahead of them. By the time they passed through the gateway in an angle of the Wall of Aurelian, in the shadow of the Pyramid of Cestius to the left, a large crowd had gathered to greet the Pope who seemed to have returned to them from the dead, and to get what was for most of them their first sight of Ecdicius, who was as much a hero here as he was throughout the West.

They proceeded north through the cheering multitudes. Sidonius would eventually resume residence at the Lateran Palace, where the popes had dwelled since Constantine had presented it to Miltiades. But first they would proceed directly to the Arch of Constantine, where Ecdicius would dramatically reveal the treachery from which he had escaped, the local troops would proclaim him Augustus in a spontaneous display (prearranged via courier before they'd left Ostia), and Sidonius would give his blessing. Later would come the opening shots in the salvo of anathemas Sidonius would hurl in the direction of Constantinople.

Sarnac, riding some distance behind the men of the hour, contented himself with sightseeing. Presently the titanic mass of the Circus Maximus loomed up ahead and to their left. Beyond and above rose the awesome imperial edifices of the Palatine Hill, which had given its name to all palaces.

As they rounded the eastern end of the Circus, he could glimpse the Colosseum far ahead. Everywhere was dense cityscape above which towered the teeming *insulae* or apartment blocks that housed the deafening mobs lining the streets.

"I hadn't expected Rome to be like this," he observed to Tylar. "Didn't the Vandals do a job on this place in 455? Has the Restorer put it back on its feet in the last decade?"

"He's done some rebuilding," came Tylar's voice inside his head. "But even in our history, the city recovered promptly from the Vandal sack, as Sidonius' letters from the 460s attest. It's sheer romanticism to think Rome went directly from classical grandeur to picturesque ruins in 455. The chariot races still draw capacity crowds over there." Tylar covertly indicated the Circus Maximus. "What really wrecked Rome in our timeline was the endless sixth-century war of siege and counter-siege as Justinian's generals tried to reconquer Italy from the Ostrogoths."

As though in confirmation of the time traveller's words, the Colosseum rose before them to the right, still in good repair and not overtaken by its medieval fate (in Sarnac's world) of serving as a rock quarry and as a readymade fortress for the local mafiosi. The gladiatorial games had passed into history as the empire had turned Christian, but the amphitheatre still hosted wild beast shows. Then they were at the Arch of Constantine, where the city's garrison stood at attention. Ecdicius spurred his horse forward and the cheering rose to a crescendo.

The fortress stood on a crag overlooking the Wesser, hugely timbered above a pedestal-like foundation of local stone, looming over this darkly forested land like the power of Rome which it represented. For this was the headquarters of the Army of Germania, as new and rough-hewn as the province itself, as elementally strong as the army which was now putting itself on display in the level area at the foot of the crag for the emperor's chamberlain.

The river barge grounded and, in comical contrast to the austere martial setting, the chamberlain's litter made its wobbly way ashore on the shoulders of bearers who seemed only too aware that every one of the thousands of waiting troops were silently praying for them to drop their burden into the shallows. But they didn't. Kai muttered his disappointment under his breath as he stepped forward.

The chamberlain Nicoles got unsteadily out of the litter, rouge running and carefully curled hair plastered to his head, fanning himself theatrically against the summer heat. Despite all that, he didn't really fit Kai's image of a eunuch; though visibly soft, he wasn't obese as they generally became after years of compensatory gluttony. *Well*, he thought, *I know men who can eat like pigs and not get fat. So why not a half-man as well?*

He got through his greeting to the chamberlain, who acknowledged in his pleasant voice. That, at least, was typical of eunuchs. As Kai knew from his mercifully brief time in Constantinople, they seldom spoke in the high-pitched screech of popular imagination. And those in high court positions had to be especially careful to make themselves personally agreeable; they cultivated pleasing voices just as they stayed scrupulously diapered.

"I trust your journey was pleasant, Chamberlain," Kai said after the formalities were over. He knew damned well it hadn't been, and wasn't particularly pleased with himself for his minor malice. It wasn't usual for him—but things had ceased to be usual on the day the news of the *Pan-Tarkan*'s death had arrived.

Nicoles fanned even more energetically, flinching from the ubiquitous insects. "Ah, my dear general, the journey has been enlightening if nothing else. I'd imagined Germania to be a land of snow and ice and freezing winds!"

"Had you come in the winter, Chamberlain, that's exactly how you would have found it." *And I wish to God you had!* "But this is unusually hot even for a summer afternoon. Why don't we proceed to the fort? At least the insects aren't as bad as they are down here by the river."

"But of course." Nicoles gazed up at the brooding walls. Then his eyes swept around, surveying the massed troops. Kai had been warned that this was no fool.

Nicoles' eyes ran over the ranks of helmeted heavy infantry with their large shields and short ring-mail *loricae hamata*. He also observed the unarmored javelin-men and archers. Some of the latter carried the oddly long bows that had appeared in Artorius' army after his rebel-quelling interlude in western Britain following the Battle of Bourges in 470. Many of the units, he knew, drew their recruits from the local population. But there were also Isaurians from Asia Minor, Franks and Gauls from the other side of the Rhine, and not a few Britons. And the formation his eyes finally settled on was predominantly British.

Sitting astride the horses that had been specially bred to carry heavy cavalry, the Artoriani seemed to embody irresistible force at rest. The history of the last three decades said the impression was not a false one. Artorius had built on the foundation of the Sarmatian *cataphractarii* from whom he was partly descended to create a force of armored shock cavalry that knew no equal, at just the time when such cavalry was coming to dominate the battlefield. Nicoles surveyed the uniformly red cloaks, the scale armor, the long lances (except for the minority of specialist mounted javelin-throwers), and the blood-red dragon standard that barely stirred in this stifling stillness; and he knew he was looking at the instrument which, wielded in precisely the right way at precisely the right time, had won Artorius the purple.

"Most impressive, General," he said to Kai. "But now, I believe I'll avail myself of your hospitality."

❖     ❖     ❖

Kai let the scroll close with a faint snap. He had learned to read late in life, but what he had just read left no room for ambiguity as to its meaning. Wilhelmus couldn't possibly have dictated it.

He raised his eyes to Nicoles. After the initial reception and dinner, they had retired to his office and the chamberlain had presented his credentials and the commands of Wilhelmus Augustus—a combination of name and title on which Kai still gagged. *That craven sack of gonads and blubber, planting his fat bottom on the throne of Artorius!* Of course he said nothing, for to do so would have been at least as much as his life was worth. But he might as well have shouted it for all his feelings were concealed from Nicoles.

Gazing blandly from across the table, the chamberlain saw a man in his forties, starting to put on a little weight but still mostly muscle. His hair and beard were coppery, but the latter—closely trimmed as was generally the case with men who had to wear the standard cavalry helmet with its adjustable cheek-pieces—was now shot through with gray, which was advancing inexorably up his temples. His ruddy, open face could hardly have been more Celtic-looking; those features held not a memory of the Sarmatian horsemen from whom he was remotely descended.

"Well, Chamberlain," he finally said, "my instructions are clear enough. And I begin to understand why you came here immediately after entering the province, before calling on the governor."

"Officially, General," Nicoles said ingratiatingly, "the reason is that the governor is headquartered further west, on the Rhine, so my route brought me here first. But I must confess that the geography was most fortuitous from my standpoint. The governor need not be concerned. Your army is now under direct imperial direction." He delicately indicated the scroll that Kai had allowed to fall to the tabletop. "I am here to help resolve any difficulties that may arise in interpreting the commands of the Augustus. You may speak quite frankly, putting any questions or concerns to me that you wish."

Kai felt a tug of conflicting emotions as his distrust of the chamberlain's word warred with his nature, which inclined him to accept any invitation to openness. "Well," he began cautiously, "my first concern is the effect these orders will have on the security of Germania. After all, I'm being ordered to strip the garrisons of the Elbe of their best troops and take them into Gaul and Britain. How will the tribes to the east react?"

"The Augustus has been given to understand that the Elbe is quiet at present, thanks to your glorious victories."

*Spoken like a true courtier*, Kai sneered inwardly. But he couldn't deny that it was basically true. Those Saxons, Thuringians and Rugians who hadn't submitted had been pushed east, where they were now reclaiming their old lands between the Elbe and the Oder from the Slavs who had filled the vacuum when the Teutons had moved west. They wouldn't make trouble, at least not immediately.

"All well and good," he said aloud, "but there may be other difficulties." His need to be frank overcame his caution. "Chamberlain, many of my officers and men are confused . . . and I share their confusion. We were all loyal to Artorius, and were prepared to be loyal to his chosen successor. Where is he now?"

Nicoles allowed himself a slight smile. This would sound good at Kai's treason trial. Not that such a trial would occur for another year or two. Right now, they needed this guileless simpleton to break the West's resistance. Afterwards, as the Augusta consolidated her power, weeding out everyone linked with the previous reign . . . "As yet, General, we can't be certain. There are, however, unconfirmed reports that he's surfaced in Italy. This is why it is imperative that the Army of Germania, led by an officer of your undoubted loyalty, move without delay to secure the West and forestall any attempt at usurpation by the traitor who conspired against his adoptive father, Artorius Augustus of revered memory."

"Yes, yes, I know. The courier brought word that he'd done that." Kai's face was like a theatrical mask representing inner agony. "But it's hard for those of us who knew him to believe it. And why would he have wanted to? The *Pan-Tarkan* was dying! All Ecdicius had to do was wait, and all would've been his."

"Perhaps, General, the late Artorius Augustus wasn't dying quite fast enough for Ecdicius." Kai's head jerked up and his green eyes went wide. Nicoles nodded gravely. "Yes. We have reason to suspect that he may have hastened the end by poison. Does not his flight from Constantinople fairly shout his guilt?"

Nicoles fell silent, shrewdly leaving Kai alone with his own torment.

*Could it be possible? Ecdicius? Well, ambition does strange things to men; I've seen it. Besides, when all's said and done the fact remains that he is a Gaul.*

*And do I really have any choice? With the* Pan-Tarkan *dead and his heir vanished, all that's left to me is the restored empire that we fought for, that* he *wanted. If I don't stay loyal to that, then what will my life have meant?*

"Well, Chamberlain," he finally said, "I'll do my best to allay my officers' misgivings. It may not be easy, considering . . . Well, you asked me to be frank. And the fact is, the new Augustus isn't too highly regarded by the army."

Nicoles smiled again. Better and better! Really, the man was like a child—he didn't even have to be maneuvered into incriminating himself. He formed an expression that counterfeited sincerity. "Actually, that unfortunate business in Wilhelmus' youth has been widely misrepresented. Remember, he was a student then, at the university Artorius Augustus had recently founded." Kai remembered the *Pan-Tarkan's* enthusiasm for the project, early in his reign. Theodosius I had closed the old University of Athens for its pagan associations, so Artorius had set out to create a Christian successor, dedicating a new university on the island of Rhodes. "So," Nicoles went on, "he had a legitimate reason for not taking up his family's traditional military calling, being at the time a Rhodes scholar. Also, I assure you he was motivated not by fear for his personal safety but by genuine misgivings about the wisdom and righteousness of the war we were waging with Persia then. So, you see, far from showing cowardice he displayed genuine moral courage."

*Well,* Kai reflected, *I thought I'd heard all the forms human hypocrisy can take! At least it's harmless, for no one could ever be taken in by such transparent self-justification. Could they?* But a resurgent caution made him hold his tongue. "No doubt, Chamberlain, no doubt. But for now, let's turn to the actual plan. I see that we're commanded to secure Britain at the same time as Gaul."

"Rest assured, General, that the Augustus does not require from you or your British troops any such display of loyalty as an invasion of your native country. Indeed, I am commanded to suggest that the securing of Britain would best be left to a trusted subordinate of non-British origin, commanding troops from other areas of the empire. Your loyalty is, of course, beyond question. But some of your British troops might experience certain . . . emotional conflicts which would prevent them from proceeding with the full rigor which law and religion alike prescribe for subjects who rebel against their rightful emperor."

Kai made no reply. Instead, he listened to a little voice he didn't want to hear: *Is this what we fought for?*

"Also," Nicoles went on, "I am in a position to assure you that your forces' landing in Britain will have the advantage of coinciding with incursions from other quarters into that notoriously rebellious island."

"What?" Kai glared at him. "Barbarians, you mean?"

"Of course." Nicoles was all blandness. "There are

innumerable precedents for hiring barbarians, not just to fight their fellow barbarians but also to chastise disobedient provincials."

"So where have the agents of the Master of the Offices been nosing about?" Kai inquired, naming the powerful official who controlled, among much else, the secret service.

"Hibernia, General. I am assured that a large-scale raid by the savages there can be arranged. Also . . ." Nicoles hesitated, and for the first time Kai thought to detect a crack in his courtier's facade, through which could be glimpsed the terrors of a thousand generations of ancestors who had stood naked to forces beyond their understanding. "The agents have been in contact with a tribe in the southwest of that island called the Formorians. In exchange for an additional subsidy, they have undertaken to supply a giant one-eyed monster!"

"*What?*" Kai barked laughter. "Oh, come, Chamberlain! Don't tell me the agent has been listening to some smooth-talking tribal chieftain. They've probably got some very big, very ugly old warrior who lost an eye in battle long ago and now frightens the local children!"

"Ordinarily, General, I'd be the first to agree with you. Only . . . I happen to know the agent in question. *He* wouldn't be taken in by some village bogeyman! I've read his report myself, and I wouldn't have believed it possible that he could have written such a document. I can only suppose that we're dealing with something beyond common understanding."

For a space, they sat in silence, their differences momentarily dwarfed by their common flesh-prickling fear in the face of the great darkness beyond their world's little campfire of the known. Nicoles finally shattered the brittle quiet with a nervous laugh.

"At any rate, General, I'm absolutely convinced of this: anything that can unnerve this agent can certainly terrify the Britons! We don't need the powers of darkness; a normal barbarian ravaging should suffice to remind these provincials where their rightful loyalty lies!"

Kai said nothing. He was still asking himself the same unanswerable question.

Sarnac leaned on the balustrade of the artificial terrace at the northeast corner of the Palatine Hill, looking out over the Forum. In the future of his timeline when the Palatine had become a place of romantic gardens, grottoes and archaeological digs, the Barberini Vineyards would cover this monumental architectural crag. Here and now, it still supported the Temple of the Deified Emperors (he couldn't remember the new name the Christians had assigned to it) and afforded the stunning view of Rome he'd been enjoying. He turned to look at the temple, and reflected that it was looking somewhat run-down; it had obviously had a low priority in the Restorer's program of rebuilding and repairing the imperial residences. Beyond it rose the palaces themselves like range upon range of mountainous architectural overload beneath whose weight it seemed the Palatine must surely sink into the Earth's crust.

He continued his turning motion and saw an approaching figure. "You sightseeing too?" he called out. "I'd have thought this was all old hat to you."

"Actually," Artorius admitted, "it's as new to me as it is to you. I never saw Rome in my own century. In fact, my counterpart didn't either."

"Huh? Wasn't he Augustus of the West for a few years before the civil war with Zeno?"

"Oh, yes. But the imperial residence was at Ravenna. He never got around to visiting Rome. Later, after the reunification, he ordered the refurbishing of these palaces—which, in our history, Theodoric the Ostrogoth did in the early sixth century. Wouldn't do to have the one-time imperial palace become dilapidated, however little it's used now. So Ecdicius at least has tip-top quarters!"

"I didn't realize you had so much in-depth knowledge about the Restorer's reign."

"I've been making it my business to acquire it. I talked to Koreel, who got to know him better while we were in Britain and in stasis. And lately I've been picking Sidonius' memories. You see, I wanted to learn just exactly how he won his way to the sole emperorship. I think I've gotten a pretty good idea by now—and it may stand you in good stead in Gaul."

"Gaul? Am I going there?"

"I think you can count on it." The man who bestrode legend grinned, took a final look around, then grasped Sarnac's shoulder. "Come on. It's time for our meeting with Ecdicius. Can't stand here taking in the scenery all day, you know!"

They walked south past the temple and entered the *Area Palatina*, the only open space left on this hill whose every cranny was filled with temples, residences, baths and warehouses. To the right were the palace edifices of early emperors. But ahead was the truly colossal labyrinth of colonnaded halls, sunken gardens, cloistered peristyles and polychrome marble walls raised by Domitian, who'd been too paranoid to enjoy it. Looking up at the raised portico which fronted the palace's entire looming facade, Sarnac was suddenly reminded of the Vatican Palaces of his own era's Rome, so magnificent inside and yet jammed together in such disharmonious juxtaposition that their exteriors could hardly even be glimpsed, much less comprehended.

They bypassed the official palace and passed through the private quarters—if the term could be applied to such an architectural wonderland, organized around upper- and lower-level peristyles—to the stadium Domitian had insisted upon. It was almost five hundred feet long, surrounded by double-level porticoes. Here, Tylar had informed them, Ecdicius had wanted to meet. And he was just dismounting from his horse after his daily exercise—he clearly considered the stadium to represent the supreme inspiration of Domitian's architects—as they arrived. Tylar and Andreas were waiting in the shade of the porticoes.

"Ah," Tylar greeted them, "you're just in time. I've gotten word from Koreel that the Army of Germania has already started to move. Of course, it will still be making its way through Germania now." Sarnac, child of an interstellar society whose messages had to be carried by ship, knew all about information lags over long distances; he was less frustrated by this era's state of communications than his twentieth-century ancestors would have been. Koreel could communicate instantaneously with Tylar, but the news he had available to communicate was limited to what couriers had brought to Constantinople. "Of course, we can't tell Ecdicius this. But he already knows that the command to invade Gaul was sent by Wilhelmus. . . ."

"Wilhelmus!" Ecdicius had only heard the last word as he approached, towelling his head free of sweat, and he snorted in derision. "I still can't get used to the idea of him as emperor. He's such a . . . a . . ." Words failed him, and Sarnac restrained himself from suggesting *nebbish*, knowing he'd get a blank stare of incomprehension for his pains. "Let's get out of the heat," Ecdicius continued, and led the way into the passageway that led, via stairway, up to the lower peristyle of the private residence. There they reemerged into a sunlight ameliorated by shade trees. Sidonius waited for them.

"Let's get right to the point," Ecdicius said, pacing in his lionish way. "Unless Kai tells the emperor—and her husband!—to go to hell, which he almost certainly won't, Gaul is looking at an invasion. Now, I think the West is quiet enough that my presence here isn't required." They all nodded. Spain and Mauretania had been informed of the plot against Ecdicius that had brought Wilhelmus to the throne, and of Sidonius' excommunication of the plotters. Those provinces had already weighed in with their support of Ecdicius' claim. "So I think it best that I go to Gaul."

"I think that's wise, Augustus," Tylar nodded. "You can raise your native country against invaders as no one else can."

"Still," Sidonius said worriedly, "Italy isn't safe either. Have we not heard rumors of a major mobilization in Illyricum?"

"Nevertheless, Your Holiness," Artorius spoke up, "the greatest threat is coming out of Germania into Gaul. And Ecdicius is uniquely able to meet it there. I'll do all I can to help organize the defense of Italy—I have some ideas on the subject. Of course I'll stay behind the scenes, in my 'Gerontius' identity, as an obscure kinsman of the Restorer. And you can inspire the people here to rise in the country's defense against an invader behind whom stand heresy and eternal damnation." Sidonius nodded slowly, and Sarnac reminded himself that this elderly, overweight cleric was the same man as that Bishop of Clermont who had, in the other history, led his flock in withstanding repeated Visigothic sieges in the name of a dying empire, with no outside help save Ecdicius and his merry men.

"I'll also remain in Italy, Your Holiness," Tylar added, "to lend whatever aid and counsel I can."

Ecdicius frowned. "I'd hoped to have you with me in Gaul, Tertullian. I don't pretend to understand everything about you. . . . Hell, *anything* about you! But I know you have sources of knowledge denied to most of us."

"I fear, Augustus, that I'd only slow you down on your journey—I'm not as young as I once was. Instead, if you wish, I'll send Bedwyr and Andronicus to accompany you."

Sarnac caught Andreas' stricken look. Ecdicius would naturally leave his family in the relative safety of Rome when he took to the field. But the young transtemporal explorer held his tongue.

Ecdicius smiled. He'd never be accused of handsomeness, but that smile transfigured his face. He placed a hand on Sarnac's right shoulder and another on Andreas' left. "Good! Tertullian, no counsel you could give me could be as great a boon as the companions you're placing at my side! Bedwyr, I understand you knew Kai once."

"I did, Augustus." Sarnac trotted out his story of having been a youth at the Battle of Angers, and Ecdicius nodded.

"Well, I fought by his side at Bourges and Pavia and on to Constantinople. It doesn't sit well to be fighting against him now, I can tell you. But between us, maybe we can read his thoughts and foresee his plans." Ecdicius gave Sarnac's shoulder a final squeeze. "It's settled, then. We'll be leaving as soon as arrangements can be made. And now, if you'll all excuse me, His Holiness and I have business before he returns to the Lateran." He and Sidonius departed, and Tylar restrained Sarnac with a light touch to his sleeve.

"I'll have a number of items for you to take along. But the most important is this." He handed Sarnac what appeared to be a long dagger or short sword.

"Oho! I remember this thing. But are you going to teach me how you get it to do its tricks?"

"I'm afraid that would call for a good deal of background orientation which you have no time to acquire. This is a special model, designed to be useable by—ahem!—one of your background."

"Must have taken some doing," Sarnac deadpanned.

"The key," Tylar went on, oblivious to sarcasm, "is what appears to be a kind of bolt here at the pommel. Twist it clockwise, and the device reconfigures into a communicator." He didn't demonstrate, in case someone should intrude on them. "It has sufficient range to reach me here in Italy—and, incidentally, Tiraena in Britain. As you know, it can trigger the short-range implants into signalling for attention."

This got Sarnac's undivided attention. He and Tiraena

would no longer be limited to second-hand messages relayed through Tylar. "I guess she's permanently out of stasis by now?" he asked, attempting offhandedness.

"Oh, yes—and hearing some disturbing rumors." Tylar himself looked disturbed, which was so rare an occurrence as to be alarming. But the time traveller proceeded before he could ask any questions.

"As I say, there's more. But we'll have time to go into that before your departure. What's most important just now is how you're going to deal with the military threat to Gaul. In these matters I will, of course, defer to Artorius."

The former High King seated himself on a marble bench, and they all followed suit. "Remember, Robert, that I mentioned I've been making a study of my counterpart's reign? I wanted to pinpoint what gave him his military edge in the post-470 period."

"I've wondered about that myself. I know how good you . . . er, he was. And having served with the Artoriani, I know how good *they* were. But he was up against some top-flight opposition in Italy and later in the Eastern Empire, including *lots* of professional heavy cavalry."

"Ah, but before that—just after the diverging of the timelines and his defeat of the Visigoths at Bourges—he was called back to Britain to put down raiders from the western region known to you as Wales. Naturally, he recruited among the friendly tribes there; and on his return to the continent, with some of those recruits in tow, it was widely noted that his army's archery had improved dramatically. Does this suggest anything to you?"

"No," Sarnac replied, clueless. "Oh, sure, I remember how mediocre the archery was at Bourg-de-Déols. In fact, it had nowhere to go but up! But I don't see the connection between an improvement and the Restorer's rebel-bashing in Wales."

"Perhaps, Robert," Tylar prompted, "you're not aware that the English longbowmen of our history's Middle

Ages—and their weapon—came from the Welsh marches."

Sarnac started to open his mouth, then closed it and was silent for a space. "Uh, but didn't that come a whole lot later than this?" he finally asked.

"To be sure," Tylar nodded. "But it's fallacious to suppose that the English longbow suddenly appeared, in the hands of men who were experts in its use, just in time for Crécy and Agincourt. There was, I believe, a medieval adage which held: 'To train a bowman, begin by training his grandfather.'"

"Still," Artorius said to Sarnac, "you're right up to a point. We're not talking about the fully developed archery that flattened the fourteenth-century French chivalry. But that archery built on a very old tradition in parts of Wales. We now know just *how* old. They're using bows almost six feet long. And they've learned to draw them to the cheek, not to the chest." He saw Sarnac's expression and nodded. "The Restorer encountered this kind of archery in 470 and"—a self-deprecating grimace—"immediately saw its possibilities. He developed tactics for employing it in conjunction with his heavy shock cavalry . . ."

". . . which was already pretty much in a class by itself," Sarnac finished for him. "Jesus Christ! Now I can see why the Restorer went through Europe like beans through a Gringo! The Artoriani, supported by archers who know what they're doing, is not something I'd want to see from the receiving end!"

"But you're going to see it, Robert," Tylar said quietly. "You and Ecdicius. Your old comrade-in-arms Kai is about to lead the army you've just described into Gaul. And you're going to have to stop it."

After a while, Sarnac became aware that his mouth was open. He closed it, swallowed, and decided to speak calmly and reasonably. That, he'd heard somewhere, was the way to deal with a lunatic. "Tylar, I don't suppose it would do any good to ask if I can use high-tech stuff."

"Absolutely not! As I've repeatedly explained . . ."

"Okay. Okay." *Remember, calmly and reasonably! Screaming and jumping up and down would probably be counterproductive.* "So my job is to stop what's currently the best army on this planet, without any technological edge. Fine. I'm completely open to suggestions." A slight pause. "Uh . . . you *do* have suggestions, don't you?"

"Actually," Artorius said, "I do have one. It's something readily available to Ecdicius. In fact, it's so obvious that I wonder why I never thought of it, back when . . ." He gave a vague you-know-what-I-mean gesture. "What I want you to propose to Ecdicius is . . ."

# CHAPTER TWELVE

They were descending from the high pass, with the Alps looming behind them, when they heard the commotion from the baggage train.

"What now?" Ecdicius muttered, signalling a halt and turning his horse's head around. Sarnac and Andreas followed him, as did the standard bearer, and they rode back uphill alongside the column with the red dragon standard streaming in the brisk upland air.

They hadn't been able to bring many troops from Italy—Gaul would have to defend itself with its own resources—but there were enough to discourage the remaining bandit gangs in the Alpine passes. (Twenty years earlier, Ecdicius would have had to pay them tribute for safe passage.) Behind the soldiers were the pack animals laden with good-quality weapons and armor as well as their own provisions. Here an altercation was underway, with several of the drovers yelling and gesticulating with Italian fervor at one of the others, a boy. As they neared the scene, one of the men grabbed the youth by an arm.

"Hold!" Ecdicius shouted. "What is this?"

The boy twisted free and whirled to face them . . . and Sarnac saw that she wasn't a boy. It took him another instant to recognize her, behind the smudged face and hacked-off hair. By then, Ecdicius' face was a mask of fury, and Andreas' one of joy.

"*Julia!*" Ecdicius looked like he was going to have a stroke. "What . . . what . . . ?"

"I was going to tell you tonight, when we came to our first halt in Gaul, father." She faced Ecdicius unflinchingly. "Don't worry about mother—I left a letter telling her where I am."

"But, but . . . how . . . ?"

The chief drover looked acutely miserable. "He . . . er, she joined us at the last minute in Rome, Augustus. She's pretty much kept to herself the whole way, and it wasn't till now that any of us had any idea. So nothing has . . . well, you know, *happened*, if you take my meaning. . . ."

"It's true, father. Don't blame these men; they knew nothing. It was all my idea." All at once her facade began to crumble, and she looked even younger than her years. "I *couldn't* stay behind in Rome and do nothing, father! And I knew you'd say no if I asked you. . . ."

"That's God's own truth!" Ecdicius leaned forward on his saddle-bow and glared down at her. "And Rome is exactly where you're going, young lady! I'm sending you back at once!"

Her lower lip trembled a little, but she looked her father straight in the eye. Sarnac had never noticed before how much like him she was. His beak was, in her, softened into a gentle aquiline curve, and she had her mother's lighter complexion and chestnut hair. But for sheer determination, there was little to choose between in those two faces.

"How, father?" she asked. "You can't send enough men back to keep me safe from the bandits in the mountains."

"It's true, Augustus," Andreas put in helpfully. "She's safer with us."

Ecdicius seemed about to explode, but he gradually subsided. "Very well," he grated. "You can come with us, until—and *only* until—I can find some proper lodging for you. In the meantime, now that everyone knows you're not a boy . . ." He gestured vaguely in Andreas' direction. "Andronicus, I want you to guard her, and *try* to keep her out of trouble!"

"I'll do my best, Augustus," Andreas replied, all dutiful resolve to carry out his orders, however distasteful. He looked like a Roman recruiting poster would have, if they'd used them. Sarnac somehow managed not to burst out laughing.

"And now," Ecdicius continued grimly, "let's proceed. We've wasted enough time as it is." As he turned his horse around, he gave Julia a final glare—or what was intended to be a glare but fooled no one. Then he shook his head. "Where you get your stubbornness and boldness from is beyond my comprehension!"

Sarnac continued to keep a straight face, nearly rupturing himself in the process.

A group of riders came out from the Arvernian villa to meet them. Ecdicius shouted a greeting to their leader and spurred his horse forward. Sarnac followed, urging his horse into a gallop.

He'd done a little riding in his youth, which combined with the trained reflexes conferred by Tylar's implants to make him an above-average horseman of this era. He was, in fact, just good enough to recognize greatness when he saw it, as he did when Ecdicius mounted a horse and they became a single organism with a single will. There were, he reflected, a few sights in the world that were in a special class by themselves. A clipper ship running before the wind under full sail. A cheetah building up to full speed as it pursued an antelope. A stooping hawk. Ecdicius on horseback.

They met the party from the villa, and its leader dismounted and saluted. "*Ave*, Augustus."

Ecdicius flung himself from the saddle and embraced the man. "Ah, enough of titles, Basileus! It's been too long." He held Basileus at arm's length and examined him with mock disapproval. "You've gone to fat since we rode together against the Visigoths! You must breed strong horses in these parts, to find one that can carry you!"

Basileus—about Ecdicius' age, and not noticeably overweight—grinned amid the general laughter. "You'll find I can still ride, Ecdicius. So can all of us. I've sent word to others of the old Brotherhood, and several are on their way here now. We'll ride again, this time for the rightful heir of Artorius Augustus!" His men broke into a cheer, even the younger ones, who knew Ecdicius only from their elders' stories.

"Splendid! We've been spreading the word that we're all to rendezvous at Clermont next month. It'll be a reunion of the Brotherhood, Basileus."

They had first passed through the Burgundian lands and made sure of the allegiance of those Roman allies. Then they had moved on into the Auvergne, stopping at the estates of Ecdicius' fellow cavaliers whom he'd led to the victory of Bourges, not on a hopeless exercise in gallantry as in Sarnac's history. They were mostly men in their late forties like the new Augustus of the West, but Basileus was right: they could still ride like centaurs. And the response had been the same everywhere. Clearly, Ecdicius would be able to throw limitless gallantry and *elan* at the hardbitten professionalism of Kai's veterans. Sarnac wondered if it would be enough.

Ecdicius remounted, using the stirrups Artorius and his men had inherited from that Sarmatian lump in the British melting-pot from which they were descended. In Sarnac's history they had been lost sight of after Artorius' downfall, vanishing from Europe until reintroduced by the Avars a century later. Here, of course, they were part of the standard heavy cavalry kit by now. So as far as cavalry technique went, it would be a wash between them and Kai.

*Kai.* The image of his onetime friend, soon to be his enemy, came crowding in. *Does* this *Kai remember me at all? If he does, it's probably as a damned deserter! He*

*must have wondered what became of Bedwyr and his
mysterious employer Tertullian shortly before the Battle
of Bourges.*

He hauled his mind back to this late-summer day in Gaul,
to this field he was riding across at Ecdicius' side. The
rest of their party had joined them, and as they rode toward
the villa Ecdicius was undergoing the embarrassment of
introducing his daughter to Basileus. It wasn't as bad as it
had been their first few stops; they'd gotten her some socially
acceptable clothes, and her hair was growing back.

Ecdicius turned to him and smiled. "Look at them,
Bedwyr," he said, swinging his arm in a circle to indicate
Basileus and his retainers. "Have you ever seen such a
crew of madmen? Kai will know he's been in a fight!"
Then he turned serious, and seemed to echo Sarnac's earlier
thoughts. "What courage and love of country can do, we'll
do. But I can't stop thinking of what we're going to have
to face. If it were just cavalry against cavalry, I'd face it
willingly. But Kai's a master at using those damned
longbowmen of his in conjunction with his cavalry. They
can break up a formation, blunt a countercharge . . ."

*Now's as good a time as any,* Sarnac decided. "Augustus,
it seems to me that we must match him with archery of
our own."

Ecdicius' brows drew together. "But how, Bedwyr? We
can't just copy the idea of longer bows; it takes *time* to
learn to use them properly. Those men Artorius brought
back from western Britain had been doing it since they
were boys! You can't duplicate that kind of skill overnight."

"True, Augustus; it takes time to train a longbowman.
But . . ." He turned toward one of Basileus' men, who looked
like he was just back from hunting, and pointed at that
which hung from the saddle-bow. "It doesn't take long to
learn how to use one of *those*, does it?"

"Why of course not." Ecdicius looked blank. "Anybody
can learn to use a crossbow; there's little skill to it, you
sight along it and pull on the handle. Every lad in Gaul

uses them for shooting game. But what's that got to do with . . . ?"

Artorius had warned Sarnac to expect this. The Romans had had crossbows for a long time, and they were as popular for hunting as Ecdicius had indicated, not just for the relative ease of learning how to use them but also for the fact that you could leave the quarrel nocked indefinitely while stalking game and be ready to get off a quick shot as your prey broke cover. But the thought of using them in war had never occurred to anyone. They were hunting weapons, period. Why? Because that was what they'd always been. It would have surprised Sarnac before his previous brush with the fifth century, but now he knew about the conservatism of preindustrial societies.

"Since so many Gallic men know how to use them, Augustus, or can be quickly taught to do so, why not form a corps of them to give our men some missile support? Kai's longbowmen would have the advantage in range, but as you've said he has only a small number of them. We could put masses of crossbowmen into the field."

Ecdicius' expression had gone from inability to understand what Sarnac was talking about to rejection of an obvious absurdity, and then to dawning interest. "Massed crossbows in battle," he finally said, very slowly, and shook his head. "But nobody ever . . ." He trailed to a halt and thought for another moment. Then, with one of the dizzyingly abrupt movements that typified him, he leaned over in his saddle toward the man with the crossbow and asked to see it. Then he inspected the weapon in silence. When he spoke again his voice was matter-of-fact. "What about the disparity in rates of fire? A trained longbowman can release arrows a lot faster than any crossbowman can get off quarrels."

Sarnac released a quiet breath of relief. It was going more smoothly than he'd dared hope. But, then, this was Ecdicius. "I have an idea on that, Augustus. Perhaps you'll let me demonstrate it later." Actually, it wasn't his idea.

The semi-historical Sun Pin had thought of it eight centuries before, when the newly invented crossbow was coming to dominate the battlefields of the Warring States, and Tylar had passed it on. (Sarnac had once rhetorically asked his old friend Liu Natalya if the Chinese had invented *everything*. She'd pretended to think about it for a decent interval before nodding judiciously.)

He examined the weapon. It was nothing like the steel arbalests of his history's Late Medieval Europe. *Those* things were designed to pierce the high-quality plate armor of their own era; here and now, that kind of steel-smashing power wasn't needed. And, by the same token, it didn't require any elaborate mechanical gizmos to draw it—and therein lay the practicality of his third-hand idea for overcoming the problem of its slow rate of fire. (Nobody in Europe would *ever* dream up a *repeating* crossbow like the Chinese *chu-ko-nu*, and there was no time to introduce it.)

They had reached the villa and were dismounting when a dusty courier rode in from the east. Basileus had a brief colloquy with him, then gestured to Ecdicius to join them. The three of them talked for a few moments, then Ecdicius returned to where Sarnac waited. His face really was hopelessly expressive; it told Sarnac what the message was before he even opened his mouth.

"The provincial border guards on the Rhine at Strasbourg report that the lead elements of the Army of Germania are within sight of the river. They'll be crossing over soon." Ecdicius' face abruptly transformed itself with a grin. "Maybe you'd better show me your idea for using crossbows this very evening!"

The barges passed back and forth in stately lines, depositing their loads of troops on the Gallic side of the Rhine and then going back to the eastern bank for more. Kai stood on a bluff overlooking the Gallic bank and the formations that were taking shape. It would have looked like chaos to a civilian, but Kai looked it over with a professional's eye and nodded.

Somewhere nearby, he'd heard, was the field where the Emperor Julian—a good general, for all his apostasy—had smashed the barbarians at the Battle of Strasbourg and saved Gaul, over a hundred and thirty years before. But Kai had no time for sightseeing. He had to deal with a constant procession of aides with requests from his officers for orders, clarifications and resolutions of disputes. He kept things in order with half his mind. The other half was on the riverside village he'd seen. Or what had once been a village.

He hadn't crossed over with the vanguard; there had been too much organizational work yet to do on the Germanian side. But one of Nicoles' troop of officials had. Kai couldn't really blame the officer who'd allowed himself to be led by the man, who after all claimed to speak with the voice of the Augustus. But . . .

He became aware of Nicoles' litter, coming up the path to the bluff. The bearers set it down, and the chamberlain emerged. "Ah, General! An inspiring sight, is it not?" Nicoles swept an arm out, indicating the coalescing army. "The unstoppable might of Rome, on the march!" He noticed Kai's expression and reined in his enthusiasm. "I understand that you had some questions concerning the activities of my underchamberlain Theophanes."

"I don't recall ever giving him permission to cross over with the first wave," Kai said stonily.

"Oh I *do* apologize, general! Doubtless we violated military protocol by not soliciting your permission. But I felt it was important to get a *personal* representative of the Augustus onto Gallic soil without delay. I would have done it myself, but I'm under instructions from the Augustus—and the Augusta, whose compassion is exceeded only by her beauty and wisdom—to avoid exposing myself to undue danger. And Theophanes is an excellent official, if occasionally prone to overzealousness."

"But . . . was *that* necessary?" Kai gestured vaguely in the direction of the charnel house that had been a riverside village.

"Oh, that." Nicoles made a little *moue*. "Most distasteful, I agree. But Theophanes assures me that the villagers displayed insufficient enthusiasm—indeed, outright surliness—when he raised the image of Wilhelmus Augustus. They actually offered violence to the image! He felt that an example should be made. Coming immediately after our entry into Gaul, it should have a salutary effect. Your own officer, I should add, came to agree; he was, no doubt, looking to the future—and his own career." For the barest instant, Nicoles' expression slipped, and Kai glimpsed something other than courtliness in his eyes. "Great changes are coming, General. Indeed, 'change' is the Augustus' watchword. There are even those" —an insinuating smile, seeming to say "Oh, aren't we being just too, *too* wicked?"— "who feel he uses it to excess." Kai had become used to this kind of ploy, and declined to rise to the bait. "At any rate," Nicoles went on, "we must all be prepared to bend with the shifting winds, General. *All* of us."

For a moment they looked at each other in silence, for nothing needed to be said; they both understood matters perfectly. Then Nicoles spoke briskly. "I understand your lieutenant Marcellus has completed his preparations for the landing in Britain."

"Yes. He's assembled all our available shipping at his base, near the Rhine's mouth, and built all the barges he needs." Kai didn't add that in the old days the Britons would have smashed the invasion at sea. But with the Saxons and other sea-raiders conquered and incorporated, the Saxon Shore Fleet had been allowed to rot away. Marcellus would have an unopposed voyage, he thought, carefully not trying to define his own feelings.

"Excellent! If all has gone according to plan, the Irish raiders should have already begun attacking from the west. So my last correspondence from our agent there assured me. He also assured me . . ." Nicoles hesitated uncharacteristically, and swallowed. "He assures me that the Fomorians have kept their bargain—in all respects."

Kai felt his neck hairs prickle. "You mean the . . . ?"

"Yes. By the way, the agent has learned the being's name. . . ."

"Balor, Lady. That's what they call him. I saw him with my own eyes! I saw him as I lay in a ditch hiding while they passed by. May God strike me dead if I didn't!"

The Ordovician chieftain sat a the focus of a half-circle of listeners in the great hall at Cadbury, trembling in the grip of exhaustion and memory. His skin gleamed with sweat under the flaring torches.

The word had only just come that the Irish raiders, so long held at bay by the terror of Artorius' name, had crossed over in their leather curraghs and were spreading terror in Gwynedd. Just behind the news had come this man, fleeing south from his village's destruction. Now they listened to him with varying expressions: Gwenhwyvaer's unreadable, Cerdic's worried, Constantine's scornful, and Tiraena's perplexed as she tried to recall where she'd heard that name.

"So, fellow," Constantine said condescendingly, "you tell us that the Irish are led by some gigantic one-eyed man, eh?" Old Cador had died last year, leaving his son as chief of the Dumnonii. He was in an uncomfortable tangle of conflicting moods these days, afire with enthusiasm for Gwenhwyvaer's declaration of British independence but seething with resentment at having to fight alongside Saxons in defense of that independence. On one point he was absolutely certain: they needed to focus their attention on meeting the invasion everyone knew was coming from the Germanian coast. His tone left no doubt about what he thought of the distraction posed by this yokel and his wild tales.

But the man stood his ground, clearly not about to be

intimidated by any Dumnonian princeling. "No! A giant indeed—half again the height of a man, and squatty for all that. And, yes, one eye—huge, glowing with an unsanctified light in the middle of his head. But he was *not a man!*" He shuddered with a fear that had nothing to do with Constantine, then took command of himself. "He stood upright on two legs, and had two arms, but there was nothing about him that was like a man—or anything of this world! It wasn't his ugliness. It was . . ." The shakes took him again. He turned to Gwenhwyvaer. "Lady, it was his *wrongness!* He's something that doesn't belong in God's creation!"

Cerdic leaned forward, frowning. "You're saying he's a . . . demon?" The *ealdorman* had finally received baptism—without noticeable improvement, Constantine had been heard to mutter. The Teutonic paganism he'd left behind had held giants. He would have preferred one of them to a denizen of the Christian hell.

"Well," Constantine said with forced heartiness, "if he is, we've nothing to fear. The priests can send him shrieking back down into the pit from whence he came!"

"Oh, I fear not," the man said in a near-whisper. Exhaustion was quickly taking him, but he smiled up at Constantine grimly. "A priest—I'd known the old fellow, but never dreamed he had the courage of any two warriors—advanced on Balor, crying out the formula of exorcism. The savages drew back, for they fear all holy men. But Balor smashed him to the earth with the great club he carries, then grasped him by his two ankles and pulled . . ." He couldn't continue. This was a man who had lived his life on the semibarbarous fringes of this brutal world, but he was obviously gagging on rising vomit. But he again mastered himself and continued. "And through it all, the monster was silent as always."

"What?" Gwenhwyvaer cocked her head to one side. "You say this Balor is mute? How, then, does he give his commands to the raiders?"

"No one ever heard *him* speak, Lady. But he wears an amulet of curious design around his neck, from which come words in a strange tongue, sounding as though spoken by a throat of metal . . ."

"Oh, this is too much!" Constantine flung himself back in his chair. "Talking amulets indeed! Must we waste any more time listening to this? I ask, you, Lady . . ." He turned toward Gwenhwyvaer, then stopped short, for beyond her he saw Tiraena. They all followed his gaze. She was sitting like a statue, with an expression none of them could read, in a silence none of them disturbed.

Over the last six years she had been an occasional visitor to Cadbury, known to be in Gwenhwyvaer's special favor. Most people made surreptitious signs when they saw the foreign-looking woman, for it was whispered that she gave counsels beyond the common knowledge of men. (Gwenhwyvaer had known about Artorius' death, and thus been able to begin implementing her declaration of independence, before anyone else had heard the news; and the tall woman had just arrived on one of her visits at the time.) Some claimed to have seen her standing distracted, as though listening to voices she alone could hear. And . . . she never seemed to grow any older.

And now she stared straight ahead at ghosts beyond their imaginings.

At length, Gwenhwyvaer reached out and touched her arm. "Lucasta, what is it?"

Tiraena blinked and seemed to awake from nightmare. "I . . . can't be certain yet, Lady. But I think this man speaks the truth."

"What?" Constantine blurted.

Gwenhwyvaer shushed him. "Go on, Lucasta."

Tiraena shook her head. "I can say no more until I'm certain. I must ride north and see for myself."

"No!" Cerdic started to protest, then stopped. The mysterious Lucasta went where and when she would.

Gwenhwyvaer looked at her gravely. "At least take

Peredur and Cynric with you. Since I've assigned them
to you as bodyguards, they'd feel disgraced if they weren't
allowed to go along."

*And you'd just send them after me anyway,* Tiraena
reflected. She glanced at Cerdic, whose son Cynric would
be going into danger for the first time. "Very well, Lady.
But I leave at first light. There's no time to waste."

*And,* she added silently, *pray to your God that I'm
wrong!*

They stopped briefly at the town of Wroxeter, where
troops from the old legionary fort at Chester stood guard
against the raiders operating to the northwest. Tiraena,
finding little in the way of reliable eyewitnesses among
the refugees huddling there, pressed on into the hills of
Gwynedd.

Her unique mystery-woman status had enabled her to
get away with wearing a practical riding outfit. And she'd
been able to hone with practice her neurally implanted
equestrian skills in the few subjective months she'd spent
in Britain between spells in stasis over the last six years.
So she could set her two bodyguards a stiff pace. It still
bothered her to be taking them to face that for which their
background had never prepared them, for she genuinely
liked them.

It had been typical of Gwenhwyvaer to assign her a Briton
and a Saxon. Peredur, quiet and self-contained, was in his
early twenties and already a veteran of the Artoriani. Cynric
Cerdicson, fourteen and therefore old enough to be a warrior
in his culture, looked on the older man with something
akin to awe but wasn't about to show it. His adolescent
pride at being given his first responsible charge had bloomed
into a fierce protectiveness which left Tiraena uncertain
whether to laugh or cry but determined to do neither within
the sight of those worshipful blue eyes.

They topped a ridge and gazed westward. There was,
she'd been told, a village beyond the next rise, which

the Irish marauders shouldn't have reached yet and which would probably be sheltering refugees from further west. She urged her horse ahead of her guards and studied the skyline . . . and saw the rising smoke that told her that the raiders had, in fact, reached that village. . . .

She was thinking about it when, with flesh-prickling shrieks, the Irish rose from concealment in the brush around them.

They swarmed in from both sides, cutting Tiraena off. These proto-Celtic people, the Fomorians, belonged to an earlier ethnic stratum than the Gaelic-speakers who had taken over most of Ireland. But they were equipped much like them: unarmored save for small leather shields, and armed with short poor-quality iron swords or the kind of club which would one day be known as a shillelagh. Gwenhwyvaer's troops would have eaten them alive in a stand-up fight—a fact that wasn't much comfort as one of them seized Tiraena's reins near the bit and jerked upward. Her horse reared, throwing her. She managed to land with a roll to minimize the impact, and was on her feet before the Fomorians had reached her.

Looking beyond them, she saw Peredur and Cynric trying to cut their way through to her. But the press of raiders around them prevented them from building up the momentum that would have ridden their foes down; it was all they could do to stay on their horses, striking downward with their *spathas*, as the barbarians crowded around and tried to dismount them. And, off to one side, she could see more of the Fomorians running up to cut the two horsemen off.

"Peredur!" she shouted over the barbarians' cries. "Get away—you'll be surrounded! Go to Chester and get help."

Their eyes met. This was no knight-errant, and his eyes told her he knew he was looking at no damsel in distress but at a fellow soldier, and his on-scene commander. He gave a quick nod. "Cynric! Let's go!"

"*No!*" The young voice caught on a sob.

Peredur's voice was like a whip-crack. "I said get moving, *boy!*"

It was just what the doctor ordered for getting Cynric moving. His eyes flashed blue fire at the one imputation that no adolescent male can endure, and he took it out on his attackers, splitting the skull of one and kicking another in the face as he turned his horse's head around and broke free of the press. Tiraena had time to see him and Peredur get away before a big Fomorian crashed into her.

She went over, pulling her attacker with her, and brought a knee up into his groin. As he doubled over with a gasp, she scrambled to her feet, upended the nearest Fomorian with a sweeping circular kick, and ran in the only direction open to her: up a slope toward thick woods. *Good,* she thought. *If I can get in among the trees maybe I can lose them.* . . .

Then her legs stopped pumping as they were tackled from behind, and she fell heavily to the ground. Half-stunned, she kicked out at the cluster of Fomorians who piled onto her. She saw a warrior raise his shillelagh two-handed above his head and bring it sweeping down. Then the world dissolved in pain and swirling lights before being swallowed up by darkness.

She wasn't sure at first that she'd awakened, for the sickening pain and the scene around her seemed but a continuation of her evil dreams.

It was night, and the torchlight revealed the ruins of a village. It also revealed other things . . . and for an instant, reality wavered. *Are they right after all?* flashed through her reeling mind. *Am I dead and in the hell the Christians believe in?* Her consciousness focused on one detail of the scene: a little girl, no more than four, her lifeless face frozen in a mask of transcendent agony and her naked childish body in a position as grotesque as any of the other impaled forms. Then the spasms began, and after everything was gone from her stomach Tiraena kept trying to retch, as her entire being sought to reject what she was seeing.

When she finally looked up, a man was standing before her, dressed in a hooded robe of coarsely woven fabric. He regarded her for a moment, then turned to the left and spoke two words. At first they didn't register on Tiraena, not so much because of their mangled pronunciation as because of their sheer impossibility.

There could be no doubt, though. The words had been: *"Her awake."* This fifth century Irish savage had spoken in a crude parody of twenty-third century Standard International English.

"Good." This was pronounced clearly, but in a tinny, mechanical voice. A vast shadow fell across her, cast by the monstrous figure that trod into her range of vision and blocked out the torchlight.

Tiraena looked up at the Interrogator and knew she was not in the Christian hell after all. She wished she could have taken refuge there.

# CHAPTER THIRTEEN

"You," she finally breathed.

There was a long pause. Then the Korvaasha motioned to the robed man to depart, which he did with no apparent good grace. Once he was out of earshot, the translating voder pendant hanging around the alien's long thick neck began producing the human-range sounds its breathing/vocalizing slits could not. The artificial voice was as horribly inflectionless as she remembered, but with a new scratchiness.

"So you speak Standard International English. I could tell from your physical appearance that you do not belong to the same ethnic type as the inferior beings native to these islands. But since the language does not currently exist, you must be a time traveller, as I now know to be possible."

"You don't remember me, do you?" Tiraena stared up into the single eye—huge, faceted, even more disturbing to humans than everything else about the Korvaasha. She was trained to see past alienness and recognize individual members of nonhuman races, and this was definitely the Interrogator, though he was twenty-plus years older and his thick, wrinkled hide showed an unpleasant looseness. Not that there had ever been any doubt as to his identity, for there could be no other Korvaasha on this planet in this century. "You captured me on Danu—just before my people's fleet arrived and smashed yours," she added pointedly. "Afterwards, your ship overhauled mine and captured me and my companions again. Then we were all taken by . . ."

"Yes, I remember you now. In my subsequent imprisonment, I had time to reflect. I came to the conclusion that your male companion had been right, impossible though it seemed: our ship had somehow travelled back in time. After I escaped and my captured gravitic vehicle crashed, my observations confirmed this. The planet was inhabited by your species, in a primitive state of technology, and therefore could only be pre-spaceflight Earth."

Tiraena found herself thinking with odd clarity in the midst of pain and horror. The Korvaasha, she knew, was being positively garrulous for one of his race. *Naturally,* she reflected. *He's had nobody to tell his story to for twenty years! So I ought to be able to keep him going.* . . . "So," she said aloud, "you must have terrorized the locals at first. But later, some of them tried to make contact with you, and you decided it might be to your advantage to reciprocate. But of course your translator is only programmed for Standard International English, so you had to teach them an elementary version of the language."

"It was a laborious process, as they were primitives as well as belonging to your contemptible species. But I cultivated certain ones who were teachable, and who were prepared to do my bidding in all things in exchange for power over their fellows." He indicated the man Tiraena had first seen, who was standing with a small group of others, similarly robed, in the torchlight. "They became my . . ."

"Priesthood," Tiraena supplied.

There was a moment's pause while the Korvaasha digested the pendant's interpretation of this. "Most perceptive of you. Through them, I was able to mold their originally useless tribe to my purposes."

"Like this?" Tiraena looked around.

"Yes, I have introduced certain refinements. My priests have taken to them most enthusiastically. There has been some reluctance in other quarters. But after the local Druids were exterminated and their gods degraded, the warriors mostly recognized that following me was the way to victories and plunder. Their rudimentary minds are incapable of thinking further."

*Yes*, she thought, with a sickness that had nothing to do with the pain in her head. She glanced at the robed figures. *The Fomorians were just an ordinary, clean sort of savage before. Is there any limit to the degradation some humans—the power-junkies—will undergo for a promise of control over other humans? And must that particular sort of scum always float to the top?* Then an obvious question occurred to her. "How is it that your voder still works?"

"It is powered by a photoelectric cell, and was designed to last under primitive conditions. Nevertheless, it is showing signs of deterioration. I am developing a form of written language for communicating with the priests after it finally ceases to function."

Tiraena nodded slowly. Even that caused her head to hurt. "It sounds like you've done very nicely where you were. So why have you led your followers here?"

"When the imperial agents arrived and the priests explained their purpose to me, I saw at once that my opportunity had arrived. I will establish myself here, after this island is conquered. Later, I will widen my power base. Eventually, I will take over this empire, clearly a more advanced society than the mud-squatting primitives with whom I currently have to work. Then I will force the development of a technology capable of space flight and displacement-point transit . . ."

*What is this?* Tiraena thought. *He can't be joking. No*

*Korvaasha has a sense of humor—the very concept is
incomprehensible to them. But he must know that this is
all nonsense! All the Fomorians have going for them is
the terror of his appearance, and that's bound to wear
off. But even if they could conquer Rome, and even if he
was a walking compendium of technical knowledge, an
Iron Age culture simply couldn't be made to jump so many
intervening developmental stages in whatever's left of his
lifetime.*

". . . and then I will go looking for my race, which must
now be expanding through this spiral arm under the aegis
of the old Unity, but which has not yet reached this galactic
neighborhood. I will lead them here, and we will exterminate
the human race long before it can become our nemesis. I
will personally oversee the slaughter, on a vast scale. I
will . . ."

*He's mad.* The belated realization burst on Tiraena. *His
brain has turned to onion dip.* The flat, expressionless
machine-voice of the voder had disguised it at first—the
thing simply *couldn't* rave. *And besides,* she thought,
teetering so close to the edge of hysteria that she had to
suppress a giggle, *it's like a bad joke.* "An insane Korvaasha?
How can you tell?"

But these megalomaniac fantasies left no doubt. The years
of loneliness and squalor, among a race he hated but on
which he depended for survival, had worn the Interrogator's
sanity away. She wondered how much the "priests" even
bothered communicating with him any more, except when
the tribe was at war.

"This is why I ordered you spared." Tiraena's awareness
of the metallic drone returned. "Your distinctive appearance
suggested foreign—and possibly more advanced—origins.
In fact, you are something even better: a time traveller
from my own era. With your advanced technical knowledge,
you will play a useful role in my plan. Thus you will have
the opportunity to earn a quick, humane death. Of course
you realize that you cannot be left alive, any more than

can any of your species—this must be self-evident even to inferior beings. But by helping to implement my plan you will be serving a higher purpose than any to which vermin like yourself could ever have realistically aspired. For by aiding in your race's extirpation, you will be helping it atone for its great crime: hindering the eventual Korvaasha-directed unification toward which all galactic life, unless perverse, unconsciously strives. . . ."

Tiraena no longer tried to restrain herself. She threw back her head, heedless of pain, and loosed a peal of laughter that was a defiant clarion in that scene out of hell. "You fucking lunatic! 'Hindered' you my ass! In my grandparents' day we kicked you off my homeworld of Raehan and were getting ready to rid the cosmos of your perverse Unity, just before the great realignment of the displacement network. And in my own time, the time you came from, we've crushed your Realm of Tarzhgul out of existence. Oh, a few of its worlds are left—genocide would lower us to your level, if possible. But orbital stations keep them under surveillance and vaporize anything more advanced than black-powder artillery and coal-burning steam pumps. And as for you personally . . ." She laughed again and staggered to her feet. "I've got news for you: your 'escape' was orchestrated by the time travellers who'd brought us to this era—*human* time travellers, from an age when the Korvaasha aren't even a bad memory. They let you go because their job is to preserve the past—including the 'Balor' of the Irish legends. So you've spent the last twenty-one years making sure a certain body of Terran myth turns out the way future human history books say it did! How's *that* for 'serving a higher purpose,' dipshit?"

She felt her arms being grasped from behind by two unseen guards, but she hardly noticed. For she had, in the past, seen the Interrogator in what she had sworn was the grip of an intense emotion of some kind—and that paled beside what she saw now. The massive frame shook, and the neck-slits practically rippled as they vocalized below the human auditory range. But no sound came from the voder, which could only translate coherent verbalizations with Standard English counterparts. Finally he subsided, and the mechanical voice came with its unvarying expressionlessness.

"You will not be suitable for the role I had in mind. In the morning you will be used for a different purpose: a reward for the warriors. If you survive, the priests will use your body as a medium for honing their skills at techniques I have taught them to appreciate. In fact, they have already become quite expert at prolonging death."

The guards jerked on her arms and began to haul her away. But for an instant she twisted herself around and faced the Interrogator again. "Oh, I almost forgot to tell you: this is a parallel reality and you're nothing but a quantum-shadow of your counterpart in the universe from which you and I both come. There, you'll eventually be killed by some Gaelic hero, and your crazy plan will come to nothing. As it will in this universe, regardless of who kills you here!"

For a moment, she thought the Interrogator was going to kill her on the spot. But one of the "priests" stepped forward and spoke to him in mock-obsequious tones, in an English so mangled as to be incomprehensible to her. The guards hustled her away hurriedly—she could smell their acrid sweat—to a post that was all that remained of some village structure. They backed her up to it, twisted her arms around behind it, and tied the wrists roughly together. Then they tied her ankles to the post's base. By the time they were done, their spirits seemed to have risen—or perhaps they needed to banish what they had felt in the presence of the Interrogator and his votaries/manipulators, for their laughter and rib-elbowing as they felt and squeezed her bound form seemed somehow too raucous. She took it, using mental discipline techniques to remove herself temporarily from her body. After a while they tired of their play and swaggered off, slapping each other on the back a few too many times, and she was alone in the darkness.

She took stock. Her long-range communicator lay deactivated in the cave near the banks of the Cam, with the stasis-field generator and the rest of Tylar's goodies. She didn't have all that many—just things she absolutely needed and which could function in the field, like the supply of nondescript little pills that could stimulate the body to heal just about anything within reason, although you slept a lot while it was happening and were very weak and hungry afterwards. It was nothing compared to the infirmary aboard Tylar's ship, where nanoids simply took an injured body apart at the molecular level and put it back together, uninjured. (Reassembling it in an *improved* form was sternly interdicted. Tiraena gathered that Tylar's civilization had had some bad experiences with that sort of thing.) But that required elaborate equipment; the pills were Tylar's idea of very crude first-aid, and he'd cautioned her that they, like everything else, must be kept from the locals lest their cultural development be distorted. But it was all back in the cave which the folk around Cadbury had come to superstitiously shun. Just as well; the Interrogator couldn't possibly be so far gone that he wouldn't recognize high-tech artifacts for what they were. She still had the implant communicator, of course, but it wasn't doing her much good.

But that wasn't the only implant in her body. She was a survey specialist and had been given various biotechnic edges over the primitive environments she must face. There was one in particular. . . .

She twisted her shoulders, raising one and lowering the other as she tried to shift the hands the guards had tied behind the post. She could feel skin being rubbed raw by the rope, but she had to get that left forefinger pointed at the knot between her wrists, and she had to do it by feel alone. And it had to be pointing *down*, not up, which would have been relatively easy.

Finally the fingertip rested against the knot. She wasn't sure of the angle, and she'd have only one chance. *Well,* she thought as she strained to hold herself in the miserably uncomfortable position, *no time like the present.* She took a deep breath against what she knew was coming and gave a carefully trained mental command.

The almost-microscopic superconductor loop just under the tip of the finger yielded up its hoarded energy, and the tiny crystal surrounding it projected that energy as a beam of coherent photons. There was the snapping sound of air rushing in to fill the vacuum drilled through it by a weapon-grade laser. That laser left a sparkling trail of ionization which would have been visible even by daylight and which someone would surely have seen if it had flashed upward into the darkness. But it merely seared the ground, without searing her butt in the process. She clenched her teeth to hold in a cry of agony as the beam burned the flesh on the inside of her right wrist. Piled atop the throbbing pain of her battered head, it sent a wave of nausea through her. Then it all subsided a little and she gingerly tried her bonds. The laser hadn't burned away as much of the knot as she'd hoped, but after a little work the last strands parted and her hands came free. After she'd untied her feet she spared a moment to feel that fingertip, where the fortunately insensitive artificial skin had been burned away.

*Good thing I resisted the temptation to use the thing on my attackers—or later on the Interrogator,* she thought. It was strictly a one-shot capability; she would never have gotten out alive. She took a deep shuddering breath—that right wrist still hurt like all the devils of hell—then slipped away through the night.

No one was keeping watch over her, securely bound as they knew her to be. She avoided any still-wakeful Fomorians and was soon clear of the village. She didn't have her light-gathering contacts, but it was—wonder of wonders—a clear night over Britain, and a three-quarter moon was up. And the constellations weren't significantly different from those of the twenty-third century Earth she had come to know. She located Ursa Minor and set her course east.

The normal British overcast and drizzle reasserted themselves by morning. *I knew it was too good to last*, Tiraena thought in her fatigue-dulled and hunger-tormented brain as she continued toiling eastward in the dreary daylight.

She had spent the entire night putting as much distance as possible between herself and her erstwhile captors. Shortly before dawn she'd stumbled onto what this milieu was pleased to call a road. She had no idea which road it was, but it ran in a more or less east-west direction, and a map summoned up on her neural display showed all such roads in these parts converging on Chester. And it beat scrambling up and down the hills that comprised the local topography. She struggled on, trying not to let herself think about pain, or food.

By the time the cavalry column appeared to the east, she was almost beyond noticing it. Only when Peredur and Cynric were supporting her did she let herself collapse.

"So that's the story," Tiraena concluded. "It's the Interrogator, beyond a doubt. Raving mad, but still dangerous. Still capable of inflicting a lot of harm, in both timelines." Her face clouded as unwanted recollections thrust themselves upward from the storehouse of nightmares into her consciousness. "Remind me to give Tylar a piece of my mind about some of the shit he inflicts on people—primitives, yes, but still people—in the course of 'policing events.'"

"I'm also going to have a few things to take up with him," Sarnac said as he studied her face in the little holographically projected display screen that hovered in midair just above his communicator. He knew that expression, and it didn't occur to him even momentarily to doubt her. "Just before I left Rome he made some typically vague noises about 'disturbing rumors' you'd been hearing." He forced himself to defer that for later. "I never considered that *he'd* be here. But it makes sense; he escaped to Ireland before the divergence of the timelines."

"It did occur to me, once. But I dismissed it out of hand, thinking he couldn't possibly have lasted this long."

"Well, it's too late to worry about that. The important thing is that you're all right now. You are, aren't you?"

"Oh, yes. My first-aid kit took care of the laser burn, though of course I'm keeping the wrist bandaged—it has no business being healed so fast, from the local standpoint. I'm also keeping my left index finger bound up. With that little hole burned through it, the artificial skin *looks* artificial. And I'm over the exhaustion. The really important question is whether the local troops will hold when they see a Korvaasha coming at them."

"And when he gets in among them," Sarnac added grimly. The Korvaasha, evolutionary products of a high-gravity planet, were even stronger relative to humans than they were larger. The Interrogator might be getting along in years, but . . .

"I'll do what I can, of course," Tiraena said. "I'll explain to Gwenhwyvaer's troops that he isn't a demon or any other supernatural being, and that he isn't deathless. I don't have much time, though. This General Marcellus—a subordinate of your old friend Kai, isn't he?—has landed at Richborough and is advancing up the Thames valley. He's been sending couriers to the Fomorians, and we're sure we haven't succeeded in intercepting all of them. The raiders are starting to move south. They're light troops, with no discipline, but they could cause us trouble if they show up at our rear while we're engaged with the imperials."

"Yeah, yeah, right," Sarnac said, distracted. "Absolutely.

That makes it even more urgent for me to get in touch with Tylar."

"Tylar? Why?"

"To get you the hell out of Britain, that's why! It's going to get very dangerous there. So there's no point in you . . ."

"No!" Tiraena's tone stopped Sarnac in his rhetorical tracks. "I'm staying in Britain."

"*What?*" Sarnac took a deep breath. "Look, in case you've forgotten, your implanted skills don't include any fifth-century combat abilities. You're not supposed to be a soldier in this milieu! So what good do you think you can do when push comes to shove?"

"I don't know," she admitted. "But I can't help thinking that there must be *something* I can do, even though I'm not allowed to use any advanced technology. And as long as there's any possibility of that . . . Bob, I *need* to stay."

Sarnac hesitated before speaking, for he knew her well enough to know that this was nothing to be spoken of lightly. "Tiraena, I know you admire Gwenhwyvaer. And maybe you've started to take Tylar's system of trans-dimensional ethics seriously. But . . ."

"I couldn't care less about Tylar's umpteen-thousand-years-distant notions! And it's not just Gwenhwyvaer. It's all of them." She sought for the words with which to verbalize what was self-evident to her. "They're barely half a step above savagery. And they're laboring under more than their fair share of political stupidity. But if you could just be here and *know* them, Bob! And I'm not talking about the rulers, I'm talking about people like . . . oh, the two bodyguards Gwenhwyvaer has assigned to me. You'd like them, Bob: Peredur—he's one of the Artoriani; and Cynric, the son of Cerdic of the West Saxons."

"Oh, yeah, I remember. So he's the grandson of . . ." Sarnac belatedly recalled his promise to Tylar and cut himself off.

"What?"

"Never mind," Sarnac said hastily. But then he

remembered it was only Artorius that Tylar wanted kept in the dark. *Oh, what the hell?* He proceeded to tell Tiraena the truth of Cerdic's parentage.

"Oho!" she said softly when he was done. "This explains a lot about Gwenhwyvaer's feelings toward Cerdic. Typical of her, you know. Some women would hate Cerdic, in her position. But not Gwenhwyvaer. As Artorius' son, he's the closest thing to a son she'll ever have."

"You're probably right. And I understand what you're saying: these people deserve a break. Well, so do a lot of people throughout history. But you can't give it to them! You've done your part by passing on the advance information Tylar transmitted to you."

"That's just it: all I've done is pass information along! I need to *do* something!"

Sarnac tried to keep his tone reasonable. "But, Tiraena, in light of what's about to happen there . . . Tiraena, you could get *killed!*"

She grinned. "This, from a guy who was getting ready to go into battle against a Korvaash successor-state more advanced than the Realm of Tarzhgul?" There was dead silence while he sought for a reply.

"Well," he finally said, "that was my duty." *Come on!* he gibed at himself. *Is that the best you can do? If you really try, you can come up with something even more stilted!*

"This is *my* duty—to myself! And to these people. I know it's irrational to feel guilty for having been born into a better era than theirs. But I can't escape a sense of obligation to them. It's part of *me*, Bob, so it's part of whatever it is you love in me. I have to stick it out for the duration! Tylar may send his ship here, but I won't willingly go aboard. I'll stay as much in the thick of things as I can get, so Tylar won't be able to snatch me without tipping his technological hand!"

Their eyes held each other in silence, but it was a communion and not a confrontation. Then Sarnac smiled.

"Hey, if you need to do this, then do it. I'll tell Tylar not to try to pull you out until you're good and ready."

"Thanks, Bob," she said softly.

Sarnac's smile blossomed into his trademark raffish grin, and he was once again the young smart-ass she'd saved from the Korvaasha in the wilderness of Danu. "Hey, it's just the kind of guy I am!" She made a flatulent noise with her mouth. "Just promise me you'll stay in touch—and that you'll be careful."

"Aren't I always?" She signed off, her smile seeming to linger like the Cheshire cat's, before he could think of a retort.

*Well*, he thought as he deactivated the communicator and the intruder alarm he was careful to employ whenever he was using anachronistic equipment in his tent, *hopefully that little turn of the good-ole-Bob routine was what she needed right now. Too bad it's all bullshit.* But he'd done rightly, he decided. He wouldn't burden her with the knowledge that he was worried sick about her, separated from savages only by troops who'd probably bolt like scared rabbits when they saw the Interrogator. *No, there's no point in undermining her morale.* A sudden flash of self-pity: *Wish somebody'd do something for* my *morale!*

He shook free of the thought as he left the tent and strolled toward the field where the crossbowmen were honing their tactics under Ecdicius' eye. The new Western Emperor noticed him and waved.

"Ah, Bedwyr, I think these farm boys are beginning to get the point of your idea—or at least starting to follow orders with a snap! For whatever reason, we're getting off half again as many flights of quarrels each minute as we were when we first tried your idea."

"Good!" In response to their call they'd gotten more hunting crossbows, and men who knew how to use them, than they needed or could effectively use. The problem, as Ecdicius had instantly seen, was the things' slow rate of fire. He'd also seen the possibilities in Sarnac's third-hand idea, and had issued a call for the strongest men in the army. (That point had been emphasized, for it lent prestige to an unglamorous job.) They had become loaders, staying behind the fighting line and constantly cocking the surplus crossbows, which were then passed on to the crossbowmen by relays of boys who brought the discharged weapons back to be readied again.

In the armies of China's Warring States, Artorius had told him, the loaders had lain on their backs, braced both feet against the back of the bow with one on each side of the stock, and pulled the string down toward the chest with both hands while straightening the legs. That wasn't absolutely necessary with these crossbows, which weren't as stiff as the Chinese originals had been. But experiments had shown it to be the fastest loading technique, so Ecdicius had rammed it through past all the obstacles outraged conservatism could erect.

Of course, it made for an immobile formation. Artorius had expounded from historical knowledge that now extended far beyond his old horizons. "There's an ongoing debate," he'd told Sarnac over wine one night in Rome. "What would have happened if Alexander the Great had advanced eastward to China? One school of thought holds that he wouldn't have stood a chance against the armies of the Warring States, with their massed crossbows that could have made colanders of Macedonian shields. I disagree, partly because he would have had no trouble finding local allies—those warlords were incapable of uniting against a common threat, which was why Shih Huang-Ti conquered them all in the end. But there's a strictly military reason as well. You see, all that firepower was locked into rigid, inflexible formations. The only really mobile troops were the cavalry, who were just scouts and skirmishers; they had nothing like Alexander's Companions, who were the closest thing to heavy shock cavalry before stirrups. I have a theory about that: in the West, the cavalry has always been the prestige arm, through which the aristocracy displayed its prowess, while Chinese cavalry were just . . . just . . ."

"Grunts on horses," Sarnac had suggested.

"Precisely. If anything, the cavalry was socially tainted by the barbarian origins of its equipment, techniques and, frequently, personnel. So while an army of the Warring States could have slaughtered the Macedonian phalanx if Alexander had been obliging enough to march it up in front of them, they wouldn't have known how to respond if the Companions had hit them from an unexpected direction."

"That doesn't sound too good for our side, does it? Kai's going to be able to send the Artoriani against us."

"It means that high-density crossbow fire is probably going to work for you only once," Artorius had allowed. "After that, Kai will know how to deal with it. You and Ecdicius are going to have to bring him to a single decisive battle under optimum conditions for a defensive action."

They had tried, even before Ecdicius had thought they were really ready, for they'd heard news of what the invaders were inflicting on east-central Gaul as they advanced west along the Roman road from Strasbourg to Toul, things that sounded nothing like the Kai Sarnac remembered. Finally, Ecdicius had found what he considered the ideal site to give battle—the gap in the Val d'Ane hills west of Toul—and Kai had neatly maneuvered them out of position. It was a typically cautious duel of generals who knew each other, with the main armies moving warily behind screens of scouting, skirmishing light cavalry. Still, Kai's hesitancy was beyond what might have been expected, given that he commanded the clearly superior force. Sarnac had wondered about it out loud via communicator, and Artorius had explained: the Briton led unenthusiastic troops. Kai had been able to hold their allegiance for Wilhelmus, but he couldn't infuse them with a fanatical loyalty to the *faux* emperor which he doubtless didn't feel himself.

So the cat-and-mouse game went on. Ecdicius wasn't

entirely displeased; at least the invaders weren't advancing any further into Gaul, and he had more time to polish his new crossbow tactics. In fact, Sarnac was surprised he was adapting so well to a war so different from his swashbuckling norm. But sometimes, when his officers and allies weren't around, he could be seen pacing like a caged lion.

Now he turned from the crossbow practice and started to speak to Sarnac, only to stop a frown. "What is it, Bedwyr? You seem distracted."

*God, am I concealing it* that *badly?* "Oh, I'm just worried about my wife in Britain, Augustus. After all, not knowing what's going on there . . ." He *couldn't* know it, not officially, in this world whose messages moved at the speed of a horseman rather than that of light.

"Yes, you told me about your wife. Attached to Gwenhwyvaer's court, isn't she? I know you must be worried. Thank God Faustina's in Rome." Ecdicius' face clouded. "Not that Rome's safety is certain. The latest word is that the Balkan armies have finally gotten moving and are advancing on Aquileia."

*And have taken it,* Sarnac didn't say, for it was something else he had no business knowing. He'd learned only last night that the important city at the head of the Adriatic, only just recovering from its sack by Attila forty years earlier, had fallen. Now an invasion of Italy was imminent, and Tylar and Artorius were preparing to head north from Rome to do what they could.

"Yes, I almost wish Faustina were here," Ecdicius continued. "Nowhere is safe, and I'd have her with me. But of course the children need her in Rome."

"At least, Augustus, you have Julia here where you can keep an eye on her." Sarnac couldn't resist remarking.

"Yes, I certainly do! The young vixen!" Ecdicius' daughter had managed to find some logically irrefutable objection to every villa and town they'd passed through, and was still travelling with them. Now, with Kai's light horsemen roving far and wide, there was no alternative but to keep her with the army, which had adopted her as a mascot anyway. But Ecdicius' scowl was still comical.

"I'm sure she'll be safe, Augustus," Sarnac assured him. "Andronicus will guard her well." Which, he reflected, was an understatement.

"Yes . . . Andronicus." Ecdicius' expression softened. "A fine young man. Although there's something about him—something that makes him hard to place as to his origins. Like you, Bedwyr." The last was spoken casually, but the dark eyes grew disconcertingly shrewd.

Alarm bells went off in Sarnac. Ecdicius had been content to accept the mysterious origins of Tylar and Artorius. But in keeping with Tylar's rule of keeping mystery to a minimum, Sarnac and Andreas had stuck to their original cover stories, and Ecdicius had seemed to accept those too. "Why, he's from Bithynia, Augustus. . . ."

". . . and you're from Armorica. Yes, I know. But there's something I can't quite put my finger on. . . . Still, far be it from me to pry, Bedwyr!" He clapped Sarnac on the shoulder and dazzled him with a grin. "If, for your own reasons or Tertullian's, you need to pose as a simple mercenary, then so be it. And now, I've got to go iron out some dispute between the Frankish and Burgundian troops." And he was off, leaving Sarnac thinking: *That's two.*

# CHAPTER FOURTEEN

A stiff west wind, chilly with advancing autumn, was blowing in off the Bristol Channel, and the torch-flames whipped and spat showers of sparks as Gwenhwyvaer looked out over the massed troops. The torchlight melted away the ravages of fifty-six winters and ignited the last remaining embers of flame in her hair, and it was Boadicea who stood before them, it was Bellona the goddess of horses and war.

The priests had blessed them earlier for the morrow's battle, but there was nothing Christian about this night's scene. No cross loomed behind Gwenhwyvaer and her captains; the blood-red dragon standard of Artorius streamed in the wind beneath the stars, and his widow spoke words fit to summon up the elemental spirits of the land.

Tiraena, standing inconspicuously off to one side, knew where some of those words had come from.

*". . . I do not desire to live to distrust my faithful and loving people. Let tyrants fear! . . . I am come amongst you . . . being resolved, in the midst and heat of battle, to live or die amongst you all, and to lay down for my God and for my people, my honor and my blood, even in the dust. I know I have the body of a weak and feeble woman, but I*

*have the heart and stomach of a king, and of a*
*king of Britain too, and think foul scorn that*
*Wilhelmus or Balor or any emperor or monster*
*should dare to invade the borders of my realm. . . ."*

Tiraena grinned inside the hood of her cloak. *Now where
have I heard* that *before? Eat your heart out, Queen Bess!*
*Good selection on Tylar's part. This country's always
seemed to do best under female rulers: Elizabeth I,
Victoria, Margaret Thatcher . . .* She became aware that
Gwenhwyvaer was telling them of . . .

*". . . this happy breed of men, this little world,*
*this precious stone set in the silver sea. . . . This*
*blessed plot, this earth, this realm, this Britain. . . ."*

Shakespeare, of course. No surprise, knowing Tylar. *What
next?* Tiraena wondered. *"We will fight them on the
beaches" isn't exactly appropriate; it's a little late for that.*
But Gwenhwyvaer managed to speak of their finest hour
before the cheering of the troops grew too thunderous for
her to be heard.

The wind was unabated at midmorning, and had begun
to bring clouds scudding in off the Atlantic, sending waves
of shadow sweeping across the hillsides of this rolling
country near the source of the Thames.

Standing atop the highest hill in the neighborhood and
facing eastward toward the dark, distant masses of the
imperial army, Tiraena gazed down to her right into the
gap where the Saxons waited, their flanks secured by hills
where light-armed archers and slingers waited among
the trees. The valley to the east was like a funnel down
which the invaders would pour, to meet the shield-wall.
It must hold until the time was right to commit the cavalry
that waited in the shelter of the hill, to Tiraena's left.

And there, thought Tiraena with her newly stimulated
recollections of Shakespeare, was the rub. Cerdic, who

led the shield-wall, and Constantine, who would command the cavalry, were no more able to agree on when the time would be right than they were on anything else.

"Will you wait, then, until all my carles are dead before beginning your charge?" Cerdic demanded.

"The entire main body of the enemy must be locked in battle with you before the cavalry circles the hill and takes them in the rear. Otherwise, our plan's for nought. Are you Saxons too cowardly to uphold your part of it?" *The hell of it is,* Tiraena reflected, *Constantine is right. Too bad he has to be such a gigantic prick about it.*

Cerdic's glare smoothed itself out into a mocking grin. "Who was given the pass to hold while your infantry take their ease behind?" He swept an arm out toward their rear, where beyond a defile at the base of this hill a ridge line curved away to the southwest. The Briton foot lined that ridge facing north, against the possible appearance of the Fomorians from that direction. Outriders had brought word of their advance, and the terror that spread before it.

Constantine flushed. "It's important that our rear be secured, lest we be caught between two foes."

"Aye, your footmen should be able to deal with naked Irish savages well enough," Cerdic taunted. Tension didn't bring out the best in him. "But have a care who you call cowards, Welshman!"

Constantine's flush grew scarlet and his hand dropped to the hilt of his *spatha.* The Britons didn't like that word, and Tiraena could see their point. It was pretty raw, being called by the Saxon word for "foreigner" in your own country.

"For that, Saxon half-breed, I'll see the color of your guts . . ."

"Have done!" Gwenhwyvaer stepped between them. "Will you madmen fall to fighting among yourselves within sight of the enemy? I forbid all personal quarrels until the battle is over. And *I* will give the signal for the cavalry to charge."

"Very well, Lady." Constantine mounted his horse. "But we'll take this up later, Saxon!" He descended the hill to put himself at the head of the cavalry that waited in its shadow to the north.

"That we will," Cerdic called after him. He looked at Cynric, where the latter stood guard with Peredur behind Tiraena, and gave a quick wink. Then he trotted off down the southern slope to join his men, who cheered him—he'd given them their own dose of edited Shakespeare last night.

"Sweet Jesu!" Gwenhwyvaer fumed to Tiraena. "Why do the imperials even bother invading this island? Why don't they just sit back and watch us kill each other off?"

They grew silent as the enemy advanced in an ominous silence. That army included few heavy cavalry; they'd been deemed unnecessary, for Britain held only a small detachment of the Artoriani, whose main body was stationed in Germania whence Kai had now led them into Gaul. (*Where Bob will be facing them,* Tiraena ordered herself not to remember.) But this was a formidable force, the center composed of heavy infantry—Isaurians from Asia Minor for the most part, but also including many of the Franks that Kai didn't want in Gaul for the same reason he hadn't sent Britons here to face their own countrymen. On the flanks, light cavalry backed up the light-armed infantry. Behind the center were those *cataphractarii* Marcellus had.

They came on with contemptuous directness—Marcellus had encountered little resistance so far except harrying by militia, and he might well be suffering from overconfidence by now. But this was no blundering onrush. As they reached the "neck" of the "funnel" the flanking elements began to advance up the hill slopes, skirmishing with the Britons whose arrows had begun to sprinkle the imperial formations. The center continued to advance and with a blare of trumpets, hurled itself forward.

Tirana imagined she could feel an earth-tremor as the

first enemy wave crashed into the shield-wall. A hellish din, compounded of shouts, screams, weapon-impacts and shield-bosses grinding together, assaulted her. After an eternal interval, the enemy drew back, a retreating tide that left a wrack of corpses. The Saxons adjusted their line to fill the gaps left by their own dead. They hadn't given an inch.

The imperials regrouped, and Tiraena could see a coming and going of couriers. A new attack wave, more massive than the first, formed itself and advanced with seemingly unstoppable momentum. Again, the contact of the fighting-fronts was like a palpable blow even where Tiraena stood, looking down from above the pain and blood. Surely, it seemed, the narrow steel band of the shield-wall must snap under the sheer weight of men bearing down on it and the impact of swords and axes that beat on it like blacksmith's hammers. She could sense Cynric fidgeting behind her— his father was fighting in the front line as tradition demanded—but he made no sound.

Finally, incredibly, the attack drew back over ground made treacherous by the heaped dead. The Saxons, their line thinner now, stood in what wasn't really silence— there were too many wounded for that—but seemed like it after the abrupt cessation of the hideous cacophony that had gone before. They stood exactly where they had stood before, waiting. And all at once Tiraena knew, beyond any possibility of doubt, that if the day went against them there would be an unbroken shield-wall of the dead down there. They could be killed, but they could not be moved.

*I've heard the Saxons called dull,* she thought in her awe. *Maybe it's true. That much sheer guts can't possibly leave room for much else.*

"I can't give the signal yet," Gwenhwyvaer said to no one in particular. She had mounted her horse, the better to be seen by those below, and they had all followed suit. Now she sat in her saddle looking like a knife was twisting in her guts. "Marcellus is still holding his heavy cavalry in reserve. They'd be able to counter our own cavalry." Tiraena looked down the hill to the north where the British cavalry waited, the red cloaks of the Artoriani vivid among the tribal contingents. The riders' impatience was infecting the horses, she could see even from here. But Gwenhwyvaer was right.

She swept her eyes over the rest of the field. The imperial flanks had gotten bogged down in disorganized fighting on the wooded slopes. And within their main body, something was happening.

Then, with a new note of trumpets, the imperial *cataphractarii* moved forward in all their armored ponderousness, and the infantry parted ranks to let them pass. Tiraena turned toward Gwenhwyvaer and started to open her mouth, but what she saw closed it. The queen was staring fixedly ahead, as though in communion with the ebb and flow of battle, awaiting some certain knowledge that the moment had come.

The imperial cavalry built up to a charge and Tiraena silently pleaded with her to give the word. But her expression remained unchanged even as the armored riders smashed into the shield wall with a force that caused it to buckle, though not to break. Evidently someone thought it *had* broken, for a shout arose from the enemy infantry and they advanced to support the shock cavalry.

At that instant, Gwenhwyvaer sprang from her motionlessness and flung up an arm. The trumpeters blared out the signal, and in the hidden area behind the hill to their left, a horse and rider—Tiraena was sure it was Constantine—sprang forward. The entire cavalry formation followed as one, riding like the Wild Hunt.

They had a goodly way to go—any further would have tired the horses too much at such a gallop—as they rounded the hill. If the shield-wall could only hold until they appeared in the rear of the now fully engaged imperials, the enemy would be caught between the Saxon anvil and the Briton hammer. . . .

It was at that moment that the west wind brought to their ears the weird war-cries of the Fomorians.

Tiraena twisted around in her saddle just in time to see the tribesmen appear at the crest of a lower ridge just to the northwest of the one topped by the British infantry line. It was too distant to make out details of the figures, but there was no mistaking the gigantic one in their midst.

In growing horror, she watched the British line begin to waver. Never mind what the mysterious wise-woman Lucasta had told them; they knew the supernatural when they saw it. A few men began to run, and it was like the first few drops of leaking water that presage the full torrent into the hold of a doomed ship, for more and more of their comrades joined them, then the whole line dissolved in panic.

*Oh, God, it's the worst possible time. If the Fomorians hit the shield-wall from the rear while the situation is still fluid. . . .* Without a word and without further thought, Tiraena turned her horse around and plunged down the hill's western slope.

"Lucasta, wait!" Gwenhwyvaer's dwindling voice didn't register on her, for her entire consciousness had narrowed to the task of controlling her horse's wild career down the steep slope. She belatedly remembered that her implanted riding skills were only minimal, and supplemented by actual practice in only her last few subjective months, as she descended the hill at breakneck speed. *Well,* she found a fraction of a second to think, *I finally know what that expression means. Breaking my neck is exactly what I'm going to do!* Then she was in the defile, forcing her mount to scramble up the ridge. Soon she was among the fleeing troops.

"Stand, damn you!" she shouted as she rode among them. The British tongue was another subject on which she'd worked at improving "Lucasta's" minimal knowledge, and few of these men understood Latin. "He's mortal, I tell you! He can be killed!"

"Listen to her, you cowardly sods!" She heard Peredur's voice behind her and stole a glance over her shoulder. Yes, he and Cynric had followed her. He rode among the milling foot troops, beating at them with the flat of his *spatha*. "By God, do you need a woman to take you by the hands and lead you into battle? Well, here she is! Maybe she'll wipe your bottoms for you too!" An angry growling arose, but the rout slowed. "Get back up to the crest of the ridge before the Irish gain it!"

*Good thought,* Tiraena realized. "Follow me," she yelled, and urged her horse up the slope. She saw that Cynric was with her. Yes, there it was just ahead, the top of the ridge . . .

They reached it just in time to come face to face with the Interrogator.

Their horses reared uncontrollably, shrieking with panic at the sight and smell, and threw them. Tiraena managed a rolling landing that absorbed most of the impact. She shook her head violently to clear it and raised herself to a crouch. The Fomorians were scrambling up to the ridgeline, and the Interrogator was advancing toward her. He carried the great club she'd heard about in one hand; the other held a sword that must have been specially made for four mutually opposable digits, and was far too long and heavy for a human to wield anyway. It couldn't be any good, forged as it was from the low-grade iron available in Ireland. But that didn't help her much, for she had no weapons, nor any implanted skill at using them if she had.

A Saxon war-cry rang out, and Cynric rushed past her and interposed himself between her and her attacker, holding aloft his shield and brandishing the *spatha* he used in lieu of his own people's traditional weapons when on horseback. He shouted his defiance again, and the adolescent voice quavered and broke.

With a force beyond that of human muscles, the Interrogator brought his club down. Cynric screamed and went to one knee as his iron-reinforced wooden shield, and the arm holding it, shattered. Then the Korvaasha thrust with his sword at the youth's midriff. The Saxon ring-mail was surprisingly good, but the power behind that thrust sent the crude iron sword crashing through the rings. Cynric screamed again with the torment of a pierced liver and dropped his *spatha*. The Interrogator pulled his sword free and raised it for a final slash.

Tiraena was on her feet, moving through a world of horror. "No!" She shouted in Standard International English. "I'm the one you want, you Korvaash bastard!"

Because she had spoken words his translator could handle, he heard her. He redirected his sword as it descended, slewing it toward her. It sliced through the flesh and muscle of her right thigh. The leg gave way under her and she crashed to the ground and rolled a few paces. Looking up through a crimson haze of agony, she saw the Interrogator advancing ponderously toward her. Idiotically, her foremost thought was: *Bob will be so worried . . .*

There was a whinny and a shout, and Peredur, keeping his charging mount under control with the horsemanship for which the Artoriani were renowned, sideswiped the Interrogator and sent the Korvaasha staggering. The Briton brought his horse around and hauled on the reins, bringing the animal rearing up. The flailing hooves momentarily held the massive alien at bay. Then Peredur brought his *spatha* down. The Interrogator parried with his own sword and, with a metallic crack, the brittle iron gave way and the blade snapped. But then the Korvaasha thrust his club at the horse's exposed belly. Off-balance, the animal went over, crushing Peredur's left leg. The Interrogator stood over the immobile Briton and pointed the remaining length of his broken sword downward. With the full mountainous weight of a Korvaasha behind it, it punched through the scale armor and the Briton's chest. There was an obscene amount of blood.

Yet even at that moment, Peredur brought up the *spatha* he'd somehow kept in his grip. The thrust lacked the force to pierce that thick hard integument, but it slid along a leg, bringing the distinctive Korvaash blood—like human blood mixed with clear syrup—welling up.

The Interrogator made no audible sound, of course, but he was less than steady as he turned from the lifeless Briton and advanced on Tiraena, gripping his club in both hands.

Tiraena felt something hard against the tips of her fingers. It was the hilt of the *spatha* Cynric had dropped. Her grip closed around it, and she struggled to her feet. The transcendent pain that started in her right thigh and flooded her entire being seemed to burn away some impediment to clarity, for all at once reality consisted of the tormented face of an impaled little girl. But then the girl's blue eyes turned dark, the skin shaded from pale to coppery, the features shifted, and it was a little Raehaniv girl who stood terrified in a dimly lit place of horror created by the Korvaasha, a little girl who also bore the name Tiraena.

The moment ended—it had lasted no more than a millisecond. Tiraena felt no pain anymore, only a calm certainty that she was about to do that for which she had been born. As though in slow motion, the Interrogator swung his club in a stroke that would have taken off her head. She dodged the blow with an unreal ease and grasped her sword in both hands—the *spatha* wasn't intended for it, but it could be done. She rotated almost a full three hundred and sixty degrees as she brought the blade around in a perfect drawing cut, into what would have been the belly of a human.

Tiraena already knew that the Korvaasha could, with difficulty, produce a sound in the human auditory range. An extremely high-pitched Korvaash scream sounded like a distant foghorn. The Interrogator emitted a *loud* foghorn sound as he doubled over. Recovering, Tiraena brought the *spatha* down on the long neck, where the hide wasn't quite so thick.

No human strength—not even Tiraena's as it was at

this moment—could have actually severed the neck with one of this era's blades. But the Interrogator's head flopped grotesquely and the unpleasant-looking Korvaash blood fountained forth as he sank to the ground.

Tiraena collapsed with a gasp of returning pain. Funny, she thought: she hadn't noticed that a wide circle of spectators had formed around this combat, half Briton and half Fomorian, all of them now standing with their mouths hanging comically open. Then the tableau broke as the Fomorian half of the circle disintegrated, fleeing with howls of panic. The Britons followed in pursuit, striking at their country's invaders as they could not strike at their own shame. Tiraena was left alone with the dead and dying.

She tore a strip of cloth from a sleeve and used it to bind her wounded thigh. Then, using her left leg and both arms, she dragged herself painfully over to Cynric. He was breathing but unconscious; she could do nothing for him but stanch the flow of blood with a wad of cloth. Finally, she made her way to the place where Peredur lay pinned to the ground by the Interrogator's broken sword, staring sightlessly at the sky. She reached out and closed his eyes.

*Was it you, Peredur?* she wondered. *Were you the Peredur who, in my reality, made the name of Sir Percival a byword for all that's best in men? I think it must have been you. And I hope you found your Grail.*

Time passed and the distant voice of battle gradually diminished. Then she heard a clatter of hooves and looked up at Gwenhwyvaer and her attendants. The expression on the queen's face told her all she needed to know, but she asked anyway. "The battle . . . ?"

"Yes. Constantine struck at just the right instant, and Cerdic's Saxons held. The imperials were crammed together so tightly they couldn't even use their weapons. It was a butchery. We couldn't pen them all in, of course, but the survivors are no longer an army. Our militia can harry them back down the Thames." Even as she told the tale, Gwenhwyvaer's eyes kept shifting to the carcass of the

Interrogator, and several of the attendants crossed themselves as their horses shied nervously away.

"I suppose we should bury it . . ." someone began.

Tiraena stood up, heedless of pain. "No! You don't want him anywhere in your food chain!" She saw their puzzled expressions and forced herself to concentrate long enough to speak words they'd understand.

"Burn him! This earth was never meant to bear his weight. Burn him! And beg your God's forgiveness as the smoke of that burning rises into His sky!"

It was all she had left in her. She collapsed into unconsciousness. A heartbeat of dead silence passed before men started running in search of firewood.

Tiraena lay in the torchlight beside Cynric, who they'd carried back to the camp with her even though his wound was clearly mortal. Cerdic stood looking down at his son, tears making runnels in the blood and grime that caked his face. Cynric was no child, but a man according to his people's lights, and therefore a fit subject for mourning.

Gwenhwyvaer stood nearby, looking at Cerdic and his son with an expression Tiraena now understood. For her own part, she was waiting for an opportunity to pop one of the little pills in the pouch at her waist. Her wound would heal anyway, but there was no reason not to speed things along.

A horse approached, and its rider dismounted. Cerdic turned and glared at him. "Well, Constantine ap Cador, here I am, and the battle's over. Have what you will of me!"

Gwenhwyvaer seemed ready to intervene, but Constantine shook his head and looked at Cynric, who lay alternately sleeping and awakening into agony. "No, Cerdic. There's not a man alive I'd seek a quarrel with at such a time. And besides . . ." He hesitated, then continued with the awkwardness of a man saying something very difficult. "I saw the line of piled Saxon corpses that marks where the shield-wall stood." They'd all seen it from atop the hill before the sun had set, and Tiraena had thought of redcoats lying dead in square on the field of Waterloo.

"Spilled Saxon blood should be no novelty to you," Cerdic said, unmoved. "You Britons have spilled it in plenty."

"Aye, when you came as ravagers of these shores. But this day's Saxon blood was shed in defense of this land, and your dead will be buried in the soil they died guarding. So whatever has gone before, for good or ill, your people are part of Britain and it's part of you, from now until the ending of the world." And he extended his hand.

*He still wouldn't want his sister to marry one,* Tiraena knew. *But it's a start—a start!*

Cerdic met Constantine's eyes, and looked at the extended hand. Then he took it, in the Roman fashion. Gwenhwyvaer smiled, and laid a hand atop the clasped forearms.

The two men departed to see to their respective followers. But Gwenhwyvaer remained, and turned to Tiraena with a smile. "Well, Lucasta, what are the bards going to do with you? How are they going to deal with the fact, witnessed by so many, that it was a woman—and a foreign woman at that—who slew the monster?"

*I imagine,* Tiraena thought, *that hero-tales are going to have to accommodate a little more variety in this timeline. Good.* She started to say something about it, but Gwenhwyvaer was gazing down at Cynric, now mercifully unconscious, with an expression that would have puzzled Tiraena once. Then she looked up with a bitter little smile. "Ah, Cerdic," she whispered. "I think I can understand how it is—how it must be for those who can have children!"

*So that still rankles.* Aloud, Tiraena addressed the queen in British rather than their customary Latin. "Leave all thoughts of barrenness, Lady. For it's in my heart that you've given birth to a nation!"

Gwehwyvaer gazed at her for a time before replying in the same tongue. "Oh, a nation's been born, right enough. God knows there's been sufficient pain and blood this day for the birth of a giant! But . . ." Her voice dropped to a near-whisper. "But it wasn't I who gave it life. It created itself. At most, I'm the foster-mother."

She seemed about to say more, but men started arriving, asking questions and needing decisions made. A final quick smile for Tiraena, and Gwenhwyvaer was off to tend her infant titan.

Alone for the moment, Tiraena slipped one of the little pills out of her pouch and swallowed. She'd just washed it down with wine from the jug that had been left beside her when Flavian, the only surgeon for this army of thousands, arrived from his rounds. He gave Tiraena a smile which vanished when he looked at Cynric.

"There's no hope, is there?" she asked, unnecessarily.

"No." The fine-boned face, clearly more Roman than Celtic, wore an expression compounded of exhaustion and despair. "The liver is pierced. He'll die before morning. I can do nothing for him." His features stiffened with bitterness, and he swept his arm out over the whole camp with its moaning rows of the wounded. "I can do nothing for any of them except try to ease their pain. I can't stop them from dying, because while we know well enough what death and sickness look like we don't really know *why* a man is alive one moment and dead the next. We know nothing. Nothing!" He clenched his fists in helpless fury, for he took all the suffering and death in the world as a personal affront.

*Why aren't all doctors like this one?* Tiraena asked the God in whom she did not believe. *And why doesn't this one have the tools and knowledge he needs?* The universe gave no answer, but she hadn't really expected one.

Flavian departed to fight and lose yet another battle in his hopeless personal war, and Tiraena looked at Cynric where he lay beside her. He was awake again, and moaning softly. As she studied his profile—yes, there was some of his grandfather there if you knew what to look for—

Tylar's words played themselves over and over in her head. *"All obvious manifestations of advanced science and technology must be kept hidden from the inhabitants of this milieu, lest the culture's future intellectual development be distorted. It is all for the greater long-range good. . . ."*

She became aware that her hand, as though actuated by a will of its own, was fumbling in the pouch, withdrawing one of the recovery-stimulating pills. She turned to Cynric and spoke urgently, for soon sleep would take her.

"Cynric!"

The youth turned his head and recognized her. "Yes, Lady?"

"Cynric, I want you to do something for me." She took the hand of his good arm and pressed the pill into it. "I want you to swallow this."

"Swallow it?" Cynric stared dubiously at the tiny ovoid, so disconcertingly unnatural, made from no substance he'd ever seen. "Why, Lady?"

"Never mind," Tiraena said, fighting off the oncoming waves of sleep. "Just do it."

"Er . . . can't I just *hold* it?"

Tiraena took a deep breath. "Cynric, you must trust me. This is a very sacred object, blessed by a holy man in—" her mind flew back to one of the twentieth-century flat movies for which Bob had a perverse fondness "—Antioch. Its virtue is that it cures seemingly mortal wounds. But you must take it into your body, like . . . like the Holy Communion. Will you do it for me, Cynric?"

The blue eyes took on an expression that sent a realization of her own unworthiness washing over her like a wave. "For you, Lady," he breathed. Then he crossed himself and popped the pill into his mouth.

She poured a swallow of wine into him, and he lay back with a smile. Sleep came almost immediately, and his features relaxed into those of the boy he still was. She made absolutely certain he was unconscious before reaching out and tousling the blond hair.

Flavian returned and saw that Cynric was motionless. "Is he . . . ?"

"No." Though rapidly drifting off, Tiraena managed a head-shake. "He's going to be all right."

"*What?* No, Lady. It's not possible."

"Flavian, believe me. I've had a . . . a vision. Just keep an eye on him. He's gone into a deep, healing sleep that will last a long time. When he awakes, give him all the food he wants, because he'll be . . . very hungry. So will I." She roused herself for a final sentence. "And tell Cerdic . . . I think he'll want to know. . . ." She slid into a semiconscious state where speech was impossible.

The surgeon leaned over and examined Cynric. Yes, the lad was breathing—and breathing deeply and regularly! He was sleeping peacefully, and his color actually seemed to be better.

Flavian stood up and gazed at the woman Lucasta, now sinking rapidly into a deep sleep of her own, and his flesh prickled. She had a Power in her that was beyond his understanding, beyond even his desire to understand. But it could not be a thing of evil. What, he wondered, could be the thoughts behind that serene, almost beatific smile her face wore?

*Fuck you, Tylar,* she thought just before letting sleep take her.

# CHAPTER FIFTEEN

"Tylar, what the hell's *happening*? I need to know!"

"Compose yourself." In Sarnac's ghostly holo display screen, the time traveler's visage was as infuriatingly calm as ever. "I also have been unable to make contact with Tiraena. This may mean simply that she is presently unable to access her long-range communicator, which, in turn, could have any of a number of relatively benign explanations—"

The tent-flap flew open, revealing Andreas in full battle array save for the helmet he still held in the crook of his left arm. "Come on, Bob! Things are moving!"

"All right, all right! I'll be along!" He instantly regretted snapping at Andreas, but he had to find out whatever Tylar knew. The young transtemporal voyager seemed to understand.

"I'll tell Ecdicius something or other, Bob. But hurry!" And Andreas was gone, plunging back into the turmoil of the camp.

"Look, Tylar, I haven't got much time, so cut the crap! What do you know about Tiraena's status?"

"I was just coming to that, my dear fellow. Finding myself unable to contact her, I investigated the state of affairs in Britain using surveillance satellites."

"Huh? What surveillance satellites?"

"Sentient devices the ship deployed into orbit as we approached, as a matter of routine procedure. Didn't I mention them? At any rate, you can set your mind at rest. The crisis is past in Britain. The invasion has been broken, and the Interrogator is dead."

"Thank God for that," Sarnac breathed.

"Dead by Tiraena's own hand, no less! Of course, she sustained some damage in the process—"

"*What?!*"

"Calm yourself! She's in no danger. But she's still recovering with the aid of the field pharmacopeia I supplied to you both. So she's been in no position to initiate long-range communications. And now" —he glanced over his shoulder at something unseen— "I must go. Matters are coming to a head here."

*Here,* Sarnac knew, meant the marshes shielding Ravenna, and he abruptly felt guilty for keeping Tylar distracted so long from the task of blocking the Eastern armies that sought to penetrate to the city. "Uh, yeah, of course. Good luck to you and Artorius."

"I'll convey your message to him when I see him again, but he's rather heavily engaged just now." Tylar paused before signing off. "Oh, yes, I almost forgot. Be sure to keep your long-range communicator in your possession at all times."

Sarnac looked skeptically at the oblong device that fit into a custom-made pouch of authentic local leather. Carrying it would be a nuisance, but it could be done.

"Well . . ." he began.

"Splendid. Remember, it's very important." And Tylar's image vanished.

Sarnac was already outfitted. He wore a scale-armor hauberk because it was expected; he couldn't get away with going into battle in what appeared to be mere quilted cloth as he had in the good old days. Too bad—the hauberk blocked the impact armor's microscopic sensors, leaving his "cloth"-clad arms and legs considerably better protected than his torso. He attached the communicator's leather carrying case—not unlike a Civil War era cartridge box—to his belt. Then he put on his cavalry helmet and joined the cheek-pieces under his chin, and stepped out into the campground. It was an unseasonably warm day for late autumn, but blustery with the promise of rain-squalls later. He paused to take in the panoramic view of what was to be today's battlefield.

Kai had finally forced a break in the deadlock. He'd struck out boldly, advancing westward from Toul, ignoring the road system and using his superb engineering corps to ford the upper reaches of the Marne and the Aube. He'd never read Sun Tzu, but he understood instinctively the way to force engagement: "When I wish to give battle, my enemy . . . cannot help but engage me, for I attack a position he must succor." Toul had been expendable; the vital road-hub of Troyes was not.

Ecdicius had countermarched at a pace that had almost driven his army beyond endurance. But now they lay interposed between Kai and Troyes. It wasn't a defensive position Ecdicius would have preferred; this low plateau where the fortified camp lay should have anchored their left flank, but thanks to Kai's preliminary maneuvering it must hold their center. In front of Sarnac, a line of spearmen faced the dauntingly massive formation of Kai's infantry center to the northeast, beyond which rose the hill—the highest one hereabouts—where the enemy command center lay. Behind the spearmen, and a little above them on the slope to shoot over their heads, were the crossbowmen on whom so much had been staked.

To the left, where the plateau was lower, was a line of relatively light-armed local cavalry levies led by Basileus. Opposite them was a large enemy cavalry formation, behind which could be seen the array of red cloaks that marked the Artoriani. To the right, below a shoulder of the plateau, Ecdicius led the pick of his cavalry: heavy *cataphractarii*, including most of his old Brotherhood from the Visigothic wars and many of their sons. They confronted a formidable infantry formation in defensive posture.

The dangers in having the commander-in-chief on the lower ground to the right where he couldn't oversee the battle were obvious even in this era, with its rudimentary notions of command-and-control. But Ecdicius could see no alternative; he must lead the heavy cavalry in person, in an effort to break through and create the kind of fluid battle he liked.

Hopefully, the two advisers "Tertullian" had lent him would be able to help in that area. . . .

"Are you receiving?" Sarnac subvocalized.

"Loud and clear," Andreas replied from his position with the right wing. "Ecdicius is still wondering why you requested to be assigned to the left wing rather than with him and the heavy cavalry."

Sarnac mounted up. He readjusted the communicator on his belt so it wouldn't dig into his ribs and cursed Tylar mechanically. "But he bought my explanation that I could do the most good where the Artoriani are going to hit us, didn't he?"

"Oh, yes. He could see the sense in it. And he was obviously impressed by your guts."

"Nice to be appreciated." Sarnac rode toward the left, down to the lower ground. Here, it wasn't really a plateau, just a rise. Still, what little slope there was to the northeast would be in their favor. The bad news was that they couldn't just let momentum carry them downhill, lest a gap open between them and the infantry center on the bluffs to their right.

"Ho, Bedwyr!" Basileus greeted him. "What kept you?"

"I was . . . praying for my wife in Britain."

"Ah, of course. But don't worry—I'm sure she's fine." Suddenly, a noise of trumpets from the imperial formation cut short the veteran's attempts at encouragement.

"They're advancing," Basileus observed. He signalled

his own trumpeters, and the lines of mostly leather-armored light cavalry began to move.

Looking beyond the enemy battle-front, Sarnac saw that the Artoriani were advancing more slowly than the lead elements. Glancing to the right, he saw the dense masses of imperial infantry moving forward, juggernaut-like. They included longbowmen, so Ecdicius' center would have to take some nasty missile-fire before being able to respond with crossbows.

Then his attention snapped back to his own part of the battle, as the enemy horse drew closer with hideous speed. Both sides' ranks included some mounted archers. They weren't much compared to what was even now standard on the Eurasian steppe, and Genghis Khan's boys would have reacted with a disdainful "Oh, puh-*leeze!*" or its equivalent. But they could discharge arrows, some of which found their marks in flesh—generally that of horses. So the momentum of charge and countercharge had been blunted by the time the two met head to head.

From the twentieth century on, military historians had tried to reconstruct what such a meeting must have been like. They'd agreed that two formations of horsemen couldn't have simply ridden into each other at full tilt. Even if men—and, with more difficulty, horses—could have been prevailed upon to do it, the only result would have been a chaos of shattered human and equine bodies. Sarnac couldn't answer the question from past experience, for in his sole cavalry-on-cavalry clash the Artoriani had taken the Visigothic horse on the flank. But now he learned precisely what happened, and why for centuries the only answer to the knight on the battlefield had been another knight.

At the moment of contact, as though by common consent, there was a general slewing to the right, so men presented their shielded left sides to each other and began jabbing with lances and hewing with swords. Amid the hell of noise and weapon-impacts, Sarnac found a millisecond to reflect that these were *light* cavalry; the same dynamics must apply

even more to a collision of heavy *cataphractarii*. Charging
directly forward with lances at rest was for riding down
mobs of undisciplined footsloggers.

Even without his high-tech goodies, Sarnac was more
heavily armored than most in this company. He made the
most of it, laying about him with his *spatha* and stealing a
look to the right. The enemy infantry had reached the spear-
front of Ecdicius' center, but was unable to bring its full
weight of numbers to bear, for it advanced across ground
broken by heaps of its own dead. The massed crossbowmen
had done fearful execution, and the large wooden shields
being held over their heads were protecting them from the
sleet of longbow shafts that arched over from behind the
enemy front. Sarnac's heart leapt with the thought that the
center would hold.

Suddenly, he felt as much as saw a shift in the battle-
pattern, as the enemy formation partially disengaged and
began to part. Then, with a roar of trumpets and throats, a
squadron of the Artoriani thundered into the fray and rocked
Basileus' lighter-armed horsemen back. Sarnac gave ground
with the rest of the struggling crush of men and horses,
and as he did he saw with dawning horror that a gap had
opened between them and the center. *Very good, Kai*, he
thought, guiltily aware that he shouldn't be feeling proud
of his old friend. It was with no surprise at all that he caught
sight of the column of hard-riding red-cloaked figures
heading unerringly for the empty space from which they
could curve around and take the immobile infantry mass
of the center in the rear.

But they'd been aware of the danger of sacrificing
mobility for firepower by tying their main infantry body
to the vulnerable crossbow-loaders. Shouted commands
rang out from the high ground, and the center's left flank
bent itself rearward, shielding the loaders. The charging
Artoriani, like an incoming tide flowing around a seaside
cliff, thundered past the solid infantry wall toward the
lightly defended camp.

"Basileus!" Sarnac yelled across a few yards of hell. "Pull back to the camp—you'll be cut off if you stay here. I'm going back now." He wrenched his horse around, freeing himself from the melee, and galloped south. Looking to his left, he could see the flying column of the Artoriani, riding parallel with him; their leading elements would reach the camp before he did. Beyond and above them, the infantry was reconfiguring its formation with greater smoothness than he would have thought possible. They wouldn't be taken in the rear, so hope still remained. Still further in the distance to the northeast rose the hill from which Kai must be overseeing the battle. To its left were more red cloaks on horses; a squadron of the Artoriani were still being held in reserve.

"Andreas, Kai's pulled a fast one: he used some of the Artoriani to push our light cavalry back and open a space between our left wing and our center, then sent most of the rest of the Artoriani through the hole. They're headed for the camp." *Where Julia is*, he didn't add. "I'm following them, and Basileus is going to pull back. But it'll take him time to disengage . . ."

"Understood. We've pushed the enemy left wing back, but not as far as we'd hoped—they've got some longbowmen here, and they blunted our charge. I'll borrow a squadron from Ecdicius and head back to relieve the camp." The steadiness of Andreas' voice as transmitted through Sarnac's mastoid by the implant communicator would have fooled most people.

"Make it quick! Signing off." Sarnac ascended the slope to the camp, where the defenders recognized him and let him through the palisade. Without pausing, he turned his horse's head leftward toward the noise of battle.

Some of the red-cloaked riders had broken through and were riding among the tents and shacks. Sarnac found himself exchanging blows with one of them. His control of his mount slipped momentarily, and as he was regaining it a sword-slash connected with his thigh, only to glance off as the impact-armor leggings stiffened to a hardness exceeding steel at the moment of impact. Taking advantage of his opponent's dumbfounded immobility, Sarnac lunged. You couldn't see much of a man's face with these helmets— the whole idea of the cheekpieces was to leave as little of it exposed as possible. But Sarnac could see that it was a young man's face just before the point of his *spatha* destroyed it. For an instant that was like a nerve-pain of the soul, he wondered if he'd served with the kid's father.

Then he was swept along as the fight swirled on into the camp. Somehow—perhaps it was the precise tenor of the shouting—he knew that the perimeter guards had sealed the hole that had been torn in the camp's defenses. But there were still these guys who'd already gotten in to deal with. Now they had reached the innermost parts of the camp, and various noncombatants were running or trying to defend themselves—like the slender, chestnut-haired young girl who stood behind a tumble of baggage, swinging a poker from the nearby smithy in great circles to fend off the red-cloaked riders.

"Julia!" he yelled, knowing she probably couldn't hear him. "Get away!" He fought frantically to reach her, but the man he was fighting was *very* good, maneuvering his horse with his knees to minimize the force of blows while striking shrewdly with his own *spatha*. Sarnac forced himself to fight clear-headedly as he watched Julia lose her footing and go down, while the enemy swarmed around her and began to dismount.

At a speed that was reckless amid the camp-clutter, a horse and rider burst into the fight, bowling over one of the still-mounted men around Julia and sideswiping one of the dismounted ones. The others turned their attention from the supine girl to the new arrival, and one of them chopped viciously at the horse's hocks. The animal went down with a scream, and Andreas rolled free. He got to his feet and hastily wrapped his cloak around his left arm while using his right hand to menace his foes with his *spatha*.

They hesitated—Andreas was a very big man on the standards of this milieu, and obviously in no mild humor—while Julia got up into a semi-crouch and scrambled behind him. Then they rushed. Without waiting to receive the attack, he waded into them, bellowing in what Sarnac supposed must be his native language.

Deflecting a cut with his left arm, he disemboweled one attacker and continued the motion to cut a leg out from under a second one, then used his shoulder to batter a third aside. A fourth got in behind him, and slashed; but Andreas was wearing his round shield strapped to his back, often the most useful place for it in this kind of fighting, and the cut which might have severed his spine glanced off it. Andreas whirled around and brought his blade down on the man's head, crashing through helmet and skull. Then another man's *spatha* banged against his own helmet. It held, of course—like Sarnac's, it had a little field generator that strengthened the iron's atomic bonds—but the impact staggered him and he fell over backwards. The attacker rushed forward for a second, killing blow. But Julia clumsily flung the poker she still held at his legs, and he stumbled forward . . . directly onto the point of the *spatha* that Andreas had managed to bring up. He continued his forward motion, and the sword-point emerged from his back, accompanied by a gout of blood. But he managed to bring his own point down, and it pierced Andreas' shoulder, where the Model 491 scale armor covered the impact armor's sensors. Blood flowed, and Andreas emitted a scream which caused Sarnac to redouble his efforts to fight his way past his unreasonably skilled opponent.

Then two streams of horsemen converged on the scene: Basileus' men who'd fallen back on the camp, and Andreas' relief column which he'd outrun. Sarnac was separated from the man he'd been fighting, and he broke through the press to Andreas, who was lying in the death-grip of the man who'd wounded him; Sarnac rolled the corpse off him while Julia cradled his head.

"You'll be all right," Sarnac said as he bound up Andreas' shoulder and poured a slug of the army's *vin* extremely *ordinaire* into him. He couldn't mention Tylar's "field pharmacopeia" with Julia present. The fighting moved away as the remaining intruders were mopped up, but sounds of battle continued unabated from the camp's northern perimeter, where enemy cavalry waves beat against the palisade whose defenders were now reinforced by Basileus' dismounted men. The left end of the infantry center had completed its bending-back and was now linked with the camp defenses, so the front was unbroken again. It was also a purely defensive front—any hope of victory must ride with Ecdicius' cavalry on the right.

Andreas seemed to read his thoughts. "Get to Ecdicius," he croaked. "He needs all the help he can get. I'll . . . be with you in my thoughts." The circumlocution was for Julia's benefit, but the point was well taken: the army's left was now anchored on the camp, and Andreas was *hors de combat* there, so Sarnac had better get his tail to the right so they'd be able to continue their communication function.

"All right," he said, mounting his horse. "Keep your spirits up." (Translation: *Stay conscious.*) "I'll tell Julia's father she's all right." And he was off toward the east, riding out of the camp under a sky whose cloudiness was growing. An occasional spatter of rain wet his face.

Approaching the right flank, he saw that Ecdicius had indeed gained some ground there even as his left flank had been driven back to the camp. So the fighting front had rotated almost one hundred and eighty degrees, pivoting on the immovable center. So now the infantry facing Ecdicius fought with their backs to the southern slopes of Kai's headquarters hill.

He found Ecdicius organizing his riders for yet another charge. "Bedwyr! What news? Andronicus somehow learned that the camp was threatened . . . Amazing, the way you two find things out. By the way, what brings you here?"

In a few swift sentences, Sarnac described what had happened on the left. "And Julia's all right, thanks to Andronicus," he concluded. Ecdicius kept his outward composure, but slowly released his breath. "He fought like a lion to protect her. He was wounded, but he'll live."

"He'll live to receive my gratitude—if any of us live through this day." Ecdicius kept his voice low, for there were others around. He gazed forward, beyond the enemy front at the hill. Then he turned toward one of his lieutenants. "Ancelius!" he shouted, with the lightheartedness of a man out hunting. "Remember when we broke that Visigothic raiding party outside Clermont, back before you got old and lazy?"

The man, one of the veterans of the old Brotherhood— he looked slightly younger than Ecdicius—grinned back. "Aye, Augustus! That was a great day. They were drawn up at the foot of a slope, like . . ." His voice trailed off and his eyes went to the formation they were facing.

"Precisely!" Ecdicius grinned like a boy. "And that fat-gutted chieftain of theirs was looking down from the top of that slope!" He wheeled his horse around, calling to several other old war-dogs. "Continue drawing back for a fresh charge as you're already doing. But divide the center like . . ."

"Like we did that day, Augustus?" Ancelius asked eagerly.

"Not quite. Instead of two elements, I want three. The one in the very center I'll lead myself. It will consist of all of you—delegate command of your own squadrons—and a few other picked men. After the front is broken, we're going to charge straight uphill. Our objective is to kill or capture Kai!"

All their mouths hung open. "But, but Ecdicius," Ancelius stammered, "you're the Augustus of the West! You can't risk the imperial person . . ."

"Hell, Ancelius, if we don't carry the day my imperial person won't be worth an imperial damn! Have you forgotten how to hazard everything on a single throw?"

He swept them all with flashing eyes. "There's far more at stake now than when we rode against the Visigoths . . . and it seemed hopeless then."

"We were young then, Ecdicius," Ancelius said sadly.

"Yes, and can you remember what that was like? Can you remember how it was in those days? The world we'd known seemed to be coming to an end, as though the pagan Fates had turned malevolent with senility, and we rode forth to do one worthwhile thing before the dark closed in over us. And then Artorius came, carrying the dawn in his hands and giving the world another chance!" Ecdicius met all their eyes, and what passed between those eyes was like an electric arc. "Now the world needs yet another chance—and Artorius is gone. But I am his heir, and in his name, and in the name of everything that was ever dear to those young men of the Auvergne who still live inside you, I call on you to follow me. The Brotherhood rides one last time!"

Sarnac heard the storm of cheers as though from a distance, for he was seeing these grizzled, thickening men as they must have been two decades ago, just before the timelines diverged. *In my reality, they did indeed go down into the dark, after performing a gesture of magnificent, gallant futility.*

*I said it to Tylar and I meant it: in this reality, gallantry is not going to be futile.*

He urged his horse forward through the crowd to Ecdicius' side. "Augustus, I'd like to be with you in the center."

Ecdicius flashed his transfiguring smile. "I wouldn't have you anywhere else, Bedwyr. And now, let's get ready to ride, before it starts raining in earnest and the ground turns to mud."

They charged with two elite units in full *cataphract* rig in the middle of the onrushing line of horsemen. Just behind them came Ecdicius and his picked squadron:

what was left of the Brotherhood, the best of the younger men, and Rear Admiral Robert Sarnac, PHLN. Over Ecdicius streamed the blood-red dragon standard he carried as the Restorer's heir, twin to the one that floated above Kai's tent.

The enemy infantry they faced in this part of the line were Franks, stationed here and not in the center where they might have found themselves opposing their ethnic relatives, as per time-honored imperial practice. They'd long since expended the throwing axes that were their favorite weapons, but their courage was unabated. And the few longbowmen who backed them up kept up an arrow-flight that sent men and horses pitching forward to the ground. Along most of the front, the Franks held solid against Ecdicius' weakened charge.

But at its midpoint, under the concentrated impact of two squadrons of armored horsemen, that line strained, heaved, and finally gave way. The riders pressed their advantage, pushing the snarling Franks back to left and right in a maelstrom of stamping hooves and thrusting lances, and the gap widened.

Sarnac, approaching that gap with the rest of Ecdicius' chosen men, visualized how this tactic must have been used against the Visigoths, with the two breakthrough units continuing on and then wheeling around and striking their shaken enemies from the rear. But on this day, their purpose was simply to open up the emptiness he now saw yawning ahead. Then they were through, with nothing but hill-slope beyond and the battle-din receding behind them. With a shout, Ecdicius spurred his mount forward into a full gallop, and it became a mad race up the slope to the sound of hunting-horns.

Up ahead, Sarnac saw a spreading confusion along the ridge-line. He also heard trumpet-signals he remembered, and he knew that Kai had summoned his last carefully hoarded reserve of the Artoriani. *So it really is a race*, he thought as he lowered his freshly issued lance and braced his feet against his stirrups. *They'll be riding up this hill from their position on the far side, and whoever gets to the top first will have the advantage. We've got a head start, since it took Kai a little while to grasp what Ecdicius is up to. But they and their horses are rested . . .*

Then they were scrambling up the last few yards to the hilltop, and there was no time for further thought, no time for anything except weapon-impacts, noise and blood. The infantry line they encountered was a hastily improvised thing, and these were headquarters troops. They smashed through with scarcely a pause and were into the encampment beyond. Ecdicius and his standard-bearer led the way toward the command tent, toward a fratricidal meeting of dragons.

The day finally fulfilled its promise with a crash of thunder and a pelting rain. Sarnac was telling himself that the Artoriani would be slowed in their progress up the hill's opposite side, when the first of the red-cloaked riders topped the ridge and bore down on the camp. There could be no thought of tactics now, as horsemen met among the tents in a swirl of single and small-group combats.

Sarnac had left his lance in the belly of an infantryman, and now he let implanted reflexes wield his *spatha* for him as he let the maelstrom of combat carry him on through the camp. All at once, he was free of the latest struggling knot of riders in which he'd been entangled. He found himself in a large open space in front of the dragon-surmounted command tent—it must have been a parade ground or something, for there was a kind of rostrum behind which an obvious noncombatant cowered. The battle-pattern, such as it was, had left the space clear, save for a rider in high-ranking officer's armor who was engaged with one of Ecdicius' men. The officer sent his opponent reeling to the ground with a sword-stroke, then looked around for fresh enemies, and his eyes met Sarnac's through the rain. And Sarnac felt a resistless tide of inevitability take hold of him as he recognized those green eyes.

"Kai," he croaked.

The enemy general walked his horse forward, never breaking eye contact, and gave him a puzzled look. "I know you from somewhere. It was long ago . . ."

"Yes, Kai. I fought beside you at Angers." *And later at Bourg-de-Déols*, Sarnac didn't add. *And afterwards you were with me when I threw a sword into a lake, and you carried the tale back to Britain. But that was in another universe.*

"Bedwyr," Kai breathed. "It's you! So many times I've wondered what became of you. You just seemed to vanish, shortly before the Battle of Bourges. Ah, if only you'd been there, when we smashed the Visigoths!" A dull hurt entered his voice. "You didn't seem the kind to desert, Bedwyr."

The battle had moved away from them, but it hardly mattered, for they were as oblivious to it as they were to the rain that drenched them. Sarnac was peripherally aware that the foppish figure behind the rostrum had stood up and was staring at them in bewilderment, his courtier's makeup running in the downpour.

"I didn't desert, Kai. I . . ." *I didn't go anywhere, Kai. This entire continuum veered off, taking you with it, leaving me with a Kai who had to live in a world without Artorius, a Kai who never became a general of a resurgent empire. But how do I explain that to you?* "It's a long story, Kai, and you wouldn't believe it anyway. But believe this: I never deserted Artorius, which is why I'm here today, fighting for his heir."

Kai stiffened in his saddle. "His heir? Ecdicius? That damned traitor who murdered the *Pan-Tarkan*?"

Sarnac recoiled as though from a slap. "What are you talking about Kai?"

"He explained it to me." Kai pointed at the bedraggled courtier. "The Chamberlain Nicoles. He told me how Ecdicius couldn't wait for Artorius to die, so he poisoned the man to whom he owed everything!"

"No, Kai! You've been told lies. I was there, in

Constantinople, and I tell you that the men who've seized power there tried to murder Ecdicius. That's why he had to flee. Join us, Kai! The East is lost, but you can help Artorius' heir come into the Western half of his inheritance at least."

Kai's eyes fled from Sarnac to Nicoles and back again, as though seeking refuge from an insoluble dilemma. Finding none, they squeezed shut, and his entire body shook convulsively. Then a crash of thunder seemed to crystallize something inside him, and the green eyes snapped open. "No! Defend yourself, Bedwyr!" And he spurred his horse forward over the few yards that separated them.

Sarnac barely had time to get his shield up and deflect the downward-sweeping *spatha*. He struck back, maneuvering for an opening, slashing and parrying through a fog of unreality. *This is Kai, and if there was anything even resembling a God in the universe we'd be on the same side.* Then they broke apart and came together again with a clash of swords, horses rearing. Sarnac's mount foundered in the mud, and he threw himself free. Then he slithered to his feet as Kai bore down on him, striking from above. He fended off several downward blows, then dropped his *spatha* and rushed in, holding his shield over his head and grasping Kai's belt with his free hand. He tugged with all his strength, and Kai toppled from the saddle. They fell to the mud in a tangle, with Kai on top.

For an instant they wrestled clumsily. Then Sarnac slid free and retrieved his blade. They both got to their feet in the mud and faced each other warily.

Sarnac felt an odd sensation at his midriff, like a small animal wiggling against him, an animal of metallic hardness. He looked down at the carrying case on his belt, and saw that the communicator it contained was reconfiguring.

The instant of distraction was all Kai needed.

Sarnac was just looking up when his opponent's shield pushed his own aside, and a sword-blade connected with his helmet, filling his eyes with Roman candles and sending him staggering backwards. Kai pressed his advantage, and Sarnac reeled under a hail of blows, finally going over on his back. Kai was instantly atop him, drawing back his *spatha* for a killing stroke . . . and stopped.

Sarnac's first thought was that it had stopped raining. But it hadn't—at least not outside the invisible hemisphere that surrounded them. That hemisphere's boundaries were clearly marked by the still-falling rain that hung frozen outside it, each drop motionless. Within the hemisphere, there was a faint splattering sound, and the puddles of water settled into calmness after the impacts of the few raindrops that had been within the field at the nanosecond in which it had formed.

But Kai had eyes for none of this. He was staring fixedly at the glowing immaterial portal that had appeared in the middle of the parade ground, and at the two figures that had emerged from it and were advancing toward him.

"*Pan-Tarkan,*" he whispered as the first of them approached him.

"Hello, Kai," Artorius said. His face was smeared with the grime of battle, and his smile was like the sun breaking through clouds.

Sarnac, unnoticed, took the carrying case off his belt and carefully laid it on the ground. Then he got up and stalked over to the second new arrival.

"What kept you?" he asked Tylar grumpily.

"Oh, I'm frightfully sorry, my dear fellow. But we were rather busy. You'll be glad to know that the invasion of Italy has been stopped. As soon as the pursuit was well in hand and Artorius could be spared, we came here without delay."

"Yeah, by means of that 'communicator'—which evidently has a few little features you forgot to tell me about."

"Ah, yes. It *is* a rather special device. In its current configuration, it can project a portal at a distance of several yards, as you can see."

"That's not all, it seems." Sarnac gazed up at the dome of motionless rain, and beyond the parade ground at the battling figures who stood like living statues. In the distance, a lightning bolt stood suspended, moving at the speed of electricity and therefore effectively stationary in terms of the rate at which time was moving inside this immaterial hemisphere.

"True, it also generates a reverse-stasis field. You may recall this kind of time-accelerating effect, which you experienced once before."

"Vividly. But those devices you'd implanted in us only produced a field that surrounded a single person."

"This device is a good deal more powerful. I anticipated that it might be necessary to create what is in effect a zone of privacy." He indicated the scene around them. Artorius was giving Kai a version of the same story he'd used on the Restorer, and Nicoles was standing in openmouthed immobility. "What transpires within the field will occupy only a nanosecond or two from the standpoint of the outside universe, so Artorius and I will never be seen."

"Except by Kai and Nicoles, here."

"Yes, their presence *is* a problem. But it was unavoidable, for only Artorius can persuade Kai to do as we wish. And the surveillance satellite currently in a position to observe this battlefield reported that the battle had reached a crisis. And, incidentally, that you were in some personal danger."

"Sweet of you to care." Sarnac turned his attention to Artorius and Kai. The latter had fallen to his knees and removed his helmet, and seemed oblivious to the wizardry that held frozen the rain and the battling figures in the camp around them. He was listening to Artorius with the air of a man who understands nothing but needs no understanding to believe.

"But, *Pan-Tarkan*," he stammered, using the title he *knew* this man, who had by his own account never been Augustus, was entitled to, "I was told that Ecdicius had poisoned you . . ."

"No, Kai. Bedwyr has spoken the truth. The traitors who've put that poltroon Wilhelmus on the throne sought Ecdicius' life because he was the legitimate heir. And now . . ." He pointed toward the camp. Ecdicius had broken free of the battle and started toward them at a gallop in which he and his horse were now suspended. "Now I've been allowed to come to you and speak to you in this bubble snatched from time so I can tell you that he is carrying forward my work by leading the West along its own true path."

"But, *Pan-Tarkan*, we fought to restore the empire."

"And you won, Kai. And now you've seen the result." Artorius spoke with enormous gentleness. "We fought like men, Kai; nothing can take that away from us. But it has pleased God to so order things in this world that right action can sometimes give birth to wrongness. And that which dwells in Constantinople is an enormous wrongness, Kai. Ecdicius knows that. I think you know it. And I call on you in the name of what you know to be true to give your allegiance to Ecdicius as Augustus of the West."

*"NO!"*

Nicoles' quavering scream shattered the silence into which Artorius' final word had dropped. Before anyone could move, the eunuch drew a dagger from his belt and sprang forward toward Artorius' back, continuing to scream in a voice from which all sanity had fled.

Sarnac still held his sword. Without time for anything fancy, he lunged past the paralyzed Tylar, thrusting as far as his arm would reach. Nicoles, with eyes only for his target, ran onto the outthrust point, which slid into his gut.

Simultaneously, Kai rushed past Artorius before the latter could turn around, raising his *spatha* and bringing it down with all his strength and all his skill in a form of swordplay which, like a crude *kendo*, aimed at putting the maximum possible force behind a sword-edge. His blade connected with the base of Nicoles' neck at an angle, slicing inward. Blood spurted. The eunuch's mouth opened to scream but expelled a retching sound and a red spray. His body sank to the ground with both their swords still in it, and Sarnac and Kai met each other's eyes over it. Slowly, they both released their hilts.

Artorius stepped up behind Kai and grasped his shoulder. "Will you do as I ask, Kai?"

"I understand none of this wizardry, *Pan-Tarkan*," Kai said, turning to face him. "But I know you, for you've come striding out of my very memories. You may say I'm not yours to command in this time and place, but I know better. And Ecdicius is your true heir."

Artorius clasped Kai in his arms—this Kai who was to all appearances his own age. "I have one other . . . not command, Kai, but request. Tell no one of this meeting we've been permitted. There are things men are better off not knowing."

"That's an easy one, *Pan-Tarkan*," Kai grinned. "Nobody'd believe me anyway!" And with that grin, Sarnac knew this man to be his old friend—Kai with a few more pounds and some gray hairs, but still Kai. And the world seemed mended.

Artorius smiled back and they embraced one last time. Then the former High King turned and strode toward the portal.

"You'd better stay for now," Tylar murmured to Sarnac. "Your abrupt disappearance would be hard to explain. We'll come back for you and Andreas as originally planned." He followed Artorius through the portal, which vanished. At the instant of its vanishing, the rain resumed its descent onto the parade ground, pelting them, and the stationary figures throughout the camp crashed back into battle. Ecdicius plunged forward, seeming to reacquire his momentum toward them. Then he reined in, puzzled, as Kai knelt before him.

"Bedwyr, the lightning must have dazzled me—I didn't see you get up. And Kai . . . ?"

The erstwhile enemy commander extended his *spatha*

hilt-first with his left hand while giving the Roman salute with the right. "Hail Ecdicius Augustus!" he shouted. "Accept my allegiance, and the Army of Germania!"

Ecdicius' jaw dropped. Sarnac grinned weakly as the accumulated exhaustion of this day began to overtake him. "We'd better have the trumpeters signal 'Truce' and send some heralds out to stop the fighting. And let's get in out of this damned rain!"

# CHAPTER SIXTEEN

They rounded the remembered bend in the road and Sarnac saw the three approaching riders, coming from the direction of Cadbury. He bounded ahead of Tylar and Artorius as Tiraena sprang from her horse and ran to him. After a while, they heard a harrumph.

"Ah, you forgot your horse," Cerdic said. He was holding the bridle Tiraena had abandoned.

"Thank you," Tiraena smiled.

"No," the *ealdorman* said with a vehement headshake. "Let you never have any thought of owing me thanks, Lady. The rest of my life will be spent in your debt for the life of my son." He dismounted and, to Tiraena's obvious consternation, fell to his knees at her feet.

"*Cerdic!*" she exclaimed, voice rising to a falsetto squeak.

"I know not where you're going, Lady, or whether you'll ever return. But if ever you're in need of a life, the life of Cerdic of the West Saxons is yours."

Tiraena's coppery face turned a dark-red shade new to Sarnac—it came to him that he'd never seen her blush before. "Aw, come on, Cerdic," she stammered. "I'm just glad Cynric is all right." She'd said goodbye to her young erstwhile bodyguard before leaving Cadbury, where he lay raising the roof with his demands to be allowed out of bed after a

271

recovery that had the entire countryside talking of miracles. "That's all the thanks I need. Now *please* get up!"

"As you command, Lady." Cerdic rose with a smile. "My debt to you is yours to release me from. But my honor, and that of my house, is mine—and you'll never want for a shield and a sword in this land!"

Gwenhwyvaer rescued Tiraena from her tongue-tied misery. "Ride on back, Cerdic. I'll catch up. There are things I must say in private."

"Aye, Lady." Cerdic mounted and rode off, leading Tiraena's horse. Silence settled over those who remained. Gwenhwyvaer walked forward until she was within less than an arm's reach of Artorius. Silence stretched as she gazed into the face, seemingly in its forties, of him who'd died in his sixties in Constantinople last spring. The late afternoon chill deepened, for winter was coming on, but neither of them showed any signs of noticing.

"So," the queen finally said, "you're off—to a land I've never heard of, Lucasta tells me, and I can well believe it. Indeed, if I understand aright, to another world, a world of dream where you're a legend! So I've lost you twice, first to death and now to what must be magic, however much you deny it."

"Remember what I told you: you share in the legend in that world. But think not of that, Gwen. For you've grown far beyond me—beyond what I became in this world, beyond what fable made of me in the other. You've grown into what I could never have imagined, for I never took the time to truly know you." He sighed deeply and took her hands. "Ah, Gwen, the waste!"

Tylar cleared his throat softly. "We really should be getting along," he said to Sarnac and Tiraena. "We'll wait for you," he added to Artorius, who nodded abstractedly.

"What was all that about with Cerdic?" Sarnac asked after they'd rounded the bend in the road.

"A long story," Tiraena replied. "I'll tell you about it once we're all aboard the ship."

✤     ✤     ✤

Sarnac gasped for breath and held his aching sides. "The Holy Pill of Antioch!" he whooped. "I *love* it!" Then another gust of uncontrollable laughter took him.

Tylar didn't share his amusement. "You really shouldn't have, you know," he told Tiraena primly. "Still, it probably won't do any harm. There'll be so many legends associated with that battle that one more won't matter. Future generations will assume that Cynric's wound wasn't really as serious as it was initially thought to be."

"And remember," Sarnac gasped, having gotten his breath back again, "you owe her one for making sure they burned the Interrogator's body instead of burying it."

"True. A Korvaash skeleton, dug up by a later scientifically oriented age, would have been impossible to explain away. As it is, with no physical evidence, he'll be written off as just one more myth. That was well done on your part."

"I wasn't thinking in those terms at the time," Tiraena admitted. "To be honest, I don't clearly remember *what* I was thinking." She stared moodily out at the panorama revealed by the "observation deck" where they reclined on the extrudable furniture that an invisible magic carpet seemed to be carrying over the English Channel under gray skies. Then she shook herself and smiled. "Anyway, Tylar, you must admit I've been punished for my little transgression." She gestured aft, toward the receding British coastline. "I think I've just proven experimentally that it's not possible to literally die of embarrassment!"

Artorius, hitherto quiet, spoke up in an odd voice. "I'm afraid, Tiraena, that you're not quite through doing it." And, before anyone could react, he was on one knee before her, seeming to kneel in midair.

"*Artorius?!*" This time, Tiraena's voice rose above falsetto on the last syllable.

"I know not what meaning the name of King Arthur holds for you, Tiraena, for your blood is of many nations and worlds. But for whatever it's worth, you have his undying gratitude for the life of his grandson."

For the first time since Sarnac had known him, Tylar was dumbfounded to the point of being completely inarticulate. When he finally closed his mouth and opened it again, all that emerged was "But, but, but . . ."

Artorius turned to the time traveller with a crocodilian grin and spoke very clearly and distinctly, like a man who'd been waiting for years to deliver a line. "I'm afraid I haven't been entirely candid with you."

"So you're really going to stay?" Sarnac had been surprised at first, but on reflection he couldn't imagine why.

Andreas nodded. They'd left him in this Gallic villa to recuperate from his wound while they'd gone to Britain. Now the two of them strolled through its courtyard in the unseasonably warm afternoon sun. His recovery was now complete, thanks to Tylar's medical resources and Julia's TLC. And his spirit was clearly as whole as his body.

"Yes. The world I came from no longer exists, far in the future of this timeline. And I wouldn't want to go back to it even if I could."

"Are you sure you'll be able to get used to this world, though?" Sarnac asked, half-jokingly. "No electric lighting, no computers, no toilet paper . . ."

Andreas smiled. "The only thing I'd really miss is advanced medicine, and Tylar's agreed to supply me with some of that. Otherwise, I'll not be losing anything that can compare with what I've found here."

"Oh, yeah: Julia. Great kid. I don't imagine you two had any problem getting Ecdicius' blessing."

"No. All he asked was that we go back to Italy with him before the wedding. That was fine with us—it's not every couple who have their marriage solemnized by the pope! And," he added, deadpan, "I think I'll get over the loss of my estate in Bithynia."

*He really does have a sense of humor,* Sarnac realized. *It was just overlaid by the concrete of his conditioning in the world he came from. And now that that world is receding into the realms of fading nightmare, it's growing toward the sun like a flower through a cracked pavement.*

"But it's not just Julia," Andreas continued. "It's what I can *do* here. In my old world, all we had was a twilight struggle to hold back the night. But now I'm at this world's dawn. I can make a difference to its future."

"Hmm? You mean you're going to continue to work for Tylar?"

"Indeed," came the time traveller's voice as he approached with Tiraena in tow. "As the son-in-law of the Augustus of the West, Andreas will be in a position to give the course of history an occasional nudge in the right direction over the coming years. He'll be in contact with Koreel, who'll be staying on for a while in the Eastern Empire—which is going to be going through interesting times over the next few years. Wilhelmus and his, er, lady have been discredited by the total failure of their attempt to reconquer the West; I doubt if they'll survive for long."

"So you plan to continue keeping an eye on this timeline, then?" Sarnac asked.

"Certainly. From our perspective, it's an absolutely unique research opportunity. A twentieth-century astronomer, long before the days of interstellar probes, remarked that humanity would never really know anything about its own planetary system until it was able to study some others. Something similar applies to the study of history. At the same time, we'll have to guard against the temptation to intervene excessively."

"Yeah, I remember you telling me about the sensation of morally sanctioned interference with events. Quite a rush, I gathered."

"And you, as I recall, expressed concern that it might become habit-forming. I assure you that it won't. The intervention we've just concluded was justified only by dire necessity. Now, this Earth must take care of itself; the fundamental responsibility of human beings for the consequences of their own actions must remain absolute. Any society that loses sight of that ceases to be viable— as the history of your own North American ancestors demonstrates, Robert. And," Tylar continued briskly, "it goes without saying that our own timeline's past remains sacrosanct; we must continue to safeguard it as we always have."

Tiraena spoke up. "Tylar, in that connection, Bob and I have been meaning to talk to you. Andreas, would you excuse us?"

"Of course. I need to talk to Artorius anyway." He departed with a wave, leaving the other three alone in the courtyard. Tylar seated himself on a bench and raised an interrogative eyebrow, waiting.

Sarnac and Tiraena looked at each other awkwardly. The latter finally took the lead. "Tylar, we know you can't allow us to keep our memories of all this, any more than you could last time. We haven't let ourselves dwell on it, but we haven't forgotten it either. So, since it's about time for us to return to our own reality and our own era, we just wanted to say that . . . that . . ."

"That there are no hard feelings," Sarnac finished for her. "We understand that there's no alternative, and we've accepted that."

"An extremely commendable attitude. However, I've been doing some thinking myself." Tylar gazed up at them over steepled fingers. "You've both done nobly in fulfilling an ethical obligation which you, Robert, never really understood; and in which you, Tiraena, didn't share. So you have, I think, gone beyond paying your debt. Indeed, you've placed *me* in *your* debt—a debt which I believe I'll pay by foregoing memory erasure on this occasion."

There was dead silence as the reality of what he'd said sank home. Sarnac finally broke it. "But . . . but you *can't*, Tylar! I mean, if we go back to our own world knowing what we know now, it would change your history and wipe out the future that includes you. Wouldn't it?"

"I assure you that I've given these matters much thought. Consider: you really have no detailed knowledge of events in the remainder of your own lifetimes, do you? I've never told you, for example, who's going to win the next election for Terra's representative to the PHL Grand Council."

"But, Tylar," Tiraena protested, "we know the answer to the greatest enigma of our age: how the human species appeared on Raehan thirty thousand years before spaceflight! We know there's such a thing as time travel! We know time travellers from the remote future are policing history! We know . . ."

"Yes," Tylar interrupted gently. "You know a great many things. And I think you also know what the reaction would be if you were to announce your knowledge to the human race at large." The silence returned. Tylar smiled. "You're both intelligent people—too intelligent, I'm sure, to want to bring yourselves into disrepute."

"So," Sarnac said slowly, "you're saying we're powerless to change history because nobody would believe us?"

"That's one way to put it." Tylar stood up and regarded them gravely. "With this decision I am, let us say, pushing the envelope of my authority. But I believe I can justify it, when called upon to do so. You can make no practical use of this gift I'm making you. All you can do is cherish the knowledge that you were part of a legend you yourselves learned as children, and that you saved the future of an entire reality. That will have to be enough." Then he smiled in his slightly befuddled way, and was again an ordinary middle-aged human. "And now, if you'll excuse me, there are still a few matters which need my attention before we depart."

"I still wish we could have stayed for Andreas' wedding," Tiraena remarked.

"Yeah. I'll bet Sidonius pulled out all the stops for them."

Most of Sarnac's attention was on Loriima III, whose night side occluded more and more of the stars as they approached it.

As Tylar had promised, the transitions between timelines had been less unpleasant when returning to the reality wherein they belonged. They'd likewise negotiated the temportal in the outer reaches of the solar system with ease, and Sarnac had been surprised by the lump that had formed in his throat when he'd sought out Sirius and found a blue-white star of apparent magnitude -1.43. Then had come the soul-shakingly brief voyage to Loriima, and yet another temportal transit. They emerged into the very night on which a Robert Sarnac whose memories had held a large hole had departed with a mysterious character calling himself Tylar. Now he had an embarrassing notion of how much it must have cost to have emplaced a temportal simply to get him back to that night. At least, no such expensive expedient would be required for Tiraena at Naeruil II; Tylar would simply take her there at a pseudo-velocity calculated to get her there on the night of her own departure.

Tylar joined them. "We're now stationary relative to the base, and within range," he informed them. A portal blinked into ghostly existence. Within it, Sarnac recognized his office suite. "Shall we go?"

They'd had time for extended goodbyes during the voyage. Now they exchanged a quick embrace. "Hey," Sarnac said, "someday we should tell Claude and Liranni the unvarnished truth about all this. They'll think their parents are crazy old coots!"

"They already think that, Bob," Tiraena informed him as gently as possible. She gave him another squeeze. "Take care. You've still got a war to attend to, you know."

"Huh! Piece of cake!" A final kiss, then he turned and stepped through the portal with Tylar.

They were in the outer office. Tylar led the way into

Sarnac's inner sanctum. "You'll find that only an insignificant amount of time has elapsed locally since your departure," Tylar said. Then: "Well, I suppose that's it."

Sarnac took a deep breath and asked the question for which he'd awaited this time when they'd be alone. "Tylar, are you a god?"

There was a barely perceptible pause. "As you'll recall," the time traveller said mildly, "Tiraena asked me that question once, fifteen of your subjective years ago. You'll also recall that I responded in the negative."

"I know," Sarnac said flatly. "I also know you lie a lot."

Again, Tylar hesitated for such a brief instant that it was impossible to be certain he had hesitated at all. Then he spread his hands diffidently.

"My dear fellow, does the answer really matter? Indeed, does the question itself not become meaningless if it has to be asked at all? I leave you with that thought." He turned to go, then paused and faced Sarnac one last time. "I will answer your question to this extent: whatever I am, and whatever label you choose to apply to what I am, I emphatically am *not* the unknowable One, Who is as unknowable to me as to you." His face broke into a mischievous grin that made it unrecognizable. "On this point, I am being *entirely* candid with you!" And Tylar was gone.

Sarnac was left standing in the midnight dimness of his office of Loriima III. He glanced at the desk chrono—yes, it was the same date and time. Then he heard movement behind him. He whirled around, then relaxed at the sight of the figure in Fleet uniform.

"Well, Artorius—or is it Captain Draco?" he drawled. "What are you doing here? I thought you'd be with Tylar."

"Actually, Admiral, I asked him for an extended leave of absence, which he granted."

"Huh? Why?"

"Well," said the onetime High King of the Britons, "you did me a good turn, which I feel I should repay. And

I've always hated to begin a job and not finish it. And . . . well, I have some ideas for the coming campaign against the Korvaasha. It's a bloody *interesting* tactical problem."

Sarnac smiled and draped an arm over the other's shoulders. "Captain Draco, I think this is the start of a beautiful friendship."

# HISTORICAL NOTE

It's seldom advisable to take Tylar at his word, but his real-world biographical asides concerning Sidonius Apollinaris, Ecdicius, the Patriarch Acacius, and Pope Gelasius are accurate. The same is true of Cerdic of the West Saxons and his son Cynric, up to a point. The semi-historical Cerdic's personal background is, of necessity, a matter of inference. That he was part-British can be taken as a given, in light of his name. That he was from the Saxon settlements on the lower Loire is speculation, albeit a reasonable one. His parentage as herein set forth is sheer fancy.

Other fifth-century characters who actually lived include the British High King documented on the continent under the honorific "Riothamus" rather than his given name, and Constantine of the Dumnonii, although I've taken minor liberties with his dates. Many of the rest, including Gwenhwyvaer, Kai and Peredur—and, for that matter, Bedwyr and Balor—have some kind of basis in legend. The imperial couple Wilhelmus and Hilaria, and the eunuch Nicoles, are, of course, purely fictitious.

I've followed a common practice by using "Saxon" as a catchall for the various tribes of Low German speakers—Saxons, Angles, Jutes and Frisians—who migrated into

Britain in the fifth century. It would be anachronistic to call them "English." The Irish were actually called *Scotti* by the Romano-Britons. This doesn't mean they came from Scotland, but rather that Scotland (Caledonia in the fifth century) was later named after them because some of them settled there, although Ireland, where most of them stayed, is of course not called "Scotland." It's all too confusing, and too Celtic. In these pages, the Irish are called the Irish. The tribal designation "Fomorian" is drawn from legend.

As in *Legacy*, I've generally used modern place names (Chester, Bourges, Troyes) rather than ancient ones (Deva, Avaricum, Augustobona), accepting anachronism as the price of clarity. But whenever a modern name is jarringly inappropriate (France, Istanbul) and the ancient one is well-known (Gaul, Constantinople), I haven't hesitated to opt for the latter. Likewise, years are given according to the present system of *Anno Domini* dating, which didn't become standard until the sixth century.